DEATH AND THE DAMNED

SEELEY JAMES

Published by

Machined Media

12402 N 68th St

Scottsdale, AZ 85254

DEATH AND THE DAMNED, Sabel Security #3

Copyright © 2016, 2018, 2019 Seeley James

Original Publication, v1.33 November 15th, 2016

This version is v1.42 12-April, 2019

Print ISBN: 978-0-9972306-3-5

eBook ISBN: 978-0-9972306-2-8

Distribution Print ISBN: 978-0-9972306-9-7

Formatting: BB eBooks

Cover Design: Jeroen ten berge

FOR NANA

CHAPTER 1

WHO TO TRUST IS THE SCARIEST decision we make in life. I grabbed him by the hair, pulled his head back, and, cheek-to-cheek, we contemplated the sparkling stars dotting the moonless Syrian sky. I sensed his eyeballs strain all the way to the right to look at me. His fingernails dug into my forearm. Anxiety caused him to miss the grandeur of the moment. Too bad. It was stunningly beautiful. You don't see that many stars from over-lit American cities. But I tired of our two-second relationship and drew my blade across his throat, severing his carotid artery and larynx before he could scream a warning to the others. I dropped his carcass on the other jihadi at my feet. He trusted me because I speak Arabic. Bad idea.

I stared at the dead fighters and thought about how ISIL's perversion of Islam wasted so many lives.

But then, I'm hardly the guy to judge other people's religious beliefs.

Mercury, winged messenger of the Roman gods, waved to me from the narrow, dusty village lane. *Earth to Jacob. Ain't the time for contemplative yoga, dawg. That monster raped three women yesterday. C'mon now. Get your head in the game. You need to find that cowboy.*

After a decade guiding me through battles as a disembodied voice in my head, Mercury decided to make himself manifest. Some people would consider meeting god in person as a divine miracle. Others would encourage me to go back on my meds. Maybe I had taken a swan dive off the sanity cliff, but when I ponder how lucky I am to have god on my side—even if he's been surviving on unemployment benefits since the late fourth century—I count my blessings. And when he tells me to keep my eyes open for a cowboy in an ISIL-held Syrian town, I listen.

I clicked my comm link open and queried my mission teammates, scattered around the houses we were about to invade. "Anyone see a cowboy?"

Dhanpal, mission leader and former Navy SEAL, responded first. "Had him in my scope for a second. He ran into target house B."

Miguel, best friend from our years in the 75th Rangers, said, "No cowboys on this side. Ready to take target house A."

Tania, former girlfriend, former MP, and mission sniper on a roof two hundred yards away, said, "Cowboy moved from B to A; did not look like a hostage. Did not look hostile."

Fawaz, former FBI SWAT team leader, said, "Ready on target house A. I have visual confirmation on six hostages in the basement."

"Go on target house A." Dhanpal's order was the last word spoken.

Miguel blew the door open with C4. I rolled in and fired on two soldiers. One dropped, the other groaned. The survivor's eyes flashed, his life still fired by the amphetamines coursing through his veins. He raised his weapon. Dhanpal barreled in the back door and finished off the wounded man. Fawaz ran straight to the basement. Miguel watched the street.

Breeching charges are not stealthy tools. You lose the element of surprise the instant you blow up stuff. Your life expectancy begins to dwindle with each passing nanosecond as your operation transitions from covert to overt. Waiting for Fawaz to make sure the hostages in the basement were indeed the Yazidi women we came to liberate was like waiting for a bomb to go off. My spinal cord itched.

"Movement on rooftop B," Tania reported over the comm link. We heard her rifle pop twice. "Two down."

A board creaked over my head.

Dhanpal pointed up and moved to cover the ladder to the rooftop.

Desert architecture requires a habitable sleeping area when the interior becomes too hot in the summer. Tania killed the man on guard up there before we moved in, but our cowboy was still a phantom.

Mercury pointed to the ceiling. *Shoot right there and you'll nail him.*

I fired.

A man's voice howled in pain. He gasp-shouted, "American! American! Don't shoot."

Dhanpal ran up the ladder. "Hands where I can see them."

Out in the street, Miguel fired three pops at target house B. The local boys were stirring. No doubt the larger force on the other side of the village would be alerted and two hundred jihadis would drop by for a game of dodge-bullet.

"Fawaz, progress?" I asked in the comm link.

"Six hostages freed. Sending them up now. They have directions."

As he spoke, the first shadow appeared from the basement, looked both ways, and ran outside. A stream of women's shadows followed her. Women captured and kept as sex slaves by ISIL. A contingent from the Yazidi Brigade called "Force of the Sun Ladies," made up of former sex slaves intent on revenge, waited on the outskirts to take them home. Fawaz emerged last and joined me by the front door.

"Ready for B," Miguel said.

"Hold up a second," Dhanpal said. "I have an American, wearing a cowboy hat and boots, claims to be a hostage. Jacob shot him in the leg."

Mercury pointed to the ceiling. *Ah dude, you were off by half an inch. If you'd hit where I was pointing, the bullet would've gone through his groin, up his torso, and through his tiny, backwoods brain. Now you gotta drag his cracker ass back to the States.*

Mercury insists all gods are Africans, and points to the fact that humans became sentient in the Rift Valley. The way I see it, if he wants to appear as a young, buffed version of Will Smith in a porn-toga with copper wings on his helmet, fine. But jeez, you'd think just once he'd be happy I followed his directions.

"Not holding up," Miguel said. "Three of us are moving on B. You drag the guy back to the Humvees."

Miguel, broad-shouldered and as big as a bear, lumbered across the street, firing his suppressed H&K into the windows. Fawaz and I followed.

The distant screech of a siren stabbed through the desert night like an ice pick in my ear.

Miguel stood outside and fired in. I charged through the open door, over the body of a dead guy, and fired into a thin wall where Mercury pointed. Behind it, a body thumped to the floor. Fawaz ran past me and jumped down the basement stairs.

Target house B had no back door. Miguel went to the roof; I kept the street clear. Not even a cat's shadow crossed the street after the explosions, yet I kept my sights moving up and down the lane as the seconds ticked by in agonizing anticipation of the nasty firefight that was sure to come.

Sweat dripped down my temples. I could feel the approaching hordes of jihadis—their courage fired by fenethylline, the drug of choice for ISIL fighters—creeping closer and closer.

At that moment, I lost concentration and pictured my one true love, Yumi Shibata. A Tokyo detective I fell in love with during a gangster slaughter in Japan. She was spending her medical leave at my Washington DC home. She wasn't happy when I signed up for Dhanpal's special mission. She'd said, "No one come back from Syria. Ever."

Mercury waved his arms. *And you're not going to come back from Syria either unless you pay attention, yo.*

A radio squawked in the corner of the room. A commander demanded an update from a dead man in Arabic. I dug through bloody pockets until I found the radio and answered in perfect Arabic. "Malfunction. Fawaz was playing with a grenade. We beat on him for it."

The commander screamed back at me. "Who are you? Where is Mahmoud?"

Fawaz was not as common a name as I thought. I should've used a derogatory name like numb-nuts instead of my teammate's name.

"Mahmoud waits for you in *Jannah*." I said, referring to Islamic heaven. "I'd be happy to send you there too, motherfucker."

I left the last word in English just to pour salt in his wound. The commander began swearing in Arabic.

Fawaz sent eleven hostages up from the basement. Two more than we counted on. The women fled into the street, running for their Yazidi sisters.

Miguel dropped down from the roof.

"Couple surprises." Fawaz pointed at two scared young men in the hall. They asked rapid-fire questions in an Eastern European dialect I didn't understand. *"Kim jesteś? Co robimy?"*

"Polskie?" Miguel asked.

They nodded. Miguel pointed to Dhanpal, staggering in the street with the cowboy—an average-sized redneck in jeans and denim shirt—over his shoulder. They got the hint and ran to help Dhanpal.

The ISIL commander said something rude on the radio.

"Hey, want to hear the worst part?" I switched back to Arabic for him. "Mahmoud says the *Houris* are actually Catholic nuns. He must've gone to the wrong heaven."

Miguel tapped my shoulder. "What's a *Houri?*"

"The heavenly companions these clowns mistake for 'seventy-two virgins'." I left the radio mike open for the commander to hear. "But then, these guys don't know the Quran."

Fawaz gestured, *time to go.* We ran in the opposite direction from the women.

A squad fired on us as we rounded the corner. We fired and ran, leapfrogging each other down the alley.

We reached our staging area and jumped in our Humvees. Tania, Miguel, and I found the cowboy laid out in the back of ours with a makeshift pressure bandage on his leg. The wound was a clean through-and-through. Nasty and painful, but not worth bawling about.

His boots caught my eye. They were cowboy boots made for someone who worked with large animals. Solid and sturdy, no designs, a heel big enough to keep your foot from pushing through the stirrup but not big enough to pretend you're any taller than you are. Any soldier this guy's age, early thirties, would wear combat boots with double stitching, heavy soles, and thick-as-hell leather. The last thing you want to worry about in a firefight with the Taliban is your boots delaminating. Oil workers wore biker-boots with steel toes because they were always dropping big iron things on their feet. The locals wore cheap-ass knockoffs because they never lived long enough to understand their footwear mistake. This guy was from the western US. Not Texas, where fancy stitching and three-inch heels are a minimum requirement. Not the hardscrabble corridor west of there either, like New Mexico, Colorado or Wyoming. They weren't prosperous enough to worry about shoes. I was feeling Oklahoma, Kansas, on up to North Dakota.

Mercury said, *This here white boy's too lazy to work, my man. Look at that hat, a Larry Mahan, 500x felt. Hats like that are for rich folk.*

My abandoned deity was right. A silver buckle glinted moonlight in my eye. Pure silver, with "Freedom" in the middle.

Mercury said, *Whoever he is, he's an oxymoron: a rich working man. Keep your eyes open. Gangstas like this don't show up without a damn good reason.*

A bullet zipped past my ear.

Fawaz and Dhanpal took the other Humvee and the Polish boys.

I grabbed the wheel and floored the big diesel in low gear, spewing rocks and gravel at our pursuers.

It was first light, about an hour before dawn, so I turned on the headlights. We circled the town, firing RPGs and throwing their scrambled response into a state of confusion while the Yazidi women made their escape. If things went according to plan, the women would drive straight across the uninhabited desert for an American intelligence outpost a hundred miles west of Haditha.

We would wreak as much havoc on the locals as possible before leading the stragglers to a different patch of desert where a pair of Apache attack helicopters waited to end their contribution to the Caliphate.

We bounced over a rutted dirt road on the town perimeter.

Tania fired an RPG, reloaded, and fired again. Then she turned to the cowboy. "Who the hell are you?"

"Michael Larson. Oil field contractor, Energy Outfitters," he said. "Somebody shot me."

He spoke with a slow, confident drawl. Not a Southern drawl, not Western drawl, but the kind the farm boys back in Iowa affected after watching too many John Wayne movies.

"My bad," I shouted over the engine noise. "Welcome to the world of collateral damage. But cut the bullshit, you're not in the oil business."

"Who are you guys? You're sure as hell not Army. Did the Artist send you?"

"The who?" Tania asked. "No, we're Sabel Security. We came to rescue some friends of ours."

"Stop the truck." He gripped his leg. "I need medical attention."

"We stop, we die." Tania turned around, reloaded, and fired an RPG. She hit something. A fireball as big as a house rose into the sky. The shockwave knocked us into the ditch. My wheels spun in the dirt, catching and slipping, and catching again. We traveled slowly forward, half in and half out, skidding and sliding. An RPG flew by us, exploding fifty yards to our left in a cotton field.

Miguel emptied a magazine in their general direction.

"Damn it. They found us." Tania opened her door, stood on the footstep, and fired her RPG over the roof while holding onto the interior with one hand. Not an easy trick. Not exactly effective either. Her grenade sailed over our attackers.

The tires caught something solid, thrusting the truck forward. Tania fell from her precarious perch in the open door and landed on her butt in the ditch while I fought to get the ungainly machine to stop fishtailing down the dirt lane.

AK-47s opened up on her position.

I wheeled the beast around, making a large circle that almost drove me back in the ditch. Halfway through the arc, I saw fifty oil tankers lined up half a mile away. I thought the US Air Force had blown up all the ISIL tankers from drones. But here they were, big and shiny. What kind of business was our cowboy in?

Bullets brought my attention back to the road. I pulled in to block Tania from the onslaught of lead. Miguel leaned out the back door and grabbed her hand. She vaulted in like a ragdoll tossed by a giant, dove between the back seats, and landed on the cowboy. A grenade exploded over our heads, shredding our thin, sheet metal roof.

My foot slammed down on the accelerator. The Humvee is not known for acceleration. We lurched forward at an excruciatingly slow pace for a battle, but slightly ahead of the foot speed of our jilted hosts.

"Get off me," the cowboy yelled.

Tania rolled off slowly. "Dumbass, my body armor just saved your life."

I glanced over my shoulder and saw a dozen shards of metal stuck in her back.

"What were you doing in As Sukhnah?" Tania asked.

"They held me for ransom. I was working an oil field in Arar."

"Arar, Saudi Arabia?"

"Right."

Tania punched him in the face and ripped out the pistol he had taped behind his back. "If you're a hostage, why did they let you carry a gun?"

In the side mirror, I saw the headlights of two vehicles come into our lane. ISIL uses Toyotas, which aren't as well armored but are a lot faster than Humvees. My only advantage was rough terrain.

I turned our truck toward the southeast and crashed across the barren desert as an RPG sailed past our windows. "Hey, Miguel," I yelled above the racket. "I don't think they liked your hostess gift."

CHAPTER 2

PIA SABEL JUMPED ON THE low retaining wall along Falls Road in the village of Potomac, Maryland on a warm morning in late June. She ran to the end and dismounted with an aerial walkover. Landing alongside Bianca Dominguez, her former high school soccer rival, she slowed to match the shorter woman's pace.

Pia had asked Bianca to stand in for Tania and Jacob, Pia's usual bodyguards, while they ran a rescue mission for old friends from the wars. Outside of Sabel Industry's mandatory two-week training, Bianca had zero qualifications for personal security. She had been a top-notch geek for the NSA until she did a favor for Pia that got her fired. Now she was Sabel Technologies' top-notch geek.

Pia had requested Bianca to fill in, hoping they could become better friends. Tania and Jacob had proven themselves as great friends. But it was time to expand her circle.

Forging new friendships always comes with unexpected first steps and Bianca proved the rule. Bianca was a bared-soul personality.

"No matter how many times it fails," Bianca said, "you still have to love someone. That's how humans operate."

"Maybe I'm not human."

"You know what I'm talking about. 'Tis better to have loved and lost than never to have loved at all.'"

"Shakespeare?" Pia asked.

"Tennyson."

They ran in silence long enough for Pia to hope Bianca would change the topic.

But no.

"It's understandable," Bianca said. "After all, that thing with your parents had to be major trauma. It's obviously taken a toll on your love life. It's time to let go of the past and fall in love…"

Bianca's voice waned in the distance as Pia resumed her usual cruising speed.

People had no idea how much it hurt to bring it up. Just a casual mention, like Bianca's, hurled the memory of that heartbreaking morning into her head. The angry man stood in front of her, his booted feet planted firmly, his muscular arms extended in front of him, her mother's body dangling from his hands, choking and sputtering—and then the gunshot in the other room.

"PIA!" Bianca's shout brought her back to the warm summer morning. "I can't run that fast."

Pia slowed and waited. "Sorry."

When she caught up, they ran on, passing grand houses with acres of front yard demarcated by white rail fences. They crossed the small creek called Rock Run before Bianca picked up where she'd left off.

"Seriously," Bianca said, "you should be thinking about a real lover. Someone to take your mind off the past. Someone to get into fights, have babies, snuggle up with. You need someone to take you into the future."

"Someone like you?"

"No, *flaca*." A Spanish endearment: *skinny-girl*. "I don't do crushes on straight girls anymore—but if you ever want to switch teams, let me know."

Pia laughed. She had standing offers from a couple players on the women's national soccer team too. She might've been Miss Popular had she not been born straight.

"Seriously," Bianca continued after they negotiated fifty yards of torn-up sidewalk. "Anyone can see it. You're running from your traumatic childhood. You're afraid to get close to anyone."

Pia had heard that same diagnosis from everyone, professional therapists and armchair psychologists alike. The wives of her father's friends, the old ladies who staffed their sprawling estate, her teachers and coaches through the years; everyone believed she was trapped in her childhood tragedy. Everyone believed they knew why she only slept three hours a night. Everyone believed they knew why she had a temper.

Everyone believed they knew why this and that.

Knowing why didn't solve anything.

She sighed. "I'm twenty-six. I have plenty of time."

"Plenty of time before you get married," Bianca said. "But everyone has to have a crash-and-burn love first. You can't appreciate true love until you've been fooled by bad love. You know what I mean?"

"That's enough about me. What about you? Do you have—what did you say—someone to fight and have babies with?"

"You sound like my mother."

"Oh, is that it? Your mother wants you to settle down and so you figure I have to settle down?"

"Don't put this on me. Tania wants you to settle down too. And the Major."

So. It was a conspiracy of the three women closest to her. All three of them single and childless. And none of them involved in great relationships. Bianca was a notorious womanizer. Tania couldn't keep a relationship exclusive for more than a month. And the Major—she kept secrets even the NSA couldn't hack. And these women wanted *her* to settle down?

They ran in front of the Giant grocery store, heading to the intersection of Falls and River Roads, the center of town.

Pia had to admit, the triumvirate's analysis was spot on. She was afraid to love. Everyone she'd ever loved was dead. Except her adopted father—and that was a strained connection on a good day. Watching her parents die when she was four had a lasting effect on her psyche. Killing her mother's killer only compounded the issue. Thinking about the situation brought back another moment in time: her four-year-old self, stabbing the man with a kitchen knife. Stabbing and stabbing and stabbing his leg. The highest point she could reach. A voice in her head telling her higher and deeper might save her mother. Then she hit something. Blood poured out. The image that woke her up every night. Blood pouring out in a pulsed stream.

Pia stumbled and regained her stride.

Some people suffer traumatic childhoods and survive—and others go mad. Pia threw herself into sports, trying to outrun the voice in her head urging her to win the gold medal that her mother would have won had she lived another year. That hard-won gold now hung on her mantle, next to the only photograph of her biological parents.

But winning never helped reel in her endless fear.

Without noticing, she was back to her usual pace. Bianca ran several yards behind her as they approached River Road. Pia was on the sidewalk, facing traffic, the light ahead was green. She could cross without breaking stride. Her lucky day. The retaining wall on her left obscured cars in the near lane.

Likewise, it restricted the view for drivers turning right.

A Ferrari 488 Spider rolled into the crosswalk.

Two strides away, she ran straight toward him at sixteen miles an hour. Too fast to stop.

She jumped. Her left foot hit the hood above his right front tire. Her right foot landed on his windshield frame. Her left foot cleared the glass and the driver's head to land deftly on top of the convertible's roll bar. Her right foot landed hard on the ground. Her knee absorbed the impact. Her momentum carried her several staggering strides to the middle of the street before she could stop.

Wheeling around, she stabbed a finger at the careless driver. "Watch where you're going, asshole!"

"Oh, ma'am, I am terribly sorry. My apologies. I—"

As she drew a breath to yell again, she saw his face.

Her heart stopped. Her insides twisted into a knot. Her mind blanked.

It was him. Stefan.

And he recognized her. "Pia! Ohmigod. Are you all right? Are you hurt?"

Bianca came up behind him and navigated around the car.

Pia turned and resumed her run, albeit at a slower pace. Years of sports injuries taught her to walk off minor injuries. Which, normally, she would've done, but suddenly, she found herself in a hurry to leave. The result was a slow jog across the street. She wondered if Stefan thought she was trying to keep his attention.

She didn't care what he thought. She picked up her pace.

Behind her, the Ferrari's engine revved. She imagined him. Probably trying to attract the attention of other women in the area. No doubt he drove it with an air of privilege that, when combined with his natural charm and good looks, could seduce women up and down the street. Good for him. Who cares?

"Pia, are you OK?" Bianca ran to catch up with her. "Are you limping?"

Pia waited up the street half a block. Behind her several cars honked. She looked up in time to see the Ferrari inching its way through a traffic snarl to turn left from the right lane. Typical Stefan. Forcing the sea to part for him.

"I'm fine. I hope I dented his fender."

"Yeah." Bianca tried to keep up. "I can't believe that guy pulled into the crosswalk like that. I know it's hard to see around the corner, but still. Hey, wait, you know that guy?"

"No." She ran on. "Sort of. Stefan Devoor, scion of Royal Devoor Oil."

The Ferrari's roar charged up the street behind her. Stefan drove up beside her in the center lane. He shouted something. She ignored him. He gunned the engine and pulled into a driveway twenty yards in front of her. He parked blocking the sidewalk. He opened his door, unfolded his tall, thin frame from the small cockpit, and stepped forward.

"You're blocking the ... oh, whatever." She stopped and crossed her arms.

"Are you OK? I am so sorry, Pia. Really."

"Get your car out of the way, Stefan." She leaned forward. "Or is it Daddy's?"

"Mine. Actually." He backed up half a step. "I came home six months ago. I left several messages for you when I arrived. Dad forced my hand. If I want the family fortune to keep flowing, I have to keep Royal Devoor profitable. I hear your father did the same to you. You're running Sabel Technologies now, right?"

"She *owns* Sabel Industries," Bianca snarled.

Pia tossed a withering glance her way. Bianca winced.

"Sorry," Pia said. "I missed your homecoming parade."

She charged at him as if to tackle him. He backed up and fell backward over his door. He crashed across the seats, his legs in the air. She landed her right foot on his near fender, and her left on his far fender, and ran down the street. She didn't look back. She didn't care what happened to him.

The anguished memory of her first love felt like a two-by-four to the face. It all came back at once as she ran. The rush of Stefan's first kiss on her lips. Her panicked waits for his call. Her constant check of the Sabel Gardens gate for his arrival. The small, thoughtful gifts he ignored. Dressing and changing and changing again. Hours of makeup applied and wiped off and reapplied. Texting followed by endless hours waiting in purgatory for his reply. Hours spent agonizing over the appropriate signals to give—or not. None of it made any difference. He never appreciated her.

And then the horrible night of Saint Albans' prom.

She cringed as she recalled in instant and perfect detail every second of his angry, soul-crushing, public dismissal.

Ten years later and, as the fates would have it, he had grown more handsome. His big brown eyes and long lashes were disgustingly perfect. His curly black hair remained thick and full. Sadly, cosmetic surgery had Americanized his distinctive Roman nose.

She'd lived with the satisfaction of having stabbed her mother's murderer to death. But for this arrogant, overprivileged stick figure with the galvanized frat-boy smile plastered on his face, she'd never felt the satisfaction of retribution. Yet.

The Ferrari's high-revving engine note came up behind her. No other traffic remained on the road.

Stefan drove into the oncoming lane and pulled alongside her. "I'm practicing for driving in England."

"Funny."

"I'd like to apologize; make amends. Can we get a cup of coffee?"

"You apologized." Pia sensed Bianca catching up behind her. "You're forgiven."

"No, seriously. I want—"

"Why is it men always talk about what *they* want? Do you have any idea what I want?" She waited until he shook his head. "I want you to leave me alone."

He tightened his mouth, nodded, and looked down. After a moment, he shrugged and drove away.

"Harsh, *flaca*." Bianca watched his taillights. "He's funny-looking to me, so I assume he's handsome in the straight world."

"I don't care what he is."

"Then why did you blush so hard?"

CHAPTER 3

THE ARTIST SQUINTED INTO THE morning sun barreling through his office window. The day was clear enough to see the high-rises four miles down the road. He didn't care. He pressed a button and fifteen feet above him electric motors whirred into action, pulling the heavy drapes closed. He enjoyed the solitude of darkness. As irrational as it was, it made him feel secure in the belief that his employees would never hear the calls he made in the dark. He unclipped the special phone from under the mahogany desk and tapped the app that scrambled his voice and routed his connection through seven countries before finally reaching Syria's cell towers.

The NSA could listen all they wanted, but tracing it back would have them looking in one of the first three countries along the way. That is, if his wire-rimmed geeks could be trusted.

While it rang, he paced the thick carpet around his desk. Someone finally answered. "Give me Ahmad."

"He is not speaking today." The new voice had a heavy accent.

"Tell him the Artist is calling."

"To you he will speak. May Allah have mercy on your soul."

After a few minutes, the other end picked up.

"You sent them. Don't deny it!" Ahmad's voice burst through the connection. "I'll kill you."

"What are you talking about?" The Artist felt himself react to anger with anger. "I'm calling because I can't reach the Slager."

"Your people came for the Slager last night. Americans are all the same. You have no faith, no integrity—"

"What people?" Heat rose in his head. "The Slager is supposed to be under your protection. What happened?"

"Don't play with me, Artist." Ahmad spat the last word. "Only one person knew where to find him. They attacked before dawn. There were five of them. Americans. No drones, no helicopters—that spells 'private operation' in my book. You're the only one who can afford it."

Ahmad told him of the attack, the missing Yazidi sex slaves, and the disappearance of the Slager.

Every muscle in the Artist's body clenched with rage. Nine months of planning went into the Artist's strategy. Millions had been allocated through untraceable shell corporations, painstaking details hammered out, all of it hinging on the Slager staying in As Sukhnah to protect his interests. Now, all of it was slipping away because Ahmad couldn't secure his own territory.

"You're supposed to have consolidated a thousand fighters in that town." The Artist heard his voice rising. "You let five men slip through your perimeter? Did they take my tankers too?"

Ahmad ranted as if letting a squad of Americans infiltrate their town was a plot by the Artist to ruin ISIL.

"They took only our women and your Slager." Ahmad ranted in meaningless Arabic before returning to English. "You've not paid for the last shipment of oil. You were afraid we would kill the Slager. Admit it. That's why you sent Special Forces for him."

"The Slager means nothing to me." The Artist worried his secretary could hear him shouting. "He's an errand boy. I wouldn't spend a dime to save him. Doesn't matter. Doesn't matter. Where is the crew? Have they made it through Venezuela yet?"

"Consider them on hold until we get the Slager back."

That was wrong. If the crew was truly autonomous and off-the-grid as promised, how could Ahmad have put them on hold? They were supposed to send messages via third parties after crossing certain checkpoints. No one could contact them. A mutually agreed safety precaution.

"This operation means as much to the Islamic State as it does to me." The Artist lowered his voice and slowed his words. "Ask your commander if he wants the crew on hold."

"He doesn't care about you." Ahmad steamed in silence for a

moment. "Besides, you don't give us shit for our tankers."

"Who got your oil moving again? Who misdirected the drone strikes?"

Arguing with a fundamentalist was a waste of time. How many Americans could be in southern Syria? He knew how to find out. He had to keep the crew on schedule. He had to remain calm to get through this minor setback.

He glanced up at the portrait of his father. An oil baron who ruled an American dynasty without spending two minutes doing it watched him with a disapproving gaze. He turned his back on the portrait. From college on, no one seeks the approval of his parents anymore. He should have that painting removed.

"So we don't trust each other, Ahmad." He took a deep breath and squeezed the back of his executive chair until his fingers hurt. "We both need this operation to succeed. You couldn't have put the crew on hold. That means they never left Venezuela. I will track down the Slager, you will tell me where to find the crew. The Slager will shepherd them the rest of the way."

Ahmad huffed and breathed hard on his end.

"They are to strike a blow against America for the Caliphate in two weeks. You said they would get to kill the most important Americans. You said we would see it on Instagram. No tricks, Artist." Ahmad sucked in a conciliatory breath. "I'll text you how to find them. But if you fail, I'll kill you myself."

The Artist disconnected and fell into his chair.

He considered calling Chuck Roche. Where his father failed to give guidance, Mr. Roche had provided light. The great man had given him the reins of the American Petroleum Association, the APA, after running it with an iron fist for thirty years. Surely he would have some advice on how to salvage the operation. But then, Roche had taken his private security team with him, leaving the Artist with nothing. No hired killers to take care of little problems.

Roche was the kind who believed everyone could make his own way in the world. No, asking his advice would never work. Besides, Roche might not approve of the plan or the crew.

It was time to live up to his codename, the artist of manipulation. He could manipulate the entire American conversation, from TV pundits to coffee shop fools, by deploying a few terrorists whenever the public took up arms against fossil fuels. Now it was time to manipulate that contractor and make him live up to his codename: the Slager. Michael Larson would have to earn the reputation he'd claimed before he took the Artist's offer and jumped parole.

He knew how to track down his man. There couldn't be that many Americans running around Syria. He picked up his intercom. "Mary, get Admiral Tilden on the line right now."

CHAPTER 4

THE ROOSTER-TAIL OF DIRT our Humvees threw in the air made following us easy for the jihadis. The Yazidi women left no dust trail because they took a paved road for the first twenty miles, securing their escape. Half a mile away, on a course parallel to mine, Dhanpal and Fawaz, with our new Polish friends, also left a cloud of dust, forcing our pursuers to split their forces. If the worst happened, our formation increased the chance of one of us escaping while the other slowed them down in a last stand. Without the massive resources of the US Army at our disposal, we had to employ riskier strategies. My strategy was to outrun Dhanpal. So far, I had a comfortable lead on him.

We were twenty miles from our safe-zone. A little under an hour, given our rough, cross-country route.

Our Humvee bounced over little ridges and dry gullies called *wadis* that flipped one of the pursuing Toyotas and slowed the rest. But our reprieve was short-lived. The quicker Toyotas pursued us with unrelenting fervor on flat ground. And there was plenty of flat ground.

My foot cramped up from holding the accelerator to the floor. The sunrise glaring in my left eye didn't help. We bounced across a small ridge and into a big *wadi* fifteen feet deep and littered with basketball-sized stones. If we could get across it before the bastards got to the edge, we were golden. Their Toyotas would never get through.

I was churning the wheel left and right to find traction between the stones when Mercury appeared. It's not necessarily a good thing when a retired god appears.

Mercury said, *Hear that noise under the hood, bro? You're doomed. Engine's going to blow. I told you they were crap when you 'rented' these heaps from the SEALs.*

I said, *I don't recall you offering any alternatives. Can you fix it? Who do you think I am? Grease-monkey god? Fix it yourself.*

A howitzer-boom came from under the hood. Smoke billowed out on the passenger side. I leapt out and lifted the hood. With a little experience working on tractors back on the farm, I could tell we were done in one glance. A hole in the engine block as big as a dinner plate exposed the inner workings better than a technical diagram. A piston flopped out and fell to the compartment floor. I dropped the hood.

Miguel and Tania looked at me with expectant faces. Michael Larson—if that was the cowboy's real name—limped out of the back and joined them. Larson's nervous gaze and darting eyes made me want to shoot him.

Mercury stood off to one side. *Tell them the truth, dawg. Suicide is your best option. Take the honorable way out before these drugged-up jihadis get hold of you and parade your carcasses on social media.*

I said, *Not without a fight to the finish.*

It's been fun hanging with you, bro, but you don't stand a chance. Bullet to the brain, quick and easy.

I said, *What kind of god can't help his chosen one in his hour of need?*

You sound just like Jesus. 'Why have you forsaken me?' He whined out the last part.

Dissing Jesus really pissed me off. At that point, I was ready to become an atheist. Although it was hardly worth the effort in my remaining minutes among the living.

"I can shoot," Larson said with that slow, confident John Wayne imitation. He should've added, *Pilgrim.*

The three of us turned to him.

Tania spoke first. "If you think we're going to give you a rifle, you're out of—."

"No matter what you think of me, those guys saw me leave with you. That makes me one of you in their eyes. The last guy who escaped—they peeled his skin off in the center of town." He clenched his teeth and closed his eyes. "At least give me a chance. If we don't win, I can take the quick way out."

Mercury leaned to my ear. *At least one of you has some sense.*

I pledged right then and there that if I lived, I would attend church regularly. I think we were Methodists, I don't remember. Hell, I'd try a synagogue or a mosque until I found something that felt more supportive. Maybe start with the Unitarians for one-stop shopping.

Miguel pulled a revolver from his belt and held it between us and nodded toward Larson.

"No fucking way," Tania said.

"If we're all going to die," I said, "why not let him take out a couple for us? He deserves as much of a chance as the rest of us."

I pointed to the back of the Humvee. Flip up a small homemade hatch and there's an M134 Gatling-type minigun mounted for firing out the back. Jury-rigged by well-intentioned first-tour grunts, it was poorly fitted. We'd ignored it because of its limited field of fire—maybe 30 degrees left or right—but its 4,000 rounds per minute might help. Our cowboy would have a hard time turning it on us from where it was bolted to the floor.

Tania saw the wisdom in my strategy. We pushed him in place and took up our positions. Miguel by the left front, me opposite, and Tania on the hood with her sniper rifle.

The first Toyota tried to stop at the top of the *wadi* but skidded the last few yards. It teetered on the brink, slid in nose-down, and flipped end over end.

Tania grabbed her trusty MGL, a six-shooter that fires 40mm grenades. "Poke some holes in his gas tank, I'll light 'em up."

Larson opened up, dispatching the crash survivors in a barrage of 7.62mm lead that tore holes in the upside-down truck. Tania launched a grenade. The gasoline spilling out caught fire, and the flames quickly engulfed the wreckage.

Dust clouds on the ridge showed three more vehicles parked above us. With four to six soldiers each, we were outnumbered beyond hope. These guys were drug addicts with no respect for life, law, or Islam, but they weren't stupid enough to stand on the ridge and let us shoot them. They'd split to either side, lay down suppressing fire, then come at us from three sides.

Mercury was right. We were going to die.

I checked my phone. Sabel Satellites covered most of the world, but not Syria. I wanted to call Yumi and say good-bye. She was the only one in Tokyo's law enforcement community who believed in me at a difficult time last winter. We fell in love and, for the first time in my misspent, single life, I was faithful to her. No less than five months straight; a record for me. The sight of her face made my heart spin like a top. Hearing her voice soothed my savage soul. Yumi made me want to be a better man. To say she was distraught when I left would be an understatement. I hadn't yet worked up the nerve to propose to her—but I meant to. Now I was going to leave her a not-quite-widow. I just wanted to say good-bye.

Her lovely face appeared, like a vision, in front of me.

Or was that Tania?

"Why are you staring into the sky?" From the Humvee's roof, Tania kicked the butt of her rifle into my chest. "Take out those guys on the right."

I trained my rifle on the ridge and flipped it to full auto.

Mercury said, *Yo, see that glint next to the rock? He's using a mirror. Target down and to the left, put three rounds in the dirt.*

I fired and heard the last yelp of a dying man. Mercury's aiming instructions sent my bullet through the dirt at just the right angle. When the bullet exited the soft, sandy soil, it went straight into the enemy's skull. Another figure, lying next to my victim, panicked, rose from his hiding place, and ran. I nailed him in the back.

A cloud of dust to my right signaled fighters entering the *wadi* behind a dirt bank fifty yards away. Tania reported a similar telltale cloud to the left. They were setting up their pincer. Right on cue, five guys opened up directly in front of us on the ridge.

Larson's M134 had little vertical range, so Tania fired at the guys straight ahead while Miguel and I fired on the flankers.

They fought smarter in the daylight, popping out, rolling left and right, laying down suppressing fire. They used the jagged dirt berms of the *wadi* to get closer and closer to us. Rounds buzzed my ear like angry hornets. More pinged off the Humvee, jarring my nerves and raising my fear-factor.

I'd been through some nasty firefights, but this one was the worst kind. To die in a ditch in the middle of nowhere without even getting a chance to call my almost-bride pissed me off. I ran toward the approaching squad on my side and took cover behind a rock the size of a truck tire. I blasted a mag through a wall of dirt and watched with satisfaction as a body fell sideways. But his friends took advantage of my victory by closing in. Shards of rock shot into the sky near my nose. I was pinned down and they were getting closer.

Larson's M134 opened up. That meant the forward squad was coming down the bank. Miguel roared his frustration at running out of ammo for his MP5 and resorted to his pistol. Tania screamed for another mag. I had one left and was too far away to toss it. Larson managed to slay half the attackers coming straight on before he too ran out of lead.

Tania used her grenade-revolver to pump three grenades over my head and three over Miguel's. The explosions pushed the bad guys back but only staved off the inevitable for a few minutes.

After the last grenade exploded there was dead silence in the *wadi*. They knew what our silence meant. They were free to toy with us and whatever ammo we had left for our pistols. For some reason, I sensed them laughing at us.

But they weren't. They were scrambling away.

Mercury scurried over to my position. *So glad you didn't take the easy way out like you were planning, yo. Suicide is just wrong.*

What? It was your idea to—

Then I heard the fast-whump of Apache helicopters seconds before their 30mm chain guns tore one-inch-diameter holes in our enemies. A second later they flew overhead, chasing down the last survivors.

We stood up and cheered.

Being thorough, they took half an hour to secure the area and send in a Navy SeaHawk to take us back to the operations area.

But they didn't send one SeaHawk. They sent two.

That struck me as odd because the military is loath to risk recruits and equipment on a regular operation, much less private contractors. Two birds was a huge expense in fuel, risk, and personnel.

From the second bird, a Navy man ran to us. "Which one of you guys works for Energy Outfitters?"

CHAPTER 5

CLICKS FROM THEIR HEELS ECHOED through the concrete stairwell of the Sabel Industries Building in downtown Bethesda. Pia led Bianca through the artificial orange-hued lighting. The high-rise's heartless cement cloaked their conversation from the thousands of workers beyond the walls. As she climbed the cold, empty space, Pia regretted cutting off Bianca's relentless psychoanalysis. Bianca had no qualifications as a therapist yet hungered to somehow fix Pia's broken life. Pia was annoyed but welcomed the cross-examination. She excelled at keeping her emotions to herself. It took someone relentless to dig them out.

They hadn't spoken since she parked the McLaren in the underground garage. She'd lost her temper and told Bianca to shut up. Now Bianca's victimized silence was killing her. If they were going to have any kind of conversation, the seventeen-floor climb in a sound-smothering stairwell would be as good a place as any.

"Go ahead, Bianca. Tell me whatever's been needling you."

Bianca huffed, partially because of the exertion, partially as retribution. "Stefan wants to start something with you. I could see it in his eyes. And you need something started."

"He's a rich, misogynistic frat boy." Pia stopped at the eighth-floor landing and faced her bodyguard. "He thinks women should run to him when he snaps his fingers."

She wheeled around and continued up.

"Then tell him you won't accept that." Bianca took a deep breath and chased after the boss. "Make him a better man."

"Not my job."

"You need passion, Pia."

"I have passion. I'm passionate about winning. Haven't you noticed all my trophies and—"

"Oh yes, you're focused on winning—but you miss all the passion in love." She ran a few steps ahead of Pia and stopped. "That's you—always winning instead of facing your trauma. You're holding back the real you. Not just lovers; you hold back from everybody. We don't know what makes you tick."

Pia needed friends who would challenge her. Knowing that didn't stop her from losing it.

"You want to know what makes me tick?" She stuck a finger in Bianca's chest. "I'm scared. OK? I've been scared all my life. You and Tania think all my problems could be solved if I'd just get laid. Well, I've got news for you. Relationships make it worse. You know what it's like to watch your mother die? You know what it's like to kill a man? It's scary. I'm so scared I wake up screaming at three in the morning. I'm scared something bad is going to happen to Alan Sabel. I'm scared something bad is going to happen to Bianca Dominguez. I'm scared that Leroy Johnson—or someone just like him—will come back from the dead to attack the people I love."

Pia took a moment to steady her breathing. When was the last time she'd said the name Leroy Johnson out loud? The man who'd killed her mother was an ever-present ghost, haunting her for killing him.

"I channel that fear into winning." She pushed past open-mouthed Bianca.

They climbed three floors in silence.

Bianca's phone buzzed, shattering the rhythmic echoing of heel-clicks. "A text from Jacob. He wants to research oil trucks in southern Syria."

"Anytime Jacob has a question, even if it sounds pretty odd, make it a top priority." Pia pushed open the stairwell door and they emerged into her office lobby.

"I'll get right on it." Bianca turned left.

"Ah. There you are." An attorney standing at the elevator bank looked up at Pia with surprise. "Alan's looking for you. He wants you in the meeting. Here, you need to sign this."

Pia grabbed the document, scanned it, and stuffed it back in his hands.

She radiated displeasure as she led him back into the stairwell and up to the penthouse conference center on the 19th floor. The attorney struggled to keep up, clutching his folder of papers and laptop to his chest. She burst from the stairwell, crossed the lobby, marched into the searing summer daylight flooding the circular meeting room, and strode straight to her father.

"Since when do I need to sign a non-disclosure agreement to attend a meeting?" she asked.

Alan Sabel rose and gave her a quick hug before pointing to an empty chair near him at the round table. "Standard business procedure, Pia. These are very important business leaders who are proposing a few deals."

"I've given you full authority to make any—"

"You'll find their proposals of some personal interest."

He gestured around the table. Immaculate specimens of corporate America sat erect with attentive eyes. A group of mostly white males with slick haircuts and trendy suits. Two people caught her eye. To the left of her father sat her second-in-command most trusted adviser, her Chief Operating Officer, known throughout the company as the Major. Across from her, Stefan Devoor tapped a pencil on a pad of paper and avoided eye contact. She rolled her eyes and scanned the others. The only other face she recognized was Stefan's father Luuk.

"You know the Devoor boys," her father said, his booming voice projecting warmth and charm, his arms wide and expansive.

"Excuse me," said a wrinkled older man who kept a hand on a silver-handled cane. "No names until the NDA is signed."

She recognized the old man from somewhere but couldn't place his name.

Alan, the well-known alpha-dog who always maintained control of proceedings, uncharacteristically silenced himself, and bowed slightly. He turned to Pia. "If you wouldn't mind."

She took the open chair while the corporate attorney scurried to her side, laid out the single page document and pen. She took her time reading every word. Looking around the room, she counted six Sabel executives and fifteen visitors. One of the Sabel executives, a young woman named Maria, gazed starry-eyed at Stefan. Stefan glanced at the woman, twitched a polite smile, then looked away.

Stefan's gaze wandered to Pia. Their eyes met. He took a breath and leaned back in his chair, using the angle to disappear behind an executive. What was that look? Anger? Hate? Embarrassment?

Once again, she was losing focus because of Stefan Devoor. She looked at the paper.

The Major nodded at her to sign, as did her father. The wording was vague but came down to one thing: she swore not to reveal the proceedings to anyone outside the room. She signed.

Alan continued with the introductions, most of the names were followed by "attorney for" and a corporate name she'd never heard of. Before Alan reached the crepe-paper old man, she remembered him.

She interrupted her father. "You're Chuck Roche."

She pronounced his surname like the insect.

A collective inhale drew the air from the room. Some point of protocol had been breached that upset the corporate slaves.

The old man stiffened and scowled, gripping his cane as if he planned to leap up and beat her with it. "It's pronounced row-SHAY."

"Huh."

If she recalled correctly, she'd seen him near the top of the Forbes 400 list of richest people. Judging from the number of sycophants around him who lifted their chins at her ignorance, she assumed he was way ahead of her on the list.

Yippee for him.

"We've been looking to divest divisions that are outside the Sabel Industries core competencies," Alan said. "These gentlemen have an interest in two of our divisions, SPP and SCE."

"Sorry." Pia squinted. "I don't have all the abbreviations memorized."

"SPP, Sabel Paper Products and SCE, Sabel Clean Energy."

Pia's mouth fell open.

"I'm sure you have sentimental attachment to those divisions," he continued, "but they're small and we've never given them the attention they deserve. Neither of them fit into our portfolio of technology and security."

No one spoke.

Alan splayed his fingers out and held her gaze. A prearranged signal calling for her to reserve her opinions for private discussion. She nodded.

"What sentimental value could these companies have?" Roche asked in a gruff voice.

"The paper company was a middle school project of hers." Alan faced him. "When she first heard about deforestation she wanted to explore renewable alternatives to tree pulp and settled on hemp paper, so we started SPP."

"What a fortunate youth to have such wealth at your disposal for class projects." Roche turned his cold, blue eyes to Pia.

"Indulgent," she said, recalling another time she'd seen his name in print. "I believe that's what you called it in your opinion piece for the *Post* after we announced the start-up. You were railing about the indulgent parenting of the *nouveau riche*."

He chuckled. "I stand by that opinion. It was indulgent of your father to invest in a company just to satisfy a twelve-year-old. Nonetheless, it turned out to be a wise investment."

Again, Alan splayed his fingers on the table. She looked at the Major, who sat stone-faced in her gray suit, her hair pulled back in a tight bun. The emotionless gaze communicated the Major's advice: keep your emotions in check.

To hell with that.

"Without generations of Ferarri driving, alcohol-fueled playboys to guide our family in the art of success—" she stared at Stefan "—we had to muddle along."

Most of the faces at the table looked down at their papers. Roche gripped his cane. Alan closed his eyelids for a long blink. Luuk Devoor glared at Pia as if she were a heretic, then looked at Roche to see if he'd survived. Stefan glanced at his father, then at Roche.

Stefan coughed and spoke in a soft voice. "Royal Devoor is particularly interested in your high-school project. SCE, the wind farm in California."

Roche's face had grown increasingly redder since Pia's outburst. His glare hadn't moved an inch from her. He ignored Stefan. "In all my life, I've never heard such impudence in a business—"

"The caterer's here." Alan stood and gestured to the side room. "Let's take a break, shall we?"

The Major rose quickly and gestured to others, guiding them into the next room where a buffet waited. Feeling grateful for his intervention, Pia swept in line between Dad and the Major.

She looped her arms through theirs and pulled them close to her. "What do they want with my companies?"

"As long as they're paying cash, I don't care." Alan checked to make sure they were flanked by his attorneys for privacy. "We're not actively helping those companies. I don't even know if the guys at Sabel Paper are smoking the hemp or rolling it."

"Roche is not just the biggest privately held refinery company in the world," the Major said. "They also own millions of acres of forest and hundreds of paper mills. He also owns a competitor, Roche Security."

"What about Royal Devoor," Pia asked. "Why would an oil company want in on wind energy?"

"They bought National Solar last year and closed it." Alan ladled himself a bowl of albondigas soup. "Same thing maybe?"

"This deal stinks, Dad." Pia chose the shrimp ceviche, which had just run out. The server excused himself to get more.

"Smells like money to me." Alan headed for the dining area where small tables waited for the group.

While she waited for the ceviche, she assessed the attendees. Stefan stood to one side, talking to two women. Both Pia and Stefan were tall enough to look over the heads of average Americans. He looked up and caught her gaze. He half-blushed, fidgeted his fingers, then excused himself, and stepped around the ladies. His direction indicated he could be heading toward her.

She turned her back and faced the empty serving bowl, the server still missing. Voices swirled around her. She wondered if Stefan intended to speak to her. Wasn't her put-down of playboys enough to keep him away? Surely, he wouldn't talk to her after the incident on the street. She clutched at her purse only to remember she left it on the meeting table.

"I've missed being in your presence." Stefan spoke softly behind her. "You are a powerful personality."

She pretended not to hear him.

"You look absolutely stunning today, Pia." He stood closer, speaking to her shoulder. "I would appreciate it if you would have coffee with me one morning. I need to—"

"'Stunning?' Is that the kind of thing you say to your strippers?" She glanced to the side but couldn't see him without turning. She did not turn. "Tell me I'm special. Tell me you mean it."

She heard him inhale slowly and hold it. Then he said, "Legions of exotic dancers have wandered the streets in search of a new benefactor for the last couple years. Nonetheless, you are beautiful."

Pia had never believed herself to be pretty. Her buffed, athletic figure turned off as many men as it attracted. Standing a few inches taller than the average American male limited her admirers even further. On top of that, her distrust of those enamored with wealth narrowed her field of prospective romantic partners to nearly nil. But an unnecessary, acerbic reaction to a simple compliment was regrettable. She faced him.

He was already four paces away. He didn't look back.

"Ma'am?" the server raised his voice. "Did you want the ceviche?"

She thanked him and took the offered bowl and looked for an open table. Nearby, Luuk Devoor poured amber liquid from a pocket flask into drinks in a circle of outstretched cups.

Several people huddled around a TV screen at the far end of the space. Pia set her dish on a table and started toward the group watching the news. A couple attorneys stepped in front of her, speaking in hushed tones. The weight of the room began to shift toward the TV.

Chuck Roche stepped in front of her. He held his cane like an accessory meant to give him an air and not as an aid for walking. The handle was solid silver in the shape of an elephant head, with a stout trunk forming the horizontal portion.

"You may not take these proceedings seriously, young lady," Roche said, "but that boy will be an important part of the business community in the coming years. Show your peers some respect."

"Peer?" She looked down at him. "Because he chose the right vagina to pop out of, he deserves respect?"

"In time, he will control vast sums of money. That money will control large sectors of the economy. The decisions he makes will benefit thousands of jobs and hundreds of communities."

Her teeth clamped down on her tongue to keep her from asking about Stefan's qualifications for directing "large sectors of the economy," but her father's hand splayed wide in her mind. She regarded the old man carefully. "That's a fine cane you have."

"My grandfather's. I carry it everywhere to remind me of my legacy." He smiled and held it up between them to admire. "Do you carry reminders of your responsibilities?"

The scar tissue on her back twitched. She'd barely escaped an explosion caused by a rogue State Department appointee. Another wound made its presence felt. And another. She kept the reminders of her responsibilities to herself.

She nosed toward the TV where half the room stood. "What has everyone's attention?"

As Roche shrugged, she pulled up the *Post* on her phone. The nation waited for a press conference held by the wildly popular young Governor of California, Marty Maddox. He was expected to announce his intention to run for president. Speculation drove the crowd's curiosity. Some were convinced it was too late in the race to mount a serious campaign. Others urged him to run since the major parties' candidates were less than inspirational.

The Governor appeared on camera and a hush came over the people packed tightly in front of Pia.

"Ladies and gentlemen," Governor Maddox said, "My grandfather's generation was called the Greatest Generation. They grew up in the Great Depression, fought and won World War II, educated their peers through the GI Bill, rebuilt Europe with the Marshall Plan, fought segregation, and built the Interstate Highway system. They pulled together as a nation and worked hard until the United States of America was the best country in the world. They vaccinated children and stamped out hunger. They built the best education system and put the first man on the moon. Each of those programs pushed our economy to new heights.

"Fresh lettuce in Southern California is now shipped to Connecticut in the middle of winter because of their highways. Companies like FedEx, UPS, and Swift Transportation expanded the economy on the roads they built. The space race spawned new technologies like personal computers, the Internet, and big data. Everyone from IBM and HP to Microsoft, Apple, and Dell prospered. The often maligned military-industrial complex created high-paying jobs in aerospace at Lockheed, Boeing, Northrop, GE and many others. These federally-driven programs employed countless citizens in rewarding careers.

"When the Greatest Generation retired, the dedication to community service that built the greatest nation in history retired with them. For the last thirty years, we've been resting on *their* laurels. We've grown greedy, thinking only of ourselves: where is my next tax break, where is my next handout, where is my next bailout, who will build my next stadium? We've not maintained the standards our grandparents set. Our nation is no longer number one in math, we're twenty-fifth—two ranks below Russia. Nineteen below Vietnam. We don't even *have* a manned space vehicle. Our infrastructure is old and crumbling. We've spent our inheritance.

"Well, ladies and gentlemen, all that's about to change. The next generation is ready to face the problems swept under the rug a long time ago. The next generation is ready to do what it takes to solve our energy problems. The next generation is ready to take our schools to the next level. The next generation is ready to hold our nation to the highest ethical standards. The next generation is ready to make the USA number one in every field. Make no mistake about it—the next generation has arrived!"

The crowd at the California Governor's mansion erupted in wild cheers. Banners flashed on giant screens around the Governor: *Move over Republicans. Move over Democrats. The NEXT Generation is here.*

Welcome the alternative political party—NEXT USA.

The Governor shouted, "LET'S TAKE AMERICA TO THE *NEXT* LEVEL!"

Chuck Roche shouted, "Turn that crap off."

Someone complied with his request.

"Excuse me?" Pia turned to face the old man. "People are watching that."

"Since the Gilded Age," Roche shouted, "this has been a two-party nation. Introducing a third party is destructive, Ms. Sabel."

"You're pronouncing it 'sable' like the rat used for fur coats. It's pronounced SAY-bul. It's Scandinavian for 'sword'."

Pia twisted between stunned executives to the TV and turned it back on. She marched defiantly back to Roche only to find his back turned, talking to Alan. Her father listened with a concerned look, rubbing his chin.

"We can't let them succeed." Roche's voice shook with emotion as he spoke quietly to Alan. "You know as well as anyone how damaging this will be."

"I know more about satellites than political—"

"I'll gather the top men in the country. We'll meet in a few days. Be ready, Alan. We'll stop this guy." Roche pitched forward and marched to the elevator. A split second later, like a school of fish, his people turned, and followed him. Luuk Devoor saw his exodus and followed suit with his entourage.

Pia watched her father's reaction. He felt her gaze at a distance, faced her, and shrugged.

The noise of a helicopter coming in for a landing on the helipad overwhelmed the scene. Everyone stopped to stare at the rotors whirling a few dangerous inches from the glass. A Marine in full dress uniform jumped out and ran straight to Pia.

He saluted her. "Ma'am, President Veronica Hunter respectfully requests your presence at the White House immediately. A matter of national importance."

"Too bad she didn't call ahead. You'll have to return empty—"

"The President empowered me, if you were hesitant, to tell you she will answer your questions about your parents' murders to the extent of her knowledge."

CHAPTER 6

IN THE VAST CUBE-FARM OUTSIDE the Artist's office, worker bees droned on through their daily routines, their inconsequential voices chattering endlessly about their meaningless lives. Fools. The Artist creaked his leather chair back and put his feet on the desk. He reviewed the invitation list of his brother billionaires for Roche's big meeting. It was his big opportunity to gain the respect of his peers. That's what mattered in life. Wowing Roche and his cadre. And he would pull it off. By the time everyone left Rancho Mirage, they would know how brilliant he was and why he called himself the Artist.

He leaned forward and dialed the first name on the list, even though it irked him to no end. Who wanted to call the married-five-times perv whose grotesque sex life had been dragged out and publicized? Not that the Artist hadn't had a few brushes with gold diggers. The burden of billionaires.

"Buddy, you saw Maddox's announcement?" the Artist asked. "We're convening a conference."

"This is a disaster." The man sounded apoplectic. "Damn straight, I'll be there."

The Artist couldn't disconnect quickly enough. The next name was more to his liking: a man who shared the Artist's views on inheritance taxes. That call went smoothly. As did the third call to the casino king who spent half the call asking about Maddox's stand on issues.

The Artist explained that no one knew a thing about Maddox. He was young and had spurned the Artist's funding every step of his political career. Time after time, the insolent young politician had refused his offers. *No quid pro quo allowed.*

Bullshit. That's how politics works. *You want my money; you promote my industry. The APA represents companies with hundreds of thousands of employees, meaning voters and taxpayers, therefore my demands benefit everyone involved. Simple math.*

Maddox never budged.

The Artist and the gaming king echoed each other. How dare Marty Maddox call Baby Boomers greedy? Who did he think he was? A vegetarian conservative-liberal who biked around Sacramento with his wife and perfect children, benefiting from a tech sector explosion that fueled his state's economy no matter how badly he screwed it up. Like Texas and Alaska with their oil revenue, a monkey could look good running California.

As he prepared for his next call, something that should never happen—did. The phone under his desk rang.

He tossed his list on the desk, bent down, grabbed the phone from its clip, pressed the encryption button and hissed his words into the voice scrambler. "What the hell are you thinking? I'm alone, but anyone could've been in this office."

"Thought you'd want to know: the crew is stuck in Mérida." The Slager clicked off.

The Artist squeezed the phone until his hand hurt. Blood rushed to his head as his anger darkened his already-black mood. "Goddamnit!"

He blew out a breath and staggered to the window and checked his watch. Just when he gets the plan back on track, everything falls apart. As if some galactic conspiracy were trying to ruin him.

He twirled the phone in his hand. The clock was ticking. The crew was wound up tight with ideology and would self-destruct in a couple weeks. If he wanted that explosion to go off at the planned place and time. He'd have to take control of the situation regardless of the risk. There was no other way. He dialed the Slager and connected on the first ring. "Where are you?"

"Observing your Moroccan morons from a hotel room across the street." The Slager snorted.

"What do you mean, 'morons'? Are they not qualified for the job?"

"Oh, they're more than qualified." The Slager's voice took an ominous tone. "They are deeply committed to killing you, me, our women and children, even our dogs. But this is only the second time they've left home. Before they joined ISIL, they never strayed farther than the goat pen back in whatever micro-village they came from."

"What happened?" the Artist asked.

"From what they told me, Omar never saw the money so he refused to cough up the passports. They don't know how to deal with scam artists."

"No. I mean, why did you leave As Sukhnah?"

"No choice. Some outfit called Sabel Security liberated Ahmad's harem, shot me, and took me with them. Thought they were saving me."

"What did you tell them?"

"Listen up, *Artiste*," Larson said with an exaggerated snarl in the last word. "I don't like the way any of this went down. I signed up to keep an eye on your tankers because—for some strange reason—you don't trust terrorists. To me, that was worth half a million and a new life with a clean ID. But this." The Slager blew a long breath. "This is not what I signed up for."

"Tough." The Artist paced the room. These money-grubbing bastards never stop. All they want is to shake down rich people when they should get out there and work to earn their own money. "Things changed when you left your post. This is your new post. Deal with it."

"I'm the one Admiral Tilden pulled out of the dirt. I'm the guy taking all the goddamn risk. Double my payday or you can tell these guys how to act in a Catholic country."

"Don't you dare speak to me like that." The Artist felt the rage boiling in his veins. "I've risked everything to finance this."

"Then finance the fuck outta me or your Moroccans are going to sit in 'Zuela long enough for someone to ask why they pray so damned often. They were on the balcony of their rooms today."

"Shit."

"Shit is right. And I'm supposed to babysit these killers around the world?"

The Artist considered telling the arrogant prick to drop dead, but there was too much at stake. It had not been an easy plan to conjure up. Noah's Ark was neither as critical to humanity nor as well planned. Without this avenue, he had nothing to protect the APA. A half-million more wasn't going to hurt the budget anyway.

He glanced at his father's portrait on the wall. He flipped off the old man and returned his attention to the phone. "All right. All right. I'll fix this. Just get them moving."

A moment of silence followed.

The Artist realized his mistake. If you don't bargain long and hard with these bottom-feeders, they smell the money. This guy will want more and more and more. Well, it didn't matter. It was a joint account. When the plan was finally executed, the Slager would wind up dead. All that money was coming back.

"If you ever want to see your dreams come true," the Artist said, "get the passports out of Omar first thing in the morning. I'll send a formula for my next number, then burn—"

"Burn the burner, yeah. I know how this works."

"Text your status after each border crossing."

"One last thing," the Slager said. "The Sabel agents know my name."

The Slager clicked off.

The Artist stared at his phone in disbelief. Had he heard right? He gave them his name? Nothing could be worse. No greater threat existed. How could he be so stupid? They find the Slager and he would squeal on Schwartz and the program. And he knew Schwartz. That sniveling little weasel would rat him out at the first whiff of a plea deal.

He pressed his fist to his forehead. Why had Roche taken the professional killers with him when he left the APA? It didn't matter. What mattered was solving the problem. He could find a way to make it work because that's how artists do things.

He called Schwartz.

"How many resources can we move to the Washington metro area overnight?" he asked.

"From the program?" Schwartz sounded confused.

"Yes, from the program. What other resources are you in charge of? I need three agents of Sabel Security eradicated."

"Three at once? High-profile killings of—"

"You were tasked with setting up the program to have resources at the ready. Are you telling me they're not ready?"

"They're ready." Schwartz hesitated as if something bothered him about the request. "But an operation like this could take all our men. There are only so many violent offenders getting out on parole who are willing to—"

"Why would it take more than two men?"

"Because of the risk. You'd want backup to the backup. We can't have one of these men get caught and go through a DNA check. The IDs we supply them are good for fingerprints and social security cards. They can start a new life, even get a passport maybe, but if they get arrested, the DNA will lead back to my rehab program."

"That's what I pay you for, isn't it?" As soon as the words left his mouth, he realized where Schwartz was going with all this. The skinny accountant was clever, but just like the Slager, it was all about the money. This time, he had more leverage.

"I'm taking a big risk here. If anything goes wrong—"

"If you don't like risk, get a job greeting shoppers at Walmart. I'll text you the names and addresses shortly. I expect to read about the murders by morning."

CHAPTER 7

THE BEST PART ABOUT WORKING for a billionaire: when you and your buddies want to help out some folks who saved your ass during the war, she lends you her private jet. For her, sending a jet on a 16,000-mile round-trip was no bigger a deal than picking out new shoes. The jet was her old one, but it slept eight and there were only five of us, so plenty of room to go around. I slept far enough away that I couldn't hear Tania snore and managed a full night's sleep before we landed.

After an ugly deployment, a post-mission high sets in that's half retained-fear and half survivor's elation. The further you get from having cheated death, the more you lean toward elation. I was leaning in hard.

Drizzle slicked the roads as I drove home in the late-evening dark. I was high and getting higher the closer I came to seeing Yumi Shibata and my puppy, Anoshni. All I could think of was her ... and whether she'd discovered how to use plurals while I was gone. Her English needed a little work. Everything else was perfect.

Mercury said, *You know it won't last, bro. You'll blow it. Always do.*

Startled, I nearly jumped out of the car at sixty on the beltway. *Jesus Christ!*

Why you always gotta bring him into it? He's going to make you give all your money to the poor and spend the rest of your life swabbing lepers. Like he did with Millard Fuller.

I said, *Who?*

Dawg, Millard Fuller. The rich guy. I had him this close to building a pantheon just for me. Mercury held up a finger and thumb as if he were squeezing a sheet of paper. *It was going to have pillows and pools and all the gold that you could eat. Enough strippers to entertain a legion.* Mercury stared into the sky as if seeing a rainbow. *But no, the sniveling noob listened to Jesus and next thing you know, he gave all his money to start up Habitat for Humanity and dedicated his life to housing the homeless.*

I said, *Sounds like a good alternative to being left in a ditch with a blown engine and a platoon of jihadis coming for me.*

Mercury took his helmet off and polished it. *There you go again, always pledging your allegiance to any god who can fix your problems. You're as fickle as Emperor Constantine. You think we're competing for your business or something?*

Mercury looked out the window as I pulled onto my quiet suburban street. *This is going to be one tough night for you, homie. Y'know that, right?*

I ignored him, pulled into the driveway, and tugged my bag out of the backseat.

The curtain in the living room dropped back as if someone didn't want to get caught peeking. Adorable. My smile grew so big my cheeks hurt. I opened the door. Anoshni barked and scrambled his way across the slick floor to scratch at my shins.

Yumi, her jet-black hair shining under the foyer light, hung her head and stepped back.

I threw my arms open and waited.

Nothing.

My smile faded.

She looked like a statue of deep sorrow.

Maybe it was my t-shirt. It read, *US Army – Keeping heaven packed with fresh souls since 1775.* Not exactly tasteful for the Buddhist crowd.

I dropped my gear and kicked the door shut and stepped forward, inches in front of her. We'd been here before. In the wars, I had developed an immunity to horror. She had not. She had classic Post Traumatic Stress Disorder. With an emphasis on disorder. It interfered with every aspect of her life. Damaged by the carnage of mankind's cruelty, she had serious problems thinking about life and death situations. My daily routine.

Her brown eyes rose to meet mine. As if pulled by a drawstring inside, her face crumpled. I wrapped my arms around her and pulled her shaking body to mine. Her tears felt warm on my chest. I stroked her hair and did my best to coo.

Anoshni barked for attention. I rubbed him with my foot.

We stood like that until my feet ached.

"Yumi," I said quietly, "let's sit down and talk about this."

"So afraid you not…" she said. "So afraid…"

She broke down again. I picked her up and carried her to the living room where I lowered us gently on the sofa. Parked in the corner, she curled up and pushed her cheek to my chest. Anoshni nudged under the crook of her arm.

Everything about my job produced horrific flashbacks for her. I waited until her breathing calmed. "Tell me from the beginning."

Speaking slowly, she recounted the story. The American approached while she was at the far end of the emergency room. The killer pressed a revolver to the victim's forehead and pulled the trigger. Tokyo's detectives work in a civilized country and do their jobs unarmed. Even the worst of criminals obey police commands. She identified herself and ordered him to surrender. He kept his eyes locked on hers while he sidestepped to the second gurney and repeated his murderous violence. Horrified, she yelled at him but found herself frozen in place. He killed four more without ever taking his eyes off her. All her training failed her, all her instincts were gone. She had no idea what to do. When he turned his weapon on her, she ran.

"He kill all the man," she said.

Psychologists told me retelling her trauma reduced the power it held over her. Whenever she retold the story, she relived it with a little more distance and a little less fear. It lifted Yumi's spirits out of the deep abyss.

And the puppy helped.

"You feel better now?" I asked.

"No."

"I came back from Syria."

She stroked my chest and looked at me. "You body came back from Syria. You not to trust such place. It reach out to you and tug at you. Make you to come back."

"I'm here. I'm back."

"Where is you heart?"

"My heart is with you, I swear."

She put her cheek on my chest and we rested for a long time. She sighed.

Mercury came in eating an apple and did a double take. *Whoa! Hold on now. You're not going to have sex with her until after I leave, right? 'Cause that face you make is just disgust—*

I said, *Then you can leave now.*

I pulled Yumi in closer and savored her warm breath on my neck.

In that domestic moment it occurred to me that my irrational resignation from the singles field was driven by a subconscious belief that settling down with Yumi might restore my sanity. Maybe I could leave Sabel Security and finally start my career as a chef. Maybe I could say good-bye to gunfire, violence—and Mercury. What had been missing from my life all these years was not a supermodel in a bikini, a Ferrari, and a shot of tequila—it was peace, *shalom, salaam, shanti.*

My phone rang. I ignored it. After the fourth ring, Yumi pulled it from my pocket and held it to my face, giving me permission to answer.

I didn't recognize the country code much less the number. "Jacob Stearne."

A flood of an indecipherable dialect emerged from the other end. After the guy's third sentence, I stopped him. "Whoa, whoa. Do you speak English?"

The first recognizable words came across with a thick layer on top. "Is English, no?"

"Who is this?"

"*Polakami*, As Sukhnah, *tak*?"

Finally, a word I recognized, *tak*, Polish for *yes*. "You're one of the Polish guys from As Sukhnah?"

"*Tak!* Uh, yes, yes. We urgency utmost. Very *wazne*."

"OK." Whatever *wazne* meant.

He prattled on in Polish until I stopped him. "Hang on, this isn't working for me. Let me find a translator."

I put him on hold and called our translation department. After five minutes, I had her online. But my Polish friend had disconnected. I called the number back.

An American answered. I said, "I was talking to a Polish guy on this phone."

"Yeah, well it's my personal phone, and I don't want him racking up huge bills on international calls for me. Sorry, pal. Write your boyfriend a letter."

"Who are you?"

"Wrong question. Who the hell are you?"

"I'm Jacob Stearne, Sabel—"

He started laughing. "I shoulda known. They said you was bat-shit crazy. What d'you want with the Polska?"

"Who are you?"

"Remember the Apache that buzz-killed your suicide attempt in the desert couple days back? That was me."

"Kyle! Thought you sounded familiar. What's with the Polish guys?"

"Hell if I know. Their embassy's making arrangements for them, but in the meantime they've been running around talking wild shit we don't understand. I finally gave them my phone and they've been calling everybody for hours. He's pulling my arm right now."

"I've got a translator, put him on."

"Who do you think's paying for this?"

"Relax, Sabel Security will pick up your bill. Put him on."

It took a few minutes for my translator to get him calmed down, but she relayed the meaning of his message. "He said: you took the Slager but he's with ISIL. He doesn't think you know that."

"Slager? What does 'slager' mean? Does he mean slugger, like baseball?"

"It means nothing in Polish. Maybe a nickname or title."

"Why should we care who the guy is?" I wondered if he meant the cowboy.

She spoke to the guy for a long time with disbelief and shock in her voice. "He's adamant that your team took a sleeper-terrorist back to the USA."

My heart stopped. "Get all the detail—"

Some noise on the other end followed by Kyle's voice. "Sorry, Jacob. I've just been ordered to cut this call."

"Who ordered it?"

"You know I can't tell you that."

"Help me out here. They just told me about a sleeper terrorist."

"Don't ask me. Our team picked up you guys and the Polish boys. Ask Admiral Tilden, NAVSUP, about the other guy."

The line went dead. It was down to the translator and me. I thanked her and clicked off.

NAVSUP was one of the services' many acronyms, but I wasn't familiar with it. Navy was a different planet from the Army. Did we turn over a sleeper agent to an unsuspecting admiral somewhere? Or did one of the clandestine services have an agent planted deep inside ISIL and we blew his cover? Or were the Polish guys smoking crack?

Yumi's gaze dug into me like a knife. I could feel it without looking at her. Anoshni tilted his head at me in solidarity with her.

She was my focus for the night. This diversion could wait. Besides, whenever the military brings in a hostage, they take them to Germany and grind them through a battery of psych tests to avoid Stockholm Syndrome, sleeper agents, or any other problems. I had nothing to worry about.

I stowed my phone and hugged Yumi.

Everything was calm and peaceful with her in my arms. I felt like I was in some kind of magic spell that matched my heart rate to her breathing. She was my everything. Except that I was starving.

My stomach growled.

She laughed and pushed up to look at me.

The front door shook under a pounding fist. "Police, open up."

Mercury stood by the door. *You know they're not the cops, bro. Feel the electric danger in your skin.*

There were times when I ignored my extinct god. This wasn't one of them.

Pushing Yumi off me, I pulled my pistol and stared at the door. "Yumi, safe room—now."

After a second's hesitation, she ran to the back of the house, crying.

I tiptoed to the foyer and stood by the hinges. Reaching out, I unlocked the bolt silently, then covered the peephole with my hand. "Who is it?"

They were looking for the blink caused by someone stepping up to the viewer. Seven bullets tore through my knotty pine, shredding holes in my hardwood floor. They'd fallen for my bait, all I had to do was wait for them to walk in and I could shoot them in the back.

They tried the door. The knob turned. The door pushed open a tentative distance. They were unsure of the terrain, which meant they had not planned the attack. An advantage I could use against them.

Yumi whimpered in the hallway, Anoshni cradled in her arms.

"No! Get in the safe room!" I ran to cover her, blowing my surprise attack.

Yumi, shocked and relieved to find me alive after believing I was dead, turned pale and froze.

I jumped in her face and yelled. "SAFE ROOM."

It occurred to her that I had a plan and it centered on her standing behind the inch-thick steel walls in my closet. She ran.

Emboldened by the noise, the amateurs threw the door open.

Their bullets tore up my hallway. I threw myself into the kitchen and scurried out the back door. I managed to kill the lights inside and out before exiting. A bag of charcoal on the deck yielded a few briquettes. I ducked across my small yard to the bushes and hurled a lump of charcoal as far into the sky as I could get it.

Two men walked out my back door bolstered with the false sense of confidence weapons give people. They both wore black, one with Vans, the other with boots. One looked left, the other looked right. They held their pistols extended in front of them. The briquette, having completed its upward arc, returned to earth in the bushes directly in front of them with a startling thud.

The boots-guy ran forward, emptying his magazine into the dirt.

His buddy stood on the deck, aiming at the same spot but holding his fire. "You get him, Clint?"

"Nah." Clint swapped mags. "Don't see nothing."

I tossed another lump in the air with more reserve than the first to avoid drawing attention to myself. It came down three feet from Clint. Spooked, he bent down to peer between the leaves.

The weeds he stared into might qualify as bushes. They were there when I bought the place. They were either weeds or expensive bushes, I had no idea, but I trimmed them up nice and they looked good. They were about waist-high and two or three bushes deep before you reached the fence. Clint waded in.

"You in there, Mr. Stearne?" Clint asked with sarcasm. "C'mon out now and make this easy on yourself."

Mercury said, *Just shoot the bastard, bro. Why wait?*

I said, *If I keep him alive, he might tell me who sent him.*

You're such a wuss sometimes. How did you survive five tours in Afghanistan and three in Iraq? Oh yeah, now I remember. You used to listen to me. Shoot the scumbag and spare the citizens the incarceration expense of life without parole. And get Yumi out of that torture chamber she's in. She's sobbing right now.

That hurt.

Clint turned slowly and looked directly at me for a split second. In that instant, I came perilously close to taking Mercury's advice. Unlike some gods, I value human life. Even the scumbags. Clint's eyes missed me crouching behind the wheelbarrow and a long-abandoned fountain project. I'm not handy around the house. Unless you need bullet holes in something.

I tossed my third and final briquette. This one came down between the two men. Clint spun with his pistol leveled at Mr. Vans, but Vans fired first. It was an eyes-closed firing, the way people do when they let adrenaline drive their actions.

I bolted from my hiding place and tackled Mr. Vans. He heard me coming and turned his head instead of his weapon.

My body weight pounded him into the deck, his right arm still fully extended. In wrestling terms, I had him pinned. I yanked his gun-hand around to point his muzzle at his right eye.

His eyes almost popped out of his head when he saw his finger on his own trigger. He gasped.

I pressed my mouth close to his ear. "What is this, a Smith and

Wesson SD9? Ten 9mm in the mag, one in the chamber? Stainless steel barrel and slide. You know, I love guns. I own an arsenal that would make you drool. You'll never get mine out of my hands. But I believe in far stronger gun control than you can imagine. I believe you should pass a rigorous background check, a mental health evaluation, and be forced to take hours of weapons training every month just to keep your license. I think every gun owner should serve in the reserves and have to pass aiming-choices-under-extreme-pressure certifications. You know why I believe these things? Two reasons. First, I've killed a bunch of guys. And the second is because morons like you don't respect what it means to pull a trigger. When you pull the trigger, you destroy something. Maybe it's a paper target. Maybe it's a tree leaf. In your case—because you've never had to choose between two popup targets, one of a little girl with an ice cream and one of a bad guy with a rifle—you let your anxiety pull your trigger. And that's why your buddy is lying face down in my back yard. You shot him in the head."

Mercury leaned into my peripheral vision. *Homie, are you serious about your gun control plan? I mean, think about it, bro—you ain't never gonna pass a mental health evaluation.*

I said, *I could pass any day of the week. There's nothing wrong with me.*

Mercury rose into the sky. *If you say so.*

My victim gurgled and choked and spluttered. "Clint? Is he dead?"

"Unless he can survive without the back half of his skull, I'm thinking—pretty much dead, yeah."

"You sure it wasn't you?"

"My Glock is cold."

"Oh man, this is bad."

I said, "Clint would concur."

Sirens screeched in the distance.

He tried to look at me with his face mushed to the ground. "Man, you gotta let me go."

"Excuse me?"

"You gotta let me go. I'm a three-time loser. Manslaughter means I'll get the death penalty."

"You idiot." I pressed my knee into his backbone. "You're not getting manslaughter; home invasion is first degree. But lucky you, Maryland canned the death penalty a few years back. You'll have to doll yourself up and sell yourself as a prison wife for life."

"No. No way. I can't go back."

"Who sent you to kill me?" I asked.

The sirens reached my front yard and turned off. Flashing lights bathed the neighborhood in alternating red, white, and blue.

Mr. Vans tightened up. He looked into his own barrel and squeezed the trigger.

CHAPTER 8

PIA SABEL ARRIVED AT THE West Wing forty-eight hours after turning down President Hunter's first invitation. Stepping from the limo, she checked the overcast sky. Drizzle could start at any moment. Bianca ran around to join her but stopped halfway to read a text.

"NSA says the oil trucks are owned by an American firm called Energy Outfitters." Bianca frowned and scrolled through an email. "Our research shows the company has no employees, no reserves, no contracts, but they ship a lot of crude oil to Roche One Refinery."

"What does that tell us?"

"I'm not sure yet." Bianca joined her. "But something's wrong with that picture."

Chief of Staff Ron Bose greeted them in the lobby. Without an extra word, he ushered them through the corridors past the Vice President's office and his own office, to the Oval Office.

President Veronica Lodge Hunter greeted them. She showed Pia the Resolute Desk, made from the timbers of its namesake exploration ship and given to the nation by Queen Victoria. On her short trip around the Oval Office, she barely mentioned the many perfectly preserved historical antiques that lined the room.

Hunter ended the tour abruptly. "Your bodyguard can wait outside."

"She leaves—I leave with her." Pia fisted her hips. "Your people tried to kill me once."

"You really need to leave the past behind you." The president's eyes narrowed. "Our conversation is classified."

"Bianca had the top clearance at the NSA."

"Fine, she stays by the door." Hunter waved her Chief of Staff out and ushered Pia to facing couches separated by a coffee table.

"What made you change your mind?" Hunter said as she took her seat. "Did Alan talk some sense into you?"

Pia sat across from the president. "Tell me everything you know about my parents."

"First, we discuss the matter I summoned you—"

"No."

President Hunter squared her shoulders and scowled. She drew a deep breath as if she were about to start yelling, then thought better of it and let the breath out. She spoke between clenched teeth. "Young lady, I am the leader of the free world. I have a mandate from the people to run this country. I set the agenda."

"A good negotiator knows when she has the lesser hand."

Hunter bit her lip and observed Pia for a long moment. "You're quite a ... handful."

"Is that why your people—"

"We've plowed that field." Hunter leaned back, dismissing the accusation with a wave of her hand. "It was an unfortunate incident. A rogue appointee. Get over it."

Pia didn't move.

"All right." Hunter leaned forward. "I promised to tell you what I know. But I have to warn you, it was over twenty years ago." Hunter waited for a thank-you that did not materialize.

Pia rolled her hand.

"At the time," Hunter said, "I was CIA Director. The Director is the whipping boy for Congress and the Administration. She's there to take the blame when an operation goes off the rails. The real power in the agency is the Deputy Director. The Deputy tells the Director as little as possible to maintain plausible deniability. That's why I don't know as much as you'd like."

Pia nodded. "The Deputy was Bill McCarty?"

"Unfortunate that McCarty died in your 'protective' custody." Hunter gave her a cold stare. "Do you know who convinced him to commit suicide?"

"Alan Sabel."

Hunter looked surprised by Pia's candid response. "Do you know why?"

"Tell your story," Pia said.

"Fine." Hunter held up her hands. "No, McCarty was not Deputy. He was the Executive Director of Resource Management. In other words, he deployed people on covert operations, vetted intel from onsite observers, matched up spies and handlers."

The president rose to retrieve a mug from her desk and stopped. "Where are my manners? Coffee, water, juice?"

"Coffee, please. Black."

Hunter turned to Bianca, who looked surprised to be acknowledged. She requested water. Hunter ordered drinks on her intercom and returned to the sofa. "The FBI was tasked with retrieving an unpublished research paper your biological father had sent out for peer review. The CIA was tasked with retrieving it from universities outside the US—Kyoto, Hamburg, and Copenhagen." She stopped to sip her coffee.

"Why?" Pia asked.

"The CIA Director reports to the Director for National Intelligence, and that's who pushed the orders to my people. They kept me in the dark. After the murders, and knowing we'd crossed the line, I tried to look at those orders and found most of them redacted. The order originated from a group that watches technologies and industries critical to our nation's sovereignty. Funding and staff for these groups comes from the industries we protect. Sometimes these industry associations become overanxious about certain situations. Someone considered your biological father's research adverse to national security."

A neatly dressed butler entered with a tray, approached Hunter and realized he had three drinks but only two people in front of him.

"Allow me, Darrel," Hunter said. She took the tray from him. He bowed and left. Hunter extended the tray to Pia, who took her mug and waited as the president balanced the tray in one hand and poured Pia's coffee with the other. Hunter then served Bianca's water bottle with a pleasant smile before retaking her seat. "Waitressed my way through college and law school."

"Which industry wanted to kill my father?" She admired her blue-glass coffee mug's engraved presidential seal.

"We'll get to that." Hunter refreshed her coffee. "Let's stick with the timeline first—we finished retrieving data from university professors who weren't happy about us or our methods of retrieval. We were successful. But your father was quite angry. He threatened to go to the press until he realized he'd sound like a conspiracy nut. So he promised to publish his data on the Internet—and that became his death warrant.

"The net was in its infancy back then, but every grad student in the country and many others in the rest of the world could have accessed what he'd developed. It would've been the first thing to ever go viral."

Hunter's information overloaded Pia's estimation of the woman. In five minutes, she had revealed more than Alan had over the last twenty years. If it were all true, it explained a good deal. She tilted her head in curiosity at Hunter and sipped her coffee.

Hunter leaned back and smoothed her pink business skirt. "You really have no idea what your father was working on?"

"Dad—Alan, for clarity—claims he had no idea. How much could I know?"

"It was referred to as the *metacapacitor*. From what I understand, it would store electricity with a thousand times more efficiency than a battery in a fraction of the space. Since there were no working prototypes, it was theoretical, but if you believe the theory, it would mean a Tesla with a thousand-mile range was possible twenty years ago. The industrial applications are endless."

Pia felt her face pinch as her anger rose. "We could be living in a cleaner world today."

"True, but it would have ushered in the deepest, longest depression in history."

"Oh, please. Is that the oil industry talking?"

"Think of the men and women in the petroleum business: exploration, drilling, shipping, refining, distribution, gas stations, and car mechanics—all thrown out of work because an electric car became viable overnight. Hundreds of thousands of jobs—"

"Mechanics?" Pia asked.

"Gas cars have ten thousand moving parts; electric cars have a hundred."

"For the sake of a few jobs, you murdered my parents?"

"If I'd known they would murder American citizens, I would have stopped the operation." The president took a deep breath. "It's the Deputy Director who runs operations. I didn't learn of these details until last week."

"I assume you never asked until then." Pia took another sip, set her mug down, and leaned forward. "So, why last week?"

"Because your country needs your help and I knew digging up this story would help win you over." Hunter stared at her for a long time.

Pia processed the monumental scandal the story would create if she could prove any of it. She had a deathbed confession from Bill McCarty and Hunter's words, but nothing linked any of it together. Murderers and conspirators leave as little paper behind as possible. So, how can one expose a president and a conspiracy without sounding like a nut-job?

"Interesting story. Is there a shred of evidence that backs it up?" Pia asked.

Hunter's eyes remained locked on Pia as she rose. She crossed to her desk, retrieved something already set out. The folder plopped on the coffee table just beyond Pia's reach. Hunter kept a single piece of paper in her hand.

The thick, presidential seal-embossed folder had several documents sticking out with the red, TOP SECRET stamp visible.

"Don't open that just yet," Hunter said. "It will be yours if you help me. If you don't, it goes in the shredder."

Anger swirled through Pia's veins. She considered telling the president to fuck off simply for trying to coerce her. Her muscles tensed, ready to rise and leave, but the desire to read the folder kept her rooted in place. The reasons for her personal tragedy, shrouded in mystery for over twenty years, lay within reach. Yet, being manipulated made her skin crawl. Should she cave to the most powerful woman in the world? Did she have an alternative?

She came to a conclusion. Hunter's popularity was at an all-time low. She faced a grass-roots revolution in her party and looked forward to a contested convention for the nomination. No sitting president had been in such disfavor in their own party since Gerald Ford in 1976.

Pia said, "I'll help you—if you end your campaign."

Without hesitation, Hunter twirled the single sheet of White House stationary across the coffee table. She leaned back and crossed her legs.

Pia hesitated a moment before picking it up and reading it. But she didn't read the whole thing. Her eyes immediately fell to the last line: *I shall not seek, and I will not accept, the nomination of my party for another term as your President.*

She looked up at the sad-face of Hunter, who shrugged. Pia asked, "You expected me to ask for this?"

"You still blame me for your abduction, so it was an easy guess." Hunter poured herself another coffee. "Before you pat yourself on the back, it's bigger than you." She huffed. "I'm tired. Tired of the vitriol and the polarization. For nothing more than ego and idealism, both parties stalled everything I tried to do. I've decided to support Marty Maddox."

Pia's expression betrayed her surprise.

"Don't go telling that reporter friend of yours, Emily whatshername." Hunter shook a finger at her with a smile. "But even more important is the reason I've asked you here."

Pia straightened up and glanced at the folder, fighting the urge to pick it up and start reading. "You have my attention."

Ron Bose buzzed her intercom. "Everyone's ready in the East Wing."

"I'll need a couple more minutes," Hunter replied. She turned back to Pia. "Our Founding Fathers balanced plutocracy through the Senate and democracy through the House. Naturally, there have been several periods in American history where there's been an imbalance."

"Such as the Gilded Age," Pia said. "Railroads, mining, and timber trusts corrupted local politicians in both parties."

"Exactly," Hunter said. "I forgot you were a history major." She gave Pia an appreciative nod before continuing. "Teddy Roosevelt and Bill Taft busted the trusts and cleaned out a lot of corruption. Income inequality began a decline that lasted from the dawn of the twentieth century until the nineteen-eighties. Some would consider that a period of self-serving democracy and point to it as the time when America lost its competitive edge."

Pia waited a moment. "And you believe the plutocracy is back?"

"They never went away. And that's not a bad thing. Believe it or not, you are one of them." Hunter looked her over and sighed. "You don't even know it, do you?"

"We only own one senator." Pia shrugged. "Well … as far as I know."

"I mentioned the business-government watchdog groups who monitor certain industries and technologies to ensure national security. You own an industry watchdog. No one can launch a satellite without your company's approval, not even SpaceX. It's a matter of national security. If Sabel Satellites falls behind the Chinese, Russians, or Germans in technology, American communications systems could be at risk. You have a tremendous amount of power, young lady—whether Alan told you about it or not."

Pia felt a queasiness building in her gut. The president's hard stare made her all the more uncertain about what kind of information her father withheld. She inhaled and looked the president in the eye. "I'll have our people stop immediately."

"Don't do that!" Hunter laughed as she leaned back. "The Russians deployed *Istrebitel Sputnik*, their first fighter satellite, in the early '60s. It shot down our surveillance satellites. The Space Race is actually a space war that's still going on today. Your people stopped the North Koreans from taking out one of our spy satellites just a few weeks ago. Sabel Sat is doing a fine job. You're one of the good guys."

Pia felt her brow furrow. "I don't understand. What do you need me to do?"

Hunter carefully inserted a finger into her sculptured hair to scratch her head. She rose, picked up the folder Pia wanted, and walked toward the door. "Walk with me. I have a photo op with some refugees from somewhere."

Pia stood, slightly confused.

Hunter said, "Have I left the dots too far apart for you to connect?"

Pia joined her as certain pieces began to fall into place. "You mean, the watchdog group that killed my parents is still out there?"

"Think about it, Pia. Who would want your father killed and his metacapacitor research destroyed?"

"The oil industry." Pia knew what that meant. "And they can order the government to murder civilians?"

"It's a $1.8 trillion-dollar industry, bigger than Canada's GDP, and they see any viable alternative to oil as a threat to their existence. I can't prove it, but I'm sure they're the ones who ordered your father killed. You and your mother were considered collateral damage. It sounds like a callous calculation, trading a family for national security, but when we drove Saddam Hussein out of Kuwait in 1991, we expected thousands of lives lost just to keep the price of oil from skyrocketing. It's the kind of calculation leaders make every day."

The president looked out the window at a light drizzle falling in the Rose Garden. Her gaze moved to the colonnade between the West Wing and the White House. She decided the risk of getting wet was too high and headed for the interior hallway.

Pia followed her. "Something's changed, then?"

Hunter nodded, her expression grave. "The groups, unions, associations, trusts—call them cabals if you like—are beginning to work together. Alone, they look after their individual self-interests, which is a controllable scenario, but together, they become a destructive force."

"How many are there?" Pia asked.

They made their way through the Cabinet Room and passed the Press Briefing Room. Bianca followed a respectful distance behind.

"Endless numbers, one for each industry: cheesemakers, shoe makers, teachers' unions, CEO associations, retailers, and so on, with varied results according to their economic clout. The big ones are oil and gas, the financial sector, technology, bio-med, institutionalized wealth, and so on."

"Unions? Agriculture?"

"American unions missed the curve on globalization. They're busy managing a declining sphere of influence. But the international unions are stepping in, the ITUC and the Chinese trade unions. They're not supposed to control American elections but, as you well know, money is pouring in from all over the world these days. Agriculture used to mean farmers." Hunter laughed. "Now it's big food processors, bio-tech, and agribusiness."

Hunter led them into the press offices. Reporters stopped what they were doing and looked up in disbelief.

"Working hard, boys and girls?" Hunter leaned in with a big smile. "You remember my good friend, Pia Sabel?"

Several people hurdled each other to push in front of Pia with a flood of questions. The only one she heard was, "Are you endorsing Hunter?"

She smiled at the president. "That might be premature."

"That's all for now, kids. Get back to work before your bosses outsource your jobs to the Koreans." Hunter strode out while the reporters moaned.

Reaching the relative privacy of the Palm Room, Pia asked, "What do you want me to do?"

Hunter stopped mid-stride and came close to Pia. "We have credible information that one of those groups is planning to destroy our democracy. They travel and work in tight formation, so we don't know who is planning it, nor do we know who they're targeting. It appears to be something highly specific that will enrich one of those groups. Whatever is planned will happen in the next few days. We have a week, maybe ten days at the most. I want you to infiltrate them, find the ring leader, and stop him."

"What about the FBI?" Pia straightened up. "Why do you want me to do your dirty work?"

"There are things the FBI can and can't do. They've reached a constitutional wall. If our information is right—and we're not sure it is— then a lot is at stake." Hunter touched Pia's arm. "Pia, we're talking about the biggest political donors in history. If we blow the investigation, the acrimony could tear the country apart. If our intel is wrong, you have the option to walk away. No paper trail, no Freedom of Information requests to expose us tapping the phones of the richest people in the country."

"If I find something, why not turn it over to the FBI then?"

"You would never trust me with what you find out—and I'm not sure I'd trust any information you would give me. If you tell me who it is and I move to stop them, no one would believe I did it for the country. They would think I did it to get Maddox elected. Or as a favor to you in exchange for campaign donations."

They rounded a corner in silence.

Hunter squinted and lowered her voice. "Pia, Chuck Roche is hosting a conference of billionaires in a few days. Someone in that group wants to undermine the duly elected representatives of your government. We can't let them subvert democracy. Find out who it is and stop him. Do what you need, make the judgment calls on your own. I will cover for you. I'll have Special Agent Verges reassigned to you because he's the only FBI agent you'll trust. Anything else you need, I'll get it for you. But you must do this. Your country needs you."

"Why me? Why not someone else?"

"The nation needs someone we can trust. Someone who won't sell us out for a billion dollars. And, you have a personal interest in seeing this through."

Pia stared, somewhat stunned, and tried to figure out what game the president was playing. Was this a setup of some kind? Would Pia take out a billionaire only to find planted evidence and the president laughing? Would a swat team descend on her after she moved against this elusive threat?

"It's a matter of trust, isn't it?" Hunter asked. "Go to the conference. You'll understand what I'm telling you by lunch time on the first day. If you don't see it by then, go home."

Pia didn't know what to say.

"Here," Hunter said, thrusting the thick folder into her hands. "I'm giving you this because I trust you. Who you should—and should not—trust is buried on the last page."

Hunter turned and walked into the East Wing, leaving Pia staring at her back.

Bianca stepped up and together they watched the president disappear into a crowd of aides. "Whoa. That was totally heavy, *flaca*."

Pia flipped open the folder about her parents' murders. As promised, document after document, showing some growing concern from an agency whose name had been redacted with a big black marker. She flipped to the last set of documents. Stapled at the corner was a three-page list of "deployed assets" signed by Bill McCarty. Near the middle of the last page, Hunter had highlighted a name in yellow.

Pia felt herself falling into a deep well. Above her the light grew smaller as darkness enveloped her. Her breathing stopped. Her hands and knees grew weak. She felt herself gasping. Someone's hand grabbed her arm. She heard Bianca's voice, distant and muffled, asking if she were OK. She pointed to the page as all the other papers fell to the floor. It was the name of the person on whom the killers relied for up-to-the-minute reports on her parents' movements as the assassination moved forward.

It read, *Onsite intelligence, available 24 x 7: Alan Sabel, 27, neighbor.*

CHAPTER 9

ON A MUGGY NIGHT IN the mountain city of Mérida, Venezuela, the Slager watched Omar Benitez wipe sleep from his eyes and stumble into a blade of yellow light from the streetlight beyond his walled yard. A soft, warm drizzle fell on their shoulders. Groggy, Omar blinked into the darkness, looking for the noise that woke him. He spotted his dog and peered at the rope around the animal's snout. The Slager stepped out from his hiding place behind the gate and tugged the dog's leash, drawing Omar's gaze to his.

In bad Spanish, the Slager said, "Your office opens in six hours. In seven hours, the crew will have their passports or the dog dies. If you make them wait another hour, your boy dies. Then the twins. Then your wife." He smiled. "You will live to witness it all."

He tossed the leash to Omar and waited while the Venezuelan official opened and closed his mouth, unable to speak. The Slager rolled his eyes and pushed past the stupid man, taking the back steps in a single stride, ignoring the pain that seared through the bullet hole in his leg. He let himself in the back door. The bureaucrat labored up the steps behind him and slinked in, mouth still open.

The Slager opened a worn drawer, took out a carving knife that looked homemade and held it out, handle first, toward Omar. It was the Slager's *now's your chance* move. Timid people never took the bait.

Omar tacitly submitted to his will.

The Slager stabbed the knife into the kitchen table between them, raised his eyebrows, opened his arms wide, then sat down. For a moment he looked uncomfortable and wiggled his shoulders in the seatback. He leaned forward and extracted a 9mm Ruger from his lower back.

He looked at his pistol. He looked at Omar. "Maybe you should get some sleep."

Omar ran up the narrow wooden stairs.

A few hours later, long before the sun would splash into Mérida's narrow valley, Omar returned and tightened the belt of his beige slacks under an overhang of beer-gut covered by his best white shirt. He ran his fingers through his short, black hair and nodded to the Slager. "I will have them in thirty minutes, Señor. You will see."

The Slager stood, towering over his new business associate, pulled the man's tie straight and tugged his collar back. He looked Omar over, nodded his satisfaction, and smiled, leaning back. "I like you, Omar. I like you so much, I'm going to bless you with my presence for another day."

Omar turned pale. "Everything will be fine, Señor. You will see."

"Indeed, I will see." The Slager leaned in, nose to nose. "When they call me from inside fucking Panama."

Sweat dripped from Omar's temple. He looked over the Slager's shoulder at his wife, whose ankles and wrists were still bound to the chair, her mouth duct-taped, and gave her an apologetic shrug. He ran out the door.

The Slager sat down at the table and picked up his cards. He looked at them and shook his head, then set them down again. "You're a good-looking woman, Milagros. Not very good at strip poker, but we can work on that. Tell me something. What god did you piss off to end up with a slimy little loser like Omar?"

She met his gaze, saw the intent there, and tried to make herself smaller.

He ripped off the tape and squeezed her mouth with one hand.

Out of the corner of his eye, he saw a figure in the shadows. He'd hoped to have this whole business done by now. But the kids were up and now they were involved.

A quick glance at their dark forms took him back, way back, to his kids and the day the judge explained "termination of parental rights for felony convictions." His wife's smug look. Her attorney's imperious glance. Pyrrhic victory for her. After her drug convictions, the kids disappeared into the foster care system. Schwartz claimed to have them located and promised to reunite them as part of the contract for the Artist. But seeing kids, anyone's kids, made him miss Ethan and Emma more than anything. His heart ached.

Forgetting himself, he spoke in English. "Well, you kids are up early. C'mon out now."

All three of them backed up behind the room divider before he remembered his Spanish. "I am the *curandera*, the healer. I'm giving your mother a treatment to rid her of demons. She won't be mean to you anymore."

One by one, the toddlers showed themselves, slowly moving out of the shadows.

The Slager rose and stuffed his pistol in his belt. He encouraged the kids to come forward with a warm smile. Their big eyes and cherubic faces tugged at his heart.

He should never threaten a man with something he couldn't do. Killing kids was something he would never do. Omar would come through. He had to.

He made the kids a breakfast of *arepas*, a round corn-flour roll, and stuffed them with beans and goat cheese. He made sure they ate everything. They made a game of cleaning up right down to scrubbing a layer of grime off the kitchen counters.

Guarded laughter and an occasional smile lightened the mood. Something the Slager had lived without for the last few years. It was something he'd longed for without realizing it: the therapeutic warmth of a child's laugh. A hug from Emma after her first day at pre-school. In eleven more days—after he pushed ten terrorists through six more countries on three more passports—he could collect his money, his ID, and his kids.

A text came from the crew. They'd made the airport and were ready to board. So far, so good. The Slager felt a little lighter. He couldn't rest until the crew had made it through customs in Panama, proving the quality of their new passports, but they had cleared the first hurdle.

He played games with the children. Then Omar returned—early.

The short fat man stood in the backdoor, his tie undone, his shirttail half untucked the way sloppy people do. He smiled at the Slager.

The Slager's heart stopped. Omar's smile was wrong. All wrong. The man looked self-satisfied, as if he were getting away with something. The Slager knew that self-righteous grin. It was the same one he flashed at his former associates when the district attorney marched him out of jail after making his plea deal and turning state's evidence against his meth-dealing partners.

He grabbed the kitchen knife, still sitting on the table, shoved Omar to the ground, slashed through the man's Achilles tendon, and sprinted up the stairs.

He burst out an upper window, onto the neighbor's tiled roof. He ran three houses down and jumped across an alley. Three small trucks rolled down the narrow lane past him. From the edge of a flat roof, he watched six soldiers jump out and march inside Omar's house. Each with a submachine gun.

The Slager got up and ran as fast as his injured leg would allow. Jumping laundry and wires, he leapt from house to house before sliding down a utility pole and into a drainage ditch. One day he would come back to kill the lying, scheming Omar. Crossing through fetid water, he came out the other side, navigated a busy street, and ran as fast as his legs could carry him.

He had to pay more attention. There was a million bucks and a clean ID waiting at the end of this ride. But he had to make it to the end. Gotta be careful. He never should've believed that fat runt would do what he was told. Bureaucrats. Never trust one of those sleazy sons of bitches for a minute. Those cops would've killed him. And why? Because he'd been too soft on Omar. Too lenient. You can't let a guy like that think he has an option for one second. Not one second. He should've killed the dog last night. Never show mercy, never look back. There was one thing he promised himself as he ran down a filthy alley: next time, kill one of the kids first. Make sure they take you seriously.

CHAPTER 10

DR. HARRISON, IN HIS MUTED-SHADE-OF-BLAH sweater, pushed his bottle of pills into my hand. I pushed it back. My puppy, Anoshni, took my side in the struggle and barked. Our game of push-of-war nearly escalated to the shoving stage as Yumi watched us.

"Doc," I said, "even I know Oxycodone causes more anxiety problems than it cures. I've seen what it can do to vets. She won't be taking anything stronger than tea."

He backed into my foyer and pocketed his poison. Tossing his keys in one hand, he whispered to me. "Have you seen your god lately?"

"Time to go, Doc." Someday I will learn: never trust a psychiatrist with personal problems. "Thanks for getting Yumi calmed down, but we'll take it from here. There's a school down the street; I'm sure you can get top dollar for the pills."

"Seriously, can you introduce me? I've never met a god. Just put him in touch or—"

"Go home, Doc." I pushed him the rest of the way and closed the door behind him.

To avoid facing Yumi, I examined the workmanship on my brand-new door. Ms. Sabel sent carpenters who managed to fix everything in an hour. Though the physical signs of last night's home invasion were gone, my girlfriend's emotional scars were still raw.

When I turned around, Mercury blocked my path. *At least let me talk to the doctor, homie. He went to Harvard. Maybe he can get us a few followers.*

I said, *He'll bring you followers—on opioids. You'll end up being a tabloid god.*

You're clean and sober and look what good temperance has done you.

Mercury looked over his shoulder at Yumi, back at me, gave me a grave look, and lowered his voice. *She's right, my man. You can give up this way of life, do something less dangerous, something that won't scare the freak out of her. You could be a cop. You'd still get to shoot people.*

I said, *Cops don't call in air strikes.*

Mercury shrugged. I pushed past him and wrapped my arms around Yumi. She'd had a rough night and the morning didn't look much smoother. "Everything's fine, babe. I'm right here."

She trembled in my arms. "Detective want speak to you."

I squeezed her a little extra before traipsing through the kitchen to the backyard. Anoshni trotted alongside. I liked having a sidekick. Even though he'd spent more time with my neighbors than me due to my endless traveling, he made me feel like the king of a castle.

Detective Czajkowski waved good-bye to a crime scene guy and looked around for anything he'd missed. "The CSIs concur with your story, Jacob. Looks like murder-suicide. But, you're not off the hook until the DA says so. Until then, don't leave town."

"You're going to follow up, right? Find out who sent them?"

He leaned back as if I'd slapped him. "You want me to interrogate the corpses?"

"Trace their bank accounts, check their phone records. Someone paid them to do this."

"What makes you think this was for-hire?"

"They broke in, tried to kill me."

"Lots of people want to kill you. They were just next in line."

He shook his head and left by the side gate as my squad entered. They exchanged pleasantries.

Miguel, Dhanpal, and Tania followed me inside. Anoshni gave up on me and followed Miguel. The pup remembered the guy who stopped on the remote road on the Navajo Reservation, plucked him from obscurity, and brought him to the dog-heaven-that-is-my-home in suburban Maryland.

They lined up to give Yumi, their adopted girlfriend, a hug.

No one gave me a hug.

I kept a watchful eye on Miguel, though. I'd lost more than one flame to the big Navajo.

We moved to my tiny living room.

"So this guy we 'rescued'," Tania started the session, "Larson or Slager, whichever, said he worked for Energy Outfitters, but got his own ride on a NAVSUP bird—before we reported anything to anybody. You ask me, that's a covert operator."

"One problem," Dhanpal said. "I did some research when I got Jacob's text last night. NAVSUP is far from covert. Naval Supply Systems Command, they're supply-chain logistics—everything from laptops to fuel. Admiral Tilden leads it, HQ'd in Mechanicsburg."

"Is it possible he's connected to special ops through supplies?" I asked.

Tania squinted. "Can you order six laptops, three SEALS, and a case of staples in the Navy? Cause in the Army, all I ever got was the laptops and the staples."

Dhanpal shook his head. "The only ops they handle are milk deliveries. NAVSUP isn't connected to JSOC or SEALs or any other groups in Iraq right now. But, I made some calls and got an appointment with one of Tilden's guys."

Miguel was due at Sabel Gardens for his rotation and dropped out of the long drive to Mechanicsburg.

"You two can handle it," Tania said. She turned to Yumi. "Hey girlfriend, whaddya say we make some tea and swap stories? Does Jacob still do that special thing with his—"

"TANIA!" The last thing I wanted was my ex-girlfriend telling my current girl stories that had my name in them.

"What?" She looked at me with innocence borrowed from Anoshni. "You ain't much to look at, you've got no money, and your manners came out of a barn, but at least you're good at one thing."

Two hours later, Dhanpal and I pulled into NAVSUP's offices where we were passed around until we landed in front of Captain John Behan. He was a proud guy who used to work out a lot before he took the desk job. He had the swagger and confidence of a man who was a lot less pudgy. He stared with a tough glare and didn't bother with small talk.

We explained our private rescue operation in Syria and the what's-wrong-with-this-picture cowboy we found.

"What does any of this have to do with NAVSUP?" Behan asked.

"We want to know why Admiral Tilden exfiltrated that guy," I said.

Dhanpal glanced at me, then Behan. "And, was he taken to Landstuhl for a full debriefing?"

"You know I can't answer that." He glanced at me. "You're Jacob Stearne?"

"Yes sir."

"I looked up your record before you arrived." His face turned smug. "You current on all your medical requirements?"

He referred to a stipulation in my discharge that I maintain constant mental health evaluations through the VA. Ms. Sabel substituted Dr. Harrison at her expense, since the VA isn't known for actually *seeing* patients. Technically, I was in violation of my discharge conditions.

"Yes sir." A white lie. "But the question is about this cowboy running around inside ISIL territory."

"If there was a NAVSUP agent of some kind in Syria, you know damn well I can't talk about it. Even if you had authorization and a need-to-know, I wouldn't tell a guy with questionable mental health."

Prejudice thrives. You talk to one has-been god and everyone thinks you're nuts.

I felt my fists balling up. "Your organization doesn't have a damn thing to do with special ops or infiltrated operatives and you know it. Dhanpal was a SEAL and I was a Ranger; we've been on missions we can't talk about until 2058. I doubt you've even seen a Top Secret rubber stamp unless you were delivering it. Neither of us ever heard of getting a ride home on a NAVSUP bird. We think something's gone wrong here."

"This division's operations are none of your concern."

"We're telling you a couple Polish guys swear this cowboy is a sleeper agent, and you're telling us not to worry?"

"You're bringing me second-hand information from a couple Polack do-gooders you don't even know the name of, and you raise your voice at me?" He stood up and pointed at his office door. "I've heard enough out of you."

Ever the good sailor, Dhanpal rose and made for the door.

Never the good soldier, I pressed my fists to his desktop and leaned across. "I'm telling you there's a possible sleeper agent walking around the USA and your division gave him a free ride back to the States. If this guy opens fire on a school bus in the name of the Islamic State, I'm going to blast you and your admiral all over the press."

"Fuck you, Stearne."

"Ask the SEALs onsite for a blood sample from the Humvee we borrowed. Check it for a match in AFRSSIR. If he's legit, he'll be in there."

"Match the what?" Behan asked.

Those of us who've drawn combat pay know what AFRSSIR stands for and joke about it with a touch of gallows humor. As in, *we're gonna get so wrecked they'll have to ID us in AFRSSIR.* You can slur it like a drunk addressing an officer, *affer-sir*, or spell it out one letter at a time in a sing-song voice for fun. It stands for Armed Forces Repository of Specimen Samples for the Identification of Remains—the military DNA database. A pencil pusher—while definitely instrumental in keeping bullet-chewers like us supplied with bullets, toilet paper, and body armor—wouldn't be as familiar with the acronym. They give their sample on day one and forget about it. But those of us who sifted through the rubble for hours to find nothing more than Joe's little finger (and weren't even sure it was Joe's) are very familiar with it.

"DNA database," I said with too much heat and anger. "Do it to cover your admiral's rear end."

"You're done here."

"Listen, Behan, just check it out." I calmed myself. "Check it out, find out why you guys were on this op, satisfy your own curiosity. Ask the Admiral if the guy was legit. There might be a reasonable explanation. If you think it adds up, fine. But if there's something screwy, call me. If you don't trust me—call him." I thumbed over my shoulder at Dhanpal and dropped my card on his desk. "If you don't trust him, call Pia Sabel."

"The soccer star?" He looked me over as if I were someone new. "You know her?"

"I'm head of her special projects team."

Behan was visibly impressed. "Is she as big as they say?"

"You mean, tall?" I asked. Certainly a middle-aged guy like Behan would know better than to use the word 'big' when referring to a female unless he's looking for arsenic in his coffee.

"I mean buff." He hunched his shoulders and clenched his fists together like a muscleman—which he was not.

"She's a world-class athlete." I looked him over, trying to determine if he had been listening to anything I'd told him.

He grinned. "But is she tough like they say?"

"If you're intimidated by a woman who could break you in half, try not to worry about it. She wouldn't waste her time on a runt like you."

He looked insulted.

"Let's keep focused on national security for a moment." I took a deep breath. "The cowboy might be just another cowboy. Or your admiral might've helped an ISIL terrorist into the country. If that was an accident, let your admiral fix it before it blows up in your face. If it was intentional, think about how ignoring it will earn you a chance to swab decks in Guantanamo."

I gave him my exit-nod and turned. Behind me, Dhanpal had his phone out, aimed at the two of us.

"Hey, what the hell do you think you're doing?" Behan asked.

"Recording Jacob's warning for posterity," Dhanpal answered. "It's on you now."

"Delete that!" Behan turned explosive-red.

Mercury stepped up behind him. *Bravery is often mistaken for unwavering courage when in fact, it's the utter miscalculation of the insurmountable odds stacked against you.*

I said, *Wha?*

Run, muthafucka, run!

Behan took a deep breath, preparing to bellow at full strength for back up.

Trusting my down-and-out god appealed to me in that moment. I moved and pushed Dhanpal ahead of me. We bolted down the hall while Behan's voice shook the walls as if some ancient monster had woken from hibernation. Heads poked out of offices. Our feet spun like cartoon characters' as we rounded the bend on the over-waxed floor and slid past the receptionist.

In the Navy, a captain is an all-powerful entity. He commands all he surveys and doesn't care about the Fourth Amendment of the Constitution prohibiting unreasonable search and seizure. We would win a court case against him, but only years after he had "accidentally" destroyed Dhanpal's phone and any video recordings that might be on it.

We dove for the car and raced out of the lot.

Dhanpal uploaded the video to the cloud and transferred a copy to my phone for backup. He erased the transfer from his phone by the time the guards stopped us at the gate.

The sergeant stepped out stretching a corded phone cradled on his shoulder. "Mr. Dhanpal Singh? I need your phone unlocked, sir."

Dhanpal handed it over.

"Yes, sir, I've found the video." The guard juggled the phone on his shoulder with the one in his hand. "I've permanently deleted it sir. Yes sir, I deleted the cloud copy as well. Thank you, sir."

The guard flipped the phone back to Dhanpal and waved us through.

We didn't speak for a mile just in case the conspiracy theorists are right about the black helicopters and drones.

When we hit the highway, I said, "He didn't seem like he was covering for the Admiral. Maybe the Poles were wrong about the cowboy."

"Institutional denial." Dhanpal opened a bag and pulled out a round ball of something fried. "Want one?"

"What's that?"

"Kachori, snack food from the old country. My grandparents just got back."

He handed me one. I took it and bit into it. A shell filled with beans and spicy as hell.

"What does 'institutional denial' mean for Behan?"

"He's unwilling to admit to himself that NAVSUP could be involved in any way. Like what the Catholic bishops did with child molesters. They weren't trying to protect them; they were trying to convince themselves it hadn't happened by making it go away."

Dhanpal popped another kachori in his mouth and handed one to me. Then he backed against the door to better face me. "We're not going to wait for Behan to wake up and smell the terrorists, are we?"

CHAPTER 11

PIA THREW OPEN THE DOUBLE doors to her father's office so hard they bounced off the stops. She strode to his expansive mahogany desk without glancing at the men arrayed around him in the meeting. Someone was in the middle of a sentence. "…which led to my recovery a couple years—"

She said, "We need to talk."

Bianca, uncertain of bodyguard protocol during a family fight, left the office and pulled the doors closed behind her.

Alan's wide smile shrank to a thin line. After a glance at the men arrayed around his desk, he looked at her. "We're in the middle of a meeting. Could you give me a minute?"

"No."

"Good morning, Pia." Stefan's voice came from behind her.

He still rubbed her the wrong way.

"Everyone out," she said without looking over her shoulder.

No one moved.

"Pia," Alan said, "Luuk and Stefan Devoor have invited us to a conference—"

"I have questions." Pia dropped the folder on his desk.

Alan Sabel's eyes dropped to the presidential seal on the folder. He sat up and lost the color in his face.

"Gentlemen, would you mind waiting outside for a few minutes?" Alan rose and addressed his guests. "Or perhaps we can reschedule for later this afternoon?"

Luuk Devoor's polite cough did not draw Pia's attention, so he spoke to her back. "I'm sure there is a reasonable explanation for this rudeness. We'll wait outside, provided we can continue the discussion with both of you."

Alan nodded without a word. The others left.

When she heard the door close, she pointed to the folder. "I've always known you were holding something back."

"What…" He choked. "What does it say about me?"

"You're listed on McCarty's personnel assignment sheet as the onsite intelligence."

Alan sank into his chair and buried his head in his hands. She didn't move. They left a long silence in which Alan's breathing was the only sound in the room. Always the big, broad chested, effusive man with the endless smile, he sat hunched over. The captain of industry who people begged for an appointment. The executive who hired and fired relying on his razor-sharp instincts. She heard him inhale and sigh.

"I… I'm sorry, Pia." He was still unable to look at her. "I'm s-so sorry. They lied to me."

"I'm sure there's a good explanation for what happened. And I want to hear it. But what hurts the most is that you never told me."

With an unfamiliar detachment, she watched the man of stone fall apart as if he were a stranger. She felt no emotion and all emotions. Hate and anger and betrayal and revenge swirled in her head, but she couldn't bring them to bear on him. For whatever else he did, he'd saved her life.

Only a young grad student, he kept her from the life of an orphan tossed about in the foster care system. As she grew up, he challenged her to do her best because *your mother is always with you*. He challenged her to excel in school because *your father would be proud*. He tucked her in many nights and read books to her. He built one of the largest privately held corporations in the country and kept most of the shares in trust for her. He never let his busy schedule keep him from the sidelines of her soccer games.

Which raised her lifelong question: *why?*

She leaned across his desk. "Who were they?"

"CIA… they told me." He coughed his words. "They had credentials. I checked them out… I thought."

"You never told me." She stared. "Why not?"

"How?" He sniffled and pulled some tissues from his desk drawer. He inhaled long and deep and pulled himself together. "How do you tell someone you love that you were an accessory to the murder of her parents? And if you figure out how, when is she old enough to understand? At six? Ten? Fourteen?"

"You wanted me to love you like a father so you could feel better about what you did."

He nodded, his head still hung. "True enough."

She longed for eye contact. She wanted to look at him and see the man she trusted with her life as recently as yesterday. She wanted to tell him she still loved him. She didn't. "Who came to you? McCarty?"

"Leroy Johnson." Alan swallowed hard.

"The man I killed?" Which is how she preferred to remember him, as opposed to the more painful but equally accurate *the man who strangled my mother.*

"He and two others came to me because I lived next door and babysat from time to time. They told me your father was working on classified materials and they had a tip he'd been talking to foreign nationals about the project. They asked me to keep an eye on their movements. Report in when they left and when they had guests. They were especially interested in who the guests were."

"How long did you spy for them?"

"Five days. Long enough for them to predict when your dad would be home." Alan looked up with red, swollen eyes. "I had no idea what they were planning."

She'd never seen him so distressed. He had been more calm and reserved the time she found him tied to a bomb. The nurturing side of her welled up, wanting to embrace him and absolve him of his sins.

Since that day, everything he had done was for her benefit. She couldn't stand the thought of cutting off her last connection to her biological family. But in her rational mind she could not give in to a man who had withheld so much for so long. She crossed her arms over her suit jacket.

"I was writing a grant proposal," he said. "My house was quiet; my roommates were gone. I heard breaking glass but couldn't tell where the noise came from. Then I heard the sounds of struggle. I ran downstairs and out my back door. That's when I heard the gunshot. From outside, I could see Leroy strangling your mother and you stabbing away at him. It took a minute to understand what I was seeing. By the time I kicked the kitchen door open, you'd hit his artery. He was bleeding out."

"They duped you?" Pia moved around the desk and stood over him.

"I don't blame you if you don't believe me. But think about this: Before the ambulances and police arrived, it was just the two of us."

"You felt guilty enough to adopt me?"

"Guilty enough to feel responsible for your future."

She moved to the window and stared blankly at the Bethesda skyline. In her dim memory of the incident, she remembered Alan grabbing things from her father's office and running them over to his house. Then he came back to hug and console her.

Her gaze took in his mahogany office. "All this—Sabel Industries—was atonement?"

Alan Sabel rose and stood next to her. He took a deep breath and straightened his posture. A little of his color came back.

"I checked to see what the killers had taken. It was only one hard drive. I knew enough about your father's projects to know there were two more projects they'd left behind. I hid them at my house. I built Sabel Satellites from one set of his notes and Sabel Technologies from the other. That's why the stock is all yours. I could never replace your mother and father, but I could protect their legacy."

He moved closer, watching her eyes.

She stepped away.

"And Sabel Security?" she asked.

"When Satellites and Tech were pumping out cash, I started the other companies. Security was my first for obvious reasons. One of the killers got away. I didn't want whoever sent him to come for you."

"Did you look into the murders?"

"Yes. I had an investigator who worked it for almost a year. One day, he called me unexpectedly and told me in a frightened voice to stop looking into it. He died in a road-rage incident five minutes later. We never caught his killer." He paused. "I tried to get the names out of McCarty when Jacob brought him in last year. He said he'd rather commit suicide than tell me."

"That's why you gave him a gun." She nodded and looked out the window.

Anger had powered her all the way from the White House to his office, leaving her emotionally exhausted. There were a thousand more questions in her head, but after waiting twenty years, they no longer came to her. The facts seemed almost trivial. Only the hurt remained. Maybe the past didn't matter. We can't change it or fix it, we can only balance ourselves on what we know about it, and move forward.

She heard herself sigh with resignation.

She said, "Veronica says the murders were ordered by a cabal."

"I've always thought it was oil interests, but I have no proof."

"She says several cabals are holding a conference soon and that one of them is planning something horrific."

"Don't call them cabals," Alan said. "Most are simply industry associations. Virtually all of them are legitimate. Some of them work well, some are ineffective, and a few put their industry's welfare above the national good. I try to keep ours in the first group." He sighed. "But a few may be actively engaged in questionable activity. What does she want you to do?"

"She wants me to discover who is plotting to undermine the government."

"That's a constant. Someone must be undermining her."

Alan held his hand out, palm up, between them. It was a thing between them. One holding out an empty hand, the other slipping their hand in and squeezing. When either of them had a bad day, they would hold hands in this unspoken way. A form of solidarity, the two of them against the world and anything it might bring. It had been a natural reflex for as long as she could remember.

She slid her hand into his.

For the first time, it felt different.

"No politician can resist the grandeur of saving the country," Alan said. "We'll need to come up with a plan and a contingency plan to deal with Hunter's endgame."

"That's the other reason I'm here." She faced him and tugged his hand. "How do I get into the conference?"

"Devoor invited me." Alan faced her. "I turned him down moments before you came in. Stefan was entertaining me with his life-journey, European education, ups and downs." He paused a moment. "Can you forgive me?"

She pulled her hand away.

They ushered the Devoors and their associates back into the meeting. Alan retook his seat behind his desk; she leaned her rear against the front edge, off to one side, crossed her arms, and watched the men. Stefan gave her a tense smile.

Luuk Devoor led her through a brief run-down on the conference.

"Everyone has a special interest," Luuk said. "We get together every now and then to look for areas of common interest. Chuck Roche will be there. I know you had a strained conversation with him the other day, but when you get to know him better, you'll understand what an infallible and benevolent leader he really is. Ritchie Skaite and the other hedge fund kings will be there. Sean Addison from Vegas. Tech sector leaders, the meat packing industry, oil, That's just the start."

"As I said before, I'm booked this week," Alan said, his gregarious personality back in full swing. He spread his arms wide, including Pia and Luuk within his gesture. "But it would be good for Sabel Industries to be represented. I'd appreciate it if you could attend this one for us, Pia. What do you say?"

Pia glanced out the expansive windows at the pewter skies and rain. She faced the visitors and smiled. "Rancho Mirage, California? Sounds perfect on a day like this."

Pia stayed behind after the group left.

She stared at Alan and he stared at her. She said, "I don't intend to be harsh. It's a lot to absorb, and—"

She didn't know what she wanted to say. Was there a way back to where they were yesterday, father and daughter?

She wanted to give him her customary peck on the cheek, but couldn't. "We'll talk later."

She walked out, her folder shoved in her shoulder bag, trying to imagine herself in his shoes during the murders. She was about the same age as he was then. Would she fall victim to CIA employees operating off-hours on an unsanctioned agenda? His story was plausible, and it answered a few questions she had about that tragic day. She would need to corroborate his story before she could trust him. Or was that too cynical? Would a man spend half his life building a fortune for someone else if atonement wasn't his aim?

Bianca stood by the elevators and pressed the down button as Pia approached. Having an MIT grad serve as a bodyguard might not be the best use of personnel, but she liked Bianca's company. And Bianca wasn't complaining.

"Energy Outfitters uses only contract employees." Bianca talked while they waited. Pia's mind had been far away. Bianca picked up on her confusion. "Energy Outfitters owns the oil tankers that Jacob found in Syria. They're a private company, so we can't access their records, but their shipping arrangements are odd. They send their oil to Roche One in Louisiana—and only to Roche One. It's the original refinery that built the Roche company, but everyone in the industry considers it a dated relic and ecological time bomb."

"Maybe I should diversify into the oil business." Pia tapped her chin. "Find out who owns it and have one of our people research the value."

"Which, Energy Outfitters or Roche One?"

"Both." Pia shrugged. "And set up a call with the Coushatta tribe in Louisiana."

Stefan headed for the elevator from the opposite hall, his head down, preoccupied. He glanced up, saw Pia, and frowned with his mouth drawn tight. The elevator pinged, Bianca stepped inside, Pia stepped inside. Stefan rocked back on his heels, an unspoken word in his mouth.

"Going down?" Bianca asked. She welcomed him in with a wave.

Reluctantly, he stepped into the only empty space—between the women. "Garage, third level."

Bianca pressed the buttons and the doors closed. "We're on two."

"Oh." Stefan stared at the floor.

Bianca caught Pia's gaze and gestured with her face and hands, *talk to him.*

That would've been easier before she humiliated him several times.

Besides, why should she? Just because Roche said he would be a big-time executive someday? Or because he was painfully handsome?

On the other hand, she could be nice to him. Carrying a grudge was letting your antagonist win a piece of your psyche. And, as her father and the Major were always telling her, never leave an enemy in business. Yes. It was up to her to fix this. What's the harm in having a business relationship? Especially with the handsome factor thrown in.

She considered conversation starters like, *how's the weather been since prom?* Wrong. How about, *have you dissed any nice women lately?* Wrong.

Damn.

He rolled up on his toes and glanced her way. "Laurence Dacade?"

She felt her face bunch up with curiosity before remembering her designer shoes. Her gaze fell to her feet. She'd picked them because they had the lowest heel and worked well with business suits. Pia's height, combined with her attitude, intimidated businessmen, so she wore flats as much as possible. But fashion rarely comes in flats. The ankle-boots caught her eye for their retro look and low heels. They'd quickly become her favorites. Not that any male had noticed before.

"Yes, they are. Hard to find good..." She lost interest in explaining her shoe problems to him.

Stefan, a string bean who stood six-five, smiled down at her. He moved a step closer.

"We'll be spending the weekend together. I hope you'll give me—"

"Don't characterize it like that."

"I meant—" he moved closer, nearly touching "—that we'll be attending the same retreat, which will put us in close proximity, and I—"

"Your proximity is too close right now." She felt the first flush of anger rise through her neck.

"Hey." He touched her forearm lightly. "I only want to apologize for—"

Her anger flashed over. Everyone wanted to apologize. What good does that do? Why not just think before doing something stupid? Why not check out CIA agents to see if they intend to murder people? Why not keep your stupid Ferrari out of the intersection? If you think first, apologies wouldn't be necessary, would they? She felt her face squeezing down, eyes narrowed. She willed herself to keep her mouth shut but she couldn't.

"Like an apology is going to fix anything?" She shoved him with both hands. "You think I care about losing everything? You think I care about public humiliation? I let it all go. And you want to bring it back so you can feel better by saying 'sorry' because it's all about you. I forgot we live on planet Stefan."

Stefan's mouth hung open a moment before glancing behind him and realizing she'd shoved him into Bianca. He stepped forward, giving the bodyguard a little room. Then he glared at Pia.

"It's not just an apology. I need to make amends." He opened his arms, palms out. "I owe you an explanation. The demons of my—"

"Demons, Stefan? You spoiled, privileged brat. What do you know about demons?"

The elevator pinged and slowed to G2.

"Jesus, Pia." Stefan grabbed her wrists before she could shove him again. "That's what I want to tell—"

She ripped her hands free, grabbed his throat and slammed him against the wall as the elevator doors opened behind her. "I don't care what you want."

She turned and stomped out. For the first few paces she noticed that Bianca's footsteps were not behind her. Then her friend's footfalls caught up with her, stomping at an angry pace.

"That was mean, *flaca*," Bianca said.

Pia held up a hand to silence her friend. Her mind raced through her encounters with Stefan.

Amends. Demons. Recovery.

The words clicked for her. His continuing request to apologize. His earlier claim that he stopped carousing two years ago. His education in Europe where touching and close proximity are norms. Stefan was speaking when she'd first entered her father's office. It was his voice uttering the word *recovery*. It all added up to explain why he'd been so erratic and mean at that prom so long ago. He was a recovering alcoholic. He had a spiritual need to make amends for his past mistakes.

He was desperate to seek out everyone he'd hurt in life and make those amends.

Deep shame flooded up from her toes. She turned in time to see the elevator doors thump close.

CHAPTER 12

THE ARTIST PUT ON HIS darkest sunglasses, planted both feet on the ground, and pulled himself up by the limo's door frame into Rancho Mirage's blazing sunlight and baking heat. He ignored the valet holding his door and followed his entourage through the Ritz lobby. They rode the elevator to his floor, where he inspected the suite to make sure everything was done according to his prior instructions. He couldn't stand an assistant who left clothes too close together in the closet; they creased each other.

"Migraine. Everyone out." He turned to his people. "Except you, Schwartz."

The men filed out the door, parting around a small, thin figure with a furrowed brow who stood with his hands clasped behind his back. He was the kind of man no one noticed but still gave everyone the creeps.

When the door closed, he turned to Schwartz. "They're both dead?"

Schwartz nodded.

"The Sabel agents knew your people were coming for them?"

Schwartz shook his head. "Stearne got lucky."

"Well, fish some more men out of the program and finish the job." The Artist went into the bathroom and ran water over a washcloth.

"It's not that easy."

"Make it that easy, damn it." He came back and turned one of the chairs so it faced away from the window. He fell into it and put the wet washcloth over his face. "How hard can killing three miserable mall cops be?"

"Sabel agents aren't mall—"

"Shut up. I know who they are." He tilted his face to the ceiling, covered his face with the washcloth, and dropped his hands to the arms of the chair. "Surely there are some men in the program who're up to the task. These Sabel guys could upset something I've been working on for months."

"Maybe if I knew what you were working on, I could find people better suited—"

The Artist jumped from his seat, tossing the washcloth aside. "You think I'm dumb enough to trust you, *Schwartz*? Do you want me to dump you back in the program? Get your old identity back? Can an accountant who shot three men in the back of the head last another year in prison?"

"I didn't mean anything by it." Schwartz met his gaze with pleading eyes. "It would make my job easier if I knew the end game, that's all."

"Or you could buy your permanent freedom by turning me in. Well, my end game is simple: I'm going to save the country. That's a good cause, isn't it? So just do what I ask and don't worry about anything else."

"Yes sir." Schwartz lowered his gaze and hunched his shoulders. "I'll find better men this time."

The Artist patted him on the shoulder and turned him around. "They were poking around the Navy's supply chain operation yesterday. I don't like that. So get moving."

He shoved Schwartz forward.

As soon as the door closed behind the little man, the Artist streamed the news on his phone. Immediately, his anger boiled up.

Marty Maddox's opening poll numbers outranked all the primary candidates from both parties combined. Rallies for the new third party filled football stadiums to capacity. That would piss off Roche. The old man hated Maddox as much as he hated Hunter. Good thing he left the Artist in charge of the APA.

The Artist turned on the TV news. Maddox was speaking in Dayton, Ohio, hinting at his promised economic program. The candidate said, "I have a strong plan that I will reveal at the proper time. It's a plan that requires hard work from the American people. It's a plan that America must do. And, most importantly, it's a plan that, when America stands united, we *can* do."

Every time he delivered a concept, Maddox asked the crowd, "Who are you?" And the crowd shouted, "We're the NEXT USA!"

The Artist paced his room. What kind of arrogant clown would make such a statement? And what was his economic plan—some socialist agenda he'd hidden beneath a conservative governorship?

He checked his watch. Time to check on the Slager. He dialed.

"Your man Omar burned me," The Slager said. "I need clothes, money, ID."

Just as he'd expected, another shakedown. If there is one thing you can count on with the little people in this country, it's them trying to take every penny you have. He resolved to put a stop to it right then and there. "You have plenty of money. Get an extra ID from the next contact. Where are you?"

"The fuck you think I am? Panama. Your towelheads don't know low-profile from *salat*. Had to beat one of them." They were silent a moment. "Is there enough extra cash for Ignacio? He's going to be like Omar when he sees ten Moroccans in person."

"What's *salat*?"

"When they throw a prayer rug on the ground five times a day. Guess what the airlines think of that shit when they do it in the aisle?"

"Yes, by all means, make them stop that ridiculous nonsense." The Artist wondered what, if anything, Ahmad had told the crew about their mission. "You'll have to negotiate the best deal you can with Ignacio. Do that first and buy whatever else you need from the remainder."

"How generous of you." The Slager's sarcasm dripped from the last syllable.

"Your attitude is unnecessary. Keep your eyes on the prize, Slager. You need that new life, especially now. If you pull this off, Schwartz might get your brats back before they're crushed and destroyed by the system."

"You fail to appreciate the risks I'm taking here. My itinerary follows these guys halfway around the world. Facial recognition software is going to place me with them. My new face is probably on wanted posters by now. Freedom and a new life won't do me any good. The authorities will come looking for me. If they find me, I'm going—"

"We can't have these men show up in the USA with Syrian passports.

They need to originate from a respected country. To get them into that country, we must pick an anonymous route. Your itinerary was planned from a verified selection of airports without video surveillance. This has all been worked out. Stick to the plan." He paused. The Slager did have a point. The man could stop at any police station in the world, tell them what's going on and everything would be ruined. Convicts were known for self-destruction and he had less than ten days left. "I'll include a little extra money for you. You can get your own doctor and change your look again."

"What about those Sabel agents?"

"I'm working on that. The first guy was better prepared than expected."

"What're you telling me? Your boys are dead?"

"These agents are more skilled than I first presumed."

"Five of them got out of As Sukhnah without a scratch; what d'you expect?" The Slager exhaled loudly. "Let me guess—your guys came from the same rehab project you found me in?"

"As a matter of fact, the program exists to grant me access to men of your … caliber." The Artist admonished himself for telling the Slager anything. Who was the employee and who was the boss? He had to be more careful. These unsavory characters would turn on him in a New York minute if he didn't keep the leash taut. He asked, "What name did you give them?"

"My real name. Michael Larson."

"Damn you, they could trace that back to me! What were you thinking?"

"I was thinking I had a bullet hole in my leg. She asked and I answered, auto-reflex. I damn near gave her my inmate number. Fuck it. I gotta go. Your Moroccans are arguing religion in the street."

CHAPTER 13

PRETENDING THEY DIDN'T KNOW ME, Miguel and Tania crossed Atlantic Avenue in Virginia Beach during a gentle rain on the longest day of the year. Tania's multi-racial hair exploded in waves of tight curls bordering on mega-Afro. I thought she looked great, but apparently it wasn't the style she was going for. She wrangled it into a ponytail. They were heading for a small, unassuming bar called The Raven. The modest, one-story beach restaurant was a favored haunt of Dhanpal's in his SEAL days.

Things had not been going well in the forty-eight hours since my home invasion, Yumi practically lived in Dr. Harrison's office ranting hysterically about Americans, our serial-killer culture, and our idolatry of violence. Miguel was attacked by a pair of men with AR-15s. Only his bulletproof Mercedes G63 saved him. Tania fought her way through a similar ambush but lost her car. Enraged that her inner circle had become targets, Ms. Sabel assigned the four of us to track down and eliminate the threat.

While Miguel and Tania slurped drinks and nibbled appetizers to make sure no uninvited guests crashed our dinner meeting, Dhanpal and I spent a good hour across the street pretending to watch carvers make wooden birds at the Atlantic Wildfowl Heritage Museum. Our real objective was to count the cars arriving at the Raven.

Mercury showed up wearing a respectable toga instead of his usual off-the-shoulder, micro-length stripper-toga. He looked like Augustus, with a red band flowing around the hem and over the shoulder. He waved his hand between the carver and me. *Back in 'Nam, Old Ed here listened to me all the time, bro. Then one day, I was telling him taking point is no big deal for a real hero—and he goes and switches teams on me. Bought into the whole Jesus thing. See where it got him? Hasn't killed anybody in forty years. Sucka.*

Ed-the-carver looked up, caught my gaze, and gave me an old-guy wink.

I shivered and turned away. Could I spend the rest of my life carving ducks?

If it meant keeping Yumi sane ... maybe.

I said, *Why're you all dressed up?*

Mercury leaned back as if avoiding a slap. *Meeting some old friends before the gods convention in San Diego.*

I said, *Gods convention? Don't tell me things like that. It makes me think I'm slipping over the edge. Maybe I should take those meds.*

Dude, always overreacting. Mercury threw his hands up. *It's no big deal. Just the annual get-together where we brag about how many followers we have, and whose disciples make the biggest sacrifices. Watch the big-timers like Buddha and Jesus strut around. You know, same ol' bullshit.*

Dhanpal nudged me. "You OK? You look seasick."

"Fine."

"My guy showed up. He's alone. Let's go."

The rain came down harder when we crossed the street. Summertime in a beach town. The Raven was in full swing. The bar was crowded, the tables were filling, and the noise level was rising with every beer the patrons put away. Miguel and Tania were already talking to our contact.

Brent had just returned from Iraq where his SEAL unit had been on standby to extract or rescue American advisers working with the Iraqi army in the event the adviser's unit was overrun or surrendered to ISIL.

"You're the guy who blew up my ride?" Brent said.

He also happened to be the guy who loaned me the Humvee.

"Good to see you made it back from deployment safe and sound," I said.

Dhanpal put a hand on each of our shoulders and pushed us into chairs. He quickly moved into small talk about their old COs and other annoying things in the Navy.

Brent played the top-secret card, and the need-to-know card, and everything else he could to avoid telling us anything about his mission.

"Cut the crap," I said. "Everyone at this table's been on classified assignments. We're not asking for mission specifics. We're asking about oddities, and Michael Larson's story is pretty damn odd."

Brent took a big slug of beer and thought for a moment. "Yeah, beyond odd. It's all wrong."

Miguel finished off an artichoke. Brent looked around the room and grabbed the last shrimp. He was about to cross the line and tell us something out of the gray-area of special ops. Stuff that happened outside of the mission that would give nothing away but felt wrong to talk about anyway.

"Not that it matters to me," Brent said, "but the Iraqis were pretty steamed about you guys rolling in and out of there like that. The Yazidis made quite a stink about it. They leveraged your success to grab more autonomy and a bigger slice of the military budget from Baghdad."

Tania, a captain in the MPs before coming to Sabel Security, leaned forward. "There's something you want to tell us, but you're not sure where it stands on the secrecy scale. That's OK. Take your time. No pressure. We just want to satisfy our consciences about the story. I mean, we gave Larson a ride. If he's a sleeper and goes on a rampage stateside, that would drive me nuts. Y'know what I'm saying? But that's not on you. That's just what we're living with."

We were pushing the gray line about what was secret and what was not. Other than Dhanpal, Brent didn't know us and telling us anything was against the nature of any special ops veteran.

Our food arrived. We ate in silence as thick as a family fight at Thanksgiving.

Dhanpal changed the subject to lighter topics for a while, but Tania's words hung between every question and answer. Brent cleaned his plate and downed his beer and looked at Tania.

"I don't know Larson from a lizard," Brent said. "First I heard of him was when Dhanpal called. I checked around and word is, NAVSUP was not connected to our deployment in any way. We carry our own supplies when we're deep like that. We keep them out of harm's way, right? So no one knew how NAVSUP got there or how they knew Larson was there."

"We checked with every oil company in Saudi Arabia," Tania said. "There are twenty-four Americans in Arar and none of them went missing."

"I checked the guy's name in the system." Brent sighed and crossed his arms. "There are seventeen Larsons in the military, all with detailed assignments. As you know, when you deploy on a classified mission, your duty roster shows the most basic stuff: a no-name base with a no-name assignment. The Larsons each had detailed status, so—no covert operators."

He shrugged and ordered another beer.

"Could've lied about his name," Miguel said.

"Nah, I saw his face," Tania said. "I could tell he instantly regretted saying it."

"Where'd they take the Humvee?" Dhanpal asked. "We want to grab a DNA sample."

"It's right where you left it."

We sighed in unison. We were damn lucky to walk away from that mission. No way in hell we were going back. And the military wasn't about to risk the lives of their guys either.

"There is one thing that might be related," Brent said. "The day before you arrived, the Iraqis tracked ten ISIL guys from As Sukhnah who were heading south just outside of Rutba, Iraq. They were on course for Arar, in Saudi. Our analysts figured they were Moroccans trying to back out of the jihad and get home. It happens."

We thought about that but didn't see a connection.

When the check arrived, my team looked at me.

I said, "What?"

"You're Pia's pet," Dhanpal said. "You're picking up the check for us, right?"

"That's why everyone ordered lobster?" I looked them over. "For the record, I am not her 'pet.' And don't talk about Ms. Sabel like—"

Miguel and Tania laughed.

"Why you always calling her MIZZ Sabel, anyway?" Tania asked.

Mercury leaned over her shoulder while she stared at me. *Go ahead, tell 'em, bro. You're afraid if you get too familiar, you'll fall in love and try to kiss her and she'll fire your ass—which she will—and then you'll end up working as a chef for the rest of your life, in the grease and alcohol and cigarette-infused kitchens of second-rate diners. Don't think I'm sticking around for that action.*

I said, *What? You'd leave me?*

Hell yeah! I'm only here hoping you'll convince Pia-Caesar-Sabel to talk to me. If you think I'm gonna watch you concoct more dishes like the 'deep fried mashed potatoes in mint sauce', you're crazy.

I said, *That ... just had too much salt.*

"What's salt got to do with it?" Tania asked.

I grabbed the check from the center of the table and gave them all a glare on behalf of Ms. Sabel's accountants—because they were right, she wouldn't care.

Before we left, I overheard Dhanpal and Brent talking quietly about being each other's "battle-buddy." Suicide rates among soldiers skyrocketed in 2005 and have remained high ever since. The cause and cure are still hotly debated among brass and civilians. In the meantime, most veterans look after each other. Many of us pledged to call someone we'd served with—a battle-buddy—if we were ever thinking about it. Brent and Dhanpal were closer than I'd realized.

I guessed he didn't want to tell me for fear I'd push the friend button harder to get more information. He was right. I would have.

We didn't get back to the DC area until nearly midnight. After dropping Tania and Dhanpal at their places, I stopped at the guard house at Quarry Springs, Miguel's new condo, and gaped at the opulence. He must've gotten a bigger bonus than I did.

The guard motioned he wanted to talk.

I buzzed down the window as the guy leaned in and spoke across me. He said, "Mr. Rodriguez, your trainers wanted to meet you in your apartment but I told them to wait in the fitness center. Hope that was OK."

We glanced at each other and shrugged.

"You did the right thing," Miguel said.

When the window went back up, I looked at my pal. "I am sick of being shot at. I'm going to take these guys down and trace them back to the source. There has to be a connection with Larson."

"I'm with Detective Czajkowski on this one," he said. "These guys are just next in line to kill you."

Nice to know who believes in you.

I drove ahead while Miguel checked his Glock. I parked out front and checked mine.

"You got any darts?" Miguel asked, referring to the patented Sabel Dart, a bullet filled with a nonlethal dose of Inland Taipan snake venom and a heavy sedative. The venom produces instant flaccid paralysis long enough for the sedative to put you to sleep. The cartridge is interchangeable with a regular bullet but holds less gunpowder due to the longer payload. Ms. Sabel doesn't like wrongful death lawsuits and insists we use them in situations where civilians might end up as collateral damage. Most veterans laugh at the idea of using them.

"Hell no," I said. "Why?"

"I just got accepted here and moved in two weeks ago." Miguel winced. "It's all rich, ancient Caucasian dudes."

We entered the lobby with our weapons drawn and held discretely behind our legs. An older couple—he in a tux and she in a sequined gown—popped out of the elevator and chatted their way across the lobby. Suddenly they stopped moving and talking. Which meant they'd seen our weapons. Miguel looked back over his shoulder and put a finger across his lips to shush them. They weren't used to being shushed by a six-five Navajo with a ponytail and a gun in his hand.

They ran.

We proceeded down the hall to the fitness center.

Mercury leaned against the wall near the glass door. *Two guys, heavily armed, homie. I suggest you skip the debate and go straight to the shooting competition.*

I said, *I want to know who's behind these guys.*

I can answer that: Desert Eagle, .50 caliber, Mark XIX. By the way, there's a lady in there watching TV on a stationary bike with the earbuds so loud she doesn't know she's got company. Try not to kill her—she's planning on going to her granddaughter's birthday party tomorrow.

DEATH AND THE DAMNED

The Desert Eagle was a bad choice of weapon on their part. The pistol—a fantasy gun for soldier-wannabes, favored in movies and video games—is heavy and unwieldy in real life. The .50 holds only seven rounds, each with a significant kick that forces the shooter to reacquire his target before firing a second shot. Aiming a five-pound brick at the end of your extended arm isn't easy if you're in a hurry. The large caliber had some serious stopping power, but anyone who'd seen action in real life would go for something nimble like the Glocks that Miguel and I carried.

I stood next to the glass door, my back against the wall. Miguel stood on the other side. He reached over and scratched his muzzle on the glass, producing an eerie noise. It took three long scratches before one of them got up enough curiosity to investigate.

A stubble-headed guy with poorly executed tattoos on his face came to the glass and tried to get a look, then opened it. Miguel grabbed him by the neck and shoved him into the wall opposite. The man struggled, but Miguel put him in a headlock, kicked the guy's foot out from under him, and rode him to the floor in a flurry of violence.

That forced me to confront his co-conspirator, still inside. I spun around the open glass, my weapon leading my view into a spacious and fully outfitted fitness center. Free weights, interval training machines, and treadmills were lined up in tastefully appointed rows. I found him, casually sitting on a stationary bike next to the old lady. They were watching a *Downton Abbey* re-run. I snuck up closer, hoping my boots didn't squeak on the polished oak floor.

Cheap exercise-machine headphones couldn't hide the thick, black swastika tattoo on his neck. He peddled the bike with little enthusiasm, his eyes on the screen. I yanked him backward and threw him on the floor. The giant Desert Eagle flew out of his belt and spun across the wood. I jumped on him, landing my knees on his kidneys.

Excruciating pain groaned out of him. I pressed my Glock to his cheek so he could see the weapon. "Who sent you?"

After he gasped for air, he managed to ask, "What the fuck, man?"

I kneed him in the balls. "Who sent you?"

"I'm just watching TV."

Noises from outside the fitness center caught my awareness but didn't distract my attention.

He reached for his pistol. My Glock smashed his fingers before snapping back into place at his cheek. "Who hired you?"

"Don't know what you're talking about."

Behind me I could hear someone approaching. I pressed the muzzle in tighter to keep my prisoner from contemplating a move and glanced over my shoulder.

Two security guards with big yellow things in their hands approached me. One of them yelled, "TASER, TASER, TASER!"

The shock was incredible. My body instantly spasmed into full rigidity while my mind remained clear.

They were talking to each other. One of them took my Glock. The other tried to kick me off the swastika-guy. The pain stopped for a split second and my muscles began to respond to my brain. I felt exhausted but managed to reclaim my grip on swastika-guy. I got another jolt of pain and felt my muscles lock solid again.

Swastika-guy crawled out from underneath me, thanked the guards, and left.

CHAPTER 14

WALKING INTO THE MEETING IN progress left Pia feeling like an ancient castaway having to learn a native language to survive on some distant island. At least this island—her office tower high above Bethesda—was familiar. She would soon be marooned in Rancho Mirage among her father's class, the indigenous billionaires.

Soccer and business are the same games played on different fields with the same reliance on teamwork and finely honed skills. Pia knew this and yet longed for the smell of grass and the heat of the sun rather than the foreign environment of glass and steel. Listening to attorneys dissecting paragraphs and division presidents brag about their quarterly results would drive her nuts one day. The coaches who directed her balance or stance without sugarcoating it or rambling were people she understood. You could see the results of your actions the instant the ball left your foot. Return on equity, leveraged assets, liquid capital, and the rest of the jargon meant nothing to her.

She would have to learn.

A chair at the head of the table waited for her, next to the Major. She dropped her purse and took her seat.

The Major pushed a folder full of papers to her. "On your right are the executives from SCE, and the team from SPP. On your left is our corporate attorney. This is an internal discussion about Devoor's offer for the SCE wind farm, and Roche's offer for SPP, the hemp-paper maker."

The Major turned to a lawyer halfway down the big table, who glanced back at her laptop and resumed talking from where she'd left off, mid-syllable.

"Do you think I should sell?" Pia asked the SCE president,

interrupting the attorney.

Middle-aged, chubby, and balding, he looked surprised by her question. "Obviously, the decision is yours. If you're asking what I'd prefer, I'd like to stay in the Sabel family of companies. But I understand business and the opportunity to cash in—"

"Why do they want to buy SCE?"

He shook his head. "They see an opportunity, I guess. They didn't tell me."

"Yes they did." Pia let her words sink in for a second. "They didn't say it out loud, but at some point in your meetings, they went from 'meh' to 'let's do this'. What were you discussing when Luuk Devoor got excited about the project?"

Every face in the room turned to the man, causing him to blush slightly while he glanced at the ceiling and recalled the meetings.

"Our patents were approved for our new generator coils." He paused while a small titter went around the room. "But it wasn't Luuk. It was Stefan who evaluated our assets. I doubt his old man could ... well. They liked the patents."

"Patents for what?"

"Coils. Basically, we discovered a process that makes the coils in wind turbines 40% more efficient. They'll compete—"

"Thanks, I get it." She turned to the woman in charge of SPP. "And you?"

"Our genetic patents were approved last week," she said. "Our hemp hybrid can make paper products indistinguishable from tree pulp at a lower cost. We're just trying to snap up land for production."

Pia turned to the attorney. "Thank you for sending me the proposals from Devoor and Roche. I'm fine with your changes, but I'd like you to add something. I'll leave it to you to work out the language. Are you familiar with the sale of Rolls Royce to Volkswagen and BMW?"

"Vaguely."

"Rolls Royce sold their production plants to VW but sold the brand name to BMW. VW could build Rolls jets and cars but they couldn't call them Rolls Royces. It was considered sneaky, but the best deal for Rolls investors." Pia stood. "I'll sell these companies, but not the patents. If they want to buy these companies because they believe in the industry, they will go forward. If they intend to suppress the technology—which would benefit their investors but not the country—they won't. I'm meeting with Devoor and Roche over the next few days. I'll close these deals." She nodded at the division presidents. "As for the employees, Sabel Industries will retain any employee who wants to stay with Sabel regardless of the deal's terms. We will find a place for you. Thank you."

With that, she left the room. In her wake, she left the same stunned silence that greeted her arrival.

The Major caught up with her as she opened the stairwell door. "Pia, did you talk to Alan about this?"

"Sorry to be so abrupt, Major. I should've been in Rancho Mirage an hour ago. I'll call him and fill him in."

The older woman edged into her path. "You can call me Jonelle."

"Dad calls you Jonelle, Major."

"Fine. You look stressed. Is everything OK?"

Tania stepped out of the restroom and joined them. "Damn straight she's stressed. Bianca says she beat up Stefan Devoor. Now she's going to spend the next several days with him. She has to apologize. You know how hard that is for Ms. Perfect?"

Pia squeezed her eyes shut and turned to the stairwell.

Tania stuck her arm out to block her. "Stairs are exercise, I get that, but you wanted wheels-up an hour ago and our bags are back at Sabel Gardens. We gotta move, sister."

Pia turned to the elevator and gave the Major a sheepish finger-wave good-bye.

When the doors closed, she turned to Tania. "Bianca talks too much."

"Girl, you are in more dire need of a quickie than any white woman in history."

Pia glared at her. Tania glared back.

Pia said, "What happened to Jacob and Miguel last night?"

"The usual. Someone tried to kill them. Somehow our boys managed to convince the cops they were the bad guys—while the real bad guys got away. Your old pal, Special Agent Verges, is abusing the FBI's facial recognition program to figure out who the guys are. He'll turn it over to the local police if he gets anywhere."

"No fingerprints?"

"Just like the two dead guys at Jacob's house. The 'assailants' burned off their fingertips, so no prints."

They both grimaced at the thought of criminals so extreme they would disfigure themselves.

"Did they find the guy from Syria they were looking for?" Pia asked.

"You're thinking their inquiry into Larson and the attempts on their lives are related? We thought about that too. The only thing tying them together is the timing. We're not ready to jump to that conclusion. There're too many people who want to kill Jacob."

"It might be a good idea for them to leave town. Go search for the guy." Pia thought for a moment. "If they don't have leads, have them move into the guest wing. Especially poor Yumi. She's not getting the right impression of Americans."

"She's getting the right impression of *her* American. Jacob is no kind of Mr. Wonderful."

The elevator stopped on the way down, the doors drew open, and Alan Sabel joined them. "You're still here? Aren't you supposed to be in California? Roche's not the kind of guy you should keep waiting. You're going into my world out there. So, a little advice. Keep your ideas to yourself and don't act on anything until you've thought it all the way through. And try to be nice to these people, even if you don't like them. But don't overdo it. Once you've tested them and know who you can trust, earn their respect and stick to them. Don't make deals with everyone you meet. And whatever you do, don't beat up any of these guys."

"Too late," Tania said.

"What?" Alan asked, turning to her.

"Go on," Pia said.

He turned back. "Listen to everyone who wants to talk, but answer only what is necessary. Hear their opinions but don't give them yours." He looked her over and felt the fabric of her business suit. "Good, you're dressed well; quality, not flash. These guys are a bunch of peacocks. Don't do any leverage deals for our companies and don't leverage any of theirs. After all, credit swaps are how the country ended up in the mortgage crisis. Above everything else, if you want to be honest, start right here." He pointed to her heart. The elevator pinged and slowed to a stop and the doors opened. "Got it?"

"Yes, Polonius-Dad." She squeezed his arm.

PIA AND TANIA GOT ON the jet in Maryland during a downpour and stepped off in the overpowering sunshine of Palm Springs. Heat radiated off the apron, burning through the soles of their shoes as if they were entering Dante's *Inferno*. For the first time since agreeing to the mission, Pia thought about what kind of demons she would meet in this desolate desert. The rich and powerful men she knew were outgoing and extraordinarily charming at charity balls. What were they like when they pursued their business goals? Where did they fall on the *Hare Psychopathy Checklist*? These men did not build fortunes by passively waiting for success. They lived in a constant state of motion, rabidly pursuing their plans.

In that regard, she shared a degree of their psychopathy.

But how dangerous were they? In fiction, businessmen were portrayed as evil monsters. In real life, they had such a singular focus on their business that it eclipsed any other consideration. Investors, customers, and employees alike relied on their singular focus to keep the industry moving forward. Most successful companies had excellent leadership, expanded the economy, and created high-paying jobs, like Facebook, AT&T, Netflix, and IBM.

Once in a great while, someone in business would make a terrible miscalculation and lives were lost. Massey Energy's mine disaster in 2010 resulted in at least two criminal convictions. Union Carbide's Bhopal tragedy ended nearly 4,000 lives. Fraud at Enron Corp and Madoff Investments collectively destroyed $100 billion of investor equity, more than all the armed robberies in American history combined. But none of those disasters endangered the nation.

Yet President Hunter believed one of the Rancho Mirage attendees was planning to do just that.

A limo carried them from the Palm Springs executive terminal up the long winding driveway to the Ritz-Carlton in Rancho Mirage. Muscle-bound security guards wearing green sport coats emblazoned with Roche Security emblems stopped them at the door to confirm their status. Tania checked in and escorted the luggage to their adjoining suites.

Pia spotted her top priority sitting alone on the patio. She crossed the lobby to the outdoor cocktail lounge. Under large triangular awnings, an air conditioner blew cool air across the patrons.

She strode toward Stefan Devoor. Stefan kept his head down, ignoring the desert vista behind him. Dressed in a pale linen shirt, he read a magazine and sipped an ice tea, doing his best to go unnoticed.

She pulled a heavy iron chair opposite him, sat, and leaned toward him, elbows on her knees.

He spoke first. "How do the locals live with all this sunshine? It gives me a headache."

She smiled, muttered yeah, and rubbed her hands together. "I'm here to apologize to you. I hope you're better at listening than I."

He leaned back, rolled the magazine tight and squeezed it. "Not necessary."

Under his chin she could see a light blue bruise. She winced and looked away. Five older men laughed at the bar. Amber liquids sloshed over ice in their glasses. They waved cigars. Their smoke wafted downrange and yet the stench still reached her. She turned back to see his piercing stare.

"I'm sorry." She picked up her meek voice. "I misread you. You're a different man from the boy I knew ten years ago. I get that. I do. I..." This was way out of her comfort zone. Beating up bad guys was no big deal, but using violence for the wrong reason hurt her principles, which in turn tarnished her pride. On her list of faults, pride ranked first. But he wasn't making it easy. "I fucked up. I own that. I should've listened to you. I should've forgiven you years ago."

He didn't move.

She looked away and found the old guys again. One of them she recognized, the man wearing a designer Panama hat and dark sunglasses:

Luuk Devoor. The others were what she thought of as *21ˢᵗ century minstrels*: like medieval minstrels, they followed the ultra-rich, singing their praises and reaping rewards like rides on the private jet, vice presidencies with few responsibilities, and invitations to lavish parties. She heard Stefan sigh.

He tossed his magazine on the table and leaned forward. He nodded toward his father. "Role model. Fourth-generation inherited wealth, chairman of a privately-held global company, benefactor to politicians, museums, hospitals—and lifelong alcoholic."

Pia looked back as Luuk Devoor waved his glass at the bartender. His squad followed his lead.

"He's rarely shit-faced," Stefan said, "but he hasn't been sober since he went to boarding school forty years ago. The term is 'maintenance alcoholic' or, clinically speaking, he's a 'Delta'. They're erratic and unpredictable, and shocking because you never realize how drunk they are until someone pulls back the curtain and reveals their secrets. It wasn't until I stumbled into an AA meeting two years ago that I understood why my upbringing was full of contradictions. He loved me or hated me, depending on the hour or how much I reminded him of my discarded mother."

Pia looked into his eyes and saw a flat expression. From her own experience she knew that telling a difficult story many times makes it less painful and more casual.

"I started drinking at fourteen. A couple shots of vodka before school. Another at lunch. I quickly became a Delta, just like my old man. We're adept at hiding it, making you think we're fine when we're not. When you and I dated, I treated you badly from beginning to end. I berated you in public. I humiliated you at the Prom. I cannot undo that, I cannot forget it, but I do—sincerely—apologize for the pain I caused you."

She let his words sit for a long time. "You've been sober for two years?"

"Twenty-seven months, two weeks. Consider me your designated driver." He smiled weakly. "I slipped a few times early on, but I earned an eighteen-month chip last week."

He sighed. "Step Eight: Made a list of all persons we had harmed, and became willing to make amends to them all. Step Nine: direct amends to such people wherever possible, except when to do so would injure them or others." He paused. "I've been making amends. Making my rounds. The more I do it, the easier it gets. By the time I found you, I was taking it lightly. Too lightly. And too insistent. For that, I also apologize."

"I see."

She believed in redemption. It was the basis of her favorite charity for homeless families. But there on the patio, her experience failed her. She had never met a recovering alcoholic her age. With no frame of reference, or personal experience, she had no idea how to gauge his sincerity. She felt uncertain about the proper response or the next step for her.

He sensed her indecision. "After my grandfather died last year, my father ran the company into the ground. I hoped to fix him but only Luuk can fix Luuk. I've spent the last few months pouring over my heritage; how the family came to America mid-nineteenth century, discovered oil, and became filthy rich." He laughed. "My mother came from a humble background, so naturally I've only researched the Devoors. Anyway, I had to save the company, so I've taken a more active role. Like this conference for example. Do you know what it's all about?"

"People don't like Marty Maddox. They want to stop him from running. But I don't get why."

"Maybe we can figure it out from who's here." Stefan tapped the table top. "Roche is here because Marty Maddox failed to kiss his ring. The oil industry follows Roche like robots. The tech guys are here too, but I have no idea why."

"I saw some hedge fund people and that online gaming guy." Pia noticed they'd both leaned toward each other. She also noticed a certain amount of sincerity behind his long lashes. Beneath the recovering frat boy was a serious young man doing his best to do the right thing.

Stefan glanced at his watch and opened his mouth to say something but never got the words out.

"What did President Hunter want with you?" The voice behind her startled Pia.

She turned to find Chuck Roche pointing his silver-handled cane at her.

Pia said, "She asked, 'Who will rid me of this troublesome billionaire?'"

Roche scowled, creasing his red-tinted, translucent skin. He dropped the point of his cane to the ground and squinted down his razor thin nose for a moment. Then he laughed. "Was she referring to me—or you?"

He waved his hand at an empty chair nearby.

An aide appeared and moved the chair to form a triangle with Pia and Stefan, then disappeared.

"If you'll excuse me," Stefan said as he rose to leave, "I have an appointment."

He gave her a short bow and a smile and walked away.

Roche tested the cushion with his cane and, finding it passable, sank slowly into it. His cane remained at attention next to his right knee with his hand resting on top. "We have something in common, young lady. Know what it is?"

"Why don't you join me?" she asked.

"We can't wait to see the backside of Veronica Lodge Hunter." He laughed and pinched a few nuts from the dish on the table.

"Not an interruption at all."

"Thank God she decided not to run again." He popped a couple in his mouth and chewed. "Word on the street is, we have you to thank for that."

"No, I insist. Have a seat."

"Did her whitewashed story about killing your parents satisfy you?"

Pia found it hard to look solemn when someone reached deep inside to tweak her central nervous system. She caught her breath and stared hard at the old man. "Shame you can't stay. I wish I could say it was nice to see you again."

"What makes a good businessperson is their ability to find common ground with friend and foe alike." Roche pushed his palm hard on his cane and rose off his haunches and teetered to a standing position. He was neither weak enough nor old enough for such theatrics, but he played his part well. He combed the thin swatch of white hair over his head with his free hand. "Good day."

CHAPTER 15

JET ENGINES HUMMED THEIR MONOTONOUS tune, the airframe vibrated with the subdued strains of flying at five hundred miles an hour, and everyone around the Slager slept through the night on their journey to Papua New Guinea. He was pinned between an obese, snoring man and an overweight lady. Between the two, he had to pull his shoulders forward to avoid contact.

The lady had been eating Xanax like candy. She would wake up every twenty minutes to munch down a bag of junk food and take a pill. A disgusting pile of empty wrappers, half-eaten carbs, and yet-to-be-consumed carcinogens littered her tray. She scarfed down a bag of potato chips, her munching drowning out the engines, and went back to sleep.

The Slager had far too much on his mind to sleep anyway. At least the plane change had gone well. His Moroccans had followed his instructions to act like strangers to each other; never speak to anyone; pretend to read books in English; wear nothing that could be associated with Islam; and limit the daily prayer ritual. So far, so good. No one paid any undue attention to them.

He pulled up the email on his phone as the fat lady turned and twisted and snorted beside him. The lone email from the Artist was laconic: *Omar reported himself as the victim of extortion. Two Sabel agents arrived in Mérida on a Sabel corporate jet; Stearne and Rodriguez. Doubtful they could follow beyond Panama. Watch your back. Extra funding wired to ensure silence in Port Moresby, Myanmar, Pyongyang, and Shanghai. Use it wisely. You're one step ahead; keep it that way.*

Extra funding. That was nice. And easy. Too easy.

He outsmarted the Mexican cartels by thinking like them: what would he do if an uninvited stranger took over distribution from the Red River to the Missouri? That's how he ended up killing their men in Laredo. Don't even let them land on your turf. But how could he think like a guy he'd never met? One who calls himself the Artist?

A codename like that was conceited and smacked of intellectual snobbery. The money this Artist spent on his creation meant he was rich or at least had access to vast sums of money.

But it was Schwartz who had approached him at the halfway house. *What would you do for a fresh start in life?* A practiced pitch. An easy sale. No doubt Schwartz had a few more ex-cons in his program. Which meant the Artist didn't care how much money was involved. Michael Larson, the Slager, would never live to spend it.

The jet engines droned on, the airframe vibrated, the passengers slept and the Slager thought.

He deserved it. Being murdered. It would be the fitting end to a man who betrayed everything in his life. He distributed tons of crystal meth up and down the Mississippi. He sold out his business associates, the very guys he'd dragged into the business. He'd lost his kids in the ultimate loser's custody battle. And to get out from under all those crimes, he was shepherding ten fucking terrorists around the world. What was that all about? Ultimately, he knew they were going to kill Americans. And soon; probably in a week. That would be the final betrayal. And he thought he could escape his past with a new ID? Pretend to be a guy who could adopt Ethan and Emma from foster care with his new, impossible-to-fail background, and his new cosmetic surgery?

Could he live with that on his conscience? Was that the kind of dad Ethan and Emma deserved? He remembered Emma crying when the cops hauled him away from the house. She'd grabbed his leg and squeezed so hard they had to pry her loose. What would she do if she found out about this? Hate him. What kid could love her dad if he aided terrorists?

There was only one way out. Schwartz had been kind enough to provide the solution to his problems. He pulled the small tinfoil packet containing the cyanide tablet from his pocket and held it in his hand. Schwartz had said, *In case you get arrested—you'll pass facial recognition but DNA is DNA.*

Ain't it though?

He choked.

Ethan and Emma smiled at him. Caught in the wrapper's tiny creases was the picture of the kids he kept in the same pocket.

He unwrapped the pill and held it in his right hand. He held the photo in his other.

Was it easier to do the Artist's bidding, participating in whatever horror show he had planned, pretending all the while to be a passive slave, driven by the whims of the rich and powerful? Or was it his calling to fight them, turn them in, go back to jail, and lose everything? But then, there was the third option: the pill. Suicide. To die and damn them all to rot in the hell of their own making. That could be the sweetest way, to drift off into oblivion. And what would that oblivion be? A dream world? A spirit world? Heaven? Hell? Or is it just an end to the pain and suffering—like a lightbulb switched off?

Who knows? The dead never come back to tell us anything. It's that fear of the unknown that turns everyone into a coward. Who wouldn't end the humiliation of life, the heartbreak of a cheating lover, the unfairness of the legal system if they knew what lies beyond the final curtain. Why put up with all of life's bullshit? Why not just swallow the pill?

He looked again at the picture. Ethan grinned with an arm draped around his little sister. The boy was barely big enough to kick a soccer ball last time he saw him. To Ethan, Dad was a hero. He was the man who tamed dealers from Tulsa to Grand Forks. Ethan's dad never backed away from a fight. Never let a cheater live. Never let the other guys get ahead. Never lost. Never.

Fuck the Artist.

And fuck the government that locked him up and took his kids.

He looked at the pill. It looked like the fat lady's Xanax. He tossed it into her trash pile.

Killing himself was just what they wanted. What they didn't know about him was: he never did what anyone wanted. Michael Larson was in. All in. Diving off the cliff with his eyes closed.

The Artist expected him to die in the end, which meant getting more money out of him was no problem. All he needed to know was how much the Artist had—and he'd take it all.

He looked up real estate in Argentina on his phone. Every country has extradition; what he needed was a place with crooked officials. Rural Argentina might have a few of those. What would they cost, ten grand a year? First thing he found was a ranch in the mountains, fifteen hundred acres, only two million USD. Hell, he was halfway there already. The kids could learn Spanish. They could live out their lives and never look back at the country that screwed them at every turn.

He looked up Cayman banks and transferred a small sum to a new account. Not enough to draw notice. Just enough to see if there would be a reaction. Was the Artist watching the withdrawals? If not, just keep taking it. Keep taking until the fuckwad complained, then turn to blackmail and get more.

He smelled something putrid. A few more sniffs led him right to the spot. He knew what it was. Rotten flesh.

The Slager stood up and kicked the fat guy next to him. The man woke with a start and took a moment to comprehend, then waddled into the aisle to let him out. The Slager got to the bathroom and pulled down his pants. Yellow puss dripped down his leg.

He peeled the homemade bandage off and looked at the torn sutures. Jacob Stearne had put a bullet right through his thigh, an inch shy of his femoral artery. He was lucky the bullet had lost a lot of velocity coming through the roof before hitting his leg. The net result was a clean through-and-through that hurt like hell—but only when he moved.

The stitches came out easily enough. Dabbing the entry and exit holes went smoothly, but god only knew what kind of primordial soup stirred around in the six inches he couldn't reach. He would need antibiotics at the next stop. He improvised a new bandage from the feminine napkins he took from the last hotel and pulled his pants back on.

He sat in the spacious—compared to his middle-seat—bathroom and thought.

Maybe, after everything was working the way it should, he would find whatever crack house his ex-wife was selling herself out of and put her out of her misery. The stupid bitch won the divorce battle but never kicked her habit and thus lost the war. Before he put a bullet through her crystallized brain, he'd even repeat her own words back to her. The ones that started them both down the road to eternal damnation. "Ever watch *Breaking Bad?*" Maybe he'd even add the words he thought at the time but never said, "Remember how it ends?"

What was wrong with selling insurance in Kansas? Maybe he should've finished that application to join the Army. He could've been a captain or major by now. Not good enough for his bad-girl wife.

No sense blaming her. He'd wanted that yellow Corvette as much as she did.

No sense thinking about the past either. It was time to keep focused on the future. Run this deal through until the Artist stopped giving him money. Then kill the motherfucker. And Schwartz. Yeah. No more worrying about anybody else's problems. From now on, the only thing that mattered was getting the kids to a new, safe place. He brought them into this world, he owed them that much. He felt much better. And much more relaxed.

The Slager's head dipped and his eyes closed for a minute. Maybe he could get some shut-eye in the bathroom where he had enough room to relax his shoulders. He felt himself falling asleep. He was back in his cell, remembering his fourth day in the big house, after he lost his spot in the medium security prison. His head was in a headlock, being battered into the wall. Another guy twisted his right arm, and a third guy pulled his pants down to his ankles and yelled, "Yeehaw!"

But it wasn't "Yeehaw!" It was the pilot's voice telling everyone to stay in their seats.

He blinked and looked around his cramped space. It would be a wonder if he ever slept again.

That thought train arrived at a new station—his most immediate problem. Sabel Security in Venezuela. How did they get there? Nothing Omar said would be taken seriously by the US since the country was deemed as reliable as North Korea. Was it Tilden? The Artist? Did it matter? Omar would send the Sabel guys to Panama, but they would never find Ignacio. That ship had sailed.

He laughed.

Although, he should never underestimate the Sabel agents. The guys he saw operating in As Sukhnah were serious dudes. They did not fuck around. There was no fat on those bones, no hesitation in their decisions, no fear in those eyes. No wonder Schwartz's guys lost. Couple of gangsters who'd roughed up a few addicts, maybe pulled a trigger four or five times, but spent most of their adult lives living the prison-porn-dream would never take out those Sabel agents.

The Slager was on his own, pursued by some ass-kicking, black ops soldiers who could probably kill him through telepathy.

He thought through several different options until the last one hit him like a ton of bricks. He had better killers than prison scum. He had ten holy warriors who would die for Allah. All he had to do was dream up a convincing story. And he could do that better than Henry V.

The plane shook and dropped what felt like a thousand feet.

The pilot calmly gave instructions to use the seatbelts during the turbulence.

A flight attendant knocked on the door. He rose, like a condemned man, opened the door, and faced the stern-looking woman in uniform. Suddenly, she was plowing into him as the plane shook violently. Together they gripped the nearest seatback. She explained the drill: *return to your seat, put on your seatbelt, remain calm.* They hit another hole in the air and bounced several times. The flight attendant fell backward. He stuck out a hand but fell on top of her.

Someone screamed.

The plane flew straight and smooth. They scrambled to their feet, slightly embarrassed, and moved up the aisle toward a commotion in his row.

The Slager stopped in his tracks. The people screaming were clustered around his seat looking at the fat lady.

"She's dead!" a voice called out.

CHAPTER 16

PICO BOLÍVAR, THE HIGHEST PEAK in Venezuela at over 16,000 feet, loomed over us as we walked the streets of Mérida in a cold rain. Miguel's Spanish wasn't great, but it was better than mine. We were trying the cheap hotels, hoping to find someone who saw ten Arabs milling around looking for purses to snatch or whatever terrorists do in their down time. Complicating our search was the unknown-to-us fact that the University of the Andes was in the center of town, filling the place with fifty thousand college kids. Looking for dark-haired young men of varied skin hues proved to be a long slog.

The ninth hotel yielded results. The manager remembered them. She told Miguel they prayed on their balconies several times a day while they complained about someone named Omar. Across the street we found another hotel manager who remembered an American associating with the Arabs. After discussing things with him for a while, he remembered finding a phone in the guy's room. Naturally, that led to sifting through a giant trash can until we found the SIM card from the phone. It had been snapped in half.

Mercury walked up the street with a curvaceous woman who wore serious earrings and a colorful, geometric-patterned dress. *What're you doing in South America, homie?*

I scratched my head. *Uh. Well. Ms. Sabel said we could use her old jet and we couldn't find anything more on Larson, and Miguel had some trouble at his fancy condo, so we're tracking ten Moroccans who left As Sukhnah. The SEALs traced them to Riyadh where they booked flights to here.*

Mercury shook his head in disgust. *Just took her jet, huh? Abusing her trust. You should be ashamed, yo. Just because Pia-Caesar-Sabel says you can use her jet doesn't mean you have to.*

I said, *I couldn't let it go to waste. Besides, we might have found the guy we're looking for. So, who's your girlfriend? Are you going to introduce me?*

He stepped back. *Hey now, dawg. She's seriously outta your league. Meet Pachamama, Inca goddess of fertility—and possibly my date to the gods convention.* Mercury stepped up close and leaned in with a conspiratorial whisper. *You'll give us a lift back to the States on the jet, right? I mean, you'd be helping a brotha impress his girl here, ya feel me? I'll even help you out in return: call Bianca for help on the SIM card.*

I said, *Oh, so it's OK for you to use the jet?*

Mercury tossed a glance at Pachamama, and whispered, *A little sensitivity, bro. Not every god has wings.*

I called Bianca. "Can your team read a broken SIM?"

"Snapped in half like they do on TV shows? No problem," she said. "The only way to destroy them is with an arc furnace."

"Can I tell if that's what he did? Where would I find one of … whatever you said?"

"You can make one out of an old microwave and multi-cell batteries. It's easy, I can show you. But the card would be a puddle of melted plastic if he did that."

"Just broken in half. I need to know who this guy was talking to and when."

"Bring it over, I'll get it working."

"I'm in Venezuela."

"How did you get there? Or do I want to know? Never mind. Watch your back, friend. They have the highest murder and kidnapping rates in the world."

"How do you know?"

"I used to head up the Latin America desk at the NSA. You know that. Hey, did he make any landline calls?"

The manager told us the guy took a couple incoming calls. We put him on with Bianca and she got the pertinent details from him. She clicked off to call in some favors with her NSA buddies. We had a little time to kill until she called back.

Her warning about crime made me think about my surroundings. Miguel was dressed for Third World travel: rumpled t-shirt and worn-out jeans without brand names, Converse knockoffs. I broke the cardinal rule of traveling to dangerous places: pricey fashion. I had an Under Armour t-shirt with their logo stretched across my chest, True Religion jeans, and neon Air Jordans on my feet. The only thing missing from my ensemble was a sticker that read: I'm-a-rich-American-needing-to-be-kidnapped.

Flying private made me feel invincible, especially since I felt like the owner of it and not the owner's muscle. I'd let my guard down. Arriving on a jet also allows you certain smuggling privileges. We carried Glocks, and being armed also gives you a false sense of security. We'd been searching through the seedy part of town without thinking about personal safety.

I took a more detailed inventory.

Two- and three-story buildings huddled over a crowded narrow street. Graffiti—or artwork, depending on your understanding of gang signs—covered every surface reachable from the thin sidewalk. Overloaded telephone poles leaned this way and that, nearly falling into the street. Walls once painted in now-faded blues or whites or yellows leaned against each other for support.

We'd seen soldiers with AK-103s at the executive terminal, but no other sign of law enforcement. The city was full of beautiful smiling people who gazed at us with intelligent eyes and upturned faces when we were nearer the university. In this block, voices were muted, faces were downcast, people were lean—and not because they'd gone gluten-free. Hugo Chavez and his socialist revolution brought the same results as most revolutions: the rich got richer and corruption flourished.

Half a block down, one of the lean and hungry watched me through his eyebrows. A young man with a scraggly beard and an angry posture kept his piercing gaze nailed to me while he spoke on a cell phone. I crossed the street with my back to him and saw a car carrying four men coming toward me. When I reached the far side, I checked the young man. He knew I made him. He spun away. The car sped up.

Getting into a gunfight in a country known for its anti-American sentiment was not my ideal resolution to Venezuela's crime wave.

I ran back and pushed Miguel inside the hotel. The lobby was twelve feet by fifteen feet, no wasted space. A standing desk blocked the manager's door. A tight staircase led to the second floor. The manager was gone.

"Damn it. They voted me out of the condo. They're going to buy back my place." Miguel stared at his phone. "Anglos got no sense of humor."

"Worry about that later. We gotta go."

The stairs led to a narrow hall with eight doors for rooms that faced the street. No fire exits. No back doors. No rooftop access. Miguel followed reluctantly and grabbed my shoulder, asking for an explanation.

We heard rushing footsteps in the lobby.

A middle-aged woman came out of a room halfway down the hall. I pushed her back in, shushed her with a finger across my lips, and ran to her window. She shrieked like the Wolfman's first victim. Below us, a car at a 45-degree angle blocked the street. Miguel gave the lady a hug, wrapping her up in his big frame. For some odd reason, it worked and she quieted down.

"Jacob, why are we terrorizing this poor lady?" he asked.

Boots clomped up the stairs.

I pointed at the sound. "Desperados."

"Why don't we say hello?" He handed the woman to me.

She resumed screaming. I get that a lot.

Miguel stepped into the hall and paced to the top of the stairs where a guy with a rusty revolver charged into the hallway.

The average Venezuelan male is around five feet four inches tall. This guy was dragging down the average. Miguel is tall even by Navajo standards. The differential was more than a foot.

The poor guy's jaw dropped as his eyes traveled up Miguel's torso. Our would-be assailant noticed the look in Miguel's eye.

My buddy spent his early years on the Navajo Reservation (known as the Rez) but moved to El Segundo, California in fifth grade. On the Rez, his birth name was as common as Joe Smith but *Two-Feathers Begay* was the subject of constant ridicule in California public schools. Everyone mistook him for a Mexican, and spoke to him in Spanish, even his teachers, so his father changed the family name to Rodriguez and renamed him Miguel. That capitulation to the Anglos' so-called civilization sparked the repressed warrior inside him. He cultivated his heritage in boot camp and channeled it to ace Ranger School at the head of his class. He believed he was a skinwalker, an ancient warrior-wizard able to change himself into a bear for battle. Normally, a calm and collected thinker, the skinwalker came out of hiding whenever someone came at him with more aggression than he thought appropriate. He sucked in a lungful of air and bellowed his war whoop.

The first of the four attackers wilted.

Miguel snapped the barrel of the revolver backward, twisting the man's finger in the trigger guard. The man's finger snapped like a twig. I heard it. So did the screaming woman—who stopped screaming. Miguel lifted the guy by the neck and held him in mid-air for a moment before hurling him down the stairs. The whole squad fell like dominoes to the landing and scrambled over each other to escape the pent-up wrath of a pissed off Native American. One guy stopped to look back up the stairs. Miguel bellowed a second whoop. The straggler slipped, fell, jumped back up, and fled.

I faced the screaming-woman, who—no longer screaming—stood behind me with her mouth open, her eyes wide. I dusted off her shoulders and patted her. "Sorry."

She slapped me. Hard.

A heavily accented voice floated up the stairs. "Easy now. Easy. I am Lieutenant Rosales. Unarmed."

I peered around Miguel's side to see to open palms reaching around the wall. An official-looking badge in a plastic holder dangled from his fingers, proving his claim. I said, "What can we do for you?"

"Nice work, señor." The scraggly bearded guy from the street stuck his head around the corner. "May I come up?"

"How about we come to you?" I asked and glanced at my new girlfriend. "We're scaring the residents."

We descended the steps.

Rosales noticed as I examined his scruffy look. "I refuel planes at the airport on my days off. *Inflación es muy* ... ehm, inflation is big."

Miguel looked out the front windows. We heard the distinct crunch of a fender-bender, followed by the roar of a small hotrod.

"You followed us?"

"Si." He grinned and shrugged. "You arrive on the Sabel jet, no? I think maybe you need special *agente* in Mérida, no?"

"Yeah, Rosales. We're thinking, between the protests and the government crackdowns, some executives might want ... independent protection. But Americans aren't keen on moving here. So, we thought we'd get a look at the local talent. Test a few guys out. See what they can do."

Miguel shot a disdainful look over his shoulder at me. He never liked making things up.

Rosales's eyes lit up. He straightened up and almost saluted. "*Si. Agente* Rosales can do anything."

Miguel raised an eyebrow and tilted back.

"We tracked a few Arabs and one American here. They were trying to get in touch with a local guy named Omar."

"This is a common name." Rosales turned to the hotel manager and rattled off a stream of Spanish that made my head spin.

I'm pretty sure it's the fastest language in the world and he was going for a record. The manager spat some back and waved his hand, dismissing the matter, then disappeared into his tiny office. Rosales faced me and smiled but said nothing.

Ten awkward seconds later, the manager reappeared and handed a slip of paper to Rosales before going back to his office and closing the door. The lieutenant pulled out his phone and dialed the number on the paper. He kept his eyes on me and smiled while he waited. When someone answered, he asked for Omar. He gave me a thumbs up.

Then he dove into a stream of Spanish again, stopped and listened, started again, then stopped suddenly, and pushed his phone in his pocket. "*Señor*, I have found Omar."

"Awesome, Rosales." I gave him my best impression of officers when you brag to them about some petty task you completed as if you'd won the decathlon. "Can I speak to him?"

He looked concerned and stroked his chin. "Does Sabel pay in dollars or bolívars?"

I'm no genius at foreign affairs, but most of the times I was jailed on leave, it started by misreading the signals at the intersection of foreign officials and money. Or women. Or some combination of the three.

I said, "Let's make sure we have a clear understanding of the rules of engagement before we discuss money. I'm interested in meeting this guy. I'm willing to hire a guide. I'm willing to pay cash. American dollars. But, I'm not willing to break any rules or insult anyone's honor."

He smiled. "Understood, *señor*. Then take a look at the map, I'll show you where we will go."

He retrieved his phone and held it away from the door, which I thought was odd. Miguel leaned over our shoulders. Rosales texted someone the single word, *rápido*. Miguel and I looked at each other.

Ten soldiers kicked in the front door with AK-103s leveled at us. One of them deferred to Rosales and called him *teniente*. Lieutenant.

"I'm sorry, *señor*. You must come with us."

As he pulled my Glock and phone, I smelled jet fuel on his clothes.

ROSALES SPENT THE FIRST TEN minutes of my incarceration smashing my left shoulder with a rubber hose every thirty seconds. He had a timer set on his phone. He said nothing, just stared at me until the timer chimed; then wound up like he was going for a home run, hit me, and reset the timer. I mentioned how cliché it was for Latin America but he was no slave to fashion trends in torture. I would've laughed at him. But cliché or not, it hurt like hell and my mouth was too swollen to talk from all the times he slipped off the target.

I was handcuffed to a chair in a classic film noir interrogation room: gray concrete all around, stains on the walls, a cheap table and rigid chairs. Rosales turned off his timer and offered me water. Then he left.

A couple hours went by.

Then it got worse.

Mercury strode in, still wearing his formal toga. *Thought I'd stop in to say good-bye, homie. I wish I could say it's been fun ... well, that one time in Kabul with Fawzia was straight up a great time. She was nice. Why didn't you stay with her?*

I said, *She dumped me. Her family didn't approve.*

Yeah, sucks to be you, bro. You shoulda told them about me. If they knew you were a god's main man, maybe we'd still be there, all peace and harmony with your little Afghan babies running around your grave. Mercury looked to the ceiling. *You think the Taliban would've put your head on a spike? Or used it for a soccer ball?*

I said, *What does Rosales want?*

You think you got it bad. Mercury whistled. *You should see what Rosales is doing to Omar. From where he sits, he's got an American spy and a bent passport official.*

Rosales really is a lieutenant? Why's he working at the airport?

What he told you, dude. Oil is down, bolívar is worthless, kids to feed. Good thing you didn't fall for the bribery entrapment. Rosales is the last honest man in uniform in this country.

Just my luck.

The door opened and Rosales strode in without a rubber hose. He tossed a pad, pen, and his phone on the table and sat down opposite me. "Why are you really in Venezuela, Mr. Stearne?"

"I'm looking for ten Arabs and an American named Michael Larson."

"You're an imperialist spy, then?"

Call me cynical, but I didn't like the sound of that. I explained our rescue operation and running into an American where one didn't belong. I told him about the call from the Polish guys and the ten Arabs who left the region for Venezuela. He kept his arms crossed and scowled but listened.

"Rosales." I leaned forward with my best trust-me look. "You're a smart man. You know that governments come and go. If the food riots are any indication, the current regime is none too popular. I'm betting you're a little like me. When I had a government job, I had a backup plan—just in case a bunch of pacifists took over and started treating veterans badly. An insurance policy. I'm not talking about cash. I'm talking about favors. I did favors for important people in Pakistan, India,

England, Kuwait. If things get ugly for me back in the States, I can visit a friend and stay a while."

That wasn't exactly true. Miguel was the one who did favors for people in other countries. I spent my free time finding women and trouble. But never underestimate the power of good bullshit.

Rosales squinted. "I don't care about impressing some stinking *gringo*."

"Student protests don't amount to much—sometimes. But sometimes they do. What would happen if a bunch of students—angry at the police—took over Mérida for a week? You could go to Caracas or somewhere. But what if it spread there too? Where would you go? Where are your friends?"

"You say something like this now. When I knock on your door, will you answer? Capitalists will say anything to get what they want."

"I'm not talking about me. I'm talking about my company. Call the Sabel Security office in São Paulo. Ask the manager if she got an email from Jacob Stearne, asking her to give you and four other people sanctuary, what would she do?"

Rosales leaned back and studied me. "And you expect me to give you freedom, just like that?"

"No. All I want is five minutes with Omar. You can sit with us, listen to the whole thing, no codes, no passing notes, no subversion. I have nothing to hide."

He went quiet while he searched my eyes to discern if I were lying. I never broke eye-contact with him.

Finally he asked, "What is the number?"

I gave him the international toll-free number. He dialed.

While he waited for it to connect, I said, "Her name is Bianca Dominguez."

When she answered, I telepathically willed her to lie for me. After all, he was right: capitalists will say anything to save their asses. Just like communists and socialists and feudalists and everyone else. She got the message and told him what he wanted to hear. I could tell because somewhere in the rapid-fire Spanish, he began to smile.

Rosales put the phone down and looked at me. "I will do this. No harm could come from it, right? Maybe I learn something."

He left the room and took a nap or something because no one came back for what felt like hours. My wrists were chafed and my butt was sore.

Eventually, the door opened and a disheveled guy with a big gut stumbled in. The door closed behind him. Someone had been working him over for a long time. The bruises distorted his face. Some were fresh and red, some were already turning blue, while others had gone purple. That meant his torture had been going on for two or three days. They had been on to Omar long before I arrived.

Omar took the only chair in the room, the one opposite me.

His eyes started to angle toward me, then he thought better of it and twisted to the side.

The door opened and Rosales came in carrying a chair. He dropped it with a bang that made Omar jump. He sat and pushed his phone to the middle of the table. "Go ahead, ask him questions. I'll translate."

I asked my questions about the Arabs and Larson. Rosales translated. Omar said nothing. I repeated and Rosales patiently translated. Still nothing.

I tried a risky approach.

"There is a reward leading to the capture of these terrorists," I lied. "In the US, that is. If your government allows it."

Rosales glared at me for a long time, then translated. He and Omar went back and forth about something. Negotiating his reward, judging from the tone of the exchange.

Omar didn't look too happy at the end, but he met my gaze for the first time. His swollen eyes were heavy with impending doom.

Rosales translated. "He doesn't know the American's name, but he was insistent that the Arabs reach Panama. He threatened Omar's family and scared his wife a great deal. For a small amount of money, Omar provided them with fake passports. They were going for new passports in Panama, then going on to other countries until their backgrounds looked clean. He doesn't know all the places they were going, but the Arabs bragged they were going to kill the American president."

Mercury leaned across the table. *Holy shit, dude. You gotta stop them. Or not. After all, she tried to kill Pia-Caesar-Sabel.*

I said, *No fucking terrorist is going to kill any president on my watch.*

Well then, we gotta get you out of here. I'll get Bianca to call the Embassy.

Rosales and I rechecked Omar's story several times, trying to poke holes in it. It held up to scrutiny.

When I was satisfied I'd learned all I could, I thanked Rosales. "Omar did the right thing. You'll send him home, right?"

"Worry about paying the reward."

"No problem. I'll see they send a check shortly."

"We found a good deal of cash in your wallet," Rosales said and faced me. "We will give it to his wife on your behalf."

"But, uh, that was my personal—"

"You're not a lying capitalist, are you, *señor?*"

"Yeah, that's fine." Except it wasn't. "You'll turn him loose then?"

"Certainly not. He is a corrupt official and will be sentenced according to the law. This country is falling apart because of greedy pigs like Omar."

Mercury leaned against the wall behind Rosales. *You're not going to win this battle, homie. Omar helped terrorists for cash—that's a death sentence in your book. You can trust Rosales; he's the only clean officer between here and Tierra del Fuego. Your money will go to Omar's widow. It's all good.*

I nodded at Rosales and held my cuffed hands out. "I'm sure you'll do the right thing with him. Now, uncuff me. I need to get to Panama."

The rubber hose came out of his pocket so fast I didn't have time to turn away. It landed on the side of my head, crushing my ear and stinging my brain. The pain was so intense I nearly puked. Omar flinched in his seat and gave me an empathetic glance.

Rosales played with his phone. "Señor, you are not going anywhere. You threatened an officer of this country with a student uprising."

"What? Never."

He played my words back to me. *Student protests don't amount to much—sometimes. But sometimes they do. What would happen if a bunch of students—angry at the police—took over Mérida for a week?*

CHAPTER 17

PIA WALKED DOWN THE HALL on the third floor of the Ritz-Carlton in Rancho Mirage as if her room were nearby. She smiled at the Roche Security guard outside the room she had intended to break into. It took a seriously paranoid executive to have someone guarding the hall. Pia kept her people nearby, but not that close. She put her head down and turned right at the corner. She stopped and pressed her back against the wall. She squeezed her eyes shut and whispered into her earbud. "Guard in the hall, standing next to his door."

Bianca replied from Sabel Technologies headquarters. "This is a terrible, unethical, and illegal idea. Just keep walking."

"This is important to me."

"OK." Bianca blew out a breath. "Give me a minute to come up with plan B."

Pia could hear Bianca typing away in the background, accessing her hack into the hotel's security system.

"Tell me the truth: did you leak the story to Emily at the *Post*?" Pia asked.

Bianca hesitated for one telltale second. "What story?"

"Don't equivocate." She paused. "Veronica's decision not to run."

"No comment."

"Tania thinks you used the scoop to win Emily over."

"What? No." Bianca's anger was palpable. "Emily's different. We've been dating for a couple weeks already."

"Can I trust you, Bianca?"

Pia heard her friend sigh. She let the silence stretch.

"Maybe I talk in my sleep," Bianca said. "She's been pestering me about what you meant when you told the White House correspondents it was premature to endorse Hunter. I got a little excited, that's all. I'm sorry. I'll apologize to the president."

"No need. Veronica figured it was you and sends her thanks. Your leak brought more reporters to the press conference than she'd seen in the last ten combined." Pia could feel Bianca's anxiety subside. "Did you tell Emily anything about the rest of that conversation?"

"No way. That's your story. I purged my memory banks the moment we walked out."

"I need to trust you, Bianca."

"Suite 3412," Bianca said. "It's right behind you and you can cross over the balcony. It's occupied, but the TV is off and there's no one accessing the Internet, so I'm pretty sure they're out of the room."

Pia found the door and waited until she heard the electronic lock clack open. She turned the handle and slipped inside the dark room. The sliding glass door to the balcony stood wide open. Gauze curtains wafted in a hot breeze. The room's contents gave away the suite's owner: Roche's security team. Bullets, magazines, stun guns, even a cattle prod lay in the open. If these guys operated like Sabel Security, they owned rooms on both sides of the boss, alternating between them for off-duty and on.

The suites faced the mountain, away from the hotel's central pools and courtyard. She checked the open space in front of her. A vast, empty desert stretched across the Coachella Valley. Mountain ranges blasted upward from the dry valley floor, reaching to alpine altitudes. No one could see her.

The railing was thin and meant for leaning against, not climbing on. She hopped up, teetered on the edge, and peered around the divider separating the two balconies.

Chuck Roche sat in a chair, an arm's length from her, his cane in one hand, his other clasping a phone to his ear, facing away from her.

She stepped down and away from the edge. She pressed her ear to the woven wood partition. Roche spoke in a patient voice, doing more listening than talking.

"Why don't we have someone in her camp?" Roche asked whoever manned the other end of the call. After a lengthy pause, he continued. "I tossed a challenge her way this afternoon. She'll come after me; count on it."

She heard Roche sigh with thinning patience as he listened to the response.

"Listen to me, Howard," Roche said. "What she did to the Devoor boy, I'm going to do to you if she gets inside my organization without me knowing about it." He paused again until he lost his patience. "ENOUGH EXCUSES! YOU FIND OUT WHAT SHE KNOWS. FIND OUT WHAT HUNTER TOLD HER. DO IT NOW OR YOU'RE FIRED."

Heat from his angry outburst radiated through the divider. She could hear his phone skitter across the concrete balcony where he threw it.

"Begging your pardon, sir." A new voice stepped onto Roche's balcony. "Messrs. Addison and Cameron are downstairs waiting."

"Hell, I'm five minutes late. Why didn't you say something?" He got up from his chair with relative ease and exhaled all his anger. She could sense him forcing a mood change from angry boss to amiable friend.

She hopped up on the railing again. Gripping the divider, she leaned her weight over and peered around it. The sunset was on the opposite side of the building, casting gloom on her side. Two men milled about the suite, nothing but shadows within the shadow-filled room. To avoid being discovered, she reached her phone around to record a few seconds of video.

Behind her, the door to the room she was in opened. Her heart stopped. A quick look over her shoulder assured her the suite's owner would not see her unless he came to the balcony. He spoke to someone in the hallway about the opening night dinner.

The railing crunched an inch forward with a metallic noise.

Pia quickly dismounted. A bolt securing the divider stretched half an inch from its anchor.

She backed to a corner of the balcony and listened intently to the most immediate threat: the owner of the room she'd broken into.

Beyond the divider, on Roche's side, she heard someone come to the sliding glass door and stop.

Pia pulled her Glock 33 from her fanny pack and, as quietly as possible, chambered a Sabel Dart. She held her breath.

Behind her, the room's owner stood four feet away, his toes on the edge of the sliding-door track. She flattened herself against the wall. He looked and listened.

His phone rang. He pulled it out of his pocket. "Bob, you ready to party? Meet me in the State Fare Bar."

The rest of his conversation cut off as he slid the door closed with a bang.

Pia almost blew a sigh of relief—then she heard a bodyguard on Roche's side of the divider. "Nah. I smell perfume."

Pia wasn't wearing any perfume, but she had showered with the hotel's body gel and knew most men couldn't tell the difference.

He sniffed near the divider.

Someone inside his suite yelled at the guy to move. He grunted and went inside, slamming the door behind him.

Pia stood perfectly still for a long time, listening to the sound of silence and sweating out the summer heat. She could feel sweat seeping from her body, only to evaporate before it formed on her skin.

Satisfied both rooms were empty, she tried the door to the room behind her. Locked solid.

She jumped to the railing and felt it give another inch. Committed, she swung onto Roche's balcony.

They were gone. The sliding door had bounced back a quarter inch from the auto-lock. His guards were better about locking their own doors than the boss's.

A glint caught her eye. On the edge of the balcony lay Roche's phone, right where he'd tossed it. She checked it out. Scratched and cracked from landing on its face. She typed in the number to Sabel Technology's remote software site. She retrieved and installed their spy software, then sent the spy-virus to Roche's cloud where it would infect any other devices he used. She wiped her fingerprints and put it back where she'd found it.

She slid the door open and pushed past blackout curtains to the dark interior. Since it was designed like her suite, she had a feel for the furniture and layout but reverted to her phone's flashlight for some help.

A case of new mobile phones lay open on the coffee table, minus one. Roche tossed enough phones around to warrant carrying spares.

She carried a couple spares herself for the same reason. But a case of them?

Roche's laptop sat on the desk. She inserted her USB key into it and powered it on. It beeped loudly. Was the guard still at the door? She held her finger on the interrupt button to choose boot options. It opened to the BIOS screen, where her software took over the start-up sequence. Her software inserted itself in the hardware before security software scanned for viruses or spyware. She could hack almost any system as long as she could reboot it twice, which was a time-consuming and noisy process. Especially if she were caught in the act. After it successfully loaded, she powered it down. Somehow, she fumbled the USB drive.

The lock clacked and the door handle dropped.

Pia slid behind the blackout curtain and pulled her pistol. She risked one eye peering out from the edge.

Someone entered the suite's foyer. Footsteps, heavy and quick, crossed the marble to the seating area. The shadowy figure flipped on a lamp and grabbed a folder from the desk. A young man, early twenties, glanced at the floor and looked around the room as if he sensed her presence. He sniffed the air.

He scanned the room slowly, starting with the kitchen, turning left.

Pia pulled her exposed shoulder and eye back from the edge and held her breath. The silence roared in her ears. Seconds ticked by like hours. She heard nothing from him, no sound of movement. She had no idea if he were approaching her or passing her by.

His phone buzzed. "Yeah, got it. I'm on my way. It's just... that perfume I smelled—"

Pia understood why dogs rolled in horseshit before hunting.

The front door slammed closed behind him.

She remained frozen in place. She let two full minutes elapse before bursting from her hiding place with her pistol drawn. The room was empty.

In the bathroom, she found the hotel's body gel, the same she'd showered with earlier. She tossed it on the floor near the sliding glass door and stepped on it until it broke open and squirted gel. Hopefully, the guard with the clever nose would find it and think that was the source of his curiosity.

She grabbed her USB drive, pushed in her earbud, and dialed up Bianca. She tried to keep her voice from sounding too frantic. "Do they have video feeds on this floor?"

"Yes, and the guard is still out there." Bianca clicked some keys. "Can you scale the outside to the ground floor?"

"Are there people in the rooms below?"

"Don't know. Everyone's supposed to be at the big reception before dinner."

Pia heard voices in the hallway. She bolted out the back and slid the door back to the place she found it, wiping prints as she went. She flipped over the edge and lowered herself to the next floor. From there, to the next, until she landed on the ground at the back end of the hotel.

She snuck a peek around the corner, where she smelled cigarette smoke. Two men in green Roche Security jackets joked about how they'd gotten women drunk to take advantage of them. Listening, she could hardly contain her outrage. She wanted to ask if they were really such low-lifes that the only way they could reproduce was through date-rape. Instead, she visualized her father's hand, splayed wide, telling her to save it for later.

She waited until she heard them leave. When it was quiet, she turned the corner and found one guard remaining with his back to her. The cigarette was an offense of self-destructive stupidity, but the misogyny called for a powerful rebuke.

Alerted by her footsteps, he looked over his shoulder.

Pia's palm slammed into the man's temple with enough force to spin him around. He staggered to the wall, put a hand out to steady himself. She kicked the back of his knee, sending him into a crumpled stance. She waited until he started to look up, then planted her knee in his nose.

"The next time you get a girl too incapacitated to say yes or no, go home—or I'll find you again."

She kneed him again hard enough to bounce his head against the wall. His eyes fluttered, his toes shook. Solid concussion.

Pia marched toward the resort's back door.

Her victim's partner burst back out with a big grin on his face and a bottle of booze in his hand. "Hey, Brett, look what I—"

He choked at the sight of his friend as Pia walked by.

"Whoa. Did you see what happened?"

She stopped, looked down at the shorter man, and then over her shoulder at Brett. "Feral Girl Scout attack. Heard reports they're running in packs out in the desert." She leaned in close to his ear. "Be careful how you treat them."

PIA'S FASHION SENSE WAS LIMITED to a nice dress, heels, jewelry, a clutch, and very little makeup. A modest side slit showed off her only source of confidence: her legs. Tania's prep time took longer. While Pia waited, she called the Major.

"What's the latest on Verges and the FBI's facial recognition? Did they figure out who's after my agents?"

"They identified the first two from Jacob's house; a pair of parole violators with no connection to Sabel Security that we can find. Whoever hired them knew what they were doing. Using unassociated deadbeats for assassins makes the trail impossible to follow. The cameras at Miguel's place didn't get a very clear picture of their faces for the program. It'll take time to refine it."

"Any word from the Coushatta tribe?"

"They liked your proposal," the Major said. "It's been sent to the Tribal Council. What is that all about?"

"Solving problems."

Pia's next call was to her hacker, Bianca. She explained Roche's plan to hack Pia's systems. "So, how secure are our computer systems?"

"Every computer works on a binary system: 0's and 1's in multiples of 8. Same for the Internet and all the traffic going through it. Hackers know this and worm their way in through ports in routers and other openings. Sabel Technologies developed a ternary system: negative 1's, positive 1's, and 0's. Most scientists gave up on it back in the '70s, but

Alan Sabel used it for secure satellite technology. When I was with the NSA, no one knew how to break the 'Sabel code'. Not even the Chinese have cracked it. Anything inside our system is safe from hackers, like this phone call and our texts and emails. But anything coming and going from our ternary system out to the regular Internet is hackable."

Tania walked in, her wild, curly hair flowing free, and gave Pia an impatient look, as if it had been Tania who'd waited for hours. Pia clicked off and grabbed her clutch, lost in thought about how to outsmart Roche. They left the suite, heading for the elevators.

Pia barely noticed, but Tania had been talking the whole time.

"...and that's why you need a man. Not that you *need* a man—but you need a man. Your employees do not need another inspirational email." Tania pressed the down button and faced her. "I mean, puh*leez*, 'it takes a lot of hard work to become talented'?"

Pia stepped in the elevator and sighed dramatically.

Tania ignored her subtle cue to stop talking. "Forget inspiration, get out there and live a little."

They wound through the resort's hallways to the reception area, where a hundred billionaires chatted and drank.

"I'll get us drinks." Tania turned toward the bar. "Ima need me some alcohol to keep an eye on the egos in this room."

"Same," Pia called out to her back.

She surveyed the scene, noting she was one of ten women in the room. She'd studied profiles on many of the people here, but there were far more than she expected.

She strolled through the crowd, listening to snippets of conversations. Sean Addison and Chuck Roche argued about politics. Joe Walters and Davy Cameron bragged about vacations. Others stopped her to rail about their favorite cause.

The hedge fund magnates Josephine Seligman and Ritchie Skaite waved her over. After introductions, they asked her which political party she belonged to. She replied, "None."

Skaite said, "Can you imagine if the referees took away four of your goals and gave them to the other team? Unfair, right? You should join the Republican Party!"

Before she could respond, Seligman laughed. "Could you imagine starting the game ahead by four goals just because you're Alan Sabel's daughter? If you believe in a level playing field, you should join the Democrats!"

Pia looked at their jovial, expectant faces. "A goal only happens when everyone on the team works together. Which party relies on teamwork?"

Skaite soured. "You sound like one of those goddamned NEXT USA types. What the hell are you doing here?"

"I've not followed the news." Pia realized she'd forgotten to study the one thing that brought all these people together. "What's wrong with NEXT USA?"

"Maddox will destroy everything." Seligman looked Pia over, pitying her ignorance. "We'll end up like Italy or Brazil, with the government lurching in a new direction every year."

Pia felt a hand on her elbow. Bobby Jenkins, founder of Jenkins Pharmaceuticals and Alan Sabel's mentor, smiled at her. "Don't worry, I'll have a word with her."

He pulled her sideways.

She glanced around to make sure his milquetoast son, Jaz, wasn't with him. He wasn't.

She twisted through the crowd at his side. "What's wrong with asking?"

He smiled up at her. "Change can be a destructive force. They're scared Marty Maddox will change everything."

"Maybe we need a little change."

"What kind? Businesses have to invest years ahead. The factories that build your satellites were built five years before the first bird circled the Earth. Alan spent those years wringing his hands, scared to death a new president or a new congress would cancel the project, destroying his investment and forcing him to lay off thousands of workers. Maddox is scaring business owners because he announced a new economic strategy without telling anyone what it is. And he's popular as hell. If his polling stays this strong into the fall, he's going to be our next president."

"If he is, that would be the will of the people. Isn't that what democracy is all about?"

"The reason the Founding Fathers put the Electoral College together was to prevent the people doing something popular that was also destructive. What if Maddox takes office and pulls the plug on Sabel Satellites and gives the business to Boeing? You'd have to lay off thirty thousand employees."

An impeccably dressed man stopped Bobby with a hug and spoke with a heavy accent. "*Ciao, mio amico,* Bobby. You will stop the Maddox, no?"

He did a double take at Pia and bowed. "Ms. Sabel, what an honor. Allow me to introduce myself. Roberto Antonelli of the International Trade Union Association."

She raised one eyebrow.

"His unions manufacture my products all over the world," Bobby said. He patted Roberto on the back and led Pia away. "Workers are the first to lose when big changes happen. They have a stake in this too."

"But they can't donate to American elections. My team just dismantled Daryl Koven's dark money operation."

"You dismantled the illegal part. If global corporations like mine can shift money to Ireland for tax breaks, why can't unions shift money here for Super PACs? A new president could make a few rules changes and force jobs to move from places like Ohio or Romania to Vietnam or Canada. Roberto represents nearly 200 million workers from virtually every country in the world. But he's a good guy. What you should worry about is the Chinese Trade Union. They represent the same number of people, but guess where they want everything made?"

Tania joined them and handed a shot glass to Pia and kept a schooner with an umbrella in it for herself. "They only had Don Julio Real, *Añejo.*"

Pia tossed it back in one swallow and handed the empty to a passing waiter.

Bianca buzzed her phone. She excused herself and pressed her earbud in.

"We found something on Roche's phone," Bianca said. "A text-thread from an anonymous phone identifying the owner only as 'the Artist'. We've traced it through several spoofed phone connections to Cambodia.

We doubt that's where the sender is, but Cambodia's system is ancient. No GPS by default. We'll keep tracking it."

"I knew Roche was our guy."

"I don't think so. The text exchange looks more like a taunt than a clandestine communication. But in one, the Artist says, 'I'm here to solve your problems.'"

"Is that all he says?"

"There are many taunts about his wife and his business partners, some intended to be funny and others obviously mean. The Artist has to be close to Roche. But that one text worried us because the Artist started the thread with a murder-for-hire proposal—which Roche dismissed as a joke."

"Could Roche be replying in a conspiracy-denying code? I mean, could he be sending a message that says, 'don't do that' when he means the opposite just in case his records are investigated?"

"We looked at that. We don't think so. His tone is reactionary, as if he's pissed as hell. Roche must know the guy, but can't figure out who it is."

Pia spotted Chuck Roche surrounded by a group of minstrels. "At the moment...he thinks it's me."

CHAPTER 18

THE PORT MORESBY POLICE PUSHED the Slager out of Jackson Airport shortly after dark and tossed his empty wallet and passport to him. They'd finished with their "inquiry" into the fat lady's unexpected death. It wasn't his fault she gobbled down everything in front of her. First sign of turbulence and she ate what looked vaguely like anxiety medication without wondering why it wasn't in her pill bottle. Nothing he could do. Anxiety killed her. It was her own fault. But that's not what he told them. He was in the bathroom. No idea what happened. Best guess: choked on junk food.

The cops had no way to know any different. But that didn't stop the threats. Even the pilot had to pay. When his turn came, the Slager eagerly handed over his wallet in exchange for the promise not to fill out any reports or paperwork. The last thing he needed was a paper trail.

Still, it was sloppy of him. If he was going to pull this off, he had to tighten up his act. No loose ends. No mistakes. No unwanted scrutiny.

At least the cops gave back his phone with its all-important banking app. If they knew anything about modern electronic banking, they could've been millionaires.

There were no taxis or busses at the airport. Only a private minibus overflowing with scared-looking locals remained near the parking lot. No one traveled in Papua New Guinea after dark. The capitol once took second place as the "least livable city" in the world. The opportunistic Raskol gangs fought for territory against the more organized Bouganvilles from the minute the sun went down until sunrise the next morning.

He mopped the sweltering heat from his face with a bandana and started walking. Somewhere between the airport and Ela Beach was the

Edgewood Hotel, a fleabag recommended by the flight attendants before they gave their statements at the inquiry.

Halfway down the slope on a gravel road, a minivan rolled slowly behind him. He had to leave his Ruger in Panama, leaving him feeling less than ready for a confrontation. He faced the vehicle.

A kindly black face with cherubic cheeks and a bushy gray beard leaned out. "Where you go, da white man?"

The Slager measured the man by his smile and kept a wary eye on the periphery. "Edgewood Hotel. Know where it is?"

"Sure." His accent sounded vaguely Jamaican. "Da place be near my destination. Hop onboard, da white man."

The Slager peeled off his backpack, looked around, and opened the passenger door. They rolled slowly down the hill and up the next, enjoying the breeze through the open windows, and talking about the danger of traveling at night.

They rounded a bend where two men wearing rags over their noses and mouths jumped from behind bushes, brandishing weapons. One held a rifle, the other an ax. The old man sighed and stopped.

The gunmen approached from both sides. The man on the Slager's side held a rusty AK-47 aimed directly at him, which allowed him to sight down the crooked barrel. If there was a bullet in the chamber, pulling the trigger would be more dangerous for the gangster than for him. He held up his hands and listened while the robbers shouted instructions in some gibberish language.

"Open da door," his driver said. "Give da man ever ding."

The Slager nodded at the thieves' accomplice. He unlatched the door, pushed it slightly, then turned in his seat and kicked the door open with both feet. His assailant fell to the ground. The gun went off, aimed skyward, but half the bullet's charge exploded in the man's face.

The partner came around, his ax held high for striking. The Slager waited until the second man committed to his overhead swing before diving to the ground sideways, kicking the man's knees as he went down. The combination had the effect of locking the man's legs in place while the ax continued its unrestricted arc, landing in his own shin bone.

In an instant the Slager was back on his feet, grabbing the ax from the

DEATH AND THE DAMNED

injured man. He quickly severed the gunman's leg and the ax-wielder's wrist, then jumped back in the minivan with his bloody ax.

"Nice try, old man. Drive me to the Edgewood or you lose a hand."

His driver didn't try to argue. He drove off, watching his friends vanish in the rearview mirror.

The Edgewood Hotel resembled an American Motel 6 It was parked on a lonely street off a main road. U-shaped, the rooms faced a gravel courtyard, each window armored with heavy chain link. He checked in, tossed his backpack on a well-worn bed, cleaned his new ax, then headed back out. Two blocks away he found an ATM, and a block after that the Big Rooster café, where he scarfed down a bucket of fried chicken. Since he was something of a novelty in the neighborhood, it wasn't long before two representatives of the local gang showed up.

He raised his ax and offered to remain peaceful if they could find a nice handgun or two. They returned in twenty minutes with a policeman who offered his official sidearm, a Glock 19, for $500. They haggled and settled on partial payment until midnight when he could retrieve more cash from the ATM. The policeman left after they exchanged the pistol for his Venezuelan passport and $200.

The Slager tucked the gun into the back of his jeans and bought a cheap backpack, rags, and thin pillows. Back in his room, he lumped the bed with the pillows, left the new backpack on the table stuffed with rags to make it look full, closed the drapes, and knelt to the window's edge. He waited until a little after midnight, when all was still, then grabbed his real backpack and snuck out. A low duck-walk got him past the manager's window and out to the street. There he crossed to a house and crouched behind a dented pickup truck.

Three cops with clubs extended arrived after 1 a.m. and marched to the Slager's room.

He followed, creeping on his toes. Sweat dripped down his nose and between his shoulder blades. He arrived a few feet behind the last man, the lookout, while the other two kicked their way into his room. Pushing his weapon to the man's ear, he waited for his victim to tense, all muscles locked with uncertainty and fear. When it was apparent the cop knew better than to move or speak, the Slager lifted the officer's service weapon from its holster and helped himself to the spare magazines. The broadside of his ax hit the man hard on the head, dropping him instantly.

The noise brought Moresby's finest from his room. He met them at the door with a pistol in each hand.

They surrendered. A few minutes later, he left the three policemen handcuffed together in their underwear and locked in his room. He dropped his three new Glocks and six spare magazines in his pack and walked to the beach.

From a distance, Ela Beach looked like any other public beach. Across a road, a playground and park bordered a strip of sand. As he neared, he could see the playground lay in ruins. The rusting hulk of a steam engine sat at the center in place of a jungle gym. Large chunks of it had been cut away, leaving ragged, sharp metal edges. He found a quiet place beneath palm trees and stretched out, using his backpack as a pillow.

He relaxed when he realized he had less than a week to go before he could get his kids back.

To keep the Moroccans from turning on him in the end, the Artist's most likely plan, he needed them on his side. For that, he needed to speak their spiritual language. He studied the Quran with a flashlight and jotted notes on a notepad.

Only one band of roving teenagers bothered him overnight, but they steered clear of his quickly drawn pistol.

After sunrise, he found a street vendor cooking over an open fire and had lamb for breakfast.

Two hours later, the Moroccan crew arrived at the appointed place: an abandoned amphitheater. Their distrust, fear, and reliance on him showed in their downcast and darting eyes as they made their way down the dirt steps between rotted wooden benches. In his estimation, only one of them had ever left Morocco before their big adventure to Syria. For the rest, joining ISIL was the first time they'd set foot outside their village. The leader, Youssef, the oldest at twenty-one, ceded control to him the minute he arrived. But none of them trusted him. The Slager gestured them to a corner.

Youssef led the opening prayer, then stood to one side, ready to translate.

"Islam has been mocked by the infidels for a thousand years," the Slager said. Youssef repeated in Arabic. "The Crusades, the occupation by Christian imperialists, the creation of Israel, are well-documented historical desecrations. But that's not the worst of it, brothers. I have seen Americans burning the Quran for fun. They piss on it in the streets. They burn it before church services. A singer once tore up a picture of the Prophet on *Saturday Night Live* and everyone cheered. America didn't need to invade Iraq in 2003. They did it to kill as many Muslims as they could. They think of us as target practice. I'm telling you, brothers, every American except me hates you."

They stared in mute disbelief. All their worst nightmares confirmed by a real American Muslim.

"You will strike the most important blow for the Caliphate." He began to strut around his dirt stage, enjoying the attention. "We don't have F-15s, tanks, drones, Apaches, night vision—we have something stronger. We have you! Your brothers will sing your praises for a thousand years. In the sacred texts, *sura* 9:5 reads, 'When the sacred months pass, slay the idolaters whenever you find them, and take them captive.' *Sura* 8:39 goes on to say, 'Fight them so that sedition might end and obedience is wholly Allah's'; and *sura* 9:123 clearly states, 'Fight the unbelievers who are nearest to you, and let them taste your ruthlessness.'"

Until now, they only thought of the Slager as another American opportunist. Hearing him quote from memory brought out their admiration. Their faces turned to him, their eyes sparkled. Even Youssef smiled.

"You know," the Slager said thoughtfully, "Muhammad al-Bukhari dedicated most of his fourth volume to the holy war against infidels. He related a *hadith* of the Prophet commenting that there are one hundred stages in paradise for those who fight for the way of God. Only those who participate in *jihad* deserve paradise."

One boy spoke up, asking a tentative question in Arabic. Youssef scowled and shouted at him. The others were curious.

The Slager demanded to hear the question.

"Hakim said the Prophet once endured people who threw garbage on him and he forgave them. He even blessed a sick woman among them. He asks if we aren't supposed to be kind and benevolent. And that we're not supposed to kill anyone unless we've offered them a chance to convert."

The Slager had only read the passages that supported his speech. He had no idea what Hakim referred to. But he knew one thing for sure: leaving a seed of doubt in a group was poison. He would have to get rid of the boy and his toxic curiosity or risk losing the whole crew. And he knew just how to do it.

"Blasphemy. Idolator!" He scowled at Hakim, a pimpled boy of seventeen. "Your evil ways seek to distract us from our holy duties. Renounce this way of thinking, *Shaitan*!"

He thought using the Arabic word for Satan would seal the deal. He was right. The entire group gave the boy the stink eye. Hakim cowered.

"We must remain strong." The Slager shook a fist at them. "Ready to ignore any diversions. Let nothing take us off our path to paradise!"

They looked at each other and raised one finger in the air, the ISIL salute reserved for martyrs that referred to the one God of the *shahada*.

As he watched them talking amongst themselves, he found a new respect for the men. They were intent on making the greatest sacrifice for their beliefs. They weren't dumb or scared or useless. They firmly believed that by giving their lives to fight the great American Satan they would prevent more bombs falling on their families, the elderly, their women and children. He could respect them for their intent. Though he had no intention of dying, he was doing something similar to protect Ethan and Emma.

When they turned back to him, their eagerness radiated from them. Now the Slager had his own little army.

"Americans kept you poor and uneducated so they can use you as footstools." He ad-libbed. Even though it was dangerous—one slip could turn them into a raging mob—it felt good. "You grew up oppressed, governed by secular law and not Sharia. Americans wouldn't let you have air conditioning or cars or even lemonade. But you are courageous. You will be rewarded in paradise. There are Rolls Royces waiting for you. Air conditioning everywhere you go. Lemonade flows from fountains. And you will have Americans, like me, to use as footstools."

They nudged each other and laughed.

"But I have sad news," he said. "Something terrible has happened in As Sukhnah. A swarm of cowardly Americans attacked without warning. The fighting was fierce and many brothers died. We defended our women and our territory bravely in a massive counterattack. We killed hundreds of infidels. Yet, as well as we fought, a few of the Americans escaped. Two of them are trying to track us down."

The boys scowled and booed.

"I need a volunteer, the bravest of the brave, to stay here in Port Moresby to kill Jacob Stearne and Miguel Rodriguez. And then keep killing everyone until he is extinguished and sent to paradise as a martyr."

CHAPTER 19

I WAITED FOR MS. SABEL'S call like a condemned man. Well, not quite like a condemned man. I was hardly on death row. I was on her private jet on Mérida's runway sipping handmade lemonade. My torture at the hands of Rosales had come to an abrupt and welcomed end. As it turned out, Bianca called Ms. Sabel, who called President Hunter, and—sixteen calls later—Rosales got his ass chewed by the President of Venezuela. Someone along the US chain of command complained that I wasn't worth the million barrels of oil the taxpayers had to buy from the stinking country to secure my release, but I didn't mind.

When she called, Ms. Sabel was direct and to the point: when she told me to search for Larson, she wanted me to tell her where I was going. Not because she cared about the jet cost; she wanted to know where I went so she could send backup when needed. Apparently, she cared. Which was more than I could say for anyone at the Montgomery County Police Department, where Detective Czajkowski had an office pool going for when I'd show up on the victims list.

She clicked off after thanking me for uncovering a plot against Hunter. Even though none of us believed Omar. Terrorists getting through the Secret Service to kill a president was damn near impossible. But Hunter and her people were doubling up on security.

Five minutes later, we were airborne.

Mercury came up from the back couch in his formal, red-trimmed toga. *Homie, before you mess around in Panama, would you mind dropping us off in San Diego?*

He nodded toward the back of the jet, where Pachamama rested in a clingy multi-colored wrap that illustrated her curves in great detail. She took her role as fertility goddess seriously.

I said, *We're chasing the Moroccans. If they went to San Diego, sure, but—*

Mercury scowled. *Help a brutha out, will ya? We can't miss the opening ceremony. Everybody's going to be there, Thor, Jupiter, Brahma, Laozu. David and Ezekiel will be protesting out front, like always. It's a big deal. Starts in two days, dawg.*

I said, *King David? The Prophet Ezekiel? They're not gods.*

That's what they're protesting. They want to be let in because they figure they're demi-gods, minimum, like Nandi and Hercules. But I tell 'em: Hey, y'all read the first commandment when you signed up, so deal. He gave me his puppy-dog look. *So, what do you say—San Diego?*

I said, *No. I'm trying to save my country.*

He gave me a mean scowl and trudged to the back. *Irrumabo te.*

It was the first time I heard him say, *fuck you.* At least he said it in Latin.

Special Agent Verges, the greenest FBI agent they could spare to keep the Sabel family feeling like they were getting special attention, met us at Tocumen International Airport in Panama City.

"Thanks for requesting me." He extended a hand to me that Miguel took when I left him hanging.

"Are you leading the investigation?" I asked.

"I'm back as the official liaison between the FBI and Sabel Security. I hear you have a great lead on some terrorists. We are all over this, Jacob. All over it like white on rice."

I only eat brown rice—and the Feds only send first-year agents when they think they're chasing fantasies.

"We have a team of CIA analysts," he puffed up his chest, "reviewing all the airport surveillance and the local FBI office is combing through the manifests as we speak."

We crossed the tarmac and entered the terminal.

"That's great news," I said. He beamed with pride. "Where are you set up?"

"Right there." He pointed to the terminal in front of us.

The passport and customs area was hard to find, but we dug up a lonesome inspector. Having already been cleared, Verges waited across the line in the small area. The passport official looked us over and asked the usual questions as slowly as possible. Being his only human interaction for the morning, he wasn't anxious to let us go.

Once he'd finished, I asked, "How many airports are there in Panama?"

Across the line, Verges gestured impatiently for me to follow him.

"Thirty-three, señor." The passport official smiled.

"How many of them have flights from places like Venezuela or Columbia?"

Verges came over and flicked his head toward the exit. Miguel held up a hand.

"Seven, maybe." The official leaned back, suspicious.

"Of those seven, how many have video surveillance?"

"This one and Albrook." He frowned. "I think."

"If you were a criminal trying to sneak into Panama, where would you fly into?"

Verges dropped his impatient look and leaned in.

"Anywhere but here or Albrook." The man checked the three of us up and down. "You are the Americans looking for the Arabs?"

I nodded.

"The flight from El Edén, Columbia had to make an emergency landing in Playón Chico two days ago."

"Why?"

"Fuel line was broken."

"Did anyone get off?" I asked.

"Si. Eleven men hired a boat. They could not wait."

Miguel was ten steps ahead of me when I turned back to the Sabel jet. I looked back at Verges. "You coming?"

Our pilots complained about landing in Playón Chico the whole flight, short as it was. I ignored them until I looked out the window and noticed our wingtips skimming treetops on approach to what looked like a cow path along the water's edge. We descended like a dive-bomber from behind a hilltop and pulled up suddenly, bouncing on an airstrip last paved in WWII. Screeching tires and jet engines roaring in reverse barely stopped us in time to avoid a watery grave. When we lowered the airstair, the pilots were arguing about whether or not we could take off.

I'd seen tractor sheds bigger than Playón Chico's thatched terminal. We left the uninhabited airport and crossed a long footbridge to the island-based town. Two boys remembered the Arabs and a white man when we offered them $5 each. They led us to a shack belonging to a man who met them at the landing strip.

His wife, cooking over an open fire on her dirt floor, was distraught. She'd not seen her husband since he left with the suspicious-looking men. She had no idea where they were heading, but he never stayed out overnight. She had a bad premonition that he was dead.

Mercury leaned over my shoulder. *That lady's in good with the local gods, homie. She's right, he's dead. Now can we go to San Diego?*

I said, *Her husband's dead and that's all you can say?*

Mercury shrugged. *Humans drop like flies, bro. No sense in losing sleep over it. Hey, San Diego?*

He was pissing me off. *No, I'm going to stop the assassination of the leader of the free world.*

Yo, dead presidents. Big deal. Narcisuss strangled Emperor Commodus; Cromwell beheaded Charles I; an anarchist killed President McKinley—if you want to be a big shot, someone will kill you. No matter how bad it seems, the sun will still rise and life goes on. But your life might not go on if I don't get some fun time with Pachamama. Ya feel me, dawg?

I said, *But where were they going?*

"Could be anywhere," Verges said. "Like Brownsville, Texas. Good place to sneak across the border."

Miguel spoke to the lady in Spanish. She broke down in tears.

"No way they could make it." I faced our FBI man. "The boat she described was good for a couple hundred miles. From here, I'm guessing they went to Cartagena."

"Get your story straight, Stearne." Verges glared at me. "Are they going for President Hunter or just tourists having a look around Central America?"

He leaned toward me as if daring me to take a swing at him.

"What the hell's bugging you, Verges?"

"Your story." He turned red. "Lieutenant Rosales claims you're a CIA agitator, trying to stir up the students at the University of the Andes. Turns out your 'Omar' died resisting arrest for supplying students with fake ID."

I stepped back. "You don't believe me?"

"I don't blame you, Stearne. Hell, I'd crack if someone were beating me with a rubber hose. But this charade's gone on long enough. The FBI has to follow up on 10,000 tips a day. Most of them have some physical evidence to go on. Look. I need to get my career back on track. I was working a serious case until Hunter called my boss and asked for me by name."

"That's a good thing, isn't it?"

"Last time I got tangled up with Pia Sabel, I ended up looking like an idiot. I finally got some street cred when they transferred me to banking fraud. I was doing good; making some busts. Pulling me into this assignment was a joke, not a promotion. Now I'm working for David Watson—the Bureau's Special Asshole in Charge. I don't have any training for CI-EEU."

I tried to piece the abbreviation together but came up blank. "Speak English."

"Counterintelligence, Economic Espionage Unit."

"What the hell?" I couldn't hide my shock. "Why are they involved?"

"Cause Counterterrorism is busy working credible threats." He shrugged. "And Sabel has been on Economic Espionage's scope several times. They have a big, fat file on her."

"You have to take this serious—"

"You're the only one who saw a NAVSUP bird in Iraq." Verges raised his voice with each word spoken. "The SEALs on duty and the Apache pilots aren't allowed to talk to us about where they were and what they were doing. The Navy's chain of command is looking into it— so they say. They'll get back to us if they find anything to corroborate your terrorist unicorns. So far, not a word out of them."

He blew out a breath and turned to the beach. He steamed for a couple minutes, pissed about something he wasn't sharing.

Dhanpal was right about institutional denial.

Why couldn't Verges see the connections?

Sometimes circumstances fall the wrong way and the verification doesn't work out. And sometimes someone on the inside gets in the way and messes with the trail of evidence. I'm not big on conspiracy theories, but this one had all the hallmarks of an unseen force pushing things around.

Verges clenched his fists and spun back around. "They sent me a brief about your mental health, Jacob. Most of the details were blacked out, classified, but words like *imaginary* and *hallucinatory* were plain to read. You got something you need to explain?"

Mercury cocked his head sideways. *Why does everybody think you're crazy?*

I shook my head.

Verges went for a walk on the beach. Miguel gave the lady a hug.

I pulled my phone and called Dhanpal. "Your buddy Brent didn't make up that thing about the Moroccans, did he?"

"He told you about it because you were there," Dhanpal said. "He's not supposed to talk about his operations outside of his chain of command. Your report put him in a world of hurt—inside his unit and inside his head. Operational trust is everything to SEALs."

Losing the trust of your team was about as depressing a thing as a soldier could endure. "You're battle-buddies, right?"

"He's not in a good place. I'm on my way to his house. We never should've pushed him, Jacob."

We clicked off.

Was I losing it? Had I imagined everything? Were the ten guys who got off a plane after an emergency landing just impatient Venezuelan tourists? Did Omar tell me what I wanted to hear just to avoid more beatings? Did Dhanpal's buddy tell us about some obscure Moroccans to derail our questions about Michael Larson? Or was there a sleeper agent shepherding ten terrorists around the world?

From thirty yards down the beach, Verges yelled, "C'mon, let's go home."

Miguel shrugged. "Our ghosts could be anywhere in the world by now. May as well go home until something turns up."

We trudged back across the foot bridge.

I poked Verges. "What about the team of agents in Panama City?"

"I was supposed to lead you into the room so the local guys could interrogate you themselves." He walked a few steps before continuing. "I wasn't sent here to help you. I was sent to evaluate the depths of your delusion."

"We've worked together in the past, Verges." Miguel grabbed the FBI man by the neck, gently. "In matters of life and death, has Jacob ever steered you wrong?"

"No."

"Then why don't you believe?"

Verges yanked himself out of Miguel's grip and trudged to the jet with his head down.

Flying back to DC gave me time to weigh the anti-psychotic meds Dr. Harrison prescribed versus spending the rest of my life dealing with what could be a serious problem. I considered Yumi in my calculations. Either I had to introduce her to Mercury, or keep one great-big-gigantic secret from my soulmate. Would she understand? Or freak out? Already she thought Americans were a bunch of gun-crazed psychopathic serial killers. A title we've earned, statistically speaking. Telling her I spoke to a between-opportunities god would not improve my heroic luster. Of all the psychiatrists and therapists and friends and family I'd been honest with, only Ms. Sabel understood my problem. And I'm not sure she's on stable ground. She keeps seeing a clergywoman no one else sees.

Occasionally, I glanced at Mercury and Pachamama snuggled on the back couch like a couple of teenagers. Not that I could blame Mercury for wanting to take the Incan goddess somewhere special; my geometry was rusty but I estimated her curves in the 65 to 70-degree range. Once in a while, he caught me staring at him and flipped me off. But what was I going to tell the pilots? Would you mind detouring 2,000 miles so I can drop off a couple fairy-tale gods? Just thinking about it sealed my decision to go back on my meds.

CHAPTER 20

IT WAS BARELY 3:30 A.M. WHEN Pia closed the report from Bianca. Nothing incriminating on Roche's laptop linked him to the Artist. The Artist's texts were disturbing threats against an unknown target. But there were no specifics. He came off like a spoiled child seeking Roche's attention. Even though they dovetailed with Jacob's findings, there was nothing the Feds could do but double security for Hunter.

With nothing actionable, the Feds requested confirmation from her sources. Since her taps were technically illegal, she declined to turn over the details. Naturally, the FBI and Secret Service thanked her team for the information and went on with their work. She couldn't blame them.

Pia knew there was something sinister going on, just as President Hunter promised. She focused her investigation on Roche's constant traveling companions and closest allies: Luuk Devoor, Ritchie Skaite, Davy Cameron, and Sean Addison. Along with their many minstrels.

Despite the early hour back on the East Coast, Bianca called her. "Royal Devoor Oil owns Energy Outfitters, EO. But it's a shell company that's nested in a series of shell companies, all of them in different closed-reporting countries like Luxembourg and Panama. Anyone could be controlling it."

The news took Pia's breath away. "Who signed off on creating it?"

"You'd have to ask Stefan for details. In a privately held company, anyone might have. In a company the size of Royal Devoor, a division president or an executive vice president can create a company. Stefan and Luuk might not even know it exists."

"If they're up to something illegal, they'll never tell me. Can we hack into their systems and read their email?"

"Let me mention—again—that's illegal, *flaca*. But it doesn't matter.

They don't have any systems to hack. EO and the parent companies are just bank accounts and outside contractors."

"Think up some ideas."

"You had the right idea." Bianca said, "Buy it. We can open the accounts and see who they're paying."

They clicked off.

By first light, she finished her notes on the sale of SPP and SCE and sent them to her attorney. She shutdown her laptop, put on her running shoes, checked on Tania, who was sound asleep in her room, then took the stairs to the lobby.

As she crossed the lobby, a woman sitting in a large chair reading a book caught her eye. She was sturdy and on the young side of middle-aged, her brown hair curled over a clerical collar resting on a black shirt above a modest gray skirt. There was a glint of intelligence and kindness in her eyes when she glanced up from her book.

Pia walked over and stopped a few feet away. The woman watched her approach, picked up a coffee mug, and sipped.

"Can you explain something, Reverend?"

"Can you live with the answer?" She extended her mug halfway between them at an awkward angle.

Pia couldn't tell if the priest was offering her the mug or just holding it oddly. The arm extension, above her shoulder, would weigh her down over time. She waited for the woman to elaborate.

She said nothing.

"Someone did something terrible a long time ago. It ruined my life." Pia looked at the mug and tried to figure out why she held it in such an odd place. "He also saved my life. I could've ended up in foster care."

Pia had never said those words aloud before.

Until that instant, she had avoided thinking about what kind of life she might have led had Alan Sabel never returned to the townhouse that horrific morning. Her mind raced through events that occasionally brought her into contact with foster care children. Across the country, half a million un-aborted, un-adopted, unwanted children in foster care bounce from one home to the next, all day, every day. Every one of them eternally desperate for an ounce of compassion from anyone. With psychological scars as big as canyons, anger masks their bone-deep fears.

In that moment, while the cleric watched her, the children's stories overwhelmed her. Nine-year-old Addy, who never stopped asking where the system had sent her little brother. Seven-year-old David, who after surviving an abusive stepfather reacted to touch as if it were a high-voltage shock. Kaitlyn, the harried social worker, who burst into tears when Pia declined to adopt the burn-victim Benjamin, whose mother had tried to boil him alive.

On any given day, Pia could step up and rescue any child in the American foster care system. She knew that—and yet couldn't bring herself to endure the children's pains and difficulties. She couldn't do what Alan Sabel did when he was her age. Maybe she wasn't driven by the same level of guilt. Maybe she chased medals and championships to escape looking at the children who needed her help. She choked back a tear.

Her mental digression left her with one clear understanding: Alan Sabel had given her something greater than wealth. Years ago, he had given her hope.

The woman held a steady gaze, still extending the coffee mug. Surely her arm had fatigued by now and she would set it down. But the reverend held it steady.

Pia realized she's been silent for a long time. "Well, anyway, what I want to know is, how do I forgive him?"

"Why would forgiving him fall to you?"

"Uh." Pia tilted her head. "He asked me to."

The woman looked at the mug. Pia glanced at the hotel's logo emblazoned on the side.

"It's not heavy." The woman nodded at the mug.

At that odd an angle, Pia couldn't imagine it hadn't grown heavy over time. The woman's dark brown eyes watched her every move. She waited for the priest to explain but several long moments stretched out between them.

Finally, Pia asked, "That's what I don't understand. How can I forgive someone who helped kill my parents—no matter how nice he was to me."

"Hold this." The woman didn't move.

Pia leaned across the coffee table and took the mug. She held it as if she were offering it back. She found herself leaning over the table to an uncomfortable degree. Her lower back immediately complained. She stifled the feeling and held steady.

"It's not heavy." The woman said again, half question, half statement. She leaned back in her chair and regarded Pia, head to toe. "God has already forgiven him. His problem is that he has yet to accept it. In order to accept forgiveness, he has to admit—to himself—what has been forgiven. That's a very hard thing. Until he does, it's a burden that grows heavier every moment he holds onto it."

The woman rose and tucked her book under her arm. They stared at each other for another long, awkward moment. Pia's arm tingled with fatigue and needles of pain pecked at her spine as the coffee mug became increasingly uncomfortable because of how she leaned forward, partially bent with her arm stretched.

The woman shifted to a more casual stance. "Alan's problems are his alone. There's nothing you can do to help him."

She turned and started to walk away.

Emotions swirled through Pia like a tornado.

Finally, her arm beginning to hurt, she called out, "What should I do with this?"

The woman stopped and spoke over her shoulder. "Sometimes letting go is better than holding on."

Pia stared at her until she disappeared down a hallway.

"Wait a second. How did you know his name is—" But the minister was gone.

She tossed the dregs into the potted plant beside the woman's chair and left the mug on the table.

She began her run at a warm-up lope, running past the bighorn statue in the entryway. She ran down the long drive, gaining speed. Light blue illuminated the eastern sky. Gleams of auburn streaked upward from beyond the distant mountains. As she ran, her mind raced through the myriad paths her life might have taken had circumstances been different.

She found a trail into the desert and took it. The trail led several miles up a mountain, becoming increasingly steep and rocky. She maintained her pace despite feeling the early morning heat picking up. When she reached the peak, she paused and looked over the valley stretching twenty miles across.

Sometimes letting go is better than holding on.

Rays of brilliant orange crested the mountain range to the east and touched her with soft light and warmth. She contemplated the contrasts in her charmed and tragic life. In her head, she heard a rapper quoting from Isaiah: "No weapon formed against you will prosper."

An inexplicable sense of weightlessness came over her. As if she could float across the valley. She felt free. She threw her hands in the air the way she had at international victories, but somehow none of those events matched the mysterious triumph she felt on that lonely peak.

She ran down the slope, back to the hotel.

She showered, dressed in a business suit, and descended the stairs. She checked the conference schedule. Twenty speakers were listed, none of which remotely interested her. Except Stefan; who was nestled in the middle. The conference was designed to make people hate Marty Maddox; that much was obvious. Near the main hall, the early birds gathered around a breakfast buffet.

She joined the line behind Davy Cameron, one of Roche's inner circle. "You're in the meat business, aren't you Mr. Cameron? What worries you about NEXT USA?"

His jowls flapped when he turned to her. He tilted his crimson bald spot her way in lieu of a handshake. "I hear he's a vegetarian. Are you a vegetarian, Ms. Sabel?"

"Only when they run out of filet mignon." Pia piled fruit in a bowl.

He laughed politely and asked the chef for a bacon and cheese omelet. "Seriously, you know these damn millennials want to change everything. He hasn't announced his platform, but I'm sure the meat-packing industry will face new regulations."

Pia asked the chef for scrambled eggs.

A voice came from behind them. "Didn't Maddox relax meat-packing regulations in California?"

"Morning, Stefan." Cameron looked up at the newcomer. "He relaxed things in California, but you can't trust a vegetarian. They always think they know what's best for us. The most sanctimonious bastards on Earth—after bicyclists."

Stefan smirked and turned to the chef. "Could I have a vegan omelet please?"

The chef nodded and went to work.

"They have those?" Pia asked.

"It's amazing what you can do with soy."

Cameron retrieved his dish and scurried off without looking back.

Stefan watched the plump man trundle away then turned back to the chef. "I've changed my mind. I'll have a regular omelet, peppers and mushrooms."

She checked out his profile. Yep, still handsome. She cringed, recalling her rudeness to him. He looked trim and fit, not gym-muscled, which she liked. He glanced nervously her way and smiled.

They faced different directions together, thinking of ways to restart the conversation.

Stefan said, "I understand you got an earful of my drunken father at the reception last night."

"He wasn't so bad. He's passionate about certain issues, that's all."

"That's how people enable him. Excusing his behavior."

She couldn't think of a response to that.

They rocked from their tiptoes to their heels until the chef held up two plates.

"Who makes deals for Royal Devoor?" Pia took her plate and waited for his. "You or your father?"

"Either of us." He followed her to an open table. "Shall we close the SCE deal?"

"I reviewed my attorney's changes, added a few of my own, and sent it back. You should hear from my team this morning." She glanced around the rapidly filling ballroom. "I thought we might discuss trading one division for another."

Stefan's eyebrows rose. "Preserving capital is always a good idea. What did you have in mind?"

"Let's discuss it tonight—" she smiled "—over dinner."

Stefan leaned back, a broad grin on his face. "That makes it official—you have accepted my apology."

They found a table and talked about small things, old friends, college days, and travels. They filled in the gaps with silent gazes that dissuaded other attendees from joining them.

Eventually, all good things come to an end. Pia and Stefan's ended when a booming microphone announced the keynote speech. The room was packed. People filled in their table. Luuk joined them, sitting next to his son.

They watched a rousing speech by one of Roche's surrogates. Stefan caught her eye and surreptitiously moved his father's coffee close to Pia. She leaned toward it and smelled the alcohol. He shrugged and moved it back.

Pia's phone buzzed with a texted code word from Bianca.

She wished luck to the three people at her table who were on the speaker's list and left the conference.

She considered asking Tania to help her bug the laptops of suspects—Roche's extended entourage—but she couldn't ask an employee to do anything illegal. She had trouble convincing herself it was for the greater good.

For over an hour, Bianca guided her through the halls and rooms until she'd successfully bugged the laptops of Ritchie Skaite, Sean Addison, Davy Cameron, and their many minstrels. A maid cleaned Luuk Devoor's room. Pia prowled the hallways, circling the large hotel until the maid's cart was gone. When the hall was empty, she swung by and grabbed the door handle.

"Where are you going, Pia?" Stefan's lyrical baritone reverberated in the hall behind her.

CHAPTER 21

THE ARTIST STOOD STAGE LEFT at the great conference, watching the reactions of the guests. Billionaires listened intently, accompanied by their hand-picked executives. Some took notes; others, like Chuck Roche, memorized every detail and nuance. They were the most intimidating group ever assembled. Not that he worried about it. Roche trusted him to chair the American Petroleum Association, or APA; the rest of them would respect the great man's hand-picked successor.

He noticed when Pia Sabel left the room after the first speaker. Good thing. She was the kind who would ask pointed questions at the wrong time. She could ruin the whole conference with that mouth of hers.

The third speaker came off the stage, well over his time allowance. The attendees offered enthusiastic applause. Some speakers they liked, others were met with massive texting and side conversations. It was a tough crowd. And there were many more speakers lined up to rant their opinions. He would shine. He would stand out. They would finally understand how much he was doing for them.

He looked at his notes again as the emcee read out his résumé.

The Artist bounded onto the stage, waving a big hand in the air, beaming a big smile, soaking up the attention. Nothing a parent could say compared to the adoration of one's peers. He understood why candidates ran for office: once you take the stage under the bright lights, with a crowd of like-minded admirers applauding you, you feel like a rock star. Nothing he'd ever done compared to that moment.

The time felt right to tell everyone about his plan. *I have ten terrorists at my beck and call.* That would get a rise out of them.

Money might buy power and influence, but terrorists took the concept of power to a whole new level. Why file a lawsuit that would take ten years when you could obliterate your enemies right now—and blame it on the Arabs?

But no. He was like a real-world James Bond, saving the free world without ever getting credit for it. His secret weapon was one he would never share.

He pulled his notes from his jacket and laid them on the podium.

He began with a joke and ambled through the requisite self-deprecating humor about his CV. Then on to the good stuff. The meat.

"Terrorists could burst into this room at any minute and lay waste to us all." He looked around the room but could see little beyond the bright lights shining in his face. "Enraged immigrants could scale the perimeter and kill us in our sleep. But the scariest proposition facing our country today is exactly what Alexis de Tocqueville warned us about: the people of a democracy, their passions inflamed by greed and self-interest, could sweep a tyrant into power, destroying lives and institutions in the process."

He waited for applause.

It didn't come.

He coughed and continued. "It is self-evident that individual rights are granted by nature and not man, yet Marty Maddox wants to dictate your rights from Washington. Order in our society rises spontaneously from the people, yet Marty Maddox promises law and order from the White House. Law, money, and markets develop best when left to develop without Maddox's promised meddling. We should be free to pursue our lives—without interference from a new third party."

The Artist expected a gathering cry of outrage from the listeners. Instead, they talked among themselves, their disinterested voices growing louder. He was losing them. He tried to find Chuck Roche in the crowd, hoping to get some sign of encouragement, but he couldn't make out any faces.

The audience drank coffee, chatted, texted, and continued to ignore him.

"We do not need to engage in 'teamwork' and 'pull together' under Maddox's yoke." He raised his voice to a shout. "After all, if you're a student of history, you know that Europe's multiverse of dispersed governance led to sustained economic growth and became the backbone of Western civilization."

Still no hue and cry for Maddox's demise rose from the crowd.

Disgusted by their apathy, the Artist wrapped up his speech. He tromped down from the podium without notice and was reduced to prodding the drowsy emcee to introduce the next speaker. He gave the waiting man the requisite nod of good luck, even though the man was one of those brown fellows, and walked off to look for a seat in the main room. He'd hoped to sit next to Roche, but his mentor had not saved him a place. He found a folding chair at the end of the first row.

The brown fellow took the stage accompanied by music and flashing lights. A round of applause went up.

"Hey, folks," the speaker said. "What part of European history was he talking about? When they were city-states in the throes of the Dark Ages? Or when they stole gunpowder from the Chinese and built weapons of mass destruction to raid and pillage Africa, the Americas, and—specifically—my Aztec ancestors? European domination had nothing to do with centralized or de-centralized government and everything to do with the malevolent devaluation of human life."

The crowd roared with laughter. Many faces turned to the Artist, grinning like fools. He smiled and waved. Keep a brave face and laugh it off. Bastards. He would wipe the smiles off the faces of these buffoons in five days. Roche trusted him with the APA. The rest of them trusted him with the largest Super PAC of them all. They trusted him to spend the money defeating opposition candidates and that's exactly what he planned to do. Anyone who opposed him would be defeated. Right now, everyone in the room opposed him.

"Sometimes change is good," the speaker continued. "Those of you in banking don't like the new Internet security regulations President Hunter pushed through last fall, but I love them. Our security company made two billion, and created over five thousand new white-collar jobs this year. I say, keep those federal regulations coming!"

Some moaned, others laughed.

The Artist seethed with anger. This asshole was dumping on his entire speech. Who did the newcomer think he was? Just because his father and mother were laborers, he put himself through school working nights, and he cashed in on e-commerce early didn't give him the right to disrespect a stalwart American family.

Everyone who applauded this phony has been warned. He told them what would happen—and now it will. Ten terrorists, dedicated to killing the most important Americans alive, are coming to town. The Artist will save a couple of those maniacs just for them.

He pulled his burner, the next in the planned succession, and texted the Slager: *Speed up the operation. Skip going through North Korea. Don't reply. Just make it happen.*

CHAPTER 22

I SPLASHED THROUGH PUDDLES FORMED by days of constant Washington drizzle and felt my boots sink into the lawn as I cut across my front yard from the driveway, overanxious to make the front door. Yumi waited for me under the front gable with Anoshni cradled in her arm, equally anxious—but not enough to get her hair wet. We crushed the puppy between us when we collided. My bags fell to the ground. I wrapped my arms around her and kissed her. For the first time in ages, she welcomed me home with the reckless affection we enjoyed in those first few weeks when love was still fresh and unsoiled by semi-accurate stories told by ex-girlfriends.

Maybe Dr. Harrison was earning his keep by helping her deal with murderers crashing through my front door. I pulled back and checked her eyes to make sure Doc hadn't taken the shortcut through happy-pills. She was nothing more than genuinely happy to see me.

Behind her stood Bianca and Emily, smiling and waving awkwardly. My Sabel teammates had worked out a duty roster to keep her company while I was away. A fact I'd forgotten when I shopped for specialty items on my way home or I would've done a better job of concealing my purchases. I roped in the shopping bag at my feet so they couldn't see the contents.

The ladies stepped around us. Emily gave Yumi a peck on the cheek. Bianca leaned to my ear. "We have a car at each end of your street. You can sleep tonight. Pia said you have to drop Yumi at the Gardens if you leave town again. But Yumi's convinced you're never going to leave town again."

I thanked them, picked up my things and followed Yumi inside.

My first order of business was to keep Yumi's good mood on the upswing. I opened the grocery bags and laid out the ingredients with a magician's flair. First, I mixed the duck breast with raisins and herbs and sautéed onions. I put the duck in the oven, and prepared the artichoke and potato au gratin and put that dish in the oven.

I picked her up and put her on the edge of my prep counter where the halogen lights dazzled her hair. We chatted about her day while she ran her fingertips lightly over my bruised face and ear. I opened a bottle of Faust Cabernet 2007—one of the many gifts Alan Sabel gives me whenever he remembers how I defused the bomb he was strapped to a few months ago—and poured glasses. We toasted, clinked, sipped, and kissed.

There are moments when you know everything is so perfectly perfect you have to commit the feelings to permanent memory. One day—when all is lost and you're pinned down by enemy fire coming from all sides and they start moving in—then you can remember you had that one special moment, that one time, and you can die happy. This was that moment.

The oysters came out next. My knife snicked them open in a quick flash of steel. I laid them on the counter between us, sprinkled Korean Bamboo salt, and squeezed out a couple drops of lemon juice.

I placed my index finger under her chin and tilted her head back. I said, "Savor the sensuality."

The first oyster slid into her mouth while her eyes looked into mine without blinking. She trusted me, completely.

She returned the favor. *"Minu ga hana."*

"What does that mean?"

"Not seeing is the flower."

Sometimes it's hard to understand if the problem is with my understanding of her culture or if her English needs more work.

She saw my confusion. She pointed to her head. "Not see the flower. Don't look. See? Close your eye. Imagine. See the flower? It is better than flower in garden."

That would take some thinking. But, nobody hired me for my thinking. They hired me for my trigger finger. So, I chopped strawberries and rhubarb and covered them with a sugar-and-oil sauce, then spooned them over a small pile of spinach on each plate. The au gratin spooned in next, followed by the duck. We moved to the dining table and lit candles.

The moment was so wonderful, I felt like giving thanks—but the last time I did that Mercury slapped me upside the head for leaving out half the *Dii Consentes*. How am I supposed to remember all the gods in the flipping Roman pantheon?

We raised our glasses and drank before digging in. She ate some, then watched me eat. Stabbing a piece of the duck, she fed it to me. I returned the gesture. We relished every bite and left the dishes on the table.

She led me to the bedroom where I took off her clothes and made her wait for a moment. I found the bag that I'd kept hidden from Bianca and Emily, and pulled out the leather wrist cuffs. Her eyes went wide. I cuffed her arms and clipped them to the rope suspended from the ceiling and pulled her arms up over her head, leaving her comfortably restrained. Her eyes betrayed a little bit of worry but a good deal of excitement too. When I kissed her, her skin was noticeably warmer than usual.

Mercury and his goddess stood by the window. *Dude, you doing the dominator thing? What makes you think this is a good idea?*

I said, *I read the highlighted passages in her erotica collection on her e-reader.*

Day-yum; that's pretty smart for a mortal. Hey bro, promise me you'll drop us off in San Diego in the morning and I'll tell you where the terrorists are.

Of all the nerve. I looked over my recycled god with disdain and tried to remember how to say *Irrumabo te* when Pachamama held up her hand. She said, *Take us to San Diego and I'll tell you how to make Yumi a very happy young lady.*

No way.

I cannot be bought.

I never give in to coercion.

I said, *Deal.*

Pachamama handed me a bottle of massage oil. *Start by letting it drip from her shoulders. Then get some ice.*

Ninety minutes later Yumi and I collapsed on the bed, quivering and satisfied.

I had a new found respect for Pachamama's knowledge base. She was the kind of fertility goddess a guy like me could listen to anytime.

Yumi crossed her arms on my chest and talked a mile a minute about something. She might've been speaking Japanese for all I know. My mind wandered, drifting into surreal scenes filled with lotus blossoms blooming and porpoises swimming through caves. Somewhere wedding bells were ringing and cold water splashed on my face.

"You sleep?" Yumi said. "You sleep on me?"

I babbled something about an energy transfer and heard the wedding bells again.

Only they weren't wedding bells. My phone was ringing. Yumi held it where I could see it without moving.

The call was from Tania. I put her on speaker.

"Did you see the email?" Tania asked.

"I'm off duty."

"Michael Larson sent it to 'the team from As Sukhnah.' He wants to meet you."

CHAPTER 23

THE GREEN LIGHT ON THE suite's lock glowed in Pia's peripheral vision while she stared at Stefan. She held the door open two inches. Lying would get her nowhere. She let go and the door auto-closed with a decisive thunk. She faced him. "Your father said something to me last night that bothered me. Among his ramblings, he indicated he knew someone involved in my parent's murders."

He approached at a measured pace, his eyes questioning her words. "So, that makes it OK to break into his suite?"

"Bad idea." Pia dropped her gaze. "I thought ... maybe I'd see something that connected them. Some kind of clue about how he knew a career CIA agent. Hell, I don't know what I expected."

Stefan crossed his arms and cocked his head. After a moment, he inhaled, reluctant but thoughtful, and drew a key from his pocket. Moving around her, he unlocked the door and threw it open. "Take a look."

His voice was flat, neither angry nor supportive. She glanced at him. He shrugged and gestured inside, keeping his expressions and body language to himself.

She felt herself shrink an inch as she stepped in. She moved to the center, wrapped her arms around herself as if she were cold, and looked through the room. She saw a laptop on the table, an open briefcase next to it with little more than an old-fashioned day planner and a few pens. A book lay on the floor next to a chair, trousers on the back of it. Three airline bottles of vodka lay on the coffee table in front of the fireplace.

He watched her. "If you pat his suit in the morning, you will feel one of those bottles in each pocket. Pat those same pockets in the evening and the pockets are empty. By the time he spoke to you, he was quite drunk."

She pursed her lips. "He didn't look it."

"Visine, antihistamines, breath mints, and four showers a day."

"Showers?"

"Your body treats alcohol like a toxin and tries to metabolize it or excrete it through the skin. The shiny nose and swollen eyelids are part of that excretion. Being loaded all day leaves you with a terrible body odor." He waved around the room. "Look at anything you wish."

"Why are you so open about me looking for something?" she asked.

"I'd like to know the truth of the matter as well. Partially because I'd like you to find the answers you want. But I have reasons of my own. If my father has gone too far, it may help him see the need for rehab. So far, two interventions haven't worked."

Pia considered his words. It was nice to hear. But his admission about his family situation bothered her. Luuk in rehab would leave Stefan in sole control of a global mega-corporation. Was he a concerned son or an ambitious heir?

Stefan lifted his arms. "Do you know what you're looking for?"

Pia shook her head. She picked up the bottles and read the labels. Then checked out the book on the floor, a non-fiction book about management.

Stefan disappeared into the bedroom.

She raised her voice. "I thought you were giving a speech this morning."

"I did." His voice echoed in the marble bathroom. "You missed it."

She slid her USB drive into the laptop and powered it on. Stefan had been more than generous so far, perhaps for his own purposes, but if he caught her hacking a computer, his patience might end. There was also the possibility he was the Artist. Or that he would unwittingly tell the mastermind about her meddling.

"How did it go?" she called.

"When your audience is a bunch of old guys—who knows?"

Keeping an eye on the passageway to the bedroom, she ran the intercept protocol which took several agonizing minutes. The laptop beeped like a giant gong that echoed in the room's silence. The screen turned blue with white lettering. She looked over her shoulder. Explaining the strange screen would never fly. She willed the software to connect and erase its traces. It beeped and churned, then finally booted to the operating system and brought up the password screen.

"I don't have his password," Stefan's soft voice surprised her.

She faced him, keeping her body in front of the computer as she pulled the incriminating USB key. "I wouldn't expect—"

"Wait." He gently pushed her aside. "Maybe I do."

Her last tug at an awkward angle twisted the machine on the desk. She pushed it back while palming the key. "Oh, sorry."

Stefan watched her as he slipped into the chair. He tried a couple passwords that didn't work, then one did. Two seconds later, Luuk Devoor's desktop appeared.

Stefan rose and gestured for Pia to take over. "Good thing he's not discovered the facial recognition system in place of the password."

She could feel him watching her. As they brushed past each other, she caught his light but musky scent. A warmness came over her, a calm about his mood. He wasn't angry as she feared, but annoyed and interested at the same time. She typed "McCarty" in the *Ask Me Anything* bar and chose *My Stuff* from the options. The machine spun for a few seconds before concluding the word did not appear in the local documents.

"I know that name," Stefan said. "Who was he?"

"Bill McCarty. He was a resources guy at the CIA. He picked the men for the operation that murdered my parents. My people caught him in an illegal operation and brought him to our ops center for questioning. While he was there, my father handed him a gun and he shot himself."

Stefan drew back with a sharp inhale. "How awful."

Pia sometimes forgot how accustomed to death she'd become since taking the helm at Sabel Security. McCarty's death meant little more to her than a missed opportunity to question him in detail. As far as she was concerned, he was another dead rat in the infested warehouse of the world.

"Did you know him?" She powered down the laptop.

"Vague memories from adolescence. He might have been one of

Dad's drinking buddies. I'll ask him about it." He smiled when Pia began to object. "Don't worry. I won't tell him we searched his hard drive. I'll frame it around his behavior, 'Why did you accost my friend about this man? Who is he?'"

Pia smiled and stood. He didn't back up. They were not nose to nose, but they were not far from it.

Stefan smiled and picked up her hand in his. "Part of my recovery requires openness and honesty on my part. I'd like to better understand your dinner invitation so I don't make another mistake, or stand too close, or make any presumptions."

He dropped her hand and stepped back. She inhaled his scent again and found it pleasing.

Pheromones or imagination?

She said, "OK. Um… We'll see?"

He left a long silence until she felt uncomfortable. There was no way in hell she would blurt out something like *I want to jump your bones*. As forward and assertive as she was, she maintained an old-fashioned sense of respectability. She'd not yet crossed the line to doing more than asking a man to dinner.

"Perhaps you would like to investigate my room?" he asked. "For information about McCarty, I mean."

He gestured to the adjoining door.

She considered how much of Stefan's inner-frat-boy still governed his relationships with women. She'd fought with men in life-and-death situations. She'd beaten the inexperienced and lost to the competent. She looked Stefan over, gauging his fitness and musculature. If she had to, she could take him. But it wouldn't be easy.

She trudged through the adjoining doors. And regretted thinking about him in terms of beating him up. Why even think that way?

She looked over his desk, where a briefcase overflowed with reports, and glanced at his laptop. He stepped ahead of her and swiped his finger on the fingerprint reader. His screen saver vanished revealing a wallpaper of outer space. She took a seat.

He leaned over her and pointed at a small blue speck on the right. "Earth. It reminds me of how small my problems are."

She looked up at him to disguise inhaling more of those delicious pheromones. He looked quizzically at her when she drew too deep a breath.

She stammered. "What … kind of cologne do you wear?"

"I don't. I'm afflicted with a sensitive olfactory system and can't stand anything artificial."

She twisted quickly back to the computer to hide her blush and typed her search.

Nothing.

This time when she rose, he stepped back.

She moved close, still not quite nose to nose. "You told me you needed to be honest and careful, and you were curious about dinner, but you didn't ask me a question. What did you want to know?"

He full-on blushed. "In the old days, a man would read the subtle hints a woman gave him through her body language or the look in her eyes. That method has failed me too many times. I've made a lot of mistakes. Perhaps minds changed, but misunderstandings arose, and someone ended up angry or worse." He sighed. "We live in the days of 'yes means yes' and I don't want to be confused by a dinner invitation where we might have different hopes and expectations. You see, I dare to dream we could retry our relationship. But, I am terrible at reading subtle clues."

Part of her wanted to slap him for assuming a dinner invitation was anything other than a business discussion over a shared meal. The other part of her knew damn well why she invited him to dinner.

To hell with respectability.

She inhaled deeply, wrapped her arms around him, and pulled him to her in unambiguous terms. "Sometimes yes means now."

CHAPTER 24

THE SLAGER WAITED UNDER THE international terminal's roof and watched the rain fall in the steaming heat of Yangon, the city formerly known as Rangoon, in Myanmar, the country formerly known as Burma. A taxi splashed through water that poured across the lane. A sheet of it sprayed his way. He danced backward and considered telling the driver to piss off. But he'd waited ten minutes for this one. He climbed in and gave the driver his destination mapped out on his phone.

The driver did a double take. The Slager confirmed the undesirable destination with a nod. The cabbie got to work shifting gears.

He watched the city pass by his window without seeing anything. Second-guessing his decision to leave Hakim behind had eaten him up the whole day. For the final time, he shut down the thought process. Hakim was agitating for a kinder, gentler Islam—one that didn't fit the agenda. He knew why. Hakim's nine-year-old brother had been the star of an ISIL video in which their father gave him a blessing before sending him out on a suicide mission. Little wonder Hakim had reservations. Maybe the ghost of his brother came to him and told him it was all horseshit. Not that it mattered.

What mattered was that Hakim swore to his brothers that he would save their mission. With deep conviction, and to the satisfaction of the other hardened jihadis, he promised to eliminate the threat. There is no pressure greater than making an oath to your peer group. The boy would do his best for them.

Hakim was Jacob Stearne's problem now. If the boy managed to blow himself and his nemesis to hell, all the better for everyone involved. If the decorated veteran sent the kid straight to Allah, at least the angst of the kid's existentialist leanings would come to an end.

He needed a contingency plan in case something went wrong and Stearne caught him. Soldiers don't make much money; could he bribe him? No way. Those guys are in it for the glory.

In his youth, he'd admired the military and seriously considered a career. Had his opportunities unfolded differently, he might have been Stearne's commanding officer. He considered the soldier for a moment. They were a lot alike. Doing whatever it takes to achieve their goals. If everything went to hell, Stearne would understand him. He would know the extremes people employ to survive. They were both professionals playing cat-and-mouse at the moment, but they were friends in a strange and violent way.

Or was he becoming delusional under stress?

What stress? He was fine. He was going to take the Artist for a ton of money, get his kids back, and live in the Pampas. Wherever he found a good place. He had nine terrorists under his command. He'd never felt more powerful in his life. He was golden.

He checked his second phone for a response from Schwartz about his proposal. Nothing. Two days without a reply was a big statement. If Schwartz was going to work with him, he would have made some indication by now. The silent treatment meant the bastard was going to rat him out. He started to toss the phone out the window, then thought better of it. Maybe reception was bad. Maybe the email didn't work in Myanmar. Give Schwartz another day. Just one. He needed some kind of insurance because he sure as hell didn't trust the Artist. Especially since the Artist told him to drop North Korea from his itinerary without explaining why. He didn't like unexplained changes.

Rain sheeted across the cab's windows. A hundred inches of rain fell on the city over the average summer. That worked out to more than a half an inch a day. Outside the cab, a week's worth was coming down. Then it stopped. The heat and humidity remained, like a bathroom in a cheap hotel after a long shower.

They were in the heart of the city, crawling down a cramped street lined with merchants huddled under canvas awnings in front of multistory apartments and office buildings. His driver honked and shouted and inched past pedestrians who gestured angrily. To the right, when passing alleys, he could see a major boulevard parallel to them, gridlocked. A pretty woman smiled at him and waved something for him to buy. More women in stalls noticed the tourist passing through their territory and called out to him. The women appeared anxious for a sale. He wondered how anxious.

Yellow circles and stripes covered many of their faces. He asked and the driver told him it was *thanaka*, a cosmetic made from fragrant powdered tree bark.

He pulled the ragged snapshot out of his pocket. Ethan and Emma in better times. He kissed his fingertips then touched their images and shoved it into his passport for protection.

Honking and swerving, they turned a corner and entered a large roundabout circling the Sule Pagoda. The cabbie told him it was a shrine dating back to 500 BCE. It looked like a giant bell covered in gold. They turned into another narrow street, out of traffic. Winding through a series of side streets barely wide enough for the car, he saw buildings in dire need of renovation, some looking burned out. Their path took them through ever more dilapidated neighborhoods. Eventually, they arrived at the riverfront, with docks and stockpiles of shipping containers on one side, and filthy, crowded apartments on the other.

The driver turned down one more alley, away from the river. He stopped and pointed to a place too narrow for the cab. The Slager paid him and walked the last two blocks. Crowds flowed in all directions, bumping their way to their individual destinations with casual immunity to the crush of humanity around them.

The Slager found his destination and entered the narrow door. He climbed to the third floor, stepping over children playing as he went. When he found the blue door with the diagonal scratch, he knocked.

Three men exploded out of the room behind him and slammed him into the wall. They took the pistol from under his shirt and rifled the other out of his backpack. They pulled him back, two of them holding his arms, while the third guy pounded a bat into his stomach five times then punched him in the face. One of them handed him a handkerchief to wipe his bloody nose.

Damn.

He'd fucked up. He'd ignored his key to survival: plan the approach. Now he was in defensive mode, on his heels and rocking backward. His nose throbbed, his bullet wound was bleeding again, and his brain was cloudy. He'd have to hang on, get a feel for where these clowns thought the rest of the day was headed.

He took a careful look at the men. They were little wiry guys. Short but fit and mean looking.

They pushed him into the doorway opposite the scratched door, where a fourth man waited for him. The boss.

"*Min-ga-la-ba.*" The cheerful, short Burmese man spoke in fair English. "Good trip?"

The boss was maybe five-one and thin with ropey muscles. A fighter of some kind. His playful eyes remained locked on the Slager, gauging his reaction, timing his reflexes, anticipating his response.

The Slager slacked his shoulders and blew out a breath. "You broke my nose."

"I sure you, sir. I do no such thing." He laughed.

The door behind them slammed. The Slager looked around quickly, then slowed his reactions. They were alone. He said, "If there is one thing I can't stand, it's a dishonest crook."

The short guy's face scrunched up. "What is this *crook*?"

"What is *min-ga-la-ba*?"

The short guy burst out laughing with one of those squeaky and fast hee-haw laughs that made the Slager want to kill him.

"You want trade. That's good. OK, we trade. *Min-ga-la-ba* mean good day, any time day. Now you go."

"A crook is a dishonest person, a criminal."

He laughed that horrible laugh again. "So play words. You call me, dishonest crook. Ha ha."

The short guy pulled up the Slager's backpack. He unzipped the front panel, pulled out a wad of cash and tossed it on top of a stack of boxes that served as a bookcase.

The Slager had no interest in watching himself get robbed, so he took in the apartment. A rattan chair owned the corner, set up like a throne circled by shin-high stools and a couple pillows. A straw mat covered a worn wooden floor. Yellow tie-dyed sheets served as drapes. An alcove led to another room. Most likely a kitchen. The mat looked like his host's bed. Not a prosperous criminal.

The proceedings were going to get ugly. The four Burmese planned to empty his account and dump his body in the river.

The tactical situation was easy enough to work out. Three armed guys waited outside in the hall. He had no weapons. The short guy was feeling safe and secure. Perfect. He only needed one more thing: the passports.

The short guy found the ATM card he'd been scrounging for. He waved it like a kid who'd won a prize. "What is PIN?"

"3-8-2-5-9-6-8."

The short guy leaned back and laughed. "I watch American TV. I know that spell *fuck-you*."

"It requires a fingerprint reader, not a PIN. Since Third World countries don't have those, we'll have to walk into a bank together if you expect to drain my account."

"What about other ten men with you?" he asked, his face turning grave.

"You don't want to meet those guys."

"Maybe my guy kill one of your guy every hour until you and I get back from bank."

The Slager shrugged and turned away as if he had to think about things. "You have the passports we came for?"

"Where are your guy?"

"If you have the passports, I'll empty the account for you. I just need to get them out of here."

"You not worried about money? You must have more waiting for you when you leave Myanmar. Where are guys?"

"You're a smart businessman." The Slager scratched his chin. "I'm going to let you in on something. You know, like partners. See. I'm just a high-priced tour guide. If I get paid the same, I'll sell these guys out like that." He snapped his fingers.

The short guy stared, unblinking, as he thought over the proposal. "How much you make?"

"$5,000 American."

"How much your people worth?"

"You saw their faces when you made the passports," the Slager said. "A man of your experience knows an Arab prince when you see one, right? I have no idea how much you can get out of them before the Saudis send troops after you, but I'm thinking, you know, tens of thousands."

"Ha ha." He pointed. "You dishonest crook." The short guy's eyes lit up. "How we take them?"

"You got those passports?"

The short guy wagged a finger between them. "No, no. I am no stupid. You—"

"Just show them to me. If they're good quality, I'll tell my guys they have to get new pictures taken and we'll round them up that way."

The short guy giggled and ran out the apartment door.

In the split second it opened, the Slager saw one goon on the hinge side and another across the hall. That left the third standing on the knob side. He counted six steps pounding down the hallway. There was a pause, then six return steps. The knob turned, the short guy pushed the door open.

The Slager waited until the man's head was between the frame and the opening door before he twisted off his back foot and slammed the door closed. The short guy was unconscious before the Slager threw his body into the hallway. He grabbed the surprised guard at the hinge, tossed him inside the room, ripped the pistol from the man's belt and shot him in the head. He wheeled around, kicked the door wide open, and shot the man across the hall in the face. At the same time, he reached around the jamb with his left hand and grabbed the last gangster.

He pulled the man's forehead to his barrel. The thug, fumbling to find the safety on his own gun, dropped the weapon on the floor.

The Slager spared the man for a moment. "Show me."

The man rattled off a plea for his life in Burmese.

He pushed the guy's face into the passport lying in the hall. "Show me where he kept the rest."

With a big tug, the Slager landed his shaking victim's feet on the ground and thrust him in the right direction. They staggered five steps before the man pointed to a wall patch. The Slager pulled his trigger and splattered the gangster's brains on the floor.

He glanced back at the carnage. Had to be done. They jumped him. They were going to kill him. They deserved to die. He was making Myanmar a better place.

But he had to get moving.

Behind the wall patch were the rest of the passports in a neat stack. Perfect examples of a corrupt government official's hard work. The names were all Chinese in origin, the stamps dated and appropriately scattered through the pages, the seals were holographic. The scans would lead back to the northern province of Myanmar where the short guy used to work.

He made his way back across town to the muddy park beyond the airport where the Moroccans waited. Working with terrorists was like swimming with sharks. With two days to go, he had to keep them together, make sure they followed his orders. Like his distribution network, he needed to bond with them. Otherwise, he was just another American needing to be killed.

He saved a nice bundle of money on the passports. He could afford to buy something nice to complete the male bonding circle.

He gathered his terrorists around him. Youssef translated. "Boys, I've come to think of you as friends, brothers in the struggle. We have one long, difficult trip ahead of us to reach the USA—and fight our final battles. That means this is our last night to relax and enjoy life. You might want to leave your Qurans in the hotel room, because tonight we're going to party with the most beautiful women you've ever met."

CHAPTER 25

MIGUEL WALKED THE SAND AND I wove between the palms several yards above the sea wall on a hot sunny day at Ela Beach, Papua New Guinea. The place was populated with weekenders strolling and playing. Only children went in the water. Michael Larson was a no-show. Or maybe he got tired of waiting in the heat and went for a beer. Not a bad idea. The sun beat down us and the ocean breeze failed.

We hiked up the mile-long strand and back without finding a suspicious-looking guy the whole way. Very few white guys at all, making it unlikely we missed him. Larson's email was a plausible invitation: *I heard you're looking for me, so meet me at the playground...* etc. It looked and smelled like a trap, so we went. That's how we roll.

We turned around at the end, where a month's worth of trash wafted back and forth in the breeze. I checked my email for an update. Nothing. We cruised back toward the rusty park.

Working without Mercury pointing the way was scary and nice. Nice to have a clear head without his distracting bullshit rolling through my brain at critical moments. Scary because there was only one certainty in my life: missions without Mercury were failures. I'd been wounded, friends died, innocent people were damaged. But he was excited about taking Pachamama to the big convention. Not that I could blame him. She looked pretty damn good for a woman who's been knitting for six hundred years.

Problem was, I couldn't get my last image of Yumi out of my head. She was in tears, having traumatic flashbacks, clutching my arms as I repacked my duffel. Maybe it was time to leave all this bloodshed behind and cook.

Miguel clucked in the comm link. "Check out the teenager in the green t-shirt."

I scanned the beach and found him. Fifty yards short of the playground, the Moroccan stood out among the Papuans. He looked young, about five-six at a hundred thirty pounds—not even full grown. Miguel passed by him unnoticed.

"Wearing a thick belt under the shirt," Miguel reported. "Mumbling prayers, sweating."

"Suicide bomber."

Defusing a guy bent on killing himself in order to take you with him is an interesting trick. A well-placed Sabel Dart could have defused this deadly situation in a second. But no, we're manly men and don't carry the things with us. Damn. Miguel circled around the guy and met me near the street. The kid was young enough that he never looked more than ten yards beyond his feet. We could use that to our advantage.

"The belt is thin," Miguel said. "His blast radius is probably under thirty feet."

"Think we can coax him away from the playground? Maybe spare some kids?"

Miguel shrugged. "You see anyone watching him?"

"You think Larson set him out as bait?" I looked around. "Not a white man in sight."

We gazed at the boy. I said, "He looks young."

"Yeah. We keep him alive. Give him to the FBI. Can't see him surviving Guantanamo."

"Usual plan?"

"You mean," Miguel shook his head, "let the Indian die first?"

"Better you than me."

We split up and moved into our positions.

Something dangled from under the kid's shirt. I kept my eye on it and called out a standard Arabic greeting. *"Sabaah al-khayr. As-salaam 'alaykum."*

Good morning, peace be on you.

He looked up, a little shocked to hear Arabic so far from home. Then he recognized me from Larson's description. Fear crossed his pimpled face. Followed by anger, then more confusion: he was not quick at making decisions. His hand swung next to his leg, reaching for the dangling thing, but he missed. When he looked down, Miguel flattened him like a linebacker on a quarterback. The big Navajo wrapped him up, kneed him in the groin, stretched his arms out, and pressed his knees down on the boy's elbows.

I ran up and felt around the boy's belly until I found the ties that held his explosive belt. A quick slice from my knife freed it, and I lifted the bomb. The boy's eyes went wide and he cringed. I turned like an Olympic shot-putter: slowly at first, gaining speed in my second rotation. I threw it in a huge arc. It flew high into the air and sailed a good distance from shore.

Terrorists from Richard Reid, the shoe bomber, to the Brussels Airport bombing, used triacetone triperoxide, or TATP, for the explosives. Highly unstable, peroxide-based explosives are easy to procure and easy to cook into a powdery white substance known as "The Mother of Satan." But the unstable part—meaning it's easy to detonate—is also its biggest drawback.

The belt's arc lost altitude and turned earthward. It hit the water with a big splash and had the good manners not to detonate until the water collapsed back around it, forming a concussion wave. The explosion drew the attention of a lot of people but, muffled as it was, its deadly potential was only obvious to the three of us. After a few seconds of curiosity, the people nearest us went back to their parties, unaware of how close they'd come to dying.

"Teamwork," Miguel said.

I stuck out a fist for a bump. He obliged.

I patted the boy down and found a pistol in his belt. The grip had a stamp indicating it belonged to the local police and not our new friend. No knives or other weapons turned up. Miguel pushed him to a sitting position and clamped him in a bear-hug embrace.

My interrogation began the way my old friend, Tony the FBI agent—may he rest in peace—taught me: gently, friendly, easy. I asked his name. What part of Morocco he was from. Why he left As Sukhnah. And so on. He said his name was Hakim and sulked. Nothing else.

It was time to move into the second phase: deprogramming his ISIL dogma.

"We're going to a hotel that overlooks the beach," I said in Arabic. "And you're going to come with us. Do you like ice cream?"

The walk back was uneventful. We got to our room-with-a-view after stopping at the shop for double-scoop cones.

I kept talking in Arabic. "We're going to talk about something I know very well, the Quran. Every time you blaspheme, Miguel here is going to pray for your soul in English until you repent. How's the ice cream?"

He licked his cone and stared at me with big brown eyes full of fear. At the same time, a certain amount of submission showed in his posture. He was coming around.

Who doesn't like ice cream?

"OK. So, the standard bullshit they tell you is from three quotes: *The infidels are your sworn enemies,* sura 4:101. Then, *Prophet, make war on the infidels,* sura 66:9. And, *Never be a helper to the disbelievers,* sura 28:86. Is that what they told you?"

Hakim nodded, his eyes still big enough to qualify him for the lead in a romance novel.

"The Arabic expression in these verses is *'al-la-dhina Kafaru'*. Here is your first test question, Hakim: What does *'al-la-dhina'* mean?"

His mouth opened and closed three times without a sound coming out. He swallowed and took a deep breath. "The non-believers."

"It doesn't say, *any* non-believers, does it?"

Hakim shook his head.

"The Quran is a very intentional book. It doesn't use words it doesn't mean. It uses *'Al-la-dhina'* because that limits it to a specific time and place. Most scholars believe the passage refers to a specific group of people who were fighting the Prophet. If the Quran meant all non-believers—forever—wouldn't it have used *'Man Kafar'* for anyone who doesn't believe?"

His eyes narrowed a little and the faint trace of a smile played at the corner of his lips. The small but significant difference meant something to him. Then his face fell. As if the revelation saddened him. He squeezed his eyes shut and began to cry.

Miguel and I glanced at each other. The big guy, in position to beat the crap out of the boy in case he tried something, put a hand on his shoulder.

I asked him what was wrong. He broke out in unrestrained sobs.

We sat there watching him wail and moan in anguish and desperation for a long time. Tears streaked down his cheeks as he repeated the name Abu many times. Miguel got up and wandered around the room.

Mercury squatted next to me. *Sad, right bro? Abu was his little brother. Fills you with confidence to find out your dad wants you dead.*

I nearly jumped out of my skin. *Do not sneak up on me like that. What happened to Pachamama and San Diego?*

You know how long women take to get ready for a simple dinner and movie? Imagine the stress a goddess is under when she's dating a Roman just to make Pachacamac jealous. She's been shopping all day, then it's hair, nails, whatever. Gonna drive me nuts.

Hakim looked at me funny.

We talked about Abu and how Hakim knew, deep down, the whole suicide thing was terribly wrong. I shared a couple stories about my Muslim friends in the Army and assured him I'd never seen anyone pissing on the Quran. We talked for an hour before I asked him about his traveling companions. He hesitated before opening up. He described Larson to a T and told me about their next destination: North Korea.

CHAPTER 26

PIA ENTERED THE SUITE, BOUNCING on her toes, only to find Tania scowling at her.

"Where the hell you been, girl?"

"At the conference." Pia tossed her clutch playfully on the sofa by the fireplace.

"How come I didn't see you there? How come you don't answer your phone?"

Pia shrugged. "I stepped out to work on the deal for SCE. It's all good."

Tania pointed at the ceiling, then put a finger across her lips. She moved to the sliding door and motioned for Pia to follow her.

Pia crossed to the balcony and waited for Tania to close the door.

"Whoo, it's hot out here." Pia looked across the valley, the heat penetrating her skin down to her bones. "I thought it was a dry heat."

"Jaz Jenkins says it a dry heave." Tania leaned over, trying to catch her gaze. She whispered. "Bianca says we're bugged. There's a wireless router in your room spoofing the hotel's. Everything going over the Internet will go to whoever owns that thing."

"OK."

"What?" Tania screeched. "OK? You're not pissed?"

Pia shrugged. "Good thing we use satellites."

Tania turned her back to the valley, crossed her arms, and scowled. "Why're you so happy all of a sudden?"

Pia stared across the valley. "The French have a saying, 'What makes us discontented with our condition is the absurdly exaggerated idea we have of the happiness of others.'"

"Uh-huh." Tania waited for Pia to say something, then tilted her head to the side. "You've gone French all right."

"Maybe it's because I'm saying yes to my first deal." Pia faced her. "It's exciting. I'm getting what I want—now."

"Is that right? Is that where Stefan went? I couldn't find him in the morning meeting either. And he didn't make it to lunch. And he didn't make it to the afternoon meeting. You have any idea where he went?"

Pia turned her gaze to the ground rather than meet the cold stare waiting for her. Talking about a tryst before it had a chance to develop into something else was a sure way to destroy any chance for happiness. The best way to parry Tania's attack was with an immediate and aggressive counterattack. "You talked to Jaz Jenkins?"

"Yeah." Tania turned away. "He's nice enough."

"I wouldn't think he's your type."

"Well." Tania picked up her chin. "Maybe I'm done with bad boys. I'm sick of alpha dogs too. I've had it with losers like Jacob and Miguel. Why can't I have a rich boyfriend?"

"Cause he's a meek little mama's boy?"

"Maybe I'm ready for meek. As a matter of fact, I'm in the mood for meek. Maybe beyond-meek. I'm ready for submissive. Rich and submissive."

With that perfect match, Pia went back inside and immediately savored the air-conditioned relief.

Catching up on her emails, she found the Coushatta Tribal Council had accepted her proposal for a new casino. Her mergers and acquisitions team had the terms for swapping SCE for Energy Outfitters. And Chuck Roche sent a list of demands to complete her proposed swap of Roche One Refinery for her paper company, SPP. Something in Roche's terms sounded off to her.

She called her M & A team leader. "What is this about fifty thousand gallons of mercury?"

"Mercury is a highly toxic byproduct of the refining process. For decades, the refinery pumped it into a holding tank that leached into the waterways. The EPA has been after him for years to clean it up, so he lists it as an asset."

"Why would he do that?"

"The EPA can't force him to clean it up without paying him for the value. In its purest form, mercury is worth $3,000 per gallon. Listing the toxic sludge as an asset means the EPA has to pay him $150 million before they can clean it up."

"And this provision he has for retaining items of sentimental value, what is he talking about?"

"As the original refinery, he's claiming some items are family heirlooms. The original valves from 1890, the company's first logo, his great-grandfather's desk chair, and all that. But his people added everything that's not bolted down. The computers, the air conditioning units—the list is ridiculous."

She thanked him and clicked off.

After staring at her laptop screen for a few minutes, she typed out a reply to Roche. "Your terms are fine if you'll allow one addition. Instead of making our mutual transition teams go through a laundry list of things you want to keep, let's just say you can keep all the portable assets. Does that work for you?"

She looked it over once more, then clicked send.

It was evening when she finished working. She put on a sleeveless Roberto Cavalli wrap-dress and checked her look in the mirror. The floral print on white looked good on her but her height made it short. Too short for the ancient billionaires attending the conference. She slipped a pair of yoga pants underneath and checked her look. The yoga pants went right back in the drawer where they came from.

To hell with the creepy old guys. She was dressing for Stefan.

She grabbed a matching clutch and tucked her Surface Book under her arm and headed down the hall.

On her way to the dining room, she called Bianca. "If I buy Energy Outfitters, how long after we take them over can we sift through their records?"

"Depends on how soon you want to raise suspicions." Bianca thought for a moment. "Once it's your company, you can send an IT team to Royal Devoor HQ to analyze what records they have and where they're kept. But you'll make them nervous if you start digging through their data looking for something specific."

Pia clicked off. She didn't mind making the Devoors nervous. Her need to know who set up and controlled EO overrode nice manners.

The Edge Steakhouse swam in gold light as if everything in the room was gilded. To her left, a dark blue sky faded into a lavender sunset over a distant mountain, its shadow streaking for miles across the valley floor. The hostess led her to a table by the wall of picture windows where Stefan waited with an eager face.

Her stomach suddenly twisted in a knot. She fought an illogical urge to turn and flee. Instead, she took her seat and laid her tablet in the middle.

"The terms are fine," she said, "except for a few concessions I've spelled out. I have them commented here if you'd like to have a look."

She pointed to the tablet between them, her eyes on the document.

He didn't move.

She looked up and found his big brown eyes and long lashes directed at her. Still, he remained motionless.

"We could wrap this up before the—"

He put his hands out, palms up, halfway across the table, one on each side of his charger.

She looked at them.

"It is a romantic evening," he said.

She put her hands in his. His fingers wrapped around hers. He squeezed them gently and firmly. An expert touch that took her back in time to those few stolen hours earlier in the day. She met his gaze for as long as she could, then looked back at the tablet.

"You have to work hard for every deal," she said.

Pia felt a pang inside her chest. Was she incapable of saying anything appropriate?

Stefan began to say something. His mouth formed the shape of a round syllable, maybe an "oh" or a "what?" but he stopped himself and turned to the sunset.

She considered herself lucky that he didn't say, *you didn't make me work very hard this morning.*

Stefan turned back from the view. "It would be a sad day indeed, were it to end with a dinner that was not romantic."

She fought to get her thoughts straightened out in her mind and took in the last embers of the pale sky. It was simple: she wanted a romantic dinner without a hundred-million-dollar deal hanging over them. She wanted him to work through the two-company swap before setting it all aside to enjoy the evening. Which was logical and he'd believe it because she would tell him that. But she didn't believe it. Why were her palms sweating? Why did the sight of him make her heart beat faster?

She faced him and leaned in. "Let's get the deal done first. You'll have to start over from the beginning if you want a doubleheader."

Which, of course, was *not at all* what she meant to say.

The blush started in her chest and forced its way up her neck into her face. From the heat rising in her skin, she knew it was a fire-engine-red blush. The kind you can't hide. Her eyelids dropped. She decided to leave them closed and wait for lightning to strike or a bomb to fall.

"I would love a doubleheader," Stefan said, the corners of his lips twitching as if he were holding back a laugh, "but pretend you care about me first. Let's talk, take a long walk, enjoy the evening. There's no need to rush into the business discussions. Besides, you don't even want Energy Outfitters."

"Why don't I want EO?"

"Oil is my legacy. It's the only tangible evidence that my dysfunctional family exists. Oil means everything to me. Over the last few months, I've come to live and breathe it. You have only one energy company and you're selling it to me. You have no portfolio in the energy sector."

"Then why do you think I'm buying it?"

"The level of detail you've discovered on this deal is fascinating." He grinned and wagged a finger at her playfully. "You're up to something and I'm dying to find out what it is."

Since Pia had no intention of telling him her plans, she changed the subject. "Did you ask Luuk about Bill McCarty?"

"Frat brothers," he said. "Dad supplied the money and McCarty supplied the girls. He would've done anything for my old man."

A presence approached their table. Pia looked up to see Sean Addison, his crocodile face quivering with each step.

"This goddamn conference is falling apart." Addison grabbed a nearby diner's shoulder as if it were a handrail. "Those fool tech-monsters are going to support Maddox. Can you believe it?"

Pia looked at Stefan. They shrugged.

"Which side have you taken?" The old man shook a finger at Stefan.

"What do you mean?" Stefan looked up with surprise.

Addison moved to the edge of their table and gripped it. "Are you with us or against us?"

Pia and Stefan glanced at each other again, unsure of the question but well aware of the anger in Addison's voice. It occurred to Pia that they missed something when they ditched the meetings.

"Are you for or against NEXT USA?" the old man asked.

"Against, naturally." Stefan shrugged.

Addison turned to Pia. "And you?"

CHAPTER 27

THE ARTIST STOOD IN HIS suite's bathroom at the Ritz-Carlton in Rancho Mirage and turned out the lights in the absurd hope they would all go away and leave him alone. These charity people never go away once you give them something. Maybe he could claim a migraine. People never argued with a migraine.

Screw it, it's show time. He took a last glance in the mirror and twisted the door knob.

He crossed through the bedroom into the living area and stopped himself from gasping aloud. They'd brought several of the children with them. The idiots. The fat lady gushed on and on about his generous philanthropy. She looked like she wanted to give him a hug. He maintained his distance. He knew how illogical it sounded, but he'd always felt as if poverty was contagious. Besides, poor people are always filthy.

He could scarcely hear her words; his attention remained bolted to the grimy mutt-children. Six of them ran their disgusting hands over the fabrics and gawked at the gilded pillows littering the couch.

"Your generous gift will supply books and backpacks so these children, and many others like them, can attend summer school. They need to catch up with their age group." She stopped talking—finally—and clasped her hands beneath her chin. "We're all so happy. Thank you."

"Yes, yes, you're welcome." He backed up a step. "But thank Pia Sabel."

"You know her?"

"She put the idea in my head. I tried to sign her up for our right to life group and she challenged me to adopt several foster care kids instead."

Too late, the Artist realized he should've kept his mouth shut.

"Oh my! I didn't know you were interested in adopt—"

"Don't get any stupid ideas." The Artist surveyed the smelly runts. "My accountant said I had to fork over a donation or give it to Uncle Sam. At least now I can tell that arrogant Sabel bitch I'm involved. At some level."

He noticed the fat lady wincing at his rough language. Screw her. If it were up to him, he'd put them all in the salt mines. At least get some work out of them instead of having them leech off society for the rest of their lives.

"Well, we appreciate your, um, generosity just the same." She tried to smile. "I'd like to thank Ms. Sabel for referring you personally. Is she staying at the hotel as well?"

"That's enough." He glanced at his aide, who tugged the fat lady's elbow. "Get them out of here and make sure she doesn't stick her fingers in Sabel's pockets on her way out."

The aid ushered out the fat lady and her flock.

The Artist grabbed a tissue and swatted at the surfaces the children had touched.

A small, thin figure waited in the hall with his hands clasped behind his back.

"Schwartz, don't stand there like a vulture," the Artist said. "Come in and close the door."

Schwartz walked in and stopped in the middle of the room, his hands still behind his back.

"Don't make me drag it out of you. What do you want?"

"The FBI have identified the dead men and the pair who attacked Rodriguez. DNA for the first two, facial recognition for the others."

"So?" the Artist asked.

"Someone will have to kill them." He paused. "But the biggest problem is the program. We have to shut it down."

"You're done then? You want your bonus and your new identity, is that it?"

The thin man nodded.

"All right," the Artist said. Shutting down before the Sabel agents and the Slager were dead could not happen. It took months to build a program like that. "But not until everything is cleared. A couple more days. Five, at the most."

"You'll be in jail by then."

"Are you threatening me?" The Artist closed in and hovered over Schwartz.

Schwartz didn't waver. He held up his phone with a text displayed on it.

The Artist squinted at it, then pulled it closer to read. At the top was a vaguely familiar phone number.

The text read, "You and I have a hammer over our heads. You tell me who the Artist is, and I'll neutralize him for us both. If you don't, I'll find out anyway and you'll go down with him."

He looked up at Schwartz. "Who sent this?"

"I don't know. I thought you would."

The Artist turned around and paced away. With his back turned, he pulled his own phone and looked up the country code for Myanmar. Schwartz was right. He did know who sent that text. "I'll deal with it. Now get out."

"We need to shut the program—"

"Not before you kill those Sabel agents, goddamn it." The Artist walked away. "Three days, then pull the plug."

"Every hour the risk rises exponentially."

"Do what you're told." He turned his back on the thin man. "By the way, I suggest you destroy that phone, cancel your service, and get a new one. Immediately."

Schwartz patted his thighs, thought about saying something, thought better of it, then left.

The Artist reached under the mattress, elbow deep, and pulled out his special phone.

Before he could turn it on, his regular phone rang. The caller ID showed Admiral Tilden.

He sent the call to voicemail and dialed the Slager. "Where the hell are you?"

"Why the call?" the Slager drawled.

"Schwartz showed me your text."

From the change in background noise, he presumed the Slager stepped outside, or into a private area. "I want to know who you are. That's all there is to it."

"So you can 'neutralize' me?"

"Do you think I trust you, *Artiste*? Don't pretend I can expect to live five minutes past your crew detonating themselves. Come to think of it, I'll bet you have plans to take me out five minutes beforehand just to minimize risk."

"Nothing could be farther from the truth." The Artist wondered if Schwartz had collaborated with the Slager. "I gave you my word."

"And now that you need me to carry out your plan, circumstances have changed. Here is my demand: I want money and insurance—or I walk the crew into the nearest Embassy and turn them over to the Cultural Attaché, otherwise known as the CIA station chief."

He had to give the Slager points for effective use of his leverage. "You'll rot in prison."

"Please. I'm smart enough to ask for immunity before making a deal." The Slager huffed. "'Neutralized' doesn't have to mean you die. It means you're no longer a threat to my life. Prove to me that I can trust you."

"If I go down, you go down harder. You've been leading them all over the world." The Artist visualized his entire plan crumbling. But he was an artist who would simply create a new ending. "Let's meet. We can work this out."

"Meet? Sure. Who's the sniper that gets paid to take me down?" The Slager chuckled. "You give up your mom as a hostage—then we can talk."

"You don't know who you're dealing with and you're making threats?"

"I have nine kids ready to die for Islam and you're as good a target as any."

The Artist's heart stopped beating. His chest caved inward with intense pain. Damn it. The Slager was right. He had all the cards now.

"We can come to an understanding if your demands are reasonable." The Artist sighed. Since his budget was unlimited, it would be revealing what the Slager thought was appropriate. "I'm willing to find something mutually satisfactory. What do you suggest?"

"My crew and I have been constantly on the move. I'm exhausted and can't think. I'll call you back from the road when I have it worked out." He paused as if thinking. "But I can tell you my first demand, and this is non-negotiable: Schwartz dies."

"Well, isn't that nice? We've found common ground already."

CHAPTER 28

HAKIM WATCHED CARTOONS WHILE I stood outside on a balcony drenched with heat and waited as the last ginger rays of sunset warmed Ela Beach. Special Agent Verges called me back. He must have shown Hakim's video confession to an Arabic speaker and gotten a translation. "Stearne, what verification do you have for this kid?"

"What do you want, a diploma from his terrorist college?" My fist clenched around the phone. "Do you want a career-making bust or not?"

"You think I'm going to fly to the other side of the world, drag back some kid who we don't see on any manifests or airport cams anywhere, and expect a big promotion? Get real."

"He said Larson is leading the cell." I slid the door closed to keep the TV noise down.

"Another one of your mythological beasts. Just because you found a Moroccan in PNG doesn't mean he's connected to ISIL. Just because some guy in Syria told you his name is Larson doesn't mean it is." Verges sighed. "Look, some guys tried to kill you and Miguel. You're under a lot of stress, I get that. But don't drag me into your hallucinations."

"Hakim and Larson are not—"

"Even if I believed you, I work for David Watson now." Verges huffed. "He's old school. He insists we get one shred of independent evidence. Just one."

David Watson, Special Agent in Charge of Counterintelligence – Economic – something – something, was a jerk I'd run across before. Ms. Sabel and I ran circles around him, which didn't do his career a whole lot of good, so I began to think all this resistance was professional jealousy. Even so, you'd think he'd let Verges investigate just to keep him busy.

I pressed on with my case. "His brother was the one in that ISIL video—kissed his father's hand before he blew himself up."

"Until you told me about it, I'd never heard of that guy or that video, Jacob. Now I wish I could un-see it. How could a father do that to his own son?"

"That's what's bothering Hakim!" My voice kept rising despite my attempts to keep calm. "He has the feeling his dad doesn't like him much."

"None of that connects him to anything. He could be telling you whatever you want to hear. NAVSUP hasn't confirmed your Larson story. The SEALs don't talk about operations. You have a kid in PNG but we don't find him traveling to or from anywhere in the world. There's nothing I can—"

"Verges! There are nine terrorists heading Stateside and—"

"Deal with it, Stearne. No one believes you." Verges spoke to someone else in the background. "Look, turn the kid over to the CIA at the Embassy. They'll verify his bona fides. If he checks out, we'll talk."

Verges clicked off.

Why can't he take my word for it when I catch a terrorist and convert him? It sounded far-fetched even to me as I thought about it. Still, why not travel around the world to a Third World dump to find out for himself? For three square meals, a warm bed, and all the cartoons he can watch, this kid would tell them everything he knows. Which isn't much from what I can tell. But then, if I were an ISIL commander, I wouldn't trust anything important to someone willing to commit suicide.

Then it dawned on me. Why the hell was I chasing terrorists when I should be home with Yumi? I should quit, get a job as a chef, and start a family. Maybe the convicts-on-parole would leave me alone. Maybe not. But at least I'd be home with the love of my life. I could picture her, running across the front yard, carrying a baby in her arms.

Mercury said, *Dude, she's running to you because his diaper needs changing and she's late to meet her mom's circle at the Rocket Bar.*

I said, *No way. Rocket Bar's a meat market, a hookup joint.*

Any woman married to you will end up in the Rocket Bar looking for alternatives, trust me. Women want a man who's reliable and safe, not carrying a death wish to extremes on a daily basis. She'll fight with you every time you take a call from Sabel HQ. Yo, marriage is more than candlelit dinners and hot sex.

I said, *I don't have a death wish. Besides, you're the one who keeps telling me to blow my brains out because life is absurd, meaningless, and hopeless.*

Mercury threw his hands up. *OK, let's pretend it's not for a minute. Let me give it to you straight: you aren't good for Yumi.*

I hate it when the gods are right about stuff.

Miguel called from the lobby to announce his return. I kept my pistol ready, my eye glued to the peephole. Two minutes later, Miguel walked past my door and proceeded to the end of the hall. He knocked on a door several doors down, then came back and stood across the hall facing me. He waited.

Mercury said, *This crazy protocol for making sure no one's following or coercing him won't stop him from stabbing you in the back.*

I said, *I trust him with my life; there's no stabbing.*

I opened the door and let Miguel in.

Mercury looked over my shoulder. *Look what happened to my main man Julius, homie. If you ask me, Miguel has a lean and hungry look. He thinks too much. Such men are dangerous.*

I said, *I can't deal with you quoting Shakespeare—or flying halfway around the world to show up unannounced, for that matter. You know what this means? I'm loony, stark raving, a nutcase, out of my tree, gaga, away with the fairies, demented—*

Mercury pushed me back. *Easy there, bro. Settle on down with your bad self. I gotta pick up Pachamama at the shoe store. She's having issues finding high heels that honor her Incan heritage in a meaningful way. But—for the record—you never had a problem with Santa flying around the world.*

I said, *He was imaginary.*

Miguel tilted his head. "Who we talking about?"

"Maybe there never was a Michael Larson." I moved past him back into the room.

"Having trouble separating the visions from your day job?"

Miguel knew me too well. We served in the same platoons on several deployments. We never talked about Mercury, but he'd figured out a few things and respected my religious disbeliefs. Or whatever the hell I have going on.

I faced him. "What'd you learn?"

"The North Korean embassy did not issue any visas here in PNG." He grabbed a bottled water.

"They offered that up?"

"Not until I broke his nose," Miguel said. "And I may have snapped three or four fingers. I don't like North Koreans." He slid open the balcony door and stepped out. "If their ancient computer system works right, PRK has no groups of ten—in any numerical combination— coming in on any airline."

I followed. "How did you check all the airlines?"

"There are only two, Air China and Air Koryo. The only way to get there from here is through Shanghai or Beijing. Our guys didn't go from here to China." He chugged the entire bottle of water in one go. "They went somewhere else."

"Larson led us to the middle of nowhere. And you know what that means." I turned to Hakim, sitting quietly on the bed, and asked in Arabic, "Did you change your appearance at every stop?"

Hakim nodded.

"He's scrubbing his boys; and wrecking our credibility." I grabbed a water bottle and tossed the last one to Hakim. "Multiple cities, multiple forged passports, a bunch of airlines—someone put big bucks into this project."

"It's a lot more than ISIL would ever spend." Miguel nodded at me. "We're going back to Syria."

"This is definitely tied to Ms. Sabel's 'Artist'."

Miguel looked at the kid and pointed to his mouth. "Hungry?"

The kid had burned off a ton of calories while contemplating suicide. He followed Miguel like a puppy.

Miguel and I didn't need to discuss turning the kid over to the CIA. They would stick him in Guantanamo for the next five hundred years and we'd have no source of information. As long as we let him think he was going home to Morocco, he would tell us anything we wanted to know about the people who talked his little brother into giving up his life for an Islamic State led by rapists.

As soon as the door closed behind them, I called Ms. Sabel. She picked up on the first ring. I brought her up to speed on the operation. She congratulated me on taking a terrorist alive and promised to have Hunter shake the FBI tree until Verges fell out of it.

"Why doesn't he believe you?" she asked.

"It's too far outside the ISIL or al Qaeda operating procedure. They don't send people to six different countries; too expensive. Verges thinks I'm running around the globe yanking random Moroccans out of the sand because I'm nuts."

"Are you?" She paused. "Yanking Moroccans out of the sand, I mean."

"I sent him a video confession in Arabic. What more could he want?"

"Who gave him your mental health evaluations?"

"I didn't ask." I choked just thinking about it. All of my records are sealed. That's standard for special ops veterans. The brass doesn't want spies digging up personnel records through Freedom of Information Act requests. The Defense Department would never turn those over to the FBI. Someone big was screwing with me. Were they intentionally helping the Artist? Or was it jealousy over my close personal relationship with god?

Sometimes I feel like Joan of Arc.

Kinda.

Not in a girly way, though.

"Who else have you told about Hakim?" she asked.

"I copied Captain Behan and Admiral Tilden at NAVSUP and asked them to explain Larson. They haven't responded."

"Miguel's right, you have to go to Syria. Before you go, you have to tell Yumi." She clicked off.

I looked at Mercury. He shrugged. *You're so screwed right now, dawg.*

CHAPTER 29

PIA SAT AT THE TABLE on her balcony at the Ritz, typing emails and reviewing documents in the dim predawn light with dried sweat from her morning run still clinging to her skin. She glanced inside the glass at Stefan, sound asleep in her bed. Would showering wake him? If so, in what kind of mood? A playful smile spread across her face. Tania had been wrong; she had not been in need of a quickie. She had been in need of a slow and thoughtful romance.

She glanced at the time—not even five. Was it cruel to wake the non-insomniacs of the world? Yes. The shower would have to wait.

She returned to her email. In his assessment of her proposal to buy Roche One, Alan Sabel wrote, "You noticed he rejected your demand that Roche pay the $100 million EPA fine before finalizing the deal. How do you propose to handle it?" Scrolling through the rest of his other comments, she found his bottom line. "If you don't mind paying the fine, you'll make money in a hundred years, but why do you want a refinery?"

She appreciated that he didn't give her orders but instead asked her thought-provoking questions.

Next up was the report from Bianca's crew monitoring the communications of Luuk Devoor, Ritchie Skaite, Davy Cameron, and Sean Addison. Nothing incriminating from any of them unless she was interested in Addison's and Cameron's extramarital affairs. The Artist had not contacted Roche since the GPS tracking began.

A note from the Major relayed the Coushatta tribe's interest in moving forward with the casino as soon as possible.

She finished off a slew of more mundane emails.

Stefan slid the glass open and stood on the sill in a thin robe, blinking at the early light.

"Good morning," she said. "Leave the door open. Let some fresh air into the room."

"You really are an insomniac." He staggered to the empty chair at her table, his eyes swollen with sleep. He echoed her greeting as best he could in his pre-conscious state. "Rumor has it that you wake up screaming in the middle of the night."

She nodded toward the mountain towering over the western end of the valley. He turned to see long fingers of daylight stretching from the east, crossing above the dark valley to light up the peaks in the west.

"Dazzling," he said before facing her again and snuggling into his chair.

"Sometimes I have horrible nightmares." She reached behind her and rolled the room service cart to them. She picked up a coffee pot and poured him a cup. She warmed hers as well. "I woke up more relaxed this morning."

He smiled and took his coffee. "Why are you interested in the Roche One Refinery?"

"You're in the oil business. I'd like to be in the oil business too. You're not worried about the competition, are you?"

"You know about his people dumping toxic sludge into the bayou?"

"Dad tells me to solve problems—not stress over them."

He looked her over, waiting for her to tell him more.

She smiled and grabbed his hand. "I have to take a shower."

After a long, luxurious shower that left them squeaky clean and even more relaxed, she sent Stefan to meet his dad for the conference's closing breakfast.

A text arrived on her phone. President Hunter texted, "Your request has been approved. EPA finalized it at 9EDT/6PDT this morning."

Pia went to her prearranged meeting with Chuck Roche.

He sat sideways at a table, his silver-handled cane standing at attention as he watched her approach. "Why do you want my refinery?"

She pulled her chair, adjusted her skirt, and sat opposite him. "I want to see if a change in management can make a difference."

"Why did you pull the patents out of the SPP deal?" He scowled and waved a waiter over. "What good is a hemp plant to me if I don't get the patents?"

"You don't care about the company. You want to shut down the technology."

"I have tree farms that take thirty years to mature. If your people make paper from hemp that can be grown in a single year, it will ruin me."

"Ruin you? Your empire is only paper thin?"

The waiter took Pia's order for coffee and yogurt. He left and she stared at Roche.

He squinted his meanest look. "I don't know what your advisers are advising, but I will not raise my offer."

"I'm fine with the offer as it stands now."

"Then this isn't about paper or the refinery." He leaned back. "Why did you want to meet?"

She dropped her tablet on the table and leaned toward him. "You asked if I believed Hunter's 'whitewashed story.' What should I believe?"

Her coffee and yogurt arrived. She was hungry and ate quickly.

When he didn't answer, she said, "Word is, you and Hunter were allies once. Insiders tell me you had a falling out. Is that what your comment was about, some juvenile desire to undermine her? Or do you have something substantive to tell me?"

Roche squeezed his cane and rocked it back and forth and flexed his jaw.

"You've yet to donate to our Super PAC," Roche said. He drained his cup and held it out, a foot from the table. A waiter appeared with a carafe and filled it, then disappeared. "You need to stand against NEXT USA. We need to know you're with us."

"Your Super PAC is all dark money, untraceable to the donor. Why not tell the American people what you're doing? Why the secrecy?"

"Privacy. If everyone knows who I'm backing, the politicians will never push my agenda." Roche scowled. "This is important. You noticed that the tech guys left the conference early? Damn socialists. They'll regret it when Maddox taxes them."

"What's wrong with paying taxes?" Pia asked. "You and I both own more estates than we could possibly live in. We both own stables full of cars. Instead of bragging about buying the latest Gucci or Gulfstream, why don't you and I brag about how much of our income serves the country?"

"Surely, you're joking." Roche's eyes narrowed.

"Do you think the military men and women who serve their country are joking? They don't have our wealth, yet they offer their lives to protect us."

"Suckers."

She sipped her coffee and let the moment stretch. "Chuck, if you paid 18% income tax, the same percentage as the average teacher in this country, you could fund 5,400 new teachers. If you paid the higher bracket, the same paid by surgeons, you could fund an aircraft carrier battle group for most of a year. Wouldn't that be worth bragging about?"

"Who are you kidding? We don't pay 18%. Why should we? We have havens and shelters and trusts. You have them—don't deny it."

"If a house on a hill is a status symbol, if a silver-handled cane announces your position, if building a library with your name on it brings you respect—why not show off your contribution to the nation?"

Roche reached for his coffee without taking his eyes off her. He brought the cup to his lips, his hands shaking with rage. He stopped and set the cup back down to prevent spilling it.

She leaned over the table. "Tell me, Chuck, what did Hunter leave out?"

"You know there are fines with that factory."

"I'll pay what's fair." Pia leaned back. "Whatever fines are outstanding against the refinery when I take over. But don't try to saddle it with Roche Industries' problems."

"Agreed." He snapped his fingers. An executive in a suit appeared with documents and held out a pen.

Roche signed in six places then pushed the stack to Pia. She signed. They shook hands while the executive snapped press-release photos of them. The executive handed her copies, scooped up the rest, and disappeared.

She finished her yogurt while he talked about the heat.

"If you feel threatened by someone close to you—" she put down her spoon and leaned across the table "—I can help you."

Roche choked on his coffee and hacked several times. "You've yet to contribute to the fight against NEXT USA."

He rose on his cane and left.

Pia went to the main ballroom. It had been divided into a much smaller room since many attendees had opted to leave early. The manageable size made it easier for her to find Stefan and Luuk Devoor. At one end of the ballroom, a giant TV screen showed an empty podium at NEXT USA headquarters.

Stefan leaned to her ear. "Maddox's been feeling the pressure to unveil his economic agenda, so he's called a hasty press conference. Smells desperate to me."

She shrugged.

"How did things go with Chuck?" he asked.

Before she could answer, the TV sprang to life. Marty Maddox stepped to the podium and basked in the applause of his worshippers. When quiet prevailed, he made the requisite opening remarks, thanking everyone from the top down to the groundskeepers.

"My economic plan has been challenged by the leading candidates." He smiled an infectious grin. "I'd like to remind people of what this great country can do when we pull together and work like a team. When we put aside our personal wants and dreams and make our humble contributions to the nation, we can do anything. We brought the brightest minds in physics together in the New Mexican desert and figured out nuclear fission in three years. We brought together the brightest minds in rocketry and put a man on the moon in eight years. We asked doctors to conquer polio, and they did—not for personal gain, but for humanity. Previous generations of Americans achieved every goal they set for themselves. It's time for the next generation to stand up and set a goal. America, are you ready for the NEXT step in American history? Are you ready for the NEXT driver of the American economy?"

The crowd in Sacramento cheered.

The crowd around Pia moaned. She glanced around at them. Maddox had no fans in Rancho Mirage.

"The greatest problem facing the NEXT generation is energy." Maddox motioned for quiet as he spoke. "We need clean energy and we need it to be the NEXT frontier we conquer. But guess who's number one on the path to solving nuclear fusion—South Korea. Is the USA number two? No. France is. Are we number three? No. Germany. Are we even in the top ten? No. Ladies and gentlemen, the world is desperate for clean energy and the USA is not even in the hunt. *That* is a failure."

Again, the crowd in Sacramento cheered while the crowd around Pia did not.

"What nation is the greatest? USA. What nation leads in battery technology? Korea."

The people around her booed out loud. Pia looked around. Ritchie Skaite stood and led the boos. Davy Cameron flipped a finger at the screen. Stefan bellowed for all he was worth. On all sides of her, people expressed anger and resistance.

"In the nineteenth century," Maddox continued, "the USA was an agricultural nation. In the twentieth century, we were a manufacturing nation. Both of those industries are still of vital importance to us, but they are not going to lead us into the twenty-first century. What our economy lacks today, what will drive us into the future, is the NEXT economy. The economy of innovation and invention and teamwork. The benefits of solving the fusion and battery technology issues will bring white-collar jobs, engineering jobs, new technologies, and spin-off industries that will drive our economy the way oil did in the last century. It will drive our NEXT economy the same way the space race and the defense industries drove our parents' economy. We need to take the NEXT step. Clean energy is the NEXT USA!"

Cheers at NEXT USA headquarters were drowned out by increasing boos around her. Even Stefan was standing. Pia was the only one sitting.

"We cannot move forward dreaming that the oil industry will go away. A smooth transition will be required from oil to—"

The feed cut off, the screen went blue. Luuk Devoor shouted from the back of the room. "Enough! Who's with me? Who will end this nightmare?"

Stefan turned to Pia. "Are you ready to help us?"

"No." She shook her head and stood. "Teamwork makes sense. Working together makes sense. Why wouldn't we get in front of the global economy? Why let the Koreans and French lead the way?"

"Never!" He glared at her as if she'd killed his first born. "He's talking about ruining my business. You own a refinery now. You can see he's going to close it and destroy your investment."

"I'd gladly close it if it helps my country. Some things are more important than money."

"You cannot think like that." He shook with anger. "I won't have it."

Pia clamped her jaw, turned on her heel, and strode out.

CHAPTER 30

THE SLAGER TOWED HIS CARRY-ON, following the herd, single-file down the corridor for international arrivals in Vancouver, Canada. His legs were rubber. Several days of living on airliners with twenty-hour flights back-to-back was killing him. The last time he slept in a bed was Mérida. He didn't even think about sitting down in the whorehouse in Yangon. International arrivals always make the passengers trudge up one gangway and down another, crossing the airport back and forth. He could feel them watching him. He kept his head down, looking tired as he trudged into the big room.

Everything was on the line in Vancouver's velvet-roped customs lanes. Customs is an intentional bottleneck where video cameras instantly check facial recognition software against massive international databases. The four previous fake passports would confuse the software and spit out inconclusive identification for their pictures. If the new passports were good, there would be no problem.

Shanghai customs had not been much of a test. For all the might of the Chinese police state, the volume of people they processed gave him and the crew anonymity. But Canada was not China. Vancouver concerned him more than any other country on their tour. Positive thinking kept falling to rational thinking. His Myanmar passport was a good story: an expat educating the unfortunate souls. But his crew of Moroccans posing as Uyghurs was his weakest link. Hopefully the Canadians were worldly enough to know Uyghurs were Western-looking and not as Asian as China's predominate Han.

He waited at passport control for the next inspector. To keep from drawing attention, he read a book. No one suspects bookworms. He glanced at the inspector in the booth. The inspector looked up right then and made eye contact. The Slager looked back at his book, telling himself not to read anything into it. Try not to look like a man shepherding nine suicide bombers into the country to kill god-knows-who just to get some cash and a new identity to save his kids. He felt a bead of sweat on his brow.

Negative thinking. He took a deep breath and rolled his shoulders. The Slager never loses. He yawned and wiped his face with his hand.

He was in good shape. The money was moving easily into his new account. Neither Schwartz nor the Artist had mentioned it in the last few exchanges. His transfers looked about the right size for bribes and extortion. Expenses he had been eliminating since Myanmar. Killing the contacts in Yangon turned out easier than he'd imagined. Somewhere outside of Shanghai two more corrupt officials lay in a ditch. He was OK with that. They were doing the world no favors by helping terrorists move around.

The man in front of him stepped up to the inspector. The Slager glanced around.

Two Moroccans stared at him from just two lines away.

Holy mother of god.

The Slager slipped his phone between the pages of his book and looked up their flight number. They were supposed to be through customs and waiting for him across town by that hour. His screen came up: two-hour delay. He checked the other flights. One was on time, the other was four hours late, meaning—despite his extensive planning, there were six terrorists in the same airport at the same time. Which meant, the two staring at him had missed their transportation window and lacked the language resources to wing it. They needed help.

And that meant the other four would need help. Vancouver, in all its multicultural glory, had signs in English, French, Chinese, Hindi, and Farsi. Not Arabic. Terrorists need not apply.

If Argentina was in his future, he could never appear on the same video feed anywhere near these guys. His heart started pounding into his ribcage.

The man behind him coughed and the Slager realized he was being summoned by the inspector.

He forced a yawn, stepped up, and handed over his passport. The man scanned it. Something beeped. Every country has a different system and a different method and a different beep. The only thing all countries had in common was the bored frown on the inspector's face. A second beep came from the machine and the inspector looked at him. He willed himself not to sweat. Yet he felt his body conspire a droplet on his temple.

The inspector said something he didn't hear, then stepped away from his booth. Not good. Definitely not good. The only thing to do was look bored and cranky. He leaned against the booth and yawned and wiped his face and looked at the carpet. In the corner of his eye, he saw the inspector talking to a supervisor, a tired woman with the required scowl. The two of them approached.

He looked up as if trying to keep his eyes open in the middle of the night.

They spoke to each other and pointed at the screen. The woman turned her glower toward him. She drew a breath in order to speak and he considered making a run for it. But where? An airport's international wing was sealed. Security at airports around the world tripled after the Brussels attack and it wasn't exactly light before that.

"Sorry, sir." The woman's scowl grew tighter. "Our system connection is down."

There was another beep.

"Oh," she said. "There we go. Have a nice day."

She left the booth and the original inspector stamped his passport. The Slager snatched it off the counter and walked away before his gasp of relief could be heard.

Ten yards upstream, the two Moroccans waited with expectant faces. He shook his head to warn them off and walked wide around them. He headed straight for the bathroom and glanced over his shoulder. They were not following him. They were looking around as if Cirque du Soleil might show up at any minute and they didn't want to miss the show. He snapped his fingers. Nothing. He gave a low whistle. One of them turned and understood. He tugged his roller bag after him and went in.

Three men were in the space. One at the urinal. Two washing up and leaving. The Slager typed out a message on his phone in the translator app and set it to Arabic. He flashed it in front of the first Moroccan who came in. The boy looked curious. Maybe e-translations were inaccurate. Maybe he couldn't read. His companion joined them. The second guy figured it out, tugged the first guy, and the two of them left.

Simple enough: relay the message to the other two, catch a cab, get to the meeting place. He was ready to go ahead with both plans—the Artist's plan first, his own second. If the others never showed up, he'd skip the Artist's plan and go straight for the jugular.

He took a hotel shuttle and caught a cab from there. He stopped for breakfast at a diner and enjoyed his meal at a leisurely pace. If he stalled long enough, they would wait for him and not the other way around. Once he thought enough time had passed, he moved into high gear.

First stop, the storage locker. Next, he met the crew at a shack of a farmhouse on River Road West outside of Ladner, British Columbia. There were soybeans on one side and the Fraser River on the other. It was a bit of sandy land five miles north of the 49th Parallel, the latitude that serves as the border between Canada and the US.

Once the fisherman welcomed the Slager and his crew aboard the boat, they set out due west and a little north, heading for the fishing grounds off Parksville, British Columbia.

The Slager knew what needed to be done. He also knew the fisherman was innocent and, unlike the passport forgers, didn't deserve his fate. It came down to one simple thought: he needed to get his kids out of hell. He pulled their picture and made a silent promise to take them someplace safe. It's a dog-eat-dog world and some of us live high and mighty and others get taken out by lightning. Who knows what's going to happen?

Somewhere about ten miles from shore, in the center of the Salish Sea, the Slager shot the fisherman in the head and dumped his weighted body overboard.

He turned the boat south, slipping between the myriad atolls near Vancouver Island until dark. Trusting his GPS with his life, he crossed Strait of Juan de Fuca after midnight and landed in the USA at Port Crescent.

The crew stood on the remote, driftwood-covered beach and watched as he set the boat's course northwest and sent it out into the broad Pacific. With any luck, the boat wouldn't be found for a month.

They trudged up the dirt road to the line of trees and found the van, right where it was supposed to be. In the back, between the many rows of seats, were the weapons. Stacks of parts, scattered among greasy auto parts, looking like a junk pile, were twenty automatic weapon replicas. Everything but the chambers and barrels reproduced in plastics through the magic of 3D printing. Plastic parts would get through metal detectors. The barrels slipped inside canes. The firing chambers fit inside the power adapters for laptops.

Everything was coming together.

They got in the van and drove into the night.

CHAPTER 31

BRINGING A TERRORIST INTO SYRIA was a new and ironic mission for me. Hakim was like a new puppy—I couldn't leave him alone for fear he'd shit on something and I couldn't take him with me because pet-terrorists were not welcome on top-secret bases deep in ISIL-held territory. On top of that, I was an ex-Army Ranger in a Navy SEAL camp. That's worse than being a Shiite in a Sunni camp.

Dhanpal had all the SEAL connections and made some calls from the states, but the in-country CO interrogated me about my mission for an hour anyway. If he found out I had a suicide bomber lounging on my boss's Gulfstream outside, my body would not come home in a flag-draped coffin. It would be used for target practice by B-2 bombers with heavy ordnance.

I left the pilots in charge of the boy and told them to shoot him if he went near a window.

To my surprise, the CO warmed to my plan. He was just as curious as I about why a NAVSUP admiral would exfiltrate a civilian. When I promised to share Larson's DNA sample, he gave us a couple electric dirt bikes, some comm gear, and a clear understanding that his men were not there to risk their lives for civilian idiots with death wishes. Then he waved good-bye.

We set out into the desert sunset on the silent bikes dressed like a pair of Lawrences of Arabia with night-vision visors.

We had three objectives: find the exact location of our abandoned Humvee; uncover any potential ambush; and get Larson's blood sample from where he bled in the back. We hadn't paused to check our coordinates during the firefight. We just wanted to get the hell out. Now we had to find it at night.

The only sound we made was our tires on the dirt. We zipped through the barren terrain in no time, arriving long after dark. We buzzed around a wide perimeter on the near side of the *wadi.*

Eventually, we found it. The Humvee sat right where we left it, stripped of everything of value. ISIL had commandeered a significant fleet of Humvees from the Iraqi Army early in their entanglements and ours had been used for parts. The hood was up, exposing the broken engine block. The alternator, battery, and everything else had been removed. In back, the Gatling gun was gone, as were the windows. But the one thing we needed was still there: the flatbed.

I climbed in and looked for blood. Without enough starlight penetrating the windowless back, I risked a flashlight. Sure enough, smears of dried blood covered the bed. I held the flashlight with my teeth and pulled out a baggie. There were no pools, only thin spots. I took up a little paint along with the samples and hoped that would work.

I was scraping up smudges for the third baggie when daylight-bright beams of search lights lit up the truck. I checked my body: prone on the floor, none of the light streaming in was hitting me. They knew I was there, but didn't have a target unless I moved.

Mercury climbed in next to me. *Is this how it ends, homie?*

I said, *I'm doing fine. Why aren't you in San Diego? Did your girl get her shoes picked out?*

Yeah, everything's fine now. Thanks for asking. We've decided to worship different gods together.

Ouch.

I said, *What about the rest of the convention?*

I'm done listening to Thor acting like he really looks like Chris Hemsworth, bro. In real life, the dude's a short ginger and rides a chariot drawn by goats. You see Chris Hemsworth riding around with goats?

Which explained who Pachamama was worshiping. Guess goat-drawn rides are all the rage with some ladies. I looked Mercury over, from his sandals to his winged helmet. I never felt sorry for a god before. I said, *How am I going to get out of this?*

Same as always: you're going to count on divine intervention, dawg, because otherwise you be dead meat.

The quiet *pptt-pptt-pptt* of our standard-issue Heckler & Koch MP5-SP echoed in the *wadi*. In rapid succession, the three spotlights went dark. On the far bank, two AK-47s opened up on Miguel's position, thirty yards upstream from me.

That was my cue to flee. I shoved the three baggies in my pocket, grabbed my rifle, and crabbed backward faster than a fly fleeing a frog's tongue. Falling out of the door, I crawled around the front of the Humvee and opened fire on the weapons lighting up the night on the far bank. Six more joined the first two, aiming at me.

"Let's go," Miguel said over the comm link.

I looked at the wall of rock behind me. My exit was exposed.

I ducked around the left fender and fired as if I were running away on that side. They opened up. I spun around, shouldered my rifle, and prayed they didn't have night vision. My escape went well for the first few seconds. My feet found rock and my hands found ledges halfway up the fifteen-foot bank. Then it all gave way.

Rock and dirt tumbled below me while I did the Wile E. Coyote scramble up the side. My hands and feet spun like tires in a snowbank, keeping me from dropping down—but not lifting me the last three feet.

Even without the modern miracle of night vision, the jihadis figured out where I was from the noise. Their bullets started ten feet to my left, stitching a diagonal line across the bank. They were methodically trying to pinpoint my position from my scream if one of their shots nicked me. One sound of pain and all six weapons would bear down on me.

I scrambled, hoping to find a piece of dirt that would hold my weight for a split second. I cringed, waiting for a bullet to strike one of my legs or arms. Somehow I'd managed to survive all my battles with my extremities intact while I saw plenty of good men lose theirs. That was what caused me to ask Mercury for help.

Mercury sat on top, his legs dangling over the edge. *That's all I hear from you, dawg. Save me from this, save me from that. When are you going to tell people who does all the saving around here? When are you going to introduce me to your friends? You treat me like I'm a backdoor god. And that just ain't right. Ya feel me?*

Someone was feeling low on self-esteem after losing his girl to a Norseman. I said, *Whatever. I want to live. Help me.*

Mercury leaned into my line of sight. *You gonna tell Pia-Caesar-Sabel how you got out of this?*

I said, *Yes! Anything!*

Grab that root over there, fool.

Inches above my left hand, a big white root stuck out of the dirt. I grabbed it and did the best one-handed pullup of my life. My torso landed on top of the bank. I rolled away, twirled myself into a firing position, trained my sight on a muzzle flash and took down an enemy. A split second later, I dropped a second. From his position twenty yards away, Miguel took down a couple more.

In the distance, headlights and spotlights from ISIL Toyotas flooded the desert. Reinforcements were three minutes out.

We jumped on our silent bikes and whirred through the darkness. Behind us, the Toyotas gained slowly but surely. Using the comm link, we alerted our American brothers. They were unhappy about us leading the enemy to their top-secret base and scrambled the Apache helicopters to dissuade our pursuers.

I tossed the third DNA baggie to the SEAL's CO, promised him a grand reception at Sabel Gardens when he and his team returned stateside, and ran up the Gulfstream's airstair.

My first call went to Yumi. "I'll be home in twelve hours, babe."

Nothing.

"I can't wait to see you again."

Nothing.

"Are you there?"

I could hear soft crying. I took a deep breath.

Her voice, filled with sniffles, came through soft and whispered. "I call you later."

Click.

Dead air.

My heart stopped beating. The sensation of falling through the floor overwhelmed me. I willed the jet's body to open up and allow me to fall fifty thousand feet to whatever patch of ground was underneath us.

Turkey or Greece, probably.

She'd begged me not to go. She'd told me to come straight home from PNG. I did head home. I just made a six-hour stop along the way to kill several nasty, horrible people and collect proof that one of their nasty horrible friends was going to do something nastier and horribli-er than I could imagine. That's how I roll. I clung to a small hope she would understand that.

She was a Buddhist. From a country where the last few generations renounced murder and mayhem after the atrocities of WWII. Even their criminals were relatively humane. There was a cultural disconnect I'd have to deal with when I got home. It would be decision time. What should I do with my life? Cook or kill?

Mercury sprawled on the ceiling eating a bunch of grapes. *You know how to read a recipe, bro, but your saucepan is always burned. Stick with the thing that brings you joy—killing bad guys. Let her go.*

I said, *I don't have any burned saucepans. Maybe a couple. But, she'll come to appreciate what I do for a living. It's my contribution to society. I kill bad guys. What's wrong with that? She'll get it when I sit down and explain it to her.*

That's what I love about you, bay-bay. Never let reality get in the way of your dreams!

What would a discarded god know about it anyway? His temple hasn't had a fresh coat of paint since the Visigoths vacationed there in 378 CE.

My second call went to Special Agent Verges as we raced over Europe. I set him up to meet us at the airport. Then I leaned back and tried to catch some sleep while waiting for Yumi to call me back.

She didn't.

Hours later, we landed and the pilot lowered the airstair. Our favorite FBI man greeted us. I looked left and right. Verges stood alone on the apron.

"Did you tell anyone about this?" I asked as I handed Hakim over to him. "I expected a few experts to come with you, like an Arabic speaker for the interrogation, maybe a few ISIL specialists."

Verges looked pale. "I'm all you get, Stearne."

I explained the situation to Hakim, that the nice man was going to find him a place to spend the night. Then we'd get ice cream for breakfast and find a way to get him home to his mom. He wasn't interested in going home, where he expected to be vilified for not joining the martyrs. Which was good because everything I told him was a lie. No doubt the FBI would ship him off to the CIA to be tortured on some secret base somewhere.

"Where're you taking him?" I asked Verges.

"I'm not sure."

"Do yourself a favor and take this seriously. I'm going to post his confession on Facebook and let you explain it to the world."

"It's not me," Verges said. He looked into the sky. "Look. They didn't give me this assignment because I'm qualified. They gave it to me because they think you're the mad hatter. They laughed at me when I showed him your video. They kicked me out, told me to take some time off."

"Who is 'they'?"

"David Watson." Verges fidgeted. "He remembers you."

"I outsmarted him a couple times." Out of the twelve thousand FBI agents in the world, there was only one guy at the Bureau that I hated. And he hated me. "Did Watson put you on some kind of administrative leave?"

"No." He looked at the ground. "Kind of. Maybe. No paperwork but essentially, yes. I'm an agent without a home."

He scraped his foot over the pavement between us. Then looked up at me, pale and scared. "Help me, Jacob."

The first thing I did was look up that NAVSUP guy, Captain Behan, in my contacts and sent him a copy of Hakim's video. I added a little note about handing the DNA samples over to the FBI—without mentioning their lack of interest. I left it up to him: tell me who Michael Larson is and where I might find him before I send the video to the *Post*. But I wasn't holding out false hopes for a quick response.

Then I called Special Agent in Charge David Watson and left a message about getting serious.

The four of us set out for my house. Me and my three banished friends. An FBI man with no portfolio. A Navajo not welcome back at his overpriced, diversity-everywhere-but-here condo. And, my new friend, the homeless terrorist.

I called Yumi to warn her about my unexpected guests.

She picked up with a lot of background noise.

"Babe, are you at the Gardens or back at my place?" I asked.

"I in LAX." A long pause followed. The background noise confirmed her story. "Sorry. I go home now."

Click.

CHAPTER 32

PIA DROPPED DOWN THE AIRSTAIR wearing her favorite suit at Moffett Airfield in Mountain View, California on a chilly, overcast morning. A strange sense of foreboding ate away at her. The FBI's reluctance to listen to Jacob was worse than bureaucracy could excuse. No one paid attention to the pre-9/11 warnings coming from the FBI's Minneapolis and Phoenix offices because the case was missing key details, like where and when an attack would occur. Now an equally epic failure to visualize danger was in process. The only reason given: Jacob's lack of credibility. His mental health issues were an understandable problem. But who had circulated the slanted view of him was a different question.

Tania climbed in the limo after her, texting like mad, neglecting her standard vigilant observation of the area. Pia leaned over and saw a stream of non-stop texts from Jaz Jenkins. If arranged marriages had been a thing in the US, Pia's father and Jaz's father, lifelong friends, would have betrothed her to the mild-mannered heir to Jenkins Pharmaceuticals years ago. Tania was a better fit for the boy. A little older and a whole lot pushier—she'd toughen him up.

Stefan was more of a challenge. She considered their last terse phone call. No one would tell her what or how to think. They'd left the conversation with such intractable positions, neither of them could call the other without making a total capitulation. She was far too hard-headed to give in. And she was in the right. So it was his fault.

But.

He was a great guy and a terrific lover. She shook her head. How did she let it go that far? How could she get their relationship back on track? How could she get him to realize how wrong he was?

Her limo deposited them a few minutes later at the campaign

headquarters of NEXT USA, a nondescript office building in central Mountain View donated by a tech billionaire. Secret Service agents confiscated their weapons and sent them inside, where a second round of Secret Service agents, the presidential detail, met them. Wanded, credentialed, and all but cavity-searched, they were sent to the boardroom at the end of the hall.

President Hunter met her at the glass door. Governor Marty Maddox waited a step behind her. A flock of people waited patiently behind them. Hunter made the introductions.

Pia found Governor Maddox to have that personality unique to politicians regardless of their ideology: excessive charm. Grabbing her hand while looking into her eyes with a genuine smile, he instantly made her feel special. As if no one else in the room mattered to him. He held her gaze and spoke with a genuine warmth reserved for no one else but her. She recalled the Greek historian Plutarch describing the same attribute in Julius Caesar. Someone tapped him on the elbow and he took his leave, breaking the spell. The flock left with him.

Pia felt herself breathing again.

Hunter and Tania stayed behind. Tania looked back and forth at Pia and the president, realized she was a third wheel, and excused herself.

"Your administration is not taking Jacob's intelligence seriously." Pia pushed two chairs apart at the middle of the table and took one.

"I'll shake them up." President Hunter sat opposite her.

Hunter also held her gaze, but with a weaker smile than Maddox's and no warmth at all.

Pia filled her in on the texts from the Artist to Roche, Jacob's retrieval of the DNA, Hakim's video confession, and Verges's dismissal.

Hunter typed a terse email on her phone to the directors of the FBI, NSA, and Homeland Security. She showed it to Pia. "If I have any power left in my lame-duck term, that should get them moving."

Pia liked Hunter's threat to roll heads if the video confession wasn't taken seriously. She nodded her approval and the president sent it.

Hunter rose, poured herself a coffee from an urn at the sidebar. "If I recall correctly, you take yours black?"

"What have you left out about this plot?" Pia asked.

Hunter turned with a NEXT USA mug in each hand. "What do you mean?"

"Why is Sabel Security taking the lead on this? We can't get a search warrant. We can't tap phones. We can't subpoena anyone."

"You've already done all those things." Hunter smiled and handed her a mug. "Government agencies need credible evidence to get warrants."

"How did you hear about this plot then?"

"The NSA listens to calls from terrorist camps. They traced several suspicious calls from one terrorist back to several odd countries. We believe his contact is using forwarding technology to prevent tracing. Since that lead is a dead end, we thought we'd start looking at who's calling odd countries."

"How did you narrow it to Roche and his friends? That's quite a logic leap."

Hunter took a deep breath, leaned back, and sipped her coffee. "Classified."

They stared at each other while sipping their coffee, each waiting for the other.

Hunter caved first. "We need either his permission or a court order to access Roche's phone. Since your snooping is technically illegal, we'll never get a warrant. You need to ask him permission."

"Me?" Pia sipped her coffee and turned her gaze to the window. "Right. You can't acknowledge any of this."

"Chuck Roche could be sending himself texts as a preemptive defense." Hunter leaned back and stared out the window.

There was not much of a view. Treetops, solar panels above parking lots, and a thin, gray fog.

"What are your impressions of Roche?" Hunter asked.

"He's like most of Dad's friends, a sociopath who believes he arrived at his position by divine right." Pia sipped.

"At the top of the food chain, we're all like that." Hunter paused. "Even you."

"He asked me a thought-provoking question." Pia set her mug on the table and faced Hunter. "He referred to the information you gave me about McCarty as 'whitewashed'. What did you leave out?"

Hunter sat up and looked her straight in the eye. Without a flinch or evasive movement, she said, "Nothing."

Pia thought through the next steps while Hunter watched her. Trust a president who once allowed rogue appointees to kidnap her? Or an obnoxious billionaire receiving texts from an assassin?

"Who to trust is a scary decision." Hunter leaned forward and lightly touched her forearm. "I know you don't trust me. Whether you forgive me for my role in your trauma is up to you. I've done what I can to make peace with you. The way I see it, you have to ask yourself one big question: why hasn't Roche reported these texts?"

Hunter's aide came in, announced the arrival of donors, and left.

Pia took her cue, shook the president's hand reluctantly, and found Tania at the end of the hall. They spent a few minutes talking to the NEXT USA volunteers, whose age range was broad and whose collective zeal was contagious. The longer they stayed, the more excited they became about America's future. They met college students and retirees working side-by-side. They met executives and waiters, CEOs and mechanics, all eager to move the American economy forward on nuclear fusion research.

An older woman stopped her. "Imagine the USA having a higher per capita income than Qatar. Wouldn't that be nice?"

She exited the building with Tania at her side. Low-hanging clouds darkened the day and the wet chill closed around her. The foreboding feeling chewed on her stomach.

She called Roche. "I need to speak to you again. When can we meet?"

"Your meeting with Maddox didn't go well?" Roche asked.

"How did you know—"

"You're on the news, live." He cackled. "Meet me at the Top of the Mark in an hour."

Pia looked around to find several news cameras pointed her way. She summoned her limo.

The fog thickened as they neared Nob Hill and the Mark Hopkins Hotel. The driver dropped them in front of a classic 1926 stone building towering on the hill above Union Square. Much to Tania's relief, they took the elevator to the nineteenth floor, marked with a T for Top, instead of a number. On a clearer day, the bar and tapas lounge might have given them a view of the Financial District, Chinatown, and the Golden Gate Bridge, but even the Fairmont Hotel, just across the street, was barely visible.

As she entered the room, a bulky security guard tapped Pia on the shoulder. His first mistake was beginning a pat down before asking permission. Grabbing his wrist, she twisted his arm by turning away from him and bending her waist into his torso. She bent her knees, lowering herself more, before shoving her butt out and tossing him over her shoulder.

The over-muscled man lay face up on the dance floor as the early evening patrons gasped. She wrenched his arm and landed her knees on his exposed stomach.

He nearly lost his lunch. She pulled his Beretta from his shoulder holster and stepped on his face.

She tossed the pistol on Roche's table. "Teach your goons some manners."

"You would make Queen Calafia proud." He smiled up at her and twisted his silver-handled cane.

She scrunched her nose as she pulled her chair out. "Montalvo's fictional character, the queen of the mythical Island of California? I'm insulted."

"You shouldn't be." He leaned back. "She was quite beautiful."

"She lost her war." Pia snapped her napkin.

He flinched. "As will you."

"Cherish your delusions while you can." She nodded in the direction of his bodyguard.

A waiter approached and waited in silence. Pia ordered a Casa Noble Añejo and the tuna poke. Roche ordered a bourbon and caviar.

"You've chosen to join the socialists?" he asked when the waiter left.

"Rigid polarizing statements are unacceptable. Rephrase your question."

"When did you become Hunter's lapdog?"

"When her people traced a terrorist plot to your doorstep." Pia gave him a cold stare.

He glanced up quickly. "What would a soccer player know about terrorists?"

"Gold medalist, thank you. I know a lot more than Roche Security." She lowered her voice. "I offered you help."

"Why would I trust someone dumb enough to waste millions cleaning up an old refinery?"

"Because the man calling himself the Artist is close to you—and you need all the help you can get."

Roche gave away his surprise when his breathing stopped and his hands trembled. "Who're you talking about? 'Artist'?"

The waiter returned with their drinks. Pia and Roche stared each other down in silence until he left.

"Do you want help on this problem, or will you wait until it's too late?" she asked. "Or are you involved?"

He spluttered and sipped his bourbon.

She sipped her tequila, savoring the flavor for a moment, then swallowed.

"Certainly not involved." He spat his words.

"Who do you suspect?"

"Roche One has a multimillion dollar fine hanging over it." He sloshed his bourbon around the ice.

"We believe the Artist is planning an assassination. We believe he confided or bragged to you who he plans to kill."

"It also has 50,000 gallons of toxic mercury that needs to be cleaned up."

"My people need access to your phone. With it, we can track down—"

Roche nearly leapt from his seat. "Never. Not Sabel Security, the Secret Service, or Schutzstaffel—you're all like the Nazi SS. You even have the same initials. You and your gangsters better keep away from me."

"Are you the kind of man to go back on a signed contract?" she asked.

"Never. I'm a man of my word."

The waiter arrived with their tapas plates.

"Then you should know," she said, "the Hunter administration reassigned the EPA fine to your parent company due to the refinery's failure to pay in a timely manner. I'm not paying it—you are."

His translucent skin turned red, his whole body shook with anger. He tried but could not speak.

"It gets worse," she said. "The refinery listed the mercury spill as an asset. That's why I insisted the contract be written requiring you to take all moveable assets. A tanker full of hazardous waste is, in my humble opinion, a very moveable asset. My people are delivering it to your estate. But you can't have my tanker, I'll need that back. So you'll have to come up with some place to store it. If you don't want it in your yard, my people will leave it in your swimming pool."

It took a moment for him to process what she'd done. When he caught his breath, he said, "You bitch."

"The world expects eloquence from a man like you." She smiled, rose, and hoisted her purse to her shoulder. "Now that we've established my negotiation skills are better than yours, explain to me why you want to deal with the Artist alone. If the madman does assassinate someone, you'll be the top suspect."

CHAPTER 33

THE ARTIST LEANED OVER THE balcony railing. Far below, through the fog, he could see her confident, predatory stride as she made her way from the Mark Hopkins' front door to her waiting limo. The multi-racial girl trotted to keep up with the boss. Sabel Industries would fail. What future could there be for a woman-owned business of that scale?

He answered his ringing phone and stepped inside, shutting the doors behind him. "What can I do for you, Tilden?"

"I've just watched two videos made by a decorated veteran name of Stearne. Who the hell is Michael Larson?"

The moment of truth had finally arrived. He'd used and abused the admiral for too long. The Artist sucked his teeth and made a decision. "Can I trust you, Admiral?"

"You better have a damn good explanation if you want my trust." Tilden scoffed. "You told me Larson was an ISIL captive and you'd paid his ransom. The feds don't allow that—but I helped you anyway. Now I've got a couple veterans with a Silver Star each and a bucket of purple hearts between them telling me this guy was nobody's prisoner. So tell me, goddamn it, who the hell is your guy and why did I send a bird for him?"

The Artist took a deep breath and explained his entire plan.

Tilden screamed and shouted, trying to make the Artist stop talking. He didn't. He enjoyed his game.

When he wrapped up, he allowed a second of silence. "All that targeting information you so proudly gave to the Air Force came from Ahmad. All the intelligence I fed you came straight from ISIL's command. You can't do anything to stop me without spending the rest of your life in prison, my friend. But it's all good. We're doing this to save the nation. And it's going down tomorrow."

Admiral Tilden made no reply. He clicked off.

Risk. There is no success without taking risks. And the Artist had just taken a big risk. Oddly, telling Tilden everything filled him with joy. The big secret unburdened at last. He spread his feet wide on the carpet and fisted his arms into the air. He shouted in triumph. He felt good. Really, really good.

The Artist considered making a few phone calls. Maybe he should tell everyone. They would understand his genius. Chuck Roche, Tilden, the Sabels, all of them would see what a great and wonderful thing he'd done. His proactive thinking spared the country from a second civil war.

Maybe he should keep a few terrorists on the side to dissuade anyone from arguing about his methods. Maybe he should buy a few more. Keep a steady stream of them coming over.

A knock on his door broke his reverie. The sharp noise of reality brought him back to earth. He had leverage over Tilden. He could keep the admiral quiet. The others would never understand. Their minds were too small to see the big picture.

Schwartz announced himself outside the door.

The Artist opened it.

The miserable man stumbled in with an icepack on his bruised face. "Larson found me. He wants you to call."

Schwartz held out a new burner in the palm of his hand. The Artist looked at it as if it were a rat. Schwartz flipped it at him and dropped into a seat.

"Are you bleeding?" the Artist asked. "If you are, get out of that chair."

Schwartz rose and looked back at the seat. "Call him."

"Don't try giving me orders, you—"

"He has my children." Schwartz dropped back in the silk-covered wingback. "'Symmetry', he called it. Some kind of sick payback because I arranged his kids' foster parents."

"You'd think he'd be grateful." The Artist stared at the phone in his hand. A pre-programmed number was ready to dial. He pressed send.

"Did you ask Schwartz if he gave you up?" the Slager asked.

"What do you want?"

"You're worth billions. He says you have thirty-two homes and estates, some you've never set foot in."

"I'm a collector." The Artist walked into the bedroom and closed the door behind him. "If you think I'm going to ransom Schwartz's kids—"

"Don't worry, I'm not shaking down Schwartz. His brats are my insurance policy. I get mine back, he gets his."

"Good." The Artist snapped the drapes closed. "Wait. What do you mean, 'shaking down'?"

"You need to provide two things: insurance and money."

"What kind of insurance?"

"Schwartz told me who has my kids. He arranged for a couple of your psychos from the program to provide foster care for them. That was thoughtful of you. But don't think I don't know what you have planned."

"Wait a minute, Slager. I would never hurt children."

"Who do you think these damn towelheads are going to kill tomorrow?"

The Artist drew a quick breath. He'd never considered collateral damage. "They should have strict instructions not to harm the children."

"You gotta be kidding me. Tell a terrorist to aim carefully?"

"If you want to see your kids again—"

"Listen up, fuckhead. This is what's going down. I'm going through with your plan. You're going to pay me. The ID, the kids, and an extra three million. Today. You got that?"

The Artist gripped the phone in his hand. His knuckles turned white. "I take it there's a threat coming?"

"I'm saving three of these Moroccans for you. They want to kiss your ring, godfather. Know what I'm saying?"

The Artist wanted to scream. You can't trust anyone anymore. There had to be a way out of it. His brain ran through scenarios like flipping pages in a book without reading it. The son of a bitch had flipped the script completely. He never should've trusted these parolee-rejects to do a decent job. The whole reason they were in jail was due to their laziness. Always taking shortcuts to wealth instead of earning it.

Yet, the more he thought about it, why should he care? If he ignored the insult, all the money would come home anyway. But one should never give in to the lower classes without a struggle. Being in a hurry is what gave away the scale of the Artist's resources in the first place. "What assurances do I have this will be your final demand?"

"None. Either these guys show up at your door and blow your head off, or you find Schwartz's head in a shopping bag on your back seat. Until one or the other happens, you have to live in fear of your own creation." The Slager laughed. "Kinda poetic, ain't it."

"Ironic, you moron." The Artist huffed. "OK for now. I'll send the money—half now and the rest after the job is done. But you better blow my socks off."

The Slager clicked off.

He stormed into the living room and threw the phone at the thin man. "Who told him I have exactly $3 million left in the Panama account, Schwartz?"

CHAPTER 34

WORSE DAYS WERE HARD TO remember. I've been dumped by all types of women: smart, pretty, funny, dumb, curvaceous, high-strung, passive-aggressive—you name a type, she's dumped me. But I always saw it coming. It's Natural Law, like Newtonian physics. You cheat on a girl, she dumps you.

But Yumi.

I hadn't even cheated.

Truth was, I had known it was coming. But we ridiculously optimistic mortals always think we have one more chance to pull it off.

My chances were over. She was gone.

I had no will to put one foot in front of the other.

I walked into the windowless meeting room in the J. Edgar Hoover building on a muggy Washington morning. It took my mind off Yumi to see the room packed with men in dark suits. Verges walked in behind me, ramrod straight and clean, ready to be taken seriously by his peers. Back in the hallway, an FBI agent calmed Hakim and lied to him in Arabic the same way I had. The poor kid was going to spend the rest of his life in a maximum security prison and no one could bring themselves to tell him the truth.

At the far end of the table was a face that killed my mood: David Watson, Special Agent in Charge. In the FBI, a SAC is like a ship's captain or an army colonel. On the open seas or outside the wire, they are the only god you're allowed to worship. They bark orders and you execute before the last syllable spills from their lips. Most of them were excellent operations officers, getting the most out of their people. Some of them, Watson for example, made Machiavelli look like Mr. Rogers. Worse, the guy was in charge of a unit that keeps the nation safe from military spies and intellectual property theft. A unit that had been waging war on Sabel Security for a long time.

"Who's ready to find Larson?" I asked.

No one answered. They didn't even blink. There would be no camaraderie.

Mercury stood behind Watson. *Hooboy, is it hot in here, bro? Maybe you should open a window—and jump out of it.*

I said, *We're all on the same team. They need to do the bureaucratic shuffle, formal introductions, that's all. It's how things work in Fed-World.*

Mercury said, *I feel some hating going down here, homie. The worst thing you can do to a bureaucrat is go over his head. And playing the president card is pretty far over their heads.*

The guy on my left pointed at the last seat. "Join us, Mr. Stearne. I represent the DIA."

"Why is Defense involved?" I didn't wait for an answer. "Who represents the FBI Joint Terrorism Task Force?"

"Sit down." Watson barked his order from his corner. "You're not asking questions. We are."

A lean older guy, Watson's gray buzz cut glistened under the fluorescents. He was old enough to qualify for one last promotion before being sent home to outlive his retirement savings, a fact that was visibly eating at his temperament. He crossed his arms and scowled.

I took the thinly padded, vinyl chair and rested my forearms on the scratched and marked-up veneer table. The walls lacked any attempt at decoration to break up their depressing gray flatness. Verges pressed his back against the wall, behind the DIA guy. A bead of sweat formed near his sideburn.

The introductions resumed. After the DIA guy, there was a CIA guy, a silent guy, and Watson, the others were government psychologists.

After the last introduction and bona fide, Watson asked, "Why did you bring Hunter in on this?"

As Mercury left the room, he spoke over his shoulder. *What'd I tell you, bro? Since they're going to roast you, Ima find me some marshmallows.*

"What we should be asking is: where is Larson? Isn't that what this—
"

"Why didn't you call me direct?"

"I did."

The doctor sitting next to Watson leaned forward. "I sense some hostility between you and—"

"Damn straight." I felt my blood boil. "Ask him about Kasey Earl or Donald Patterson or Violet Windsor or Shane—"

"You have history." The doctor glanced over his shoulder at Watson and sank back. "Let's try to leave that in the past and move forward, shall we?"

A text came in on my phone. I glanced at it: Captain Behan. He said, "Admiral Tilden shot himself at his desk."

I texted him back. "I need his call logs."

Behan shot right back. "No way that's going to fly, civilian."

I handed my phone to the DIA guy. Army veterans like me harbor a distrust of people outside the Pentagon. The DIA guy glanced at it, squinted while his brain-gears worked through the background on my story. He checked his notes. Then he acknowledged his understanding with a simple nod.

"You harbored a fugitive." Watson pounded his index finger on the table. "You've been coming and going from a black ops site in the Middle East like it was a garden party. That's why I'm here. And that's why these guys are here. You're spying for ISIL."

"I got my Silver Star in a firefight with the Taliban," I said. "You're suggesting I switched sides?"

Watson looked at one of the other doctors. Unruly black hair and big, thick glasses made him look like the mad scientist from central casting. The guy tossed a folder full of handwritten notes on the table and cleared his throat. "According to Dr. Harrison's notes, Mr. Stearne expresses classic symptoms of PTSD. Serious brain damage from prolonged exposure to extreme violence and many explosions has been proven to alter cognitive functions. His delusions manifest themselves—"

"Hakim said the attack is going down today. TODAY. If I'm not deluded and something big goes down, what are you going to tell the families of the dead?"

Watson's mouth clamped so tight he almost broke a tooth.

"We're behind you," the DIA guy said to me. He shot a glare at Watson. "Do you have any actionable intelligence? A location, a state, general region?"

"Not a goddamn thing." I looked each of them in the eye. "But if we put boots on the ground, FBI, National Guard, Army, cop, anyone with a pistol and general knowledge of how to use it, at every public gathering in the—"

Watson blew up. "You got shit. You know that? You got one kid you found in PNG. You've got a baggie of dried blood you found in an undisclosed location. You've got a mental health record that's been redacted. And you want to turn the USA into East Berlin?"

"My expertise is killing jihadis. Protecting citizens is yours. I want to hunt down a terrorist. The President of the United States wants me to hunt down a terrorist. Do you want to help me or not?"

An hour of yelling didn't help anything. They agreed to follow their own plans. The DIA offered unlimited resources to help me. But they insisted on having an itinerary. It was an infinitely more pleasant experience than working with Watson—but equally useless.

A few minutes later, Verges and I walked down the sidewalk in a light drizzle, heading for the Federal Triangle Metro stop.

Mercury squeezed between us, his wet t-shirt-toga clinging to his skin, forcing me to look away. *Why is everyone hating on you just cause you're insane, homie? Isn't it politically incorrect to hate on the criminally insane these days? I mean, when was the last time you killed a bunch of people? Oh yeah, yesterday.*

I said, *What good does it do talking to god? Why don't you just tell me: where the hell is Michael Larson?*

Verges glanced my way. "I swear Jacob, if I knew, I'd tell you."

CHAPTER 35

PIA WATCHED RAIN DROPS DRIP down her window pane at the Ritz in Half Moon Bay, just over the mountains from San Mateo, San Francisco, and the whole Bay Area. Lit from inside, the mirror-like drops rolled down at varied speeds, some overtaking others and consuming them.

It was time to suck it up and call him. She glanced at the time on her phone. It might be five in the morning in California, but that would be eight back East. He'd be awake.

He answered in a barely audible voice.

"Oh," she said. "I thought you were an early riser."

"Yeah." He paused and she heard him wrestle sheets. "But five is pretty early."

"You're not in DC?" She bumped her forehead with her fist. "I'm so sorry. I didn't mean to wake you."

"Don't worry about it. I had to get up to answer the phone." His loud yawn came across the line. "Let me get some coffee. I'll call you back."

She clicked off and sighed. Stupid. Dumb. Useless. Waking up three hours before anyone else always exposed her anxiousness. Ugh. And this was how she went about repairing the relationship?

Tania opened the door from the adjoining suite, yawning in a baby doll nightgown, a pot of coffee in one hand. "Bianca's report is in."

She grabbed two mugs and joined Pia at the desk. Together they brought up Bianca's email. Working backward from their phone's access towers for each call, only Davy Cameron could be eliminated. The Artist had texted Roche minutes after her meeting, warning him to "stay away from the bitch". The two phones were within one hundred feet of each other. They could've been as little as a few feet, but phone locators are inaccurate from one minute to the next. The rest of Roche's group—

Luuk Devoor, Stefan Devoor, Ritchie Skaite, and Sean Addison—were staying within a block of him on Nob Hill. Bianca ended her report with a question. "Why isn't Stefan Devoor's phone responding yet?"

"Don't tell me you didn't get a chance." Tania looked at her. "The boy was living in your room out in the desert."

"I didn't want to." She stammered. "It felt wrong."

"You didn't want to suspect him? Girl, you need to wake up on the man-thang. They're all suspects."

Jacob called from the street outside FBI HQ. "They want actionable intel. A nationwide search might panic the population, so they don't want to look for ten terrorists. This morning, Hakim gets up and tells me this is the day! What more do they want?"

Pia reassured him she would call the president again, then clicked off. She wondered about the email Hunter sent and if her lame-duck status would cause such complacency. Then she wondered what could be done. What actionable intel did they really have?

Hunter's assistant put the President on. With unbridled enthusiasm, Hunter said, "Are you calling to endorse Maddox? You know he's the right pick."

Pia hadn't expected the question, but realized she should have. It caused her to think a moment. She knew the power of teamwork. She wanted to see the country come together rather than tear apart. She liked the idea of a national goal. But she'd never seen herself as a political person. She never considered endorsing anyone.

All of which was nothing more than an interesting distraction.

She focused on the threat. "Jacob met with the FBI, CIA, and DIA, and they want actionable intelligence. We expected more urgency."

"What does he want them to do?"

"National manhunt." On saying it, Pia understood how far over-the-top it sounded. "He's adamant the attack is today."

"My people have strong opinions about your boy."

"I trust him."

"And he still had no idea where they might be?" the president asked. "Or which Larson he wants to find?"

"He gave them DNA, but it takes a day to come up with results."

"I'll have Homeland Security give a press conference and set up a call-in number."

"What good will that do?"

"We'll have the whole country looking for him." The president sounded incredulous. "Let's see, the Democrats have rallies in Atlanta and Chicago; the Republicans have events in Philadelphia, Boston, and Denver. We can focus on those cities. NEXT USA has a big rally today. Say, are you still in the Bay Area?"

"Yes." Pia watched the rain dripping down the window pane. The grounds outside the hotel were still too dark and shrouded in fog to see anything.

"Can I tell Governor Maddox that you'll join him on stage to endorse him?"

Pia wondered if Hunter had given her the impossible assignment just to drag her into the election. Was her endorsement of any real value? Blue collar workers wouldn't care what a billionaire thinks. Executives wouldn't care what a young woman in her twenties thinks. The only demographic group who might care was the three million underage girls involved in youth soccer.

Then it dawned on her. What Hunter really wanted.

"How much do you need?" Pia asked.

"As much as you're willing to give." Hunter left a moment of silence, then lowered her voice. "He's going after the industry that killed your parents."

A pang hit Pia's heart—just as Hunter intended. She felt manipulated in both the best and worst ways possible. When she'd first heard it, she'd only heard Maddox's economic plan as an intellectual question: do we want to take action and solve the problem or wait for the Koreans or French or Germans to solve it? Whoever won the race would be the richest country in the world. Saudi kings would come begging favors. But the idea that it would crush the power of the oil lobby never occurred to her. Would she get answers? Or revenge? Did it matter?

"Will $100 million be enough to get NEXT USA started?" she asked.

"I'm endorsing him via video link today." Hunter's voice was giddy with excitement. "Go to the rally. I'll introduce you and you'll make your endorsement. You'll have to give a short speech. Do you have a speech writer?"

"Uh, no."

"I'll have one of mine call you. When can you wire the money?"

Pia felt her feet growing cold. "I'll have to check with Dad."

"Do that. I have to go." Hunter paused. "Oh, and Pia, I'm very glad to have you onboard. We're going to change the world. We're going to build the future. You're going to be a big part of that."

Pia clicked off and set her phone down. She watched the larger raindrops consume the smaller ones.

Tania leaned over, trying to get in Pia's line of site. "You OK? You look like you paid $100 million to get punched in the gut."

Pia straightened up slowly. "I thought I'd at least get kissed—"

Her phone rang. Stefan. She cringed before mentally switching over to make-up mode, and clicked on. "Stefan, are you awake now? Sorry about earlier, but I thought you should be the first to hear of my decision to endorse Maddox."

In the silence that followed, she checked her phone twice to see if they were still connected.

Finally, his rumbling baritone broke the silence. "You bought Roche One. You're in the oil business now. You can't be serious about this. Maddox is going to destroy your investment."

"He said the transition was an important part. He's not going to kill a $1.8 trillion economic sector overnight. But if the Koreans get there first, they sure as hell will. We'll have the Great Depression all over again." She paused. "I'm doing this, Stefan. I'm getting up on stage this afternoon and making a public statement."

"NO!" His shout was so loud she pulled the phone from her ear. "Do not go to the rally. You cannot be there. I won't allow it."

"Who gave you the power to 'allow' anything?" She clicked off in the middle of his hasty apology.

So much for the best lover in the last year. And the only.

The rest of the day whirled around her. Homeland Security held a press conference that ended up as a footnote on the websites of major news outlets. Without actionable intel, no one wanted to discuss it. Hunter's speech writer called and worked out a very short speech.

Pia and Tania met with NEXT USA's road crew for the rally. Six billionaires lined up with her, getting their cues and marks on the amphitheater's stage. Together they memorized their speeches and places.

"I paid $20 million and I have to stand stage left?" asked the social media pioneer. He faced Pia and laughed. "You must have outbid me to stand next to the candidate."

She pretended to laugh and glanced at the latest text from Dad. "$100 million? Are you insane? I can buy all four candidates for half that much—which would guarantee White House access."

"I have White House access now." She texted back. "What good is it?"

The crowd began filling in. T-shirt vendors, water-bottle sellers, hot dogs, and cotton candy concessions popped up. The place looked like a concert or a circus. By mid-afternoon, the atmosphere was charged with electricity from the crowd below and the storm clouds above. Organizers ran around talking to the Secret Service people about rain and lightning procedures.

The warm-up band came out and played. The warm-up speakers came out and spoke. The keynote speaker came out and keynoted.

Then President Hunter's face exploded across four big screens facing the crowd. A man at the foot of the stage jumped up and down, raising his arms. The crowd exploded into cheers for Hunter. Her giant face smiled down on everyone.

A gentle rain began to fall. Umbrellas popped open.

Hunter was deep in her speech. Pia looked over her notes and tried to remember her cue. Nerves began to itch in her hands and arms and neck. No stranger to public speaking, she was an alien in the political arena.

Tania ran toward her, pointing and gesturing as she shoved her way through the backstage crew. Tania said something she didn't hear.

Hunter mentioned Pia's name. Her cue. She walked out on stage to a roar from the crowd. Few things in life are as satisfying or as life-affirming as basking in the adoration of huge crowds. The lights glared in her eyes. She smiled. She waved. The President looked down from her big screen like an adoring mother.

Tania's voice rose above the din. "He's here. Larson. I saw him."

CHAPTER 36

THE SLAGER THOUGHT ABOUT HIS new bank balance—over four million and climbing. He smiled. Billionaires might be rich, but they were dumb as posts. He turned back to his crew and ran through the operation one more time.

Each man carried a piece of the puzzle and a spare of another man's piece. They could build six automatic rifles. They only needed three. They had nine terrorists, though only three would act. Redundancy to ensure a completed operation. There was no way the Slager was going to miss his $3 million payday.

The Moroccans didn't know shit about international travel, but they prayed with dedication and took on serious demeanors when they were ready. And they *were* ready. Clean-shaven chins, neatly trimmed hair, a couple guys were dyed blond, a couple dyed red, one shaved bald. Some dressed like hippy-wannabes, some like corporate guys, and a couple went grunge.

They split up, each man taking a different route, a different train, a different bus, getting on at a different stop, changing to a different mode of transportation, and arriving at different times. They sat in different seats, or stood in different wings, or lounged on different parts of the grass.

At each man's appointed time, he would make his way to one of the three appointed restrooms, and went to the last stall. He would give the three-cough signal and, when his overture was acknowledged, he would pass his parts to the martyr in the next stall. Then each man left, with no evidence, no ID, no connection to the killers.

Each martyr would praise Allah silently and assembled the plastic parts into an assault rifle. He tossed the extra pieces into the trash can and went into the crowd with the weapon under his raincoat.

That was the plan. The Slager could only assume all these things were going on. The Artist had a different plan, one with greater loss of life for both civilians and martyrs, but the Slager had come to appreciate the power of having a terrorist in your pocket.

He had only one job left: to post pictures to a Facebook page that would let the Artist know the job was done. After that, all he had to do was rendezvous with the Moroccans who lived through the debacle and carry out his personal insurance policy.

He looked for a good vantage point and found one on a vendor's walkway off the side of the main stage. He leaned against a wall and marveled at how much makeup President Hunter wore for her close-up. On the big screen, far above his head, all her wrinkles were cavernous and puttied like an old window. He spied an ice cream vendor and treated himself to an ice cream sandwich.

He was unwrapping his bar when she caught his eye.

A policewoman in uniform was questioning one of his martyrs. His man had an umbrella under his arm, carried like a man from a desert where umbrellas were only seen in the movies. No natural movement in his walk at all. His man's face tinted red with the first sign of anger. The problem in his plan was keeping Youssef, the only English speaker in the group, separated from the others. It had to be done. But it gave the operation a higher risk of discovery. And they were about to be discovered.

The Slager tossed his ice cream in the trash, pushed off the wall behind him, and strode across the grass. He stopped back to back with his martyr and took what appeared to be a selfie. Then he looked at the picture and zoomed in on the officer's badge: Talmadge.

"Whoa. Mary, right?" He said as he turned and bumped into her. "Sorry, it was so long ago. Mary Talmadge?"

She gave him the once over.

"I'm sorry, you're Mary Talmadge, right? A friend introduced us, like, what, a year ago?" He leaned back and grinned, then let his grin sour. "Oh. I'm wrong. I'm sorry. Didn't mean to bother you, officer."

"Olivia." She squinted at him. "Who introduced us?"

Behind him, he sensed his man understand the diversion and back away.

"Anita and Juan's housewarming." He cocked his head, then shrugged. "Not you though, huh."

She shook her head slowly, her eyes never leaving his in a mean way. "You got my last name right."

"Get out." He grinned again and backed up a step to where his martyr had been standing. Empty space. "You got a sister or something?"

"Hey!" The officer pushed him aside and searched through the crowd for her quarry.

He shrugged and slipped between bodies and headed back to his perch on the walkway. Peeling a second ice cream sandwich made his mouth water, but again he was denied his dessert. A Secret Service man in body armor that could stop a missile was eyeballing Youssef. Even at a distance, he could see why. The devout Muslim was mumbling prayers. Saving the translator for the final operation was more of a necessity, so what the guy was doing in that position was inexplicable. He tossed his ice cream and trotted down the stairs to the main floor.

He bumped into Youssef, breaking his trance. "Fucking Muslims. Go home." The Slager leaned close to the terrorist and whispered. "You're giving them away. Get out of here."

The Slager moved on, threading his way through to the Secret Service agent who'd been watching Youssef. "Wow, those are some threads you got there, buddy. What is that, level IV?"

"Move on, sir." The agent scowled hard. "Or you will be removed."

The Slager feigned an insulted look, then a touch of surprise, then nodded. "Yes, sir. Sorry, didn't meant to disturb the service."

He looked around, into the rafters, as if seeing the many agents for the first time. The one thing he noticed was the gap in the very spot his martyrs needed.

The Slager returned and bought one last ice cream sandwich. He moved to a corner overlooking the stage, not too close, not too far.

Then he saw her. Across the stage, at a distance, between a hundred people, it was her. That bitch from As Sukhnah. And she saw him. Their eyes lasered each other for a moment. He smiled and waved. Why not?

The woman disappeared.

The soccer star walked out on stage. Who the hell would care what some stupid athlete had to say about who should be president?

His first martyr opened fire and rushed the stage. Ahead of schedule. The suspense of meeting his maker had proved too much for the young man. But that was OK. He'd baked in some extra time for those anxious to die.

The martyr executed his part in the drama exactly as planned, rushing an access point, stage left. Bullets sliced a path through bodies for him. His rate of fire emptied a magazine before the first sniper took a shot.

The sniper had to have been shocked when his direct hit, center mass, was stopped. Smuggled ceramic plates, placed into special pockets sewn into their t-shirts, had been a stroke of genius. The Moroccans had whined about staying up late to do women's work, but it was paying off now.

Fear gripped the crowd. Every untrained civilian, froze like a statue. Their bodies sent conflicting flight or fight decisions rushing to the brain, overloading it. *Terrorist attacks happen in France. They happen in Baghdad. They happen in Tel Aviv. They don't happen in Mountain View. Therefore, this isn't happening.*

Yet it was.

The Secret Service agents trained their sights on the first martyr. As the herd's attention turned that way, the second gunman opened up, spinning in a circle, holding his rifle above his head, aiming down. He was the tallest at six-eight. With his arms stretched high, and the special trigger they'd rigged for shooting at an angle, his bullets struck the unprotected heads of agents and police and civilians. He stood in the middle of the forward crowd, where people were packed the tightest, making him a difficult target for the snipers. His intent was clear: shoot people in the head. Front-line Secret Service agents didn't wear helmets to political rallies. This forced the Secret Service into a decision-lock just like the civilians. Should they wade into the crowd and die, or wait for the helmeted agents to arrive from the perimeter?

The first martyr turned his weapon on the agents on stage and took out two. Perfect head shots.

Everything proceeded according to plan.

Screams, delayed by utter disbelief, erupted throughout the crowd. While he watched, three brave people died trying to stop his whirling dervish of a martyr.

The crew's final act began at the height of the mayhem. His best, most fervent martyr rushed the stage from the side farthest from the first two martyrs. With all eyes on the first two, stage left, the third man went unnoticed. With the power of a gymnast, he leapt to the stage and fired at Maddox, who waited offstage in the wings. The Secret Service men assigned to protect him were still looking around the corner to determine the threat direction. Just as the Slager had predicted.

Then the unexpected happened. The soccer star ran straight at the last martyr.

She ran like a cheetah going after a deer. Starting to his right, she barreled in as he was aiming beyond the Slager's line of sight. The martyr did his job: he kept firing and ignored the girl. She slammed her forearm into the Moroccan's nose. He fell backward. She wrenched the gun from his hands and slammed the stock in his face. She pounded blow after blow into the martyr's head. The weapon broke apart the way you'd expect cheap plastic to self-destruct. She ejected the magazine and the bullet in the chamber and tossed the weapon.

The scenario had gone so horribly wrong, the Slager forgot to take pictures.

He pulled up his phone and snapped away. He posted with the message, "Massacre at NEXT USA rally."

He estimated the casualties at ten dead and forty wounded. Maybe twice that number, he couldn't tell. But the target, Maddox, was undetermined. He'd have to watch the news. Sabel stomping a martyr was a loose end he didn't need. He'd tie that one up one way or another. Find out what hospital he's in and incite a mob to a little vigilante justice. Or just walk in and shoot the asshole. Who would stop him? The cops who'd just lost a few of their own?

The crowd was already fleeing for the exits. He tossed the phone in the nearest trash can while it uploaded. He turned and joined the stampede.

Halfway out, he stopped.

His knees refused to hold him up. His feet would not move forward. Bile from deep inside him erupted like a volcano. He puked his guts out in a trash can. When he looked up, an older woman pushed him aside and emptied herself.

He stared across the mass of people fleeing the scene. What had he done? Until now, it was all just operational details on a piece of paper. Like a math problem, it was nothing more than a mental exercise in search of a solution. Numbers and ideas and timelines and contingencies were abstract, not reality. Surrounded by howling and screams and shouts and alarms, the weight of his complicity tore at him.

What the hell was he thinking?

None of this was his idea. He didn't fund it. He didn't dream it up. His only crime was ripping off some rich dude. He had his own problems to worry about.

Tugging the smudged picture out, he had a long look at Ethan and Emma and took a deep breath.

He had a higher purpose to his actions than any of these losers.

Fuck 'em.

CHAPTER 37

I WAS SHAKING OFF MY raincoat in the pantry at Sabel Gardens when Alan Sabel stormed in with hate and anger radiating off him in waves. I thought he was going to strangle me. The intensity in his eyes pushed me back. His aggressive and livid posture made me gulp. He stopped short and said, "Pia's been shot. Grab your people, let's go."

He was in shock, confused and scared, so I kept calm and pushed my melting emotions aside. Mr. Sabel needed me to keep him organized, on track, and safe. I channeled every confused thought into those priorities. Mainly because we didn't know her condition—dead or alive, grazed, wounded, or critical—and I never stress over what I don't know.

We sprinted through the evening rain to the limo and raced to the airport and ran up the airstair. The hatch clunked and chunked closed and the jet rolled down the runway and we popped out of the clouds heading into a bright sunset. It was a long flight. The Major, Miguel, and Dhanpal rode it out in silence. If we were the kind to carry prayer beads, we would've worn them out.

Mercury paced back and forth on the ceiling, beside himself with anger. *Nobody hurts my Caesar and gets away with it. You hear me, dawg? The Gemonian Steps would be too nice for these bastards. We're going Chinese on this one: Lingchi. You cut out a chunk of flesh every couple hours. The guy doesn't die for days.*

The lost god was right: Larson was my responsibility. With or without the FBI's help, I was going to track down the cowboy and ... and what? Bring him to justice? No. Lingchi sounded like a damn good idea.

Tania was also wounded. That's why we didn't get word via normal channels. The emergency room contacted next of kin. Alan mentioned that fact somewhere over Illinois. He couldn't get hold of the emergency room doctor because of the incoming crush of wounded. So he preoccupied himself dialing every doctor from Seattle to San Diego. He asked them about his daughter's chances. Most of them didn't know or wouldn't render an opinion when they were miles away.

He didn't get anyone in the emergency room on the phone until we reached Nebraskan airspace. The staff were handling more than twenty critically wounded. That was just one hospital.

He offered huge incentives for specialists to drop what they were doing, go to the Bay Area, and do whatever needed to be done to save Pia. By the time we crossed Utah, he had ten doctors booking flights to San Jose. His own, Doc Günter, sat in the back, texting everyone he knew for an update.

The news reports rolled in, constantly changing and morphing as new facts emerged and old ones lost their shine. Twenty gunmen trimmed down to three. The number of dead and wounded rose and fell by the minute. The crowd had gone nuts and tackled everyone remotely Muslim-looking: Hindus, Sikhs, Armenians, Greeks—anyone not white, black, or Latino had been turned over to the Secret Service. The use of mostly-plastic weapons emerged by the time we crossed from Nevada into California.

Then the worst news arrived: Marty Maddox was dead.

His death brought home Ms. Sabel's mortality for all of us. She'd cheated death so many times we'd come to believe she was invincible. For the first time, we considered the very real possibility that she might not make it.

No one said that out loud.

The Secret Service lost three of their own, the head of the candidate's detail among them. The breakdown in security was under review. The methods used were compared to the Paris attacks in the fall of 2015—only it was more insidious because they managed to evade the metal detectors. The spokesman cited Pia Sabel, seriously wounded in the attack, for jumping one of the attackers and keeping him alive. The killer was still unconscious from the vicious blindside blow Ms. Sabel delivered. His recovery was questionable.

The death toll rose to thirty-five, the wounded to sixty-one.

Alan waved his hands to quiet everyone. The Major muted the news.

As we taxied to the hangar in the early evening dark, he clicked off his call and jumped up. "She's alive. Abdominal wound and potential internal damage, the radiologist hasn't read the charts yet. But she's going to make it."

Everyone celebrated.

Tania called me in the middle of our shouts for joy. Only it wasn't Tania. It was a nurse. She told me Tania was going into surgery. Three bullets: one through her collar bone, one clipped her ear, and the last cracked her skull open. She could give me no encouragement.

Our collective mood soured when I relayed the news.

Two limos whisked us to the hospital. The place was crawling with cops. We had to convince them we were neither reporters nor terrorists nor vigilantes.

When we were allowed in, Ms. Sabel was sedated in a private suite. Alan and the Major went to her room. Dhanpal took first watch in the hallway. Miguel and I stood outside the emergency entrance under the overhang for arriving vehicles.

David Watson could have prevented this attack. I dialed him to tell him what I thought of him.

But he didn't pick up.

He drove up.

Three midsized sedans screeched to a stop on drizzle-slicked pavement six inches from my shins. Watson and Verges got out of the middle car. Watson steamed toward me like an angry train. Verges followed behind, making *take-it-easy* gestures with his hands.

"Why the hell didn't you turn Hakim over when you first landed in the States?" Watson shouted loud enough for the press corps to hear.

He strode straight to me, his face bunched up like a fist, going for nose to nose intimidation. But Miguel's hand shot past my shoulder, hit Watson square in the chest, and laid the agent out on the sidewalk.

He sprawled like an upside-down turtle until he righted himself and rose to standing. Wiping drizzle-splatter off himself, he moved a respectful distance from Miguel's considerable reach.

"Why are you handling this case, Watson?" I asked.

"I don't discuss assignments with you."

"Why didn't they assign the terrorism branch? At least they know what they're doing."

"They're taking over now. But they have their hands full doing the standard methodology. I'm in charge of you."

Which would only happen if the FBI Director had told him to drop everything and do the work he should've done when I came back from Syria. If Ms. Sabel weren't bleeding upstairs, I would've decked the prick a second time.

I leaned back and crossed my arms. "So you're here to work with me and this is your way of collaborating?"

Watson looked at the ground, then over his shoulder at Verges, who wore an I-told-you-so face. He faced me. "Verges vouched for you. You need to find this Larson guy."

"Me?" I leaned forward again. "You need to get hold of Admiral Tilden's phone logs and find out who put him up to this."

"We'll work the Navy. You work on finding Larson."

"Because you're scared of him?"

"You're the only one who's seen him." Watson pushed up to me, doing his best to intimidate me. "You brag about sneaking in and out of Syria. You claim to have captured one of his boys. Time to live up to all your bullshit."

"OK, I'll do your job for you." I pushed a finger into his chest. "What happened to the DNA I brought back from As Sukhnah?"

"You were right. His name is Michael Larson. Served time for murder and drug distribution, paroled out six months ago, then disappeared. Facial recognition software didn't find him anywhere in Mountain View or Palo Alto. We're still scanning." Watson reached in his inside coat pocket and pulled out a few sheets of paper, folded neatly. He shoved them in my hands. "That's his prison photo. We don't have any footage of him going into the amphitheater, but it's not hard to defeat those systems. Before she passed out, your girlfriend Tania Cooper told the EMTs that she saw Larson. She said you'd find him. So get moving."

Watson turned around and walked back to his car. Verges shrugged and joined him.

Mercury watched him leave. *Nice guy. Reminds me of Coriolanus, the traitor. Don't trust him for a minute, brotha.*

I said, *Why do I have to find Larson?*

Mercury said, *Because, it's an impossible task, so he's going to the press with the pictures and you're going to the streets to die.*

I looked at Watson's papers: all the background on Larson's massive meth operation and territorial disputes with the Mexican drug cartels. This guy fought the nastiest cartels and won. They found the bodies of his enemies spread from Oklahoma to the Dakotas. They never found the heads. No wonder I hadn't caught him yet.

Then I noticed the worst part: the picture they had of him wasn't him. Michael Larson's mugshot was the same guy but with different brow ridges and a higher nose. The Larson I shot in As Sukhnah had higher cheekbones, a razor-sharp jawline, and the kind of chin dimple that was all the rage in Hollywood.

"Hey," I shouted at Watson. "Your pictures are out of date. He's had cosmetic surgery."

"Got a better one?" He stood with his door open, one leg in, one leg out.

I shook my head.

The Feds got in their cars. Their doors slammed, their transmissions clunked into gear, and they drove away.

Miguel tapped my shoulder and pointed through the glass doors at a TV hanging high on a wall in the Emergency Room. President Hunter stood behind a podium, straightening papers and looking around at the reporters. She looked pissed.

We went inside and joined a few staff members under the screen. Six cops on duty, protecting the wounded terrorist from a lynching, huddled in with us.

Hunter cleared her throat and looked at her papers. She looked up and started to speak. But she didn't speak. She looked down at her notes again and her face turned crimson, tears streamed down her face. She looked up, her lips quivering, her face trembling. She threw her notes sideways.

"Hours ago I endorsed Marty Maddox—and now he's dead," she shouted. She glared into the camera. "Goddamn it, when a bunch of fucking terrorists kill an American candidate, they deserve to die. All of them. I'll ask Congress for a declaration of war against ISIL and anyone who helps them. Tonight. We will annihilate anyone who looks like them or says something bad about America. We'll cut them down. Kill them all."

She glared around the silent room and into the camera. She looked so scary, I jumped when her gaze fell my way.

A middle-aged lady standing next to me shoved her fist in the air. "You tell 'em, Veronica."

Miguel and I glanced around us. A cheer went up and everyone clapped.

Hunter stormed off the stage, followed by her aides and generals, all of whom looked surprised. More than surprised. They were shocked. The standard presidential response is to call for a period of mourning, pay respects to the surviving families, all that stuff. This lady went straight out and grabbed war powers.

Miguel leaned over. "Did the President of the United States just drop an F-bomb on national TV?"

"Guess she was pissed." I backed away from the nurses. "What's Larson got planned for the other six martyrs?"

"She didn't mention Larson." Miguel shook his head. "She didn't assign the Terrorism group to Hakim. She knows Roche's friends are funding this. So why is she going to war?"

Mercury tapped my shoulder. *Look outside, homie. That's the motherfucker right there. Go get him.*

I turned to see my reflection in the windows with nurses and cops behind me. *Who?*

Dude, it's the dude. Larson. He's right there looking at you.

I walked over to the wide glass doors, trying to see outside. They whooshed open in front of me. A man in cowboy boots with a Freedom buckle and Larry Mahan hat threw his leg over a Harley FXB Sturgis on the sidewalk. He took a quick, panicked look over his shoulder. Our eyes met for a split second. In that instant, I felt the purity of the fear and hate he had for me. He kicked it over and revved the Harley. With one last glance my way, he tapped the gearshift with his toe, dropped the clutch, and sped away.

CHAPTER 38

PIA COULD FEEL HER FATHER'S hand holding hers. She caught a glimpse of him somewhere down a long, gray tunnel. When she shifted her head to see him better, she saw a hint of his profile as her eyes swept past him. She tried to stop her head from moving but her muscles didn't respond. Her narrow field of vision fell to the wall. A groan of disappointment escaped.

Hands pulled her head back upright and propped pillows on either side. The only thing she could see was a glow above her head and a flickering light above her feet. After a moment of confusion, she decided the flickering light was a TV.

Her father's face came into view. Up close. He said something in a strange and muddy language. The Major leaned into view from the other side. She frowned. Maybe. Then they disappeared. All Pia could see was the back of their heads. They were watching TV.

With some considerable effort, she focused on the TV. President Hunter in a gray, cotton-candy room. Bright face and hair. Yelling. The President of the United States of America was yelling something that made everyone gasp.

Three people were in Pia's room.

She twisted to see where the third voice came from. A person next to the Major. Was it Stefan? It should be Stefan. But it wasn't Stefan. It was a woman. In uniform. Not military. Not police.

Words caught up to her slowly. The President said "fuck." Then she said "war." Pia thought it was nice to hear the President use a bad word. Maybe they should do that more often. War was not something they should say often.

Pia lifted her hand but it weighed too much. She couldn't see what they put on top of her arm to hold it down. She tried the other one. Same problem. Panic set in. Was she strapped down? She had to tell them, no war. No war. They were not terrorists, they were mercenaries. Different problem. Different solution.

She tried to scream "no war" but nothing came out of her mouth. Maybe a vowel fell out.

She tried again. Noises. Only noises.

A stranger leaned into her view. The woman in uniform. Just a flash, then gone. A nurse? Her father's face came next.

Once in a great while she felt vulnerable. Once when she was four. Again when she broke her leg in a game. After she'd been tortured by the CIA. And a few other times. Those were the times Alan came into view. Dad. He was always there when something bad happened. She felt his hand stroking hers.

She heard his soothing voice. "Everything's going to be fine. Take it easy, Princess. Go back to sleep. I'll be right here the whole time. I'll be here when you wake up."

★ ★ ★

ALAN SABEL LOOKED ACROSS HIS daughter's sheets to Jonelle Jackson, the Major, and whispered. "Could you understand her?"

The Major shook her head.

He turned his gaze back to Pia's face. So pale. He asked the nurse for a wet washcloth. She brought one. He wiped it gently across her forehead, then down her cheek.

"She's asleep again." The nurse took the washcloth.

Alan stepped around the foot of the bed and stood close to the Major, and spoke in a soft voice. "Get every available Sabel agent on this. Put out a bounty. Double any reward to whatever the cops put out. Triple it."

"Did that an hour ago." She uncrossed her arms and squeezed his shoulder.

"Yeah, right. We talked. I forgot." He crossed to the window and looked into the black night. "I didn't get her this far in life to lose her to some scumbag terrorists."

The Major joined him and put her arms around him. Inky raindrops rolled down the dark glass.

"Have you been following her latest project?" Alan hugged her. "How the hell did Hunter get her caught up in this stupid campaign?"

"It's not the 'how' that worries me," the Major said, "it's the why."

"Money." Alan leaned back and gazed at her. "Good thing I hadn't wired the $100 mil yet."

The Major scowled. "How can you think about the money at a time like this?"

"Sorry, Jonelle. It's an all-consuming thought. It's what I fall back on in crisis mode." He pulled her tight. "What do you mean, if you didn't mean money?"

★ ★ ★

PRESIDENT VERONICA LODGE HUNTER PUSHED one of the generals out of her way. "I wasn't asking if kicking their asses was a good idea. I said we're going to do it."

"That's what we're trying to tell you," an admiral behind her said. "Every ass we kick brings ten more."

"Then kill the next ten and the next and the next."

The admiral threw up his hands and turned to a colleague, another guy with three stars on his lapel. The man said, "With all due respect, Madam President, the only end to that plan is genocide. There's a reason we sent the Turks, Iraqis, and Iranians after ISIL."

"Pretty goddamned ineffective, weren't they?" Hunter jutted her jaw. "Quit stalling and start making plans."

The collective sigh from the Joint Chiefs and their aides sounded more like a hiss. They filed out of the Oval Office stooped and slumped, resigned to their fate.

One man remained on the couch, manspreading like a boss: the Chairman of the Joint Chiefs. He flashed the four stars on his epaulets. "The trouble with killing terrorists is, that's what they want."

"Happy to oblige." She gave him her best withering look. "Let's send every last martyr to Allah."

He grinned. "Separatists are a pain and a horror and should not exist. But they do. And they always have. Thirteen colonies terrorized British interests until the British went home. The Vietnamese did the same thing to us. The IRA, Basques, Taliban, Uyghurs, FARC—the list is endless. Why take on ISIL now?"

"Did you miss something?" Her voice shook with anger. "An American candidate is dead."

"A national tragedy. But so is an endless, unwinnable war in a hellhole on the other side of the globe." He rose with theatrical movements, spreading his arms in the air. "No one cares if a hundred thousand towelheads volunteer for target practice. Least of all me." He stuck his index finger in Hunter's face. "But I'm not ready to bring home a hundred thousand American coffins just so you can catapult your failed one-term presidency into NEXT USA's open slot."

CHAPTER 39

IN THE DARK RECESSES OF his suite high atop the Fairmont Hotel, the Artist pushed the room service cart into the living room to rid himself of the post-lunch stench of clams and cursed the wait staff for not moving quickly enough. "Why am I pushing this damned cart?"

The butler jumped to attention and wheeled away the offending dishes.

He closed the doors and hurried back to the TV. Reporters sifted through eyewitnesses, many of whom were fellow reporters there to cover the event. As the dispatches droned out dirges, his excitement grew. He clasped his hands and restrained his desire to jump up and down. "Oh, this is so much better than I anticipated."

Across the darkened sitting room, next to the only light bulb, Schwartz sat motionless.

"You're not happy?" the Artist asked. "You helped make this a success. We've saved the United States of America from a socialist dictatorship."

"Maddox was a centrist." The thin man leaned over and threw up into the trash can. He heaved and spluttered and spit the last. He cleared his throat, then said, "Don't say 'we.' I didn't have anything to do with this ... this atrocity."

"You better not miss that bucket." The Artist watched Schwartz dry heave. "And go flush that. Call the maid in, have her bring a new can. Disgusting."

The Artist changed the channel. A commentator echoed President Hunter's call to action, an all-out war on ISIL. A counterpoint view was given by the next commentator, that a war would be unwinnable. The Artist searched for more talking heads and found even less interest in a ground war and more yearning to follow Maddox's plan to get the nation off oil, thereby denuding terrorists of their income.

Another channel gave the day over to Marty Maddox's legacy. Half a million people turned out in San Francisco to cross the Golden Gate Bridge on foot. A million held candles on the National Mall in DC. Uncountable millions circled Central Park in an endless procession. Tens of millions around the country showed their solidarity by changing their party affiliation to NEXT USA.

"NBC is projecting NEXT USA to be the nation's largest party by next week," one of the talking heads reported.

The Artist twisted from the screen to glare at Schwartz. "Did you hear that? What is wrong with these people? It's only been hours and already everyone's out to support those lunatics."

"They were already popular." Schwartz flopped his hands on the arms of the chair. "What did you expect?"

"I expect people to rise up against their oppressors. I expect people to realize how Chuck Roche has been right all these years." He twisted back to the TV. "Maddox wasn't a serious candidate. He was going to ruin the country. We have to do something. We still have a few Moroccans left."

"What does that mean?"

"We'll send them into the crowds. We'll start the revolution the hard way."

Schwartz stood, his weak knees wobbling, and stared at his boss. "You're insane. Mass murderers like you always think they're going to start a popular uprising. Charlie Manson thought he was igniting a giant race war. Omar Mateen thought American Muslims would erupt in violence after the Orlando shooting. You're just as delusional as they were. You didn't save the country, you killed a bunch of innocent people. I'm done."

The thin man started for the door.

The Artist grabbed him by the arms. "Don't you dare walk out on me."

"What're you going to do?" Schwartz leaned his weight into his boss. "Larson said you ordered him to kill me. He still has my children. I'm a dead man no matter what I do."

There was only one place the skinny coward would go if he thought his fate was sealed: straight to the authorities. The glorified bookkeeper could ruin everything in one interrogation. It would be easy for Schwartz to piece it all together for the Feds.

"Stop thinking passively." The Artist held firm. "He insisted on murdering you because you squealed on him. Be the aggressor. Turn the tables around. We'll set a trap. Do you have any more men in the program?"

The thin man stopped pushing against the Artist.

"What kind of trap?" He took a step back.

"We'll tell him you're at my ranch. I think there's one called Mildred Ridge only a few hours away. He'll go there to kill you, but your guys will jump him before he gets there."

Schwartz nodded and thought. He paced a few steps away, then back.

"Might work." He clasped his hands behind his back. "What about his Moroccans? He turned himself into their spiritual leader."

"I'll make that part of the deal. He sends them on their last attack before he gets you. They'll have martyred themselves, leaving him alone. He'll walk into an ambush."

"No." Schwartz looked sick and moved away. "I can't be part of any more terrorist attacks."

"Don't snivel." The Artist followed and stood over his shoulder. "He has your children. You're their protector. It's time to act like a man and do what needs to be done."

The truth of the matter hit Schwartz hard. His face turned white. The gaunt little fellow's breathing hitched.

"Get them freed first. My kids." He swallowed. "Before you do anything else."

"Sure. Whatever."

"Swear to me."

"Of course, of course. Do it for the children. Hold your head high, it's a noble price to pay. Now get out of here and find the men you'll need. Get out to Mildred Ridge before he does."

Schwartz picked his raincoat off the back of a chair and slipped into it as he walked out.

The Artist paced the room with a wary eye on the news.

He couldn't believe that sniveling Schwartz. How dare the little weasel question his methods. What was wrong with a few casualties in the grand scheme of things? Did Truman hesitate when they estimated a hundred thousand civilian casualties in Hiroshima? Of course not. These are the decisions great men make when the need arises. Soon, Roche and the rest would see how his plan had been as brilliant as it was necessary. They would call for the genius who dreamed it up to come forward. Then he would bask in the glow of their adoration.

The fools who fret and whine about humanity have no idea how meaningless their pitiful lives are. What difference does it make to a great nation if a few hundred dog-walkers are missing tomorrow?

But if the US let a man like Marty Maddox run the country, the economy would collapse. After a few days of mourning over a lost fantasy, the public would move on. Whereas losing a great man like Chuck Roche—that would change the world forever. His impact on oil refining strengthened America and secured the energy sector when the market was most volatile. Who could trust a bike-riding vegetarian to guide the transition from oil to the fantasy of nuclear fusion? A change like that would cause a global depression the likes of which had never been seen in the history of the world.

Maddox was the greater threat to humanity.

Was.

Roche's face appeared on the screen. The old man looked pale and haggard and sick. The Artist turned up the volume. A reporter asked a question and Roche answered. "I was not a fan of Governor Maddox, but attacking an American candidate is an act of war against the American system of governement. President Hunter has my full support. I condemn this cowardly act with all my heart and soul."

The Artist couldn't believe his ears.

That backstabbing wretch.

He did it for Roche.

Was the old man so out of touch he couldn't see the beauty of it? Wasn't it for courageous acts like this that the APA was formed in the first place? Wasn't killing off the minor threats to the American way of life the whole reason the APA existed? Now that he was chairman, these decisions were his to make.

He called the Slager. No answer.

He left a message. "You've done well. I'm pleased with the results. Since you didn't waste the whole crew, you'll have two more attacks to finish. Then you can go and live happily ever after. Oh, and one last thing—Schwartz is plotting to ambush you. Maybe you should do something about that man."

CHAPTER 40

I PULLED MY PISTOL AS the Harley Sturgis roared off, fishtailing on the wet asphalt. A cop car parked halfway up the emergency drive denied Larson access to the main boulevard. He swerved left into a parking lot spread over several acres.

No line of sight.

I held my fire.

I sensed Miguel running up behind me. "Larson! Get the cops. He's on a Harley."

I took off running, taking a shortcut. Rows of cars packed neatly together became an obstacle course. They were side-by-side and nose to nose with decorative plantings in between. The first row was fine, but the second was packed too close to squeeze through. I jumped on a slick hood and from there onto a wet roof. Aiming where his engine roared I could see nothing more than his shadow flashing between sodium lights. Larson was running lights out.

Crossing via rooftops, minivan to minivan, sheet metal buckled under my weight only to snap back when I moved on. I slipped and hopped my way down the lane. He turned into my row, riding straight for me. I stopped on the roof of a small sedan and aimed carefully.

He fired off four rounds. An automatic weapon firing without the need for repeated trigger pulls. A military-grade weapon.

I dove to the ground and lost my Glock on the landing.

The Sturgis roared away while I scrabbled under a car to retrieve my weapon. My fingertips felt the trigger guard. I hooked it with my little finger and dragged it backward until my elbow couldn't contract any farther in the tight space. Without releasing my pinkie-grip, I pulled my body out.

His engine roared away, growing more distant by the second.

Once my pistol was secure, I ran as fast as I could, heading for the street. I vaguely recalled the parking area being recessed below a knee-high berm. His Harley was no dirt bike. With any luck, he'd have to return to the main entry.

I ran up the berm, through a decorative hedge, and came out street-side next to the big EMERGENCY directional sign, glowing under a spot light. From the sound echoing off the building, Larson had reached the same conclusion and was smart enough to know I'd be waiting for him. The approach was a sweeping turn, made for an ambulance to take at fair speed without spilling the precious cargo inside. No sudden rights or lefts that might dump a patient out of the gurney at the last minute. Larson revved the engine at the top. I crouched behind the metal signage and leveled my sights.

He dumped the clutch and pulled a wheelie, leaving me with little more than his feet and engine plate as targets.

I fired three shots. The first cracked someone's windshield and set off the car alarm. The second sparked on his frame. The third went into the darkness and filled me with dread that I'd hear the scream of a bystander wounded or killed.

People who'd never been in a real gunfight had a deeply held belief in movie-magic: when a bullet misses its target, it loses the will to live, suffers from the shame, and falls harmlessly to the ground, a hopeless failure. In reality, the bullet continues to travel forward until it destroys something. One might want to believe gravity will pull it down, but, according the NRA Firearms Fact Book, that doesn't happen for up to a mile. Anything between the shooter and the end of that mile-long range is toast.

I didn't hear anything bad. I heard something worse.

Larson firing his automatic weapon from the saddle of the Sturgis. Some shooters don't concern themselves with velocity and range of the flying bullets much less the collateral damage his undisciplined shots will cause. Larson fell in that camp. He fired in my general direction, forcing me below my signage and maintained the fusillade as he sped past me and skidded the bike into a full left turn onto the drive. His knee grazed the pavement like a pro racer.

He continued the turn, crossing Grant Street between cars in light traffic and flew down the four-lane road before I could get a bead on him.

The noisy bike wailed into the middle distance. Maybe three hundred yards away, beyond my visual range, the noise changed.

He stopped.

Then it started up again, louder and higher pitched. It thundered away. Then the sound of screeching metal on pavement and a collision reached me. Horns honked.

Miguel led two cops on foot to my position. Miguel said, "Did you get him?"

"Laid the bike down. He's waiting in the bushes for me to inspect the wreckage."

"Evil."

The cops looked at each other and at me. "Who are you guys?"

We explained and sent the local PD to look for him, but I wasn't holding out much hope. A guy smart enough to circle the globe with ten terrorists wasn't going to be caught in the endless rabbit warren of suburban California. I gave my statement to the uniformed officer, then the detective, then the lieutenant, then the captain.

Everyone wanted to know why Larson came to the hospital. My guess was he wanted to kill the injured terrorist to make sure the guy didn't talk. But the word about Larson's existence hadn't circulated to the street level yet. They gave me their suspicious looks.

Mercury stepped into the empty space. *I cannot believe you missed him. You could've been a hero, homie. I'm so disappointed in you right now.*

I said, *Why don't you tell me something useful? Like how do I find this guy?*

Mercury shrugged. *Don't play stupid with me. You know damn well how to contact this asshole.*

I looked around. A news van idled at the far curb.

I marched straight to it. A middle-aged woman sat on the open sliding door talking to a cameraman with a vape.

"Want a big scoop?"

The vape guy blew a cloud of smoke. The middle-aged woman brushed her hair away from red, swollen eyes and looked me up and down.

"I'm Jacob Stearne, head of Special Operations for Sabel Security. The shooter who just left here is responsible for the attack on Marty Maddox. He brought the terrorists into the country."

She squinted at me as she rose to standing. "Got ID? Anything to back up your story?"

I handed her my Sabel ID. "My story is proven by the fact that he just left here firing on full auto. Or maybe you missed that."

"He shot my driver." Her face was rock solid. Her makeup streaked by tears. She was in no mood for games.

Behind her I noticed a spider web of cracks in the windshield. I looked across the street and triangulated my line of fire to make sure I wasn't the killer. I wasn't.

"Fire up the camera. Can you broadcast live?"

A few seconds later, she made a tearful announcement on live TV, then introduced me. She interviewed me about why Larson came to the hospital and what caused the gunfire.

I answered her questions with a certain amount of anxiety building inside me until it exploded.

I skipped her last question and turned into the bright lights and glassy eye of the camera. "Michael Larson, the cops and the public want proof, evidence, and a fair trial. Good for them. You and I know who brought Hakim and Youssef and eight other terrorists to this country—you. I'm going to end your miserable life. Don't bother running. Don't bother trying to hide. Call me—I'll make it quick."

I held up my cell phone and gave out the number.

When I finished, there was a second of silence, then the camera guy killed the light. "We're off the air."

"I hope you know what you're doing," the reporter said. "That video's going viral and your phone's going to ring with a thousand teenaged boys, and a thousand lonely old people, and a thousand—"

"As long as I get to put a bullet in his brain, I'll talk to them all." I pushed past her and headed back to the emergency room.

Halfway across Grant Street, my cell rang. Blocked caller ID. I answered.

"Well, hello, Jacob Stearne. You're the guy who shot me in the leg back in Syria. I've got six Moroccans left and I've given them your picture and your full resume. Yeah, you should tell your company not to brag about your heroic deeds on their website, cause now my boys know all about you—and how many heroes of the Caliphate you've killed. So, c'mon, motherfucker, let's get this party lit."

He clicked off.

Larson wasn't the kind of guy to stream live TV news on his phone. Which meant he was nearby, in the shadows, watching me make my statement live.

I turned around.

CHAPTER 41

PIA LEANED FORWARD, HOLDING her rolling IV, and squeezed Tania's hand. Machines beeped the status for vital signs, medications, and solutions. The monotony of them gave her an odd sense of calm. The doctors had done their best; the rest was up to Tania. She was tough, with a survivor's force of will. She would make it. She had to. Pia needed her and Tania knew it.

Tania's eyes remained closed.

"She's heavily sedated," the nurse said. "She doesn't even know you're here."

"I know she's here." Pia stroked Tania's cool forehead.

"You shouldn't stay. You can't be on your feet too long if you want to recover."

It was an undeniable argument. Pia could feel her stitches complaining from the moment she swung her feet over the edge of her bed. Walking was a bad idea, but Pia had always pushed the recovery envelope.

Making matters worse, Doc Günter appeared in the doorway. "There you are. Not even in a wheelchair. You need to be in bed."

"I need to move." Pia stroked Tania's hand once more and faced Doc. "But I'll be a good little girl and go back for a while—if that makes everyone happy."

She took a last glance around the gloomy room. Blue daylight filtered in the window from the cloudy day outside. Ultra-clean linoleum and unscented scrubbing products left a sterile feel in her nose. An ICU was no place to recover.

With Doc Günter on one side and the ever-present nurse on the other, she shuffled her way through the maze of hallways back to her room.

The Major stood at the window, looking over her shoulder with a phone pressed to her ear. "Just a minute, Madam President. She just came back."

Pia took the offered phone and gingerly sat on the edge of the bed. "My condolences on your loss."

"America's loss, Pia." Hunter's voice wavered. She took a breath to steady herself. "A national tragedy. He could've brought us all together." She sniffled and blew her nose as discretely as she could. "But how are you? The country is proud of you."

Pia fiddled with the sheets and tossed them back. "It was too late."

"Alan tells me you're expected to recover in time." Hunter paused, but Pia didn't fill the gap. "I'm praying for Tania. How is she doing?"

"In the ICU." She swung her legs up on the bed and felt a jolt of pain through her core. "War in the Middle East is wrong and you know it."

"Unity." Hunter took a deep breath. "Some things are more important than right or wrong. When Americans pull together in a crisis, they forget their differences. Those were the goals that attracted you to NEXT USA."

"We know the enemy is an American."

"If we blame Roche's rich and powerful friends—" Hunter's voice rose in volume "—we'll create a tremendous divide without any result. Besides, we don't even know who to blame. All we have are a few texts you gained illegally. No, we won't fight phantoms. We fight the war everyone will rally around."

"That's Vietnam or Iraq all over again." Pia gingerly tucked her legs under the sheets and covered herself. "Thousands will die on the basis of manufactured intelligence."

"We do it for the good of the country." Hunter softened. "You're the heroine of the hour. The people need to hear from you. We need your support."

Pia couldn't understand the statement for a few seconds. "I will not endorse a war elsewhere when there are six more terrorists in the country right now—and you know they were financed by an American."

"Keep your eye on our goals." Hunter's voice turned harsh. "You want nuclear fusion. You know it'll eliminate our dependence on Arab oil. We're their biggest customer and they've been hijacking our planes and murdering our citizens for decades. If you don't stand with me, you're aiding these mass murderers. But if you stand up to them, you're helping put Americans back to work. You're helping us bring the country together. Taking the war to the Middle East will accomplish our dream for the nation. Pia, you must stand with me at this critical time."

"Stand with you?" Pia looked to the Major. "How do I know you're not the Artist?"

"Pia Sabel, how dare you accuse—"

"Fuck you." Pia clicked off and started to throw it at the wall. She caught herself and tossed the phone at the foot of the bed. She thought about Chuck Roche and his case of new phones.

The Major caught her eye and raised her brows. Pia filled her in on the conversation.

Stefan knocked on the door and leaned in with a big smile and a balloon bouquet. Pia pushed her hair back and sat up.

Before he could speak, Doc Günter blocked him. "She needs her rest. Perhaps tomorrow—"

"Now is fine." Pia hoped she didn't look too eager to see him.

Stefan bowed to Doc and smiled at the Major and tied the bouquet loosely to the side rail near the foot of the bed.

She offered a hand. He took it and gazed into her eyes. She took a deep breath. How do you repair a relationship as short and stormy as theirs? A thousand thoughts about what to say came into her head. Each one evaluated and rejected as either inflammatory or trite. He remained stoic—or was going through the same search for words. The net result: silence.

A group of doctors, making their rounds, stepped in and ushered everyone out. Stefan kissed her cheek, whispered something stilted about praying for her recovery, promised to return, then reluctantly left.

The doctors hooked up machines and examined wounds and changed dressings and made pronouncements and gave instructions to Doc Günter as if Pia wasn't there. Günter thanked them for coming and told them Pia would follow some instructions and not others because that's the kind of woman she was and always would be. They complained, but the Major came back and backed him up. The cadre of physicians left, grumbling.

Then the room was quiet for a moment.

A silhouette of a man stood in her open door and knocked gently. Slightly stooped with thin gray hair, he held flowers in one hand. The other rested on a silver-handled cane. "After some reflection, I came to admire the mercury-polluted water in my swimming pool."

With a glance to Pia, the Major asked if she should kick Roche out.

Pia waved her off and raised her bed. "Come in."

"Could I speak to you privately?" he asked.

Doc Günter and the nurse scurried out. The Major crossed her arms.

"That was a dirty trick to play on an old man." He approached and held out the flowers to the Major, who made no effort to help him. "But I came to pay my respects to the obstinate woman who pulled it off."

Pia stared at him.

He set the flowers on the counter nearby. "My wife says it was the kind of trick I used to pull when I was young and impetuous."

He took a long look at the Major.

She took a long look at him.

"She's my trusted adviser," Pia said. "Why are you here?"

He shook his head. "Your tackle of the terrorist went viral. I must admit, it was as impressive as it was selfless."

"You should try 'selfless' sometime. Everything you've ever done was to benefit you, your family, or your company."

"Family is important. Without it—"

"Community is more important. Without it, you're just another tribe on the plains dodging sabre-tooths. State is more important than community. And your country, if you value freedom, outranks them all. Everyone else came to that conclusion yesterday. Did you?"

Roche bit back his anger, taking a long breath, glancing out the window, before returning his gaze to Pia. "Regardless of my opinion, your actions were commendable."

"That's not why you came." She pushed up and repositioned herself to see him eye to eye. "I offered to find the Artist. You refused."

He clasped both hands over the silver handle and bowed his head. "You're right. I need help."

"Why now?"

"The FBI came to me. They asked many questions. They knew many things. But they didn't know the nickname the Artist gave himself." He paused and leaned forward. "But you knew. That means, you've been reading my texts."

"So?"

Roche straightened up, indignant. "That's illegal."

"So?"

He spluttered, looking for the right words. "I'll sue you."

"You aided a terrorist plot by not reporting it. Sue me and that's my defense. You'll win your case but the world will know what a scumbag you are. Instead of exposing one of your friends as a madman—and facing the embarrassing facts—you chose to keep it to yourself."

His translucent skin trembled and turned red. "You used that information to screw me out of the refinery and stick me with the fine."

"That's all you think about? Yourself?" Pia scoffed. "I read more than your texts. I read your emails too. You referred to unloading a 'multimillion-dollar problem on an overconfident child'. You were all for it until you realized I won that round."

He blushed. "Why were you reading my personal messages?"

"Hunter asked me to find these guys. We tracked him to Rancho Mirage. Then we hit a wall."

"Hunter?" He choked and looked up at the Major. "Is this true? The Artist was there? Next to me?"

She confirmed with a nod.

The weight of his complicity took hold. He fell sideways, grabbed her bedrail, and righted himself. His face went from red to white in a second. "How can you be—"

He broke down.

The Major picked up a tissue box and handed it to him.

He sniffled and blew his nose and sucked some air and raised his chin. Then he said, "You're sure it's someone close to me, someone I know?"

"Yes." Pia waited until he looked up. "We narrowed it to one of four people."

Roche stammered three times without producing an intelligible syllable. He stopped trying and took a deep breath. "I need your help."

Then he pulled his phone out and offered it to Pia on an extended, trembling hand.

A text from the Artist to Roche: "Because you failed to appreciate those who look out for your interests—you're next."

CHAPTER 42

THE SLAGER LAY ON A big bed in the master bedroom of the empty rental in the Marina District and watched his old mug shot flash on the screen. A reporter advised viewers to report the man to authorities. "Do not approach him. He's presumed armed and dangerous."

He wondered if Schwartz's doctor had done enough to make him unrecognizable to the average citizen. It was a good job. High quality. He didn't even recognize himself. Ethan and Emma wouldn't recognize him when he picked them up. They were young, he could explain that away.

Cops were another story. A suspicious bunch by nature, they could see a guy's rap sheet on his face, his guilt written in his eyes, they could sense his intent before he had intent. The cops would be a problem.

A noise at the back of the townhouse brought him up quickly. The Moroccans were upstairs cycling through the showers and otherwise making noise, but something caught his ear. He jumped off the bed, grabbed his pistol, and tiptoed down the staircase.

At the back door, an intruder pushed against his hasty defense, a bookcase shoved against the door. Inching through the kitchen, he grabbed a knife from the block. He backed up to the frame.

With any luck, whoever it was would give up and go away. Aside from Stearne and a few others who could ID him, he had no desire to kill anymore. But if he had to…

A middle-aged woman pushed through, cursing the cleaning crew for blocking her way.

She closed the door behind her and turned in time to see the flash of his knife before it ripped through her neck. Her eyes froze in horror, looking into his as she died. He lowered her body on the floor and let her bleed out.

She bled all over his shirt. He risked a quick look out the back anyway.

The sky was dim, the fog was thick, the rain was near.

A solitary Audi sat in the narrow driveway that slithered between townhouses to a garage in back. At least he had an extra set of wheels. Ditching the stolen Harley had left him riding with the crew. Across the way, an upstairs curtain began to pull back. Some nosy neighbor kept tabs on the tiny patch of yard. That moved the timeline up a whole lot.

He closed the door and looked at his victim. She looked like a real estate type doing a routine check on the property. Bad luck. Had to be done. No doubt about it. Like the cameraman from the street the night before. But, that was Stearne's fault. He should've taken what was coming to him like a man. Instead, he ran and hid and fired back, forcing the Slager to shoot indiscriminately. Stearne would understand collateral damage. When you fixate on your goal, there's bound to be unintended consequences.

Nonetheless, every dead body added to the risk.

He had to be more careful.

And he had to clear out.

The Slager ran upstairs, ignoring his throbbing bullet wound.

On his way, he thought about his lesson learned in Venezuela: kill the kids first. Why hang onto Schwartz' kids? They were a liability that slowed him down. He could kill them and record a greeting on his phone to show Schwartz. Just enough to keep the thin man doing what he wanted.

But killing them and leaving their bodies in the house would lead the cops to Schwartz. And he still needed the thin man. Schwartz wasn't much of a threat, but he was a clever negotiator. He'd managed to get away without giving up the Artist's name. Schwartz gave him only enough to move forward. His damn children would live at least one more day. Then he'd grab Schwartz and start pumping bullets into the brats until the bastard gave up the Artist.

Without warning, his memory recalled a triumphant return home after a few days away. Ethan and Emma ran to him, wrapped their arms around his calf, and hugged for all they were worth. Laughs and love.

There was no way in hell he could kill Schwartz's kids.

He'd have the Moroccans do it.

He jumped the last steps and landed on the third floor. The pain from his bullet wound nearly knocked him over. He staggered a couple steps and powered through it.

"Youssef." He grabbed his translator. "You take the kids in the minivan. Tape them up good. No noises. People are coming. We have to leave town right now."

"Let them come." Youssef smiled wide. "We're ready."

Was it an admirable dedication to their cause or abject stupidity that brought out the macho in these guys? What mattered was that he needed them to accomplish his goals.

"Not yet, brother." He looked into Youssef's eyes. "We need to attack in another place, at another time." He tried to think up something fast. "To make it look like there are more of us. To make them truly tremble."

Youssef nodded at the Slager's wisdom. "Yes, yes. They will tremble before us! OK. Take the minivan and children. Tape them up?"

"And meet me at 'Station C'. You still have that on your map?"

Youssef checked, nodded, and began shouting instructions to the others.

For his next move, the Slager had a decision to make: Stearne or his captured martyr? The Martyr could confirm whatever Hakim was telling them, making him a high priority. But the police coverage had been far greater than he had anticipated. The smart course of action was to abandon the Moroccans and get out. But the Artist already nixed that option by holding up his three million dollars. Quit now and he was short on the ranch in Argentina. At least the asshole agreed to change the targets, places, and times. That left Stearne and the big Indian as his top priority.

The Slager changed into clean clothes, changed the bandage on his leg, grabbed the woman's keys and phone, and backed her car down the narrow lane into the street.

Marketing a company as a brand-name operation also makes it easy to find. Sabel Security, and their minor celebrity owner, were high-profile enough that twelve phone calls to local hotels produced their location.

It took an hour to reach the Four Seasons in Silicon Valley. Sheets of glass rose into the sky, reflecting endless grayness behind an ordinary stone-and-glass building. He pulled around back to the service entrance and parked and got out and stood near the bushes overlooking the 101. He pretended to smoke and waited while several smokers came and went. Finally, a room service guy, slow and alone, came out for a cigarette. He strangled the young man behind a pickup truck and changed into his uniform. He swiped the badge on the security reader and opened the door and grabbed a cart and pushed it into the service elevator.

A maid shifted her cart to the side, making room for him. He smiled and stole her key card without her noticing.

At the fourth floor, he got off and used the phone in the service bay and called room service. He spoke in bad Spanish. "What room is Jacob Stearne? I have a delivery for him but they gave me the wrong room. Help me out before my boss finds out."

The guy on the other end told him.

He went straight to the seventh floor and peeked down the hall. No one there. He padded softly and knocked gently.

No answer.

He keyed the door and went in. Wet towels hung in the bathroom, rumpled sheets on the bed, open duffle on a chair, a bunch of funny-looking ammo on the bureau. He picked up a bullet and checked it out. Some kind of miniature dart. Three magazines of these darts lay abandoned on the bureau.

A text arrived on his burner.

In the text, the Artist named the new target, time, and location for the next attack. Grabbing a pen from the nightstand, the Slager jotted the info on hotel stationary and shoved the paper in his pocket.

He kept looking: under the bed, between the mattress and box spring, in the drawers.

The closet had something of interest. A hard-shell case, custom made with foam inserts for a small arsenal. The empty spaces spoke volumes about what was not in the room: an MP5SD assault rifle, four spare magazines, two Glocks and two spare magazines. Several different types of infrared laser pointers. A big, nasty looking knife and a boot knife. Jacob Stearne was ready for Armageddon. The Slager looked around. The only thing Stearne left behind were the darts.

He checked the room one last time. Nothing indicated where his intended victim had gone, yet he could feel the furious vibrations his prey left behind. Jacob Stearne was out, wandering the streets of the Bay Area, looking for Michael Larson. Unlike the cops and the general public, Stearne knew who he was hunting.

He liked Stearne. They were like prize fighters, circling each other.

The game was on.

He picked up the stationary and wrote Stearne a note: *Sorry to miss you. Too bad you couldn't help us take down Maddox and your boss. Meet us at the Golden Gate Bridge and you can celebrate with us. Praise Allah, brotha by anotha motha.*

CHAPTER 43

I LOOKED OVER THE EDGE of the Four Seasons' roof. A big-ass highway full of cars parked in both directions formed the northern perimeter. An office building stood to the east. A garage full of cars, some coming, some going, hemmed the south and west. It was a busy place hosting some kind of meeting for people in suits and shiny shoes.

No way in hell would I ever be a guy in a suit and shiny shoes going to a meeting. The tedium would drive me suicidal. For a moment I wondered if that was an underlying cause of the rising suicide rate among veterans. Did you wake up one day and realize you put your life on the line so guys in suits and shiny shoes could stop for a latte before going to the meeting? After you kill a hundred-forty-three people dedicated to ending your way of life—thirty-seven of them hand-to-hand—can you sit in a room and watch the riveting PowerPoint presentation, "Purchasing Perfection: How IBM Saved 6 Cents per Unit" without going mad?

Mercury said, *Aw, Homie. If you were a guy in a suit and shiny shoes going to a meeting, Yumi would be back at your crib gnawing on some Carolina ribs right now. Ya feel me?*

I said, *Don't talk about Yumi. Ever. Besides, Japanese women don't eat Carolina ribs. Too much fat.*

After all that sushi, they break like twigs before a plate of ribs, bro. You should pay attention to what Yumi needs. She needs ribs.

Ribs. Sick as it was, I couldn't even think about her. I knew why she left me. It wasn't food. I had to make a decision in life: quit this job and find a job cooking yakitori, or save the world from people like Larson.

My list of failures was long and detailed, but there was one occupation in life where I excelled: carnage.

Someday I'd face the fact that Yumi was better off marrying the sushi chef on her block. She could teach him how to tie her up and use ice cubes.

I said, *Where is Larson?*

Mercury leaned over the railing. *I'm telling you, brutha, he's down there. Looking for you.*

I said, *You sure he didn't go to Washington to kill the president?*

Mercury laughed. *Ah c'mon, brutha. Would he waste the time and ammo on Hunter? Who followed him around the world? Who kidnapped his martyr? His biggest problem is—you.*

I walked the length of the building's sweeping curve, hopping over AC ducts and leaning over periodically. The men in suits and shiny shoes (and they were predominately men—in Silicon Valley, everyone's all for equal rights as long as they don't have to hire women), hustled back and forth to the parking lot, mobile phones clamped to their ears.

If Larson and his Moroccans were going to strike an all-American target, Mercury's prediction about the Four Seasons sounded plausible. But I was losing my patience. The sooner I faced off with him, the better.

"Dead body here." Miguel's voice rolled in my earbud with an uncanny calmness. "Strangled and naked."

The wings on Mercury's helmet wiggled. *The dude is in your room right now. His guys put a bullet through Pia-Caesar-Sabel's midriff, he needs a slow, painful death. Crucifixion is perfect for this guy. You know, they don't put a nail through your hands and feet like the pictures of Jesus. They put it through your wrists and ankles. That way your weight is supported for a long time. The victim tries to hold himself up to keep his clavicle from breaking under the weight, but none of them can last more than a day or two doing that. Then—*

My wrists and ankles twitched. *Yeah. Just had breakfast. Can we come back to that later?*

I shifted my arsenal-backpack to running position and took the steps two at a time. I vaulted the bannisters at the landings. On the seventh floor, I burst from the stairwell. My feet stuck in pile carpeting so deep it almost threw me down. A swinging door was closing ahead of me.

The swinging stopped. A hand pushed it open a crack. A head poked out to look at me.

Larson.

My weapon was leveled an instant later, but the swinging door batted back and forth.

Bullets spewed out through the drywall.

Mercury said, *Shoot! Kill him!*

I said, *I can't. If I miss, I could kill a guest by accident.*

Mercury said, *So? What's a little collateral damage? Take a chance. I want this guy dead.*

Shaking off my bloodthirsty god, I backed into the concrete stairwell and shifted to the side that would give me an angle on Larson. I kept my boot in the door and my eye pressed to the small gap. He wasn't coming.

After too many seconds, I jumped across the hallway, leading with my sights. Nothing. I moved to the service door and tossed it open. Empty. An elevator hummed down its shaft.

"Miguel, he's coming down the service elevator."

"I've got his exit covered."

Back in the stairwell, I slid down the bannister and jumped over the edge. I took the steps two and three at a time and jumped the turns until I hit the ground floor. Outside, sirens wailed up the main entrance. People screamed on the far side of thick walls. A little automatic fire and the place had descended into chaos. Nerves were still sparking from the attack on Maddox.

When I popped out of the stairwell, I was in the lobby. Nowhere near the service elevator. A wall separated guests from the noise and smell of the kitchen. Cops were streaming in the main door, less than a hundred feet away.

A quick look around and I was off running to the small bar off the lobby. As I suspected, they had access to the kitchens through a swinging door.

Aiming down my sight, I crept along the wall toward the service elevator. The shaft opened into a staging area that faced away from the main kitchen. A blind corner. The perfect place for Larson to lie in wait. I stepped as far to the left as I could get, aiming and moving sideways. If you run around a corner tight to the wall, the other guy can stand next to the wall and shoot you. If you go wide, you can see his shoulder or foot and shoot through the drywall.

When I rounded the corner, Miguel aimed at me from twenty yards beyond.

The kitchen around us was silent. I looked around and saw twenty frightened faces. I holstered my weapon. "Sabel Security. We're the good guys. Did you see a man running through here?"

The first second after I asked, no one even blinked. Then someone shook his head and another joined him.

"He was in this elevator. Where else could he go?"

A big man pointed over his shoulder at the back door. A young woman pointed in the opposite direction. Another man pointed out the front.

"You," I pointed to the big man. "Pick up the largest pot you have and hold it up. If you see a guy who isn't me or a cop, drop the pot. I'll come save you."

Everyone scrambled into largest-pot-finding mode. They handed him a ten-gallon aluminum pan. He held it over his head.

"You check the back," I said to Miguel.

"Split up so he can kill us easier?" Miguel took point, heading toward the back door, the smoker's exit. "We go together."

The din of the highway drowned out any discussion when we opened the door. Nothing left, nothing right. Straight ahead, a man started up an Audi and backed up. Miguel stood in his path, I ran to the driver's window, aiming at the heavily tinted glass.

A man, not Larson, rolled the window down. I motioned for him to get out.

Holding his hands above his head, looking scared, a busboy got out.

"Is there anyone in the car with you?" I asked.

He shook his head.

Miguel checked the back and trunk.

"Why? Is it stolen?" The boy nodded at the car.

"Where did you get it?"

"A guy gave me a fifty to pick up his wife at the train."

"What guy, where?"

"A guy. Second floor, Ballroom."

"In a suit?"

"No, jeans and plaid shirt. Look." The boy pulled a folded fifty out of his shirt pocket. "See?"

Two cops came around the bend. Another pair leaned out of the kitchen door. Four weapons drawn on us.

"DROP YOUR WEAPONS NOW! HANDS IN THE AIR."

CHAPTER 44

PIA ROLLED THE IV STAND down the hall, making the fifth circumnavigation of the floor and feeling better about her recovery. In the two days since the attack, she had to spend every lucid hour chasing away nurses with pain medication so she could think. Her thoughts were more like endless questions. Could Hunter be the Artist? Why hadn't she tapped Stefan's phone? Why did Roche's friends always travel together? Why had the FBI ignored Jacob for so long? Why did Hunter ask her to take on the assignment? Why did she agree? Who could she trust?

Doc Günter stood at the end of the hallway, waving her down and pointing to her suite. Fun time was over until she could get rid of him again. Walking, running, moving was a necessity to her.

She approached the doctor. "Time for medication or something?"

"Visitors." He nodded inside, where Dad and the FBI's Special Agent in Charge, David Watson, waited for her, and walked away.

She stared down Watson. "What can I do for you, Special Agent in Charge?"

"I've advised him," Alan said, "that we'll wait for our attorneys."

"Which is your right," Watson offered. "But I have just a few simple questions."

"You can always ask." Pia sat on the edge of the bed.

"Did you tap the phones of Chuck Roche, Luuk Devoor, Ritchie Skaite, Davy Cameron, and Sean Addison?"

"No comment."

"I'm not a reporter. I'm a federal agent and this is an active investigation. You have to answer my questions."

"Then we'll defer that one for when the attorneys arrive." She tossed back the sheets. "Or should we postpone them all?"

"My group is responsible for the actions of foreign intelligence services that employ human and technical means to gather information about the US that adversely affects our national interests. My questions relate directly to that mandate. I'd appreciate your cooperation."

"And I said you can ask. Whether or not I will answer without the advice of counsel depends on your question. Would you like to try again?"

He huffed and dropped his shoulders. "Who authorized the wiretapping?"

Alan Sabel's mouth dropped open. "Wiretapping? Pia would never do a thing like that."

"You gave me the distinct impression you were President Hunter's lapdog, Watson." Pia swung her legs onto the bed. "Should we infer your loyalties are elsewhere now that she's a lame duck?"

He stiffened and lifted his chin. "I'll ignore the inference—but for the record, her polls shot up in the last two days."

"Nothing like a good war to rally the citizens, is that it?" She pulled the thin blanket over her legs.

"To whom did you communicate your wiretap recordings, Ms. Sabel?"

"Are you banking on her losing, or have you been anointed to take her down?"

"Your answers are unresponsive." Watson crossed his arms. "That won't help you."

Alan scowled at Watson. "Help her what? What are you getting at?"

"She's in this thing deep and we have the records to prove it. If she's going to shield her client, she'll go down for it. Talk some sense into her, Mr. Sabel."

"Pia? Is this true? You have nothing to gain by shielding anyone. I don't care—"

"Watson is someone's busboy." She looked at Watson as if he were gum stuck to the sidewalk. "He cleans up after others. When we know who's pulling his leash, we can decide whether we help him or not."

"There is no middle ground on crime, Pia." Alan's exasperation lifted his volume and tone. "You have to disclose whatever you know."

Pia glared at Watson, and Watson glared at her.

"This is serious stuff, young lady," Watson said. "We're talking about the terrorist assassination of an American candidate and you've withheld intelligence on the foreign powers who made that happen. You can cooperate or expect me to rain on your parade."

"Start filling your sandbags, Watson." Pia pointed to the door. "I don't do parades. I bring the storms."

"We will continue this investigation with a subpoena." Watson shot an angry glance at Alan, then turned on his heel and left.

"You're not above the law, Pia." Alan threw up his hands. "Sabel Industries has many contracts with important people. Those people will not do business with even a whiff of criminal activity involved. I'll talk him off the ledge, but you have to cooperate. I can't help you on something like this."

"You may leave."

Alan's mouth opened and shut several times.

The Major leaned against the doorframe. "We have to put her on administrative leave."

"You heard the exchange?" Alan asked.

The Major nodded.

He strode past her and shouted down the hall for Watson.

"Tania's not well," the Major said. "Took a turn for the worse last night. They're not sure either way. It's a traumatic brain injury, all kinds of things going wrong right now. Her parents arrive in a couple hours."

Pia stared at the wall for a long time. Tania had to make it. They'd been through everything together. She couldn't imagine a world without Tania. "I'll visit her in a minute."

"First, you need to come clean with the FBI." The Major crossed her arms.

Pia held up a hand to hold off the Major's imminent lecture as she dialed her phone.

The Major rolled her eyes and left.

Hunter picked up on the fourth ring. "We're in a war planning meeting. I don't have time to give you the attention you deserve. I'll call you back."

"David Watson was here." Pia heard voices behind Hunter, as if she were putting the phone down. "He wanted me to tell him who authorized the wiretap."

A few silent seconds ticked by. "I'm listening."

"Roche asked for help. That's the investigation Watson should be working."

"If you're suggesting I should contact him, Presidents don't direct employees or investigations. You aren't the first person to be investigated and I'm sure this won't be the last time for you. So toughen up and soldier through it, like the rest of us."

"What should I tell him about the authorization?"

"The truth." Hunter paused. "You're not implying that I authorized it, are you?"

"You implied Sabel Security could do things the FBI could not."

"As long as this is a free country, that remains true. However, I never told you to do anything illegal."

"You never authorized anything." Pia replayed the woman's carefully constructed dialogue in her head. "You said, '…make the judgment calls on your own. I will cover for you.'"

"I certainly hope, for your sake, you didn't think that gave you carte blanche to break the law." Hunter paused a moment. "They need me in this meeting. Good luck with your investigation. Oh, one other thing—the people at NEXT USA told me your donation hasn't arrived yet."

"Good luck with your fundraising." Pia clicked off.

She began thumbing out a text and stopped when she sensed a figure at the door.

Stefan held a box of roses under his arm and a pained expression on his face.

"Come in," she said. She tried to recall her rehearsed monologue designed specifically to repair and restart their broken relationship. Nothing came to her. Not even a syllable.

He hesitated, one foot in and one foot out, frozen mid-stride, uncertain of his desire to come in or run away.

What were those brilliant words? The ones that sounded so good in the mirror? The opening diplomatic apology, the pleasant question intended to let him talk. The repression of her dominating personality. How did it go? What should she say?

Stefan made his decision. His pained face turned angry. He tossed the long stem roses on the counter. "You hacked my father's phone? That's why you wanted to get in his room? Did you do the same for Skaite and Addison and Cameron and … everyone I know?"

Watson must have stopped him in the hall.

His chest heaved while he waited for an answer.

She didn't have one. The room and all its contents disappeared. She saw only Stefan's eyes.

"I entered his password." His nostrils flared, his eyes narrowed. "You led me to betray my father. Did you hack mine as well? Why? Did you want to know what I said about you?"

A wildcat tried to claw its way out from inside her ribcage, scratching and shredding her insides. There was no breath in her lungs to give an answer.

"Here," he tossed his phone on her bed, "read my texts. Copy my emails, hack all you want."

He left.

Nothing moved in the room. She stared at the phone next to her knee.

She finished her text to Chuck Roche. "You and your squad need to contract Sabel Security before we can help you. Have these forms signed in front of you and note the reaction of each man."

She sent it, then took another long look at Stefan's phone. A wise woman would have Bianca hack it. An insecure woman would search it for mentions of her name. A woman chasing the Artist would have it thoroughly analyzed. But a smart woman knew the Artist's phone, the one with the incriminating evidence, would never have landed on her bed.

She left it and rolled her IV stand to the closet. She changed and packed extra clothes in a bag.

She hooked the packed bag on the IV stand and rolled herself down the hall. The elevator took her to the ICU, where she ducked into Tania's room. Heading straight for the closet, she swapped phones.

She moved to the bedside and brushed Tania's face.

Groggy and puffy, Tania turned to her and smiled with her eyes closed. "You're s-s-still here?"

"I am." Pia squeezed her hand.

"You're like f-f-family. Mphf. Know th-th-that? You … always there. Whenever I hurt … y-yo-you're always there."

Pain stabbed Pia's chest. She took a deep breath to keep herself from choking up.

"Sorry. I've got to go away for a while." Pia felt a tear welling in her eye. "I need you to rest. OK?"

CHAPTER 45

THE SLAGER WALKED DOWN JACKSON Street, a few feet past Wentworth Place in Chinatown, and turned into the narrow alley between buildings. He touched both sides of the alley with his fingertips until he saw the door, just as the instructions said. Black with the Arabic letter faa, which looked Chinese if you didn't know either language. It was "Station C", one of ten prearranged assembly spots. He opened the door to a cramped storeroom. Among the sacks of rice and beans were six Moroccans armed to the teeth. At the back were two children, taped up tight and hooded.

"We have decided." Youssef stepped forward. "We start shooting here, each man in a different direction, moving away from each other."

"Oh, you decided that, did you?" The Slager nodded and smiled. "Yeah. You could do that."

The men in the room gave him their fiercest looks. They had prepared to die. And they were ready. Like a boiler about to blow, these guys wanted to detonate, and anywhere on the North American mainland would suit them.

He leered at them, jutting out his jaw. In the blink of an eye, he snatched one of the Kalashnikovs out of one man's hand, smashed his face with the butt, spun it around, and aimed it at the others.

"We're in Chinatown. This neighborhood is full of Chinese gangs, as mean as you've ever seen, and armed to the teeth. They're all illegal aliens to boot." He stared into each man's eyes hoping they didn't know he was lying. "You kill these guys and America won't be terrorized, they'll give you a medal."

Like a school of fish, they turned in unison to Youssef. He repeated the Slager's words in Arabic.

They slouched and sighed.

The Slager handed the gun back to his man and patted him on the cheek. "Listen up. We have a target: Chuck Roche and six of America's billionaires. Each one of these guys is richer than Mohammed VI." He waited for Youssef to translate the King of Morocco's name before going on. "You take those guys down and you'll be making a statement."

While the crew discussed their prospects among themselves, he wondered if he could trap the Artist in the target group. Schwartz had revealed the Artist was targeting his own clique after some kind of falling-out.

He stepped outside and dialed.

The Artist answered after several rings. "I said I would call you."

"The crew is getting anxious. I just talked them out of wiping out Chinatown."

"What do you want?"

"Your boy Schwartz should take out the Moroccan in the hospital." The Slager waited a beat. "We can't have any loose ends and I'm burned there."

"You have his kids. You call him."

"OK. Are you paying Schwartz directly?"

"I've made promises. I believe you and I agree on our top priority for the after-party: Schwartz dies."

"I want his cut."

"Figures." The Artist sighed. "Is there anyone you won't betray?"

"I want my $3 million now." The Slager put a stick of gum in his mouth and savored the first-bite rush of flavor. "Or the operation ends in Chinatown with this phone turned over to the cops."

"You'd go down for it."

"I have an escape plan all worked out. Test me, or wire the money. But don't think they won't find you." The Slager let the Artist chew on that threat for a moment. "When will the targets be ready?"

"I'll text you. Then burn the burner."

"One last thing: how will we know which guy is you?"

"What do you mean?"

"I'm just guessing you don't want the crew to kill you." The Slager slowed his words down and lowered his voice. "We'll need to know which one you are so you don't get caught in the crossfire. Believe me, these guys don't know shit, but they know crossfire. I can make sure you get out alive."

The Artist hesitated. "I won't be there."

"Won't the authorities think that's suspicious?"

He hesitated a second time. "Why would they be suspicious of me?"

"Schwartz says you're one of Roche's inner circle."

"Fuck Schwartz. Do we need him? Why not take him out today? Get on that."

"I need him." The Slager grinned, unable to contain how pleased he was with the leverage.

"What is it, money? How about another million? That makes four. Transferring it now. Take him out and leave his body somewhere it won't be found for a few days."

"I'll take the million, but you said Schwartz was the only one who knew where my kids are. I need him."

"Yes. I see. I forgot about that."

There was something wrong in that answer.

"Hey, I need proof my kids are alive." A pain struck deep in the Slager's gut. He was doing this to ensure they had the future they deserved, but he'd been focused on the money and forgot the many broken promises of proof. "I need it before we move on your friends."

"I have no idea if that can happen or not. Talk to Schwartz. Get this job done."

"I get a live stream of my kids and I can move the crew into place minutes later."

"Talk to Schwartz."

The Artist clicked off.

The Slager cursed and dialed Schwartz. "He wants me to kill you now."

They shared a nervous chuckle.

"But you need to take out that guy—"

"Hey!" A voice behind him in the alley. Two cops stood on the sidewalk, street side. "What are you doing there?"

The Slager pocketed his phone, leaving it on. He shrugged and tossed up his hands. "Looking for a place to smoke. Is that illegal in California?"

One of the cops approached him. "What was in your hand?"

The Slager held his arms out and did his best to scowl while his insides flipped over. "A phone. Do you have probable cause, officer?"

"Shut up and show me the contents of your pockets."

"Hey, I don't have to—"

"Do it now." The officer placed his hand on his Taser.

"OK, OK." He pulled his phone out with two fingers and held it aloft. He slid it back into his pocket.

"Show me some ID."

He reached behind him and, for just a second, imagined pulling his Smith & Wesson MP45. Could he take them both? No problem. But then what? Cop killing would shorten his lifespan right quick. He pulled the worn wallet and removed the license and handed it over and tried to remember the name on it. Schwartz had provided it along with several others, but this was the first time he had to produce it in the USA.

The cop took it and radioed it in from his shoulder mic. After the confirmation came back, the cop looked him over carefully and handed back the license.

The Slager took it and glanced at it. William H. Harrison, shortest US Presidency in history. The man died of a cold thirty days after giving his inauguration speech.

Schwartz had a sense of humor.

Or was it a message?

"Sorry, Mr. Harrison," the cop said. "Got a couple calls from the local shopkeepers. Said they saw a bunch of terrorist-looking guys carrying packages that looked like guns or something. We're combing the neighborhood. You see anything?"

CHAPTER 46

I STARED AT THE DETECTIVE and the detective stared at me behind the Four Seasons hotel in Silicon Valley on a cold, drizzly summer morning.

Mercury stood behind him making a pistol with his fingers that he pressed to the cop's head and pulled the trigger. *C'mon, bro, you don't have to listen to his bullshit. We gotta find that monster. Nobody hurts a Caesar and walks, ya feel me?*

A god who advocates cop-killing. Wonderful. I closed my eyes.

"Keep looking at me, Mr. Stearne." The detective crossed his arms. "And answer the question."

He was a little guy, scrawny and pissed at the world because everybody was taller, even women. Guys like him always won over the prettiest girl at the dance because they tried harder. The same goes for career moves; they tried harder and therefore went further. This guy was young and had plans to go a long way. So it follows that a guy who's always compensating is going to try harder when it comes to taking statements from friendly witnesses. Short on patience and quick with tough words, the detective didn't like me or my story.

"I didn't call it in because I wasn't the guy who found the body. When I heard about the deceased, I was busy ducking bullets on the seventh floor."

He shoved his notepad in his pocket and pushed my shoulder to turn me around. "OK, let's go look at these alleged bullet holes. While we walk, tell me about your relationship with this phantom guy, Larson."

We rode the service elevator while I told him about our trip to As Sukhnah and meeting Larson. And shooting him in the leg. And chasing him around the globe. And having the FBI tell me I'm loony. And finding Hakim. And having the FBI ignore the confession. And watching helplessly as an American presidential candidate was assassinated.

"Did that stuff happen in the real world? Or was that, like, in your head, maybe?" the detective asked with a pointed tone of voice. "You have anyone who can back up that story? I mean, sneaking into Syria? Really, Mr. Stearne?"

His arrogance disappeared when my left hand slid under his chin and pinned him to the elevator wall while my right hand stripped his Taser from his belt, his pepper spray from his coat pocket, and his pistol from his shoulder holster. His reaction time was a joke; his hands arrived to defend each item a second too late. I let him go and held his weapon between us. Before he could grab it back, I dropped the magazine out and ejected the round in the chamber, letting everything fall to the floor.

"Hey!"

"Yes. I snuck into Syria." I gave him my soldier stare. The kind of look a veteran has when he's deciding whether he should rip your head off with his bare hands or make a tuna sandwich.

The detective swallowed. He scrambled to reassemble his kit and put himself back together, then stared at the elevator door the rest of the way.

We got off at the seventh floor, where a uniformed cop inspected the detective's badge even though they knew each other by name.

My detective puffed up his chest in front of his pals, reclaiming his alpha status. "You're not in Syria anymore. You're in my house. You'll follow my rules."

"OK."

My cell buzzed an incoming text from Ms. Sabel. I didn't check it.

"Yeah." The detective squinted into a hole through three drywall layers. "Those are bullet holes all right. Lemme see your gun."

He held out his hand while continuing to stare through the hole.

I rolled my eyes. "You left it with your partner."

He gave me a displeased glance and grabbed me, shoved me down the hall to my room, and followed me. Inside, a crime-scene crew, two girls and a guy, scraped and bagged and waved at the detective. One of them handed him a baggie with a sheet of paper in it.

After a quick glance, he held it in front of me. "Explain this, Stearne."

"It's called stationary. Hotels provide it so guests can perform an ancient ritual that dates way back to the olden days before texting. People would write letters—"

"Cut the sarcasm. We're looking for a terrorist—according to you. Why does he write you a note like you're old friends?"

"Because he's feeling alone in the world."

"Get serious, Stearne—or we do this at the station."

"Listen to the man." David Watson stood in the door, giving the short guy his best scowl while holding out his FBI credentials. He waited a second for the detective to say something, which he didn't. Then he looked at me. "Why do you say that?"

"Someone put some money into this operation and it sure as hell wasn't your convict drug dealer." I took the letter and skimmed it. "He's traveling with a rapidly declining number of friends. That has to wear you down, make you feel lonely. Beating the system has a kind of high to it. But killing Marty Maddox had to have some kind of low to it."

The three crime-scene guys stopped working and listened.

"Why did you call him 'my' convict?" Watson asked.

"You linked the DNA to Michael Larson, but your picture doesn't look anything like him. Either you crossed up the DNA profiles, or I pulled the wrong scrap of blood out of that Humvee, or someone paid to have cosmetic surgery for a convicted meth dealer. Which sounds most likely?"

The little guy scrunched up his nose. "What the hell are you two talking about? What kind of high do you think this guy—"

"East Palo Alto is a small town; you don't get many big cases. So just shut up and let the adults talk." Watson grabbed the detective by the shoulder and squeezed. "Go ahead, Stearne."

"By now, Larson's come to the realization he's not going to live much longer. His benefactor won't need him after the final attack. Maybe his own terrorists are supposed to take him out. Or, maybe, he kills himself. Maybe suicide by cop. But he's an optimist, like all human beings. No matter how bad the odds, we always think we'll have one more chance. We'll get out of it. Cheat death. He's hoping if he picks a fight with me, he can beat me and get away."

"This is bullshit." The detective looked back and forth between us.

"You don't look like a psychologist. You're no profiler."

Normally I would've given him my soldier stare again. But something on the paper caught my eye: indentations.

"He's on to something." Watson looked around the room. "Let me guess, not a shred of evidence that the guy was here, right?"

"Just the letter." The detective said.

I held the letter up to the light streaming in the window. They were indentations all right. God only knows what they meant.

Watson snatched it out of my hands. "You mean this Larson-guy really exists?"

Mercury leaned over Watson. *Shoulda taken out the scrawny dude when you had a chance, yo. Now you're going to have to kill an FBI agent as well. Sucks.*

I said, *I'm not killing anyone. We have evidence. They're going to run with it this time.*

Mercury said, *Sure thing, homie. Do the Pompey thing: ask the Egyptians for refuge when you're fleeing Caesar and see what happens.*

Even though I knew better, I asked, *Why, what happened to Pompey?*

The Egyptians held a welcoming party and stabbed him in the back—literally. You gotta get away from Watson. He's never going to believe you know where they're going to strike.

I said, *But I don't know when they're going to strike.*

Watson grabbed one of the crime-scene people and shouted at her until she pulled the sheet of paper out and dusted it for prints.

"Looks like the edge of a hand," she said. "You know, like when you put your pen hand on the paper to write?"

He grabbed the paper without using gloves and grabbed my wrist and pulled up my hand and held it next to the paper. He looked, and the detective looked, and Watson said, "Could be."

"Did you write yourself a letter?" the detective asked. "Were you trying to make us believe there's another guy involved?"

Watson said, "He's been doing that from the beginning."

"What?" I heard myself screech.

I looked at the letter. The black dust for fingerprinting also highlighted the indentations. It was clear this was the sheet of paper under another sheet that Larson had been writing on. Before writing his note to me, he'd written something else.

Plain as day, it read: Mark Hopkins.

Whoever he was.

A loud knock on the open door turned our heads. My attorney stood there like a savior.

The fat man from Washington waddled in, waving a hand as if shooing flies. "Give me a moment with my client."

Everyone in the room grumbled, then backed away. I huddled with counsel by the door.

He said, "I got this. They've been filing search warrants all night. So I took the red-eye."

He crossed to Watson, ignoring the local detective. "Not only do you not have a search warrant for Jacob, you're interrogating a witness…"

All eyes were on him so I snuck a peek at my phone. A coded text from Ms. Sabel. "8 JJ f0-10 O"

Mercury read over my shoulder. *My man! Pia-Caesar-Sabel needs you. You gotta read that right now—but don't use your phone.*

I said, *I know. I got this.*

Mercury said, *Just back out slowly. They're not paying attention.*

Watson poked a finger in the lawyer's big belly. "I think your clients are in on this. Stearne just said someone rich had to be financing it. And that a lonely loser is running the Moroccans. Guess who fits that profile? Guess where all the evidence points?"

"What evidence? You have a paw print."

Even the crime scene guys were watching the spectacle. I backed into the hallway in slow motion. I crossed the hall to Dhanpal's room.

Scratching and yawning from an all-night shift, he let me in. "Wazzup, Jacob?"

"I need your tablet. Ever hear of a guy named Mark Hopkins?"

He shook his head and tossed me the tablet before falling back to his bed, face first. "Pia was up at three, buddy. You'd think she got her nails done—not had a 9mm removed from her flesh."

To tease out the clues Ms. Sabel left me, I brought up a browser and checked the US soccer team roster: #8 was Julie Johnson. I switched to

Outlook.com and entered the email address, firstname0 dash lastname0, julie0-johnson0@outlook.com. I stared at the password box until I remembered the only password she'd ever told me about: *PiaSabelGold!2012*. She used it as a reminder of her personal goal in the months leading up to the Olympics. It worked. The inbox had one email from a name I'd never heard of that read, "buy a car – pre-GPS. pick me up st. francis. no phones."

Mercury pointed at the email. *You getting the message yet, brutha? You're in deep shit and getting deeper by the minute. Larson managed to pin the whole thing on you and the boss. Ready to shoot your way out of this now?*

I said, *That's not what she told me to do.*

Mercury said, *You're going to let Larson get away with this? He's got six, count 'em, SIX martyrs ready to murder Americans and die in the slaughter. If one of those victims turns out to be our golden girl, you and me are finished, bro. Finished.*

I closed the browser tab and searched for used cars, St. Francis, and Mark Hopkins. My heart started pounding. My blood ran cold.

Mercury was right. I did know where the next attack was going to be.

Pulling Dhanpal off his bed, I shoved a Provigil stay-awake pill in his mouth and slapped him awake. "You gotta do this, Dhanpal. Go in there and tell Watson to look closely at the letter. The terrorists aren't going to the bridge—they're going to the Mark Hopkins hotel. He's not going to believe you. But you've got to tell him and make sure my attorney is a witness to your warning. Then you've got to defend the Mark Hopkins."

"Alone?" His eyes opened up. "Against six Moroccans? No backup?"

"Right. Miguel has to guard Tania. There's a chance Larson might go there."

He nodded and shook himself and took a deep breath. "On it, buddy." He held out a fist to bump. "Tip of the spear."

Bumped. "Sharpest point."

We left together.

The argument between Watson and my attorney reached a hundred decibels. Dhanpal interrupted them. I slipped my phone into the pocket of a crime-scene lady who had her back to me. She never noticed. After dumping Dhanpal's tablet down the laundry chute, I raced downstairs, grabbed my portable armament backpack from behind the bushes, and caught a cab.

The dealer accepted my Sabel Security corporate Amex and sold me a '67 Pontiac GTO Convertible. He claimed it was the original muscle car and carried a classic collector-car resale value. All I wanted was some horsepower, current plates, and no paper trail for a couple days. He obliged.

I drove around the campus of St. Francis High School until I found the football field.

Ms. Sabel rose out of the shadows under the bleachers and climbed in.

CHAPTER 47

PIA'S WOUNDS PAINED HER WHEN she sank into the Pontiac's bucket seats. Jacob looked away when she let an "oof" escape. With both bridges on the 80 and the 92 gridlocked, he drove north on the 280. She didn't ask about a destination. She turned the radio on and searched for news.

A talk-radio station gave unlimited time to uninformed callers voicing their unfiltered thoughts about Islam, terrorists, and those responsible. Hunter's war drums were beating hard. Pia spun the old-fashioned AM dial through four stations before finding one reporting live news. The station provided updates about planned memorials for Marty Maddox. President Hunter would attend several high-profile events in the cities with governors who'd backed Maddox and NEXT USA early on. She would cross the country four times in two days, like someone campaigning for office.

One news reporter said, "Florida's governor tweeted a plea for President Hunter to take up Maddox's cause and run NEXT USA, but she declined just a few minutes later."

"You have a destination in mind?" she asked as they fought traffic to cross the Golden Gate.

Jacob nodded and started to answer, but his words were cut off by the announcer on the radio.

"With me is Alan Sabel," the radio voice said, "founder of Sabel Industries and father of the fugitive."

Pia glanced at Jacob. He kept his eyes on the road.

Her request for him to pick her up was desperate enough; she didn't need to explain how deep Watson was digging her grave.

"I have a brief statement," Alan said. "Until the FBI shows me some evidence of her involvement, I believe this is a cover-up. Our employee, Jacob Stearne, delivered a terrorist and video confession to them and they failed to act. For them to blame—"

"Did she record phone conversations without a warrant?" the reporter asked.

"Citizens cannot get a warrant."

"Did she record conversations without permission?"

"I have no evidence of that."

"If the FBI produces conclusive evidence that she did, how should she be punished?"

"I would never condemn my daughter on a hypothetical question."

"In 2002," the reporter asked, "your private conversations and voice mails were recorded and published by a news outlet. Do you think she should face the same punishment today that you advocated for those reporters?"

Alan hesitated and coughed. "There is no evidence, so there is no question."

The reporter prattled on about something else.

"Not a ringing endorsement." Pia faced Jacob. "They tripped him up."

Jacob didn't answer for a mile. "He lives by the Honor Code, doesn't he?"

"I will not lie, cheat, steal, or tolerate those who do." Pia repeated in a low voice. "That would be his mantra—and mine. Usually."

"He's having a difficult time getting a grip on this."

She turned the radio off. They drove for a long time in silence.

There were few times in her life that felt as bleak as this day. She took an ethical shortcut and Watson caught her. Roche figured it out because she knew the codename before the FBI, so who told Watson? Roche couldn't have without admitting he'd ignored warnings for over a week. She said, "How does Watson know I tapped Roche's phone? Do you think he works for the Artist?"

"An FBI man?" Jacob shot her a glance. "Either he's being manipulated or he's a bureaucrat covering up his lack of interest in preventing the attack—most likely a combination of both."

She sank in the seat and closed her eyes.

The engine rumbled and the tires purred. Across the Bridge and through Mill Valley. They kept rolling north by northwest until they cleared the Bay Area and swung northeast toward Sacramento. He drove fast enough to squeeze through traffic, getting to the head of each snarl of cars and trucks, but not fast enough to draw the police.

"Why is Watson twisting this 'Larson doesn't exist' story against you?" she asked.

"First time I met him was at NIH on the bio-tech case. I made him look bad and he's never forgiven me." Jacob took his eyes off the road long enough to give her a hopeful smile that came off badly. "His strings are pulled by someone outside the FBI."

"Hunter told me industry associations push bureaucrats around. Covering up Larson would take a lot of pushing."

"You're rich, so you miss the biggest struggle in life. You don't know how desperate people are to make a thousand bucks. Every now and then someone gets caught with their hands in the cookie jar. It's always scary how little money is involved compared to the damage they do."

"Watson earned his graft this week." She sighed. "We're screwed."

Pia tried the radio again.

This time they found Stefan Devoor's words flaunted by a radio host. "This headline is a shocker: Stefan Devoor, one of the wealthiest young men in the country, flatly states, 'I let Pia Sabel into our hotel rooms where she bugged our phones and laptops.' He goes on to say he can't believe he fell for her tricks. He called her a ... well, let's listen to him."

The host played a recording of Stefan. "She's like a modern Mata Hari, using her charms to seduce even the most vigilant—"

Pia snapped it off. She crossed her arms and pushed back in the seat. "Want me to drive?"

"Do the antibiotics make you drowsy?"

"More like sick to my stomach." She leaned against the window.

They passed Vacaville and took the 505 bypass and rolled north. They learned from a large billboard that the long Central Valley of California stretches from Bakersfield to Redding and produces half the nation's fruit and vegetables. Nothing else interesting presented itself for observation on the long road to nowhere. Pia tried the radio again.

She found David Watson's voice, mid-sentence. "...a damned terrorist into this country on a private jet. He's armed and dangerous. The public should not confront him but call the FBI..."

She clicked off. "Have you talked to Yumi since she left?"

"How does everyone know she left?"

"Surprise—women talk to each other."

"No, I've not talked to her." He sighed. "I know why she left."

"Because everything we do ends in a lot of death?" she asked.

"I'm thinking of giving it up. I can cook. Run a restaurant. Something."

"You're not going to call her until you decide?"

He shrugged. She turned the radio back on.

This time they found a reporter's update on the terrorist Pia tackled. The man was conscious but suffering post-traumatic amnesia from a severe concussion. The doctors were offering no estimates of when the terrorist could be questioned. It could be hours or days.

"Wow, you really decked that guy," Jacob said.

"I was going to beat him to death with his own rifle when it occurred to me the FBI might want to question him."

"So you stopped?"

"No. I kept beating him—but his weapon fell apart."

The announcer switched to a different reporter. This time it was the Major. "I'm not sure where Mr. Watson gets his information. Jacob delivered the terrorist to the FBI. For them to issue a warrant for his arrest—"

"Other than your employees, Ms. Jackson, do you have any one who can confirm that's what Mr. Stearne—"

Pia switched it off again and turned to Jacob. "We don't have a lot of friends right now."

"We'll be fine. Probably."

CHAPTER 48

THE ARTIST UNFURLED AN UMBRELLA on his balcony at the Fairmont Hotel on Nob Hill and looked down on the Mark Hopkins' entrance. The perfect view. Maybe he should record it on his phone. The ultimate payback was about to unfold and they brought it on themselves. A giddiness overtook him. They laughed at his speech in Rancho Mirage. They didn't heed his warnings about Maddox. They didn't trust his profound solution. And the unkindest cut of all: Roche failed to see the brilliance in his plan.

They would suffer the consequences for their lack of vision.

All of them.

He glanced at his watch. He needed a drink to steady his nerves. Just one. He went back inside, dropped ice into a glass, poured a scotch from hotel's decanter, and swirled it. No. He set it down before taking a sip. Bad idea. A clear head was required at times like these. He poured the liquor down the sink.

Behind him, the light faded as the drizzle turned to rain coming down hard. A sigh escaped him. It would've been a sight to behold—the ambulances and police cars—but he wasn't going to stand in the rain to watch.

A knock on the door startled him. Even more startling that the butler announced a Roche Security guard. The guard delivered a request to join Chuck Roche for cocktails. A request he could neither accept nor decline. The Slager was due any minute. He couldn't be there. Nor could he refuse his mentor's invitation.

There was nothing he could do but keep a stiff upper lip and maintain appearances. He took a moment to grab a coat. The security guard waited in the living room while the Artist grabbed his special phone. He dialed the Slager. No answer.

The security guard knocked on the bedroom door and raised his voice. "He wants to see you right away sir. He requests only a minute or two of your time."

There was one possibility: get in and get out before the shooting started. Or maybe an urgent bathroom break if time was tight. With a deep breath, he squared his shoulders and left.

He followed the guard to the elevator, down to the lobby, out to Mason St., and crossed the intersection to the Hopkins. The guard marched him straight to the lobby lounge where Roche's entourage stood at the bar. The gathering was a typical evening for the group. Drinks, dinner, more drinks, off to their respective suites. Some took young ladies with them for entertainment. Roche usually drank little and worked his phone throughout the evening.

The guard pointed to a small round table in the corner. Roche waved him over with a tip of his silver-handled cane and a grin.

He took his assigned seat like a condemned man. After all, he was a condemned man. Condemned by his own hand. He glanced around, half-expecting to see Moroccan terrorists running in the front door.

Realizing his unpleasant appearance, he smiled and picked up his attitude. "Sorry, I'm suffering from a bit of indigestion."

"How sad." Roche waved at the bartender. "Unusual for you to miss dinner with the gang. I thought it was a girl."

The Artist scowled at the suggestion. Roche laughed at him. The bastard just sat there and laughed at him. All those years of thinking he was the greatest American, the achiever who took a few pipelines and refineries and turned them into a global conglomerate through sheer force of will—when it had been nothing but inheritance and luck. He never should have listened to Roche. And now, by summoning him, the old man was putting him in danger.

The bartender coughed next to him.

For a moment, he had no idea why the man was staring at him. Then he remembered himself. "7-Up."

He admonished himself to keep it together, act normal, forget that six Moroccan terrorists would burst into the lobby at any moment and gun down everyone in the room.

"You must sign this release," Roche slid a paper and pen across the table in front of him.

He glanced at the paper, but felt Roche's intense interest in him to such a degree that he looked up. "What is this?"

"Sabel Security is doing a little research for me." Roche palmed his stupid cane and smiled. "They need to look through your phone records."

The Artist felt anger consuming him. Blood rushed to his head so hot and fast, he worried it was visible. The words on the paper disappeared in a swirl of lost concentration. The son of a bitch hired Sabel? What kind of research? They had to be searching for the Artist. That meant he could no longer taunt Roche. They would find him. Roche's final betrayal. He had arranged the old man's execution. Maybe it was fitting he be here to witness it.

A defense came to him. "You trust that lousy outfit? Isn't that girl wanted by the FBI?"

"For some reason, I thought you liked her." Roche's gaze pierced him like a javelin.

The old man still knew how to keep him off balance. He resented it like never before. Yet he had to get out of there before the killers came and mowed everyone down. Sign it and leave. Sickness, migraine, meetings, something like that.

Roche's voice sounded distant. "I have reason to believe the allegations against her will be dropped in a day or two."

Impossible. Watson assured him that end would be wrapped up shortly. But the FBI is a big organization; another branch may have stepped in. He would have to come up with a new story to keep Watson going after her. And Watson was growing more reluctant every day. He needed Schwartz to quit stalling and provide more men from the program.

The bartender arrived with his drink on a small silver tray, which he swirled with a good deal of panache.

The Artist took the glass and sipped a gulp, while his eyes instinctively glanced around the lobby for the imminent arrival of mass murderers. He spluttered his drink. Bad form. Definitely bad form. He pulled the loose threads of his anxious thoughts together and focused on the paper. "This is backdated."

"My mistake." A mischievous grin spread across Roche's face. "I engaged them a few days ago and forgot the paperwork. I trust you'll overlook that."

Roche was the sharpest businessman he'd ever met. There were no details missed. Something in his leering smile was terribly wrong. Whatever malevolence hid behind the old man's face, the real danger would burst through the front door any second. The tension was making him sick. Still, he couldn't make his hand pick up the pen to sign. It would be like signing a confession.

"She endorsed Maddox." The Artist took another sip. "How could you do business with such an airhead?"

"I'm a convert." Roche leaned in with a twinkle in his eye. He lowered his voice to a conspiratorial whisper. "Remember that old refinery I've been trying to unload? She bought it and screwed me royally on the deal."

He roared with uncharacteristic laughter.

The Artist was shocked beyond words. How could anyone best Roche, and why would he laugh about it? What could possibly be funny about getting screwed by a pinhead athlete?

Screams echoed through the lobby. The Artist shoved over the marble table and dove to the floor. Three quick and quiet pops followed. After a short pause, three more. Then a full second of silence. Screams erupted again.

"CALL 9-1-1! CALL 9-1-1!" The shouts came from several directions.

The Artist peeked between his fingers to see Roche standing, calm and collected, leaning around a column.

"I'll be damned. He was right!" Roche looked back at the Artist. "You see? You're a convert now too, aren't you?"

"What?" He pulled his hands away, wondering when the rest of the shooting would start.

"Look, man, look!" Roche pointed toward the lobby with his cane.

The Artist rose on wobbling knees and hobbled a step to the column.

He leaned around it.

Three men lay on the ground with rifles in their hands. A short dark fellow stepped over them, a rifle on his shoulder and a pistol in his hand, and kicked their guns away, one at a time. Blood oozed out of their heads in wide pools around the bodies.

Onlookers cowered in corners of the room. Someone threw up. Behind him, the bar patrons rose from the floor and returned their spilled drinks to upright.

"Sabel Security agent by the name of Dhanpal Singh." Roche pointed with his cane. "Indian fellow I would guess, but damn good anyway, wouldn't you say?"

The Artist seethed with anger. His men were dead. Months and millions wasted by a mall cop in the lobby? Roche looked smug and satisfied. The traitor. To think he'd once idolized the ridiculous fool. Roche had no vision.

But the danger was far from over.

The Slager and three more Moroccans were out there.

At least, they were supposed to be.

The Artist looked to the street. "There could be more."

Beyond the glass front doors, a bellman and two guests picked themselves off the sidewalk, checking each other, and staring at the dead men. Inside, people were rising to standing, pointing and clicking pictures with their phones.

"Damnedest thing," Roche said. "Sabel wasn't hired for protection, but a couple hours ago, this guy comes in here with a convincing story about the terrorists. My guys were outraged, asked about the FBI, said the same things you did about Pia. So I told the guy he could perch up there on the balcony. Didn't see any harm in it. You didn't even notice him when you came in."

People don't look up when they enter a room; certainly not his Moroccans. How did the Sabel guard know about the attack? Had the Slager told him? Schwartz? Wiring the money in advance had been a mistake. Betrayed at every turn. By friend and foe alike. He felt as if someone were tying up his stomach with twine and squeezing it, tighter and tighter.

He was alone in this endeavor. No more compromises. No more capitulations. The Slager had to die. And Schwartz too. The only question left was how.

The Artist would find a way.

Roche waited for the bartender to set the table back upright, then sat. The Artist followed suit.

"Where were we?" Roche asked. "Oh yes—you're about to sign this."

He stared at his death warrant. Or was it? Sabel could run through his calls but they'd never find the burner. Naturally, the upside to working with suicidal maniacs was the drastically short lifespan. If Schwartz and Larson were dead, no one could connect him to the Moroccans.

Roche watched him closely. "You're not going to give me a hard time about the release, are you?"

CHAPTER 49

A RAINBOW OVER THE CASCADE Mountains lifted our low spirits as we left Redding, California on our way to a ranch near Indian Spring about fifty miles south of the Oregon border. We tried the License Plate game, but it didn't break the shroud of helplessness. Neither had the occasional radio reports. Even though Dhanpal was credited with stopping three suicide bombers, the media separated that Sabel victory from the actions of the owner and her number-one henchman. My attorney blew so much hot air about my rights I sounded guilty.

The Major was no help either. She let her anxiety slip in one sentence and the news outlets played it over and over. Alan Sabel backed further away from us with each new interview. After he told one reporter that sometimes parents have to "face facts", we decided not to listen to the radio anymore.

Rounding a bend on I-5, a massive mountain of granite called the Castle Crags rose six thousand feet above the volcanic Cascades. I took the exit and drove several miles into the dense ponderosa pines before turning onto a dirt road where we stopped for a livestock gate. Ms. Sabel drove through while I dragged the gate closed. She drove the remaining six miles up the rough road until we came to an open space. A large turning circle surrounded by a bunkhouse and sheds greeted us. At the circle's center was a corral, horse barn, and a two-bedroom ranch house. Between the house and bunkhouse stood a black bell mounted on an eight-foot post. We got out and stretched.

I knocked on the door and called out without hearing anything but birds and the wind in the pines. I rang the bell three times slowly, to make it sound intentional. Then we parked our butts against the Pontiac's fenders and waited.

Mercury sat on the roof. *Whoa, homie, nice spread this guy has. If you'd stayed in the service a couple more years, you could be living large like this.*

I said, *I mustered out because of you, thank you very much. Hartman inherited this place.*

The wings on his helmet fluttered him to the ground. *There you go, blaming me for everything. Everybody knows you don't go telling an Army psych that you listen to the voices in your head. That's just plain crazy.*

I said, *Why are your wings wiggling? You told me that was for bad news.*

Yeah, well here it is, bro: Hartman has Internet, and he's not hearing nice things about you. He might not be feeling the brotherhood-thing like he should.

A voice shouted from the trail behind the metal barn. Sergeant Major Hartman rode a palomino around the side and edged up to us. The horse stopped and peed ten gallons while Hartman dismounted.

"Sergeant Major Hartman—" I gestured to the boss "—allow me to present Ms. Pia Sabel."

He didn't even glance at her. "What the hell you doing here?"

"We've come seeking help." Ms. Sabel stuck out a hand.

He looked at it, then looked her over. Five years outdoors had aged him more than the wars. His denim shirt and jacket hung on him like a wire hanger. His boots were military, not cowboy. His hat was all cowboy, though. Even had a rattlesnake skin on the band.

"You've heard the stories—but you know me." I offered my wrists. "If you believe what you've heard, take me in."

His gaze swept over me, recalling the firefights, the mad scrambles, the trust you put in another soldier to get your wounded ass off the battlefield.

He squinted at Ms. Sabel's hand and shook it. "Wish I could say it was a pleasure to meet you, ma'am. But this ain't pleasant for neither of us."

Her mouth tightened up. She nodded.

"We can't ask you for shelter." I tossed my nose at the granite mountain looming over the landscape. "I was hoping you could give me some suggestions and a head start."

"The Stearne I served with wouldn't never have brought a terrorist into the country." He took a deep breath, looking me up and down. "But years and war can change a man."

We said nothing.

"Running ain't gonna solve your problems." He stared first at me, then at Ms. Sabel. When we stood quiet a long time, he understood. "I see. Smart people don't run unless they know something's going to break their way. Is that it?"

We declined that question as well. Partly because we hadn't discussed it, and partly because we weren't that smart. We did run out of pure desperation.

He waved his hand for us to follow and led his horse across the way to the metal barn. He slid open a large rolling door that revealed sixteen stalls and a tack room around a wide-open center. The strong smell of large animals, leather, and hay struck me. Memories of a farm back in Iowa, a long time ago, flooded back to me. We kept horses. Horses and humans have a primordial symbiosis, comforting and therapeutic.

A curious fellow with big round eyes stuck his head out of a stall. I patted his nose.

He tried to bite my elbow.

I leaned conspirator-close to Ms. Sabel and whispered. "Are you well enough to ride?"

"I'll have to be."

At the back were two trucks, a new one and a 1946 Dodge pickup. I knew the model because Hartman carried a picture of it on every tour. It was his grandfather's first car. They restored it a year before the old man died.

He took the saddle off his horse and put him in a stall and rubbed him down and gave him a carrot.

We waited.

He stepped out of the stall and closed the gate behind him. He leaned against it. "How much of a head start you want?"

"Twenty-four hours should work," Ms. Sabel said.

I snapped a glance at her. Where did that number come from? Watson was going to crucify me tomorrow or the day after, or next week, whenever it would save his career. All the evidence was on a Lazy Susan. I put it there, all he had to do was turn it to point at me instead of the mythical Larson.

Sergeant Major Hartman pushed off the gate and stood between us. "You two know how to ride? I'll assume you think you do. These here are trail horses, docile as they come. They get rode twelve hours a day so you should be fine. You take them on up to Colter's Cabin, over the pass, southeast of Bear Ridge about a mile. Red markers on that trail, can't miss it. Saddle up Santana and Circe. I'll pull a few things together for you."

He walked away.

We looked at the stalls. Neat name tags guided us to our mounts. We were far from experts, but memories from the farm helped. We figured out the blanket and saddle arrangements. We found hackamores with our steeds' names on them. By the time we were done, Hartman returned with saddlebags and bed rolls. He checked and fixed our work without ridiculing us, which we appreciated. We led the horses out to the paddock and mounted.

"Reality is what it is, not what you want it to be, soldier." He held us by the hackamores. "You go on up there. Have a good long think about what's really going on. If you see a way forward, ride on into Quartz Valley, Klamath Reservation, see Anthony Tsotsie. He'll take care of you. But if you come to grips with this thing and you done what they said—do your country a favor."

I stared at him and he stared at me.

Then Ms. Sabel whistled and tossed the car keys in a nice, soft arc. "Take the car for rental on the horses. It would look nice next to that old pickup."

She rode out as he started to object. I leaned over. "It's a matter of scale. The car's value is less to her than lunch money to you and me. Take it and say thank you."

He called out his thanks as I caught up with her. A broad trail led up the hillside behind his compound. Colored ribbons—red, green, blue, yellow, pink, and black—hung on branches overhead, color-coded for city slickers like us. One by one, the different colors branched off. We kept with the red.

A mile up the hill, she asked, "What did he mean, 'do your country a favor'?"

"*Seppuku.* Suicide."

She nodded. A hawk screeched overhead and winged away to the south.

A barren ridge gave us a view of the larger landscape. Far behind and below us, Hartman used a water truck to cover our tracks from the main road to his house.

We clomped along a trail worn into the granite down to a stream trickling between ferns at the bottom. We didn't have much to say that we hadn't said in the car. Except for the things we avoided saying. We rode in silence. Saddles creaked and horses sighed and breezes whispered in the branches. The birds resumed singing sometime after the hawk left the area. We rode until late afternoon.

"What the hell is wrong with Watson?" I yelled into the trees when the pressure built up enough to explode inside me. "He screwed up. Why not just admit it? The terrorism division is already working on Hakim." I turned to Ms. Sabel. "The guy you tackled will corroborate his story. Watson has nothing. What will he get from torturing us instead of looking for Larson?"

"You provided DNA for a guy Hakim couldn't identify. That would make anyone suspicious."

"Yeah, sucks to be me. But why you?"

"Whoever pulls his strings also ordered my parents' murders. It doesn't surprise me they sent Watson after me. In my case, industrial espionage is his area." She let her horse eat some daisies. "How does Larson expect to get out of this alive?"

"The Artist must have promised him a big payday."

"More than a payday. He'll be more hated than Benedict Arnold. We have to find the connection. What clues did he give you?"

"He wore cowboy gear, expensive hat, serious boots, and belt. I can't think of anything else."

My horse started to wander off-trail. I pulled him back and we rode in silence a lot longer.

We found the cabin next to a good-sized stream and turned the horses loose in a small corral at the back. It had two rooms, a bedroom and a great room. Inside was all Hartman, sparse and severe: a wooden table and chairs, a bookcase with six books, a mantle with nothing on it, windows with plain fabric for drapes. A stack of firewood lay near the stone fireplace. A kitchen furnished with enamelware and silver in tightly sealed containers. No raccoons allowed.

I emptied the saddlebags to find a fishnet, two lemons, butter, salt, fresh green beans, sliced almonds, half a head of lettuce, a tomato, a sprig of thyme, four eggs, four slices of bread, and a tomato. Dinner and breakfast—nothing more than we asked for.

I took the net out to the stream. Just out of sight from the cabin, Hartman had dammed up a small pool and stocked it with rainbow trout. Campers might think he's quite the fisherman. It took me a couple tries, but I managed to snag a couple.

A hundred yards short of the cabin, I stopped and drank in the view. The sun pushed orange-red beams between two peaks and across the bottoms of the low-slung clouds. Everything around me was bathed in a pink-orange light. Ms. Sabel stood in the paddock, looking at the same sunset. Then, a few wordless minutes later, it was over. We went back to work.

Cleaned and gutted, the fish sizzled in a grilling basket over the fire. Ms. Sabel followed my instructions for lemon, salt, and thyme. It quickly filled the cabin with a hunger-inducing scent. I tossed a salad and boiled the green beans. We ate at the table.

Food tastes best when you're roughing it. Even if the cabin wasn't all that rough.

We ate in relative silence, the crackling fire our only music, the smell of burning pine our incense.

We washed the dishes and she went to bed in the other room. I tossed another log on the fire and sacked out on the couch.

Sometimes life feels absurd and hopeless. I was trying to save the country and failing. Chased by an FBI boss intent on salvaging his career. Running from justice barreling at me like a runaway train. Fleeing into the Cascades with no plan for exoneration. My life was over. All the medals and citations would mean nothing in the end. If anyone remembered Jacob Stearne, it would be a couple ex-girlfriends when they talked about lousy lovers: *One time I dated this loser...*

Sure, I'd had some good times. I'd enjoyed the scent of lemon and thyme on fire-seared trout. I'd seen the moonrise over a dew-covered alfalfa field. I'd had good friends like Ms. Sabel and Miguel. At critical times in my life I'd been helped by mere acquaintances, like Hartman. I'd seen people help others for no reason beyond an intangible thing called "kindness." I'd seen soldiers fight and die so Americans could shop at the mall. I'd breathed in the crisp freshness of mountain air and heavy beach breezes. I'd felt the beauty of our cozy cabin in the woods. I'd felt the selfless and immediate love Yumi gave me—even when it had no future. My life had not been absurd and hopeless. It had been worth living.

Her voice floated in from the bedroom, "You know what we have to do tomorrow."

"Find and kill Larson—or die trying."

CHAPTER 50

BIANCA DOMINGUEZ PICKED UP HER tablet and crossed the length of the Sabel Technology building in Columbia, Maryland. People greeted her in the halls, even though she had only been with Sabel a few months. She wondered how much of the respect they showed her was due to her friendship with the boss and how much was due to the difference in esprit de corps between the Sabel companies and her former employer, the NSA. Not that she could complain about her NSA career. After winning a CIA-sponsored hacking contest in high school, the NSA tracked her down and gave her a scholarship to MIT. She took the money and happily began serving her required ten years with the Feds. Then President Hunter fired her.

That firing stung. It stung almost as much as the reason for the task force she created that morning. Bianca was a firm believer in strict adherence to the law. At the NSA, her coworkers were as nerdy about the rules as they were about their surveillance. Why she willingly sent Pia Sabel the NSA's high-resolution photographs of rural China was something of a mystery to her. But that's what got her fired. If a government employee at any level had asked her for the same thing, she would've gone ballistic.

All self-deception aside, she knew why she did whatever Pia asked. She'd had a crush on Pia Sabel since high school and would do anything to impress her. Every gay girl has an unrequited crush on a straight girl. It's one of the sad facts of gay life. Not unlike the straight guys who harbor lesbian-fetishes. Or the woman who dreams about bringing her two boyfriends together. The whole world lusts for something unworkable.

It was that very crush on Pia that drew her into tapping phones. She did it without a second thought. Jumped right in after making one feeble objection. Bianca could've been Pia's lifeline to reality, the helpful friend who counseled her to think about the consequences of her actions. Instead, she was a co-conspirator. Now the corporate attorneys were shielding her from the FBI's demands.

How long would that last? When it came right down to it, if the attorneys couldn't make the whole thing go away, she'd have to tell the truth. Pia did a bad thing for all the right reasons, but that wouldn't matter in the eyes of the law.

She turned the corner and entered the dark, windowless meeting room. Sixteen high-back chairs surrounded a marble, football-shaped table. Fifteen of the finest minds at Sabel Tech sat in those chairs. Carter and Tyler, the most outspoken of the group, bookended an empty chair. Their stoic faces turned to her and the room went quiet.

She cast her tablet's screen to the wall-sized monitor at the end of the room and remained standing. Mapping software pinpointed six color-coded triangles in an animated sequence. "The hunt for the Artist, the architect of the NEXT USA slaughter, is in full swing. Some of you have been working on this already and the rest are aware of it. From today forward, you're assigned to my team. We're going to find the person who financed this attack and bring him to justice."

"Excuse me." Carter raised his hand and tossed back his shoulder-length hair. "Are we working with the FBI on this?"

"Yes and no." Bianca stared down the people who grumbled. "The FBI Terrorism division is pursuing the attackers' origin. The Counterintelligence division is hyper-focused on Pia and Jacob. President Hunter made war her top priority. We're pursuing this angle—"

"Out of self-preservation?" Tyler asked.

"You mean boss-preservation," Carter said.

A cynical titter ran through the group.

"Both," Bianca answered. "I'm not going to kid you; this is a serious threat to the company."

"Could you boys shut up?" a woman's voice at the end of the table asked. Bianca didn't see who spoke, but her antagonists put their hands in their laps and faced the screen.

"As you know," she continued, "these triangles are the movements of Chuck Roche, Luuk Devoor, Ritchie Skaite, Sean Addison, Davy Cameron, and, from fairly sketchy data, Stefan Devoor. We've eliminated Davy Cameron from the list when he flew to New York. Chuck Roche approached Pia for help, but we shouldn't rule him out. What we need is a quick and accurate method of figuring out who the Artist is from the data we have. Anyone have an idea?"

No one said anything right away.

"Obviously, trace the calls," Bianca said. "But they're burner-hopping and using a complex relay system that's tough to unravel."

Tyler raised a hand for a second before speaking. "I'm not comfortable invading people's privacy. This might be standard procedure at your old job, Bianca, but you've already dug out a ton of personal—"

"We have written permission from each of the people." Bianca touched her screen to open the attachments in Outlook. "They've been filed."

"And they weren't coerced? They all agreed voluntarily?"

"That is correct." Bianca decided not to mention that more than one of them was incredulous about the backdating. And then there was the fact that they never breached Stefan's phone in the first place.

"These permissions are light on specifics," Tyler said. "Do these people know we're reading their emails or plotting their positions by the minute?"

"What is your problem?" The voice from the dark spoke up again. "We're looking for the financier of terrorism. Someone who attacked our democracy."

The voice was Teri, a heavyset middle-aged woman with short, black hair. Bianca had met her before and was impressed with her quick grasp of complex projects.

"It doesn't matter," Tyler said. "What matters is the Big-Brother factor. Five of these people are innocent. Some or all could be victims. We need to protect their privacy from the White House and the FBI."

"Terrorists don't get privacy." Teri slapped the table.

"Five of them are not terrorists."

"Then they won't mind us ruling them out."

"Why are we even doing this?" Carter asked. "What makes it OK for Pia Sabel but not OK for the government?"

"I'm not Pia Sabel and I'm not the government." Bianca stared Carter down. "I'm a citizen who is livid that an American thinks he can get away with this. We have the means to find this traitor, therefore we have a moral obligation to do it."

"That's the same excuse the Stasi used."

Bianca held a hand up to stop the conversation. She took a deep breath and crossed her arms.

She started to talk, but Teri jumped in ahead of her. "Carter, you stated your usual paranoid conspiracy theories. But I've known you since you started here and you've always been the first to help Pia or Alan. Something else is bugging you. What is it?"

A long silence followed while everyone stared at Carter.

He blushed and fiddled with a stylus for his tablet. In a quiet tone, he said, "We have a unique and powerful system here. We have the power to do what Bianca wants. But I have a big problem with who has access to our system. I've always had a problem with that. Not just in this case, but in any and all cases. If misguided people have access to our system, this would no longer be a free country."

Some of the senior employees nodded their agreement.

"We can read your mail and track your position better than the NSA." Carter glanced around the table. "That's why they contract our resources. Until now, everything has remained proprietary. The liability we have is our boss. She's a 'person of interest' in a terrorist attack. With the power of a subpoena, the government can do a search of our systems and steal our encryption-cracking algorithms, the keys to privacy in America."

"If they're going to catch terrorists," Teri said, "that's OK with me."

"That's a big 'if'. Would it be OK if President Hunter used our algorithms to open the email of Democrats and Republicans? She could outmaneuver her competition at every turn. I mean no disrespect to Hunter. It could be anybody in any party. Imagine your least favorite politician, whatever ideological persuasion you hate the most, having that power. The USA could turn into East Germany circa 1964 in thirty seconds with our algorithms."

It was a debate Bianca had been embroiled in many times at the NSA. Are we protecting or repressing freedom? Are we doing the bidding of the party in power or tracking and catching dangerous people? Checks and balances were in place, but abuse is never more than a keystroke away.

"Here's what we do." Bianca rose and paced. "Find the guy, then find a way to prove it outside of our system. Then destroy all our communications and emails, any paper trail that could be subpoenaed—before the subpoena arrives."

Everyone considered the concept for a moment.

Then Tyler raised his hand briefly again. "Hunter is already using us—"

"That may be, but there are three more terrorists out there. Americans are about to die. Let's do something to stop them and worry about Hunter later." Whispers went around the circle until she added, "Nothing gets back to Hunter. Nothing."

Carter and Tyler looked at each other, then nodded.

"We have the official dweeb blessing," Teri said. "Can we please get started now?"

Bianca restarted her meeting and took them through all the information she'd gathered. They hammered out squads to tackle each of the probability patterns and the logistics issues. They split up to retrieve personal effects from their regular desks to move into the group space. They knew they'd work without sleep until they caught the Artist. It was how they always tackled big problems.

Bianca retraced her way through the corridors.

Her phone rang with the caller ID of the receptionist. "Ms. Dominguez, there are five FBI men here. They say they have a subpoena."

CHAPTER 51

THE ARTIST TROD DOWNHILL TOWARD the Embarcadero in a sour mood, slipping in and out of pools of tangerine streetlight. The wet, chilly air carried the endless smell of frying Chinese food. Traffic hissed past him. He shoved his hands deep in his jacket pockets and trudged onward with no destination in mind.

The police and FBI had asked endless questions. *Did you see anything? Why did you drop to the floor so quickly?* He played dumb. But there was no denying it—they were getting closer. The Slager had put him in that position. Was Schwartz working with him? Where were they? Why didn't the Slager answer his phone?

All around him, everything was written in Chinese. Even the damned Bank of America branch had its name spelled out in scribbles. Proof of the great American decline. Everyone clamored to open the floodgates for these hordes of rat-people. Political correctness would drive English to extinction and the country would be babbling some child-like language before long. The Artist would stop this nonsense. The country would raise a statue in his honor one day. A park, an airport, maybe a stadium. All of the above.

He pulled out his burner and tried the Slager again. What game could the son of a bitch be playing?

The whole reason for his walk was to clear his head. Find some way out of this mess. He had to think. And think hard. Ideally, the Slager and Schwartz would kill each other. It was his best hope. But how? Maybe send that Sabel agent Jacob Stearne after the thin man. How big a risk would it be to phone Stearne and tell him where to find Schwartz? Sure, it could work. He could pretend to be one of the convicts hired to kill Stearne but decided to change allegiances.

Stearne would buy it. He was dumb enough to sign up to be an army bullet-chewer.

The Artist sighed.

If Stearne took Schwartz alive, the sniveling little worm would talk. He was a savvy negotiator, after all. He managed to testify against his Mafia bosses and wound up with only two years for three cold-blooded executions.

He stopped and looked around. The Federal Reserve Bank of San Francisco loomed over him. A dark and severe building surrounded by filthy beggars after the executive class cleared out. One of the vagrants held out a hand. The Artist scowled enough to push the man back without uttering a word. Roche's cane was handy for sidewalk encounters like that. A quick swish through the air always silenced bums. He should get a cane.

He decided to stick to his original plan. Put the Slager and Schwartz in a room and let them kill each other.

One fact he would have to face: the final death would come at his hand. It would have to. And who would he rather face? An accountant who could kill when cornered or a meth dealer who cleared a territory from St. Louis to Santa Fe? No question there.

Then a new idea came to him. He used the burner to dial Schwartz.

The thin man answered.

The Artist said, "Do you have the men we need?"

"I could only get two," Schwartz said. "And your Slager still has my kids."

"Quit worrying about your problems and do what I told you." The Artist reined in his anger. "Lure him out there. Exchange your children for my name. Just make sure you kill him. I can't have him escape knowing who I am. Now, I want to meet these men you've hired."

"For weeks you pound me about your 'insistence on distance' and now you want to meet them?"

"Things are becoming critical. The Slager has done something disloyal. He must be eliminated in twenty-four hours."

"They aren't here." Schwartz hesitated. "I can bring them in tomorrow."

"Not to the hotel, you idiot!" Again he tried to calm himself. He looked around. "Find a dive in Chinatown, one without cameras. Text me at this number."

"We're well beyond the scope. You need to—"

"Yes, yes, of course. How much?"

"Three million."

THE SLAGER SIPPED HIS COFFEE amid the clatter and clank of dishes and orders hollered between a waitress and a cook on a cold, wet night in San Francisco. Across the table from him, Schwartz clicked off and slipped the phone in his suit pocket. The thin man smiled in a way that gave him the creeps. The sooner he got rid of the damned accountant, the better.

"Plenty more to come," Schwartz said. "He replenished the Panama account. He has to pay whatever we want."

The Slager nodded and looked out the window. Beyond the reflection of himself was nothing but blackness. Somewhere in that endless dark, some ex-felons were fostering his kids. Maybe Ethan and Emma were better off. Would that fucking Stearne or the FBI ever quit looking for him? Not now. Not after five terrorists were dead and two in custody. Eventually they would confirm Hakim's story and have enough leads to find him. He could see the worst scenario: Everything goes great, he picks up his kids, starts a new life, drops them off at school one morning, and—BOOM—a SWAT team drops out of the sky. *That's right kid, your dad masterminded the most traitorous terrorist attack in American history.* There were other attacks with more massive body counts, but this one was an attack on the democracy itself.

How could he consider getting his kids back with that hanging over his head? He was better off killing himself. Leave the money for them and jump off a bridge. Who could he trust to give millions to his kids? Not their mother, that was for sure.

A pair of fingers snapped in front of him. "Did you hear me? Millions more."

"Does it bother you?" The Slager held the cup with both hands, stared into it, and inhaled the aroma of cheap, thin coffee.

Schwartz looked around the room and leaned across the scarred laminate table. "Of course it bothers me."

The waitress appeared at their booth, snapped her gum, and waited for recognition that didn't come. She quit waiting. "You boys ready to order?"

"Pancakes," the Slager said.

"Toast," Schwartz said.

They handed over their plastic-coated menus. She refilled their mugs and trundled away.

Schwartz leaned over the table again, a fierce look in his beady eyes. "What's done is done. Forget it. Let's move forward, get what we need, and go our separate ways. We have a plan—stick to it. Can you kill Stearne?"

"I've got that handled. He's dead by this time tomorrow." The Slager could only hope. He'd beaten meth-addicts and cartel assassins but never a special ops veteran. Stearne had a PhD in death. His hands trembled. He shoved them in his jacket pockets.

"You better have this handled," Schwartz hissed. "I'm counting on you. You don't look like you've got your head in the game."

The Slager scowled and watched the thin man's eyes. He growled, "Shut up and show me my goddamn kids—with a copy of today's newspaper in front of them."

"I'm working on it." Schwartz leaned back. "I can't force them to send me pictures. Besides, I'm not sure these guys know what a newspaper is."

"Great."

"Let me see mine."

"I'm not changing the deal. Mine first." The Slager sipped his coffee. It was hotter, but still weak. "Where's my new ID?"

"We're not changing the deal—says you. You get your kids, I get mine, you kill Stearne, I give you an ID, we both kill the Artist."

"Why not just tell me who he is?"

"I'm not stupid. That's my last card. Once he's dead, neither of us needs to worry about killing the other. Until then … trust is elusive."

348

Their food clattered to the table in front of them. The waitress bustled off without a word. Around them people chatted and ate in the half-filled diner. The Slager dug in and ate half his stack before washing it down with coffee.

"I still need those other two Sabel guards done," he said.

Schwartz glanced his way. "We ran out of program participants."

"What happened?"

"The police traced them back to the program. They're looking for an upstanding member of the community who looks like me but going by the name Andy Biggs."

"Where you going to get two convicts to meet the Artist?"

Schwartz nosed out the window at the bus station across the street. "A hundred bucks, a few coached answers, I'm solid."

Without knowing how gullible the Artist was, he had no way of knowing if that plan would work. Again he considered his bridge-dive option. Plant one of the burners on Schwartz, call in a tip to the authorities, jump into oblivion. Nice and easy. No more worries.

The appeal of 'no more worries' grew on him. His whole life had been fear-driven. From the moment he killed the Kansas City meth dealers and took over their operation, he'd been racing to meet his maker.

Schwartz's phone beeped. He pulled it out and smiled and pushed the screen to the Slager's face.

A blond boy and an auburn girl sat on either side of a newspaper. They were bigger. Fat from cheap food, but grown bigger, too. Their faces were exactly the same, only longer. Ethan and Emma. They were alive. But they didn't look happy. Emma was on the verge of tears, her face pouting, her fists clenched. Ethan looked pissed off, his eyes narrowed. They needed him. He owed it to them to win this game, pick them up, give them hugs, bring them home—somewhere.

"My turn." Schwartz interrupted his reverie.

"What? Right now?" The Slager looked up. "I don't let the crew carry a phone. The morons would be dialing 1-800-Praise-Allah every ten seconds."

Schwartz grabbed his collar, lightning fast, and yanked him closer.

"Are they alive?"

The real Schwartz was staring him in the eye. The Schwartz who loved his kids as much as he loved Ethan and Emma. A profound regret came over him. He never should've taken this man's kids. He and Schwartz were brothers in this nightmare. It was time to trust his brother.

"They're alive." He took a deep breath. "Tell you what. Let's cut the plan down to the essentials. I have enough money to bug out now. I'll go so far away, the Sabel guys will never find me. You find a way to get the Artist to the warehouse in the morning, I'll kill him—and you can have your kids back. We wave good-bye right then and there."

CHAPTER 52

SOME GODS ARE KIND. SOME gods are thoughtful. Some gods save their beleaguered followers when they're persecuted. Mine is just annoying. He was shaking me. The last log on the fire was still glowing. I checked the time on my phone. Only I didn't have a phone because we didn't want anyone following us.

I rubbed my eyes. *What time is it?*

Mercury said, *Thirty seconds before Pia-Caesar-Sabel wakes up screaming, yo. That means it's time to get up and get to work. You've got some terrorists to catch and a ringleader to kill.*

I said, *What are you talking about?*

Mercury paced away and back to me and threw his hands in the air. *You know what I'm talking about, Dawg. She wakes up screaming at—*

No, I mean what work is there to do? The cops want to kill me and I don't have a clue how to find Larson. My eyes focused. He was soaking wet. His toga clung to him like it was wet-toga night at a gay bar. *What happened to you?*

He nodded at the window. *It's raining outside.*

I waited for an explanation.

He said, *I saw Venus out there. The goddess of love herself. Only—it wasn't Venus. It was a Venus Castina. A cross-dressing guy posing as Venus. Not my thing. Hey. Don't judge, dude. Togas look alike in the dark. But don't worry about that. You gotta get back to the city. You know how to find Larson.*

I stared at him for a moment, wondering how far he went with Venus—but then decided there are some things you don't want to know about your god.

Suddenly, it struck me like a hockey puck shot into the stands. I jumped up and ran in the other room. Ms. Sabel tossed and turned under a heavy comforter—the condition that preceded her screaming herself awake.

I shook her shoulder.

She sat up fast, her eyes wide open and searching mine. "What is it?"

"I know how we can find the Artist. I can't believe I didn't think of it earlier. We need to find a phone."

She pulled one out from under the sheets and tossed it to me as her legs swung out from the bed. She made bedhead look good. She grabbed her yoga pants and jacket and pulled herself together. She pulled up her t-shirt and looked at her bandage. Blood seeped through. Our gazes met. She shrugged and dry-swallowed a handful of antibiotics.

I turned the phone on and recognized the screen as Tania's. "You think they've noticed you swapped phones?"

"Not for a while." She pulled her hair back in her trademark ponytail. "It's been off since we left. Use it, shut it off again."

Through the cloud, I accessed my text messages and found Captain Behan's phone number. He didn't answer. It went to voice mail. "Captain Behan, that video where I told you about the terrorist is on the cloud. It goes live on the *Post's* website unless you tell me: who asked Admiral Tilden to extract Michael Larson? I'll call you later and expect an answer."

My muscles were twitching in readiness to start the endgame. I didn't know who I was after or where he was, but he was going down. Just as I was about to pull the battery, Yumi's pretty face popped into my head. She must have emailed me. I risked taking another minute online and accessed my email. Scanning through a thousand special offers, two emails caught my attention. Yumi sent a short novel about her feelings and Michael Larson sent another challenge.

Prioritizing, I scanned Yumi's tome first. It stung like a knife in my heart. Her point was clear from the opening sentence. Life with the *Shinigami*, spirit of death, kept her in a state of constant paralysis. In the beginning, she'd hoped to change me. As time went on, she came to realize I wasn't the spirit—I was the victim. The *Shinigami* were chasing me. My life was a constant battle against the unstoppable onslaught of death. She wanted me to stop inviting the *Shinigami* into my life.

Yeah. Well. I can do whatever I want. The twenty-eighth amendment to the constitution guarantees my right to invite evil spirits into my life. Murder and mayhem is the great American pastime. Don't believe me? Turn on the TV.

Mercury pointed at the screen. *She got that right, brutha. You're a marked man. If not for your favorite god, you'd be ashes in the wind right now. Speaking of Shinigami coming for you, let's take a peek at the one from Larson.*

First I replied to her. "TL;DR. I've an appointment with a *Shinigami* right now, but I'll call you after, 'K?"

Mercury said, *Don't press SEND. Don't press SEND. Don't press SEND. Aw, dude, you pressed send. You know you're going to regret that in the morning.*

I said, *She dissed my profession. And she left me. I'm pissed.*

Larson's email went straight to the point. "Next Rave: Quesada & Fitch, warehouse district, 9AM. Be there or be talked about, motherfucker. PS: Tried to call you—are you ignoring me? Hurts, bro. I'm guessing you peed your pants and ran away without your phone."

We were 300 miles away on horseback. I needed to stall for time to change our mode of transportation. I replied, "Deepest regrets, Princess. Calendar shows too many overlapping parties. Can we make the after-party? Say 9PM? PS: Don't be so sensitive about the sends-to-voicemail. I live to kill guys like you."

Ms. Sabel was looking over my shoulder this time. "Did he really think you'd walk into an ambush?"

"Yes, because I would. Anytime."

"Won't he think we're sending the FBI?"

"He's planning to sacrifice his pawns, the remaining terrorists."

She looked at me as if she was impressed with my intellectual capacity. I struck a pose that I thought was the kind of pose smart people strike. I savored the moment.

"May I?" She tugged the phone from my hand and turned her back to me. "Before we go dark, I just have to check a couple things."

No secret what she was checking after she saw Yumi's email in my inbox.

I went out in the dark to check on the horses. They were sound asleep. I looked at the stars and figured it was about 3:30 a.m., ninety minutes before daylight. Back inside, she'd turned the phone off and stowed it. We made breakfast and ate and cleaned up the place for the next guests.

We went outside and woke the horses and tossed them some hay. Saddled and ready to ride, we decided to walk them until first light. Flashlights kept us moving for the first hour. The pale blue predawn helped us farther. There was plenty of light, but no sunshine an hour later. The mountains obscured direct beams from the sun, but the sky had cleared and the morning warmed.

An owl swooped in silently behind Ms. Sabel to check us out. She never sensed its presence. It glided to a tree and hooted.

After an hour of silence, I had to ask. "What did Stefan have to say?"

"A few profanities and a lot of unpleasantness." She sighed. "He complained about the backdated forms; said he found them dishonest. His second round of texts was uglier."

Once we decided the horses could see well enough, we rode several miles to the reservation.

There wasn't a town so much as a dirt road with a string of houses along it. It was still early, not much moved, not even the birds. Finally, we found a man walking toward us. Anthony Tsotsie called out and waved. "This way."

We followed him into the trees to a small clapboard house in need of a paint job. Behind it was a split-rail paddock, weathered and warped. An old Honda was parked in front. Next to the Honda was a '67 Pontiac GTO Convertible.

Hartman stepped out to the porch holding a cup of coffee. He watched us turn the horses into the corral without saying a word. We approached him with one-part excitement and one-part consternation. Like being called to the principal's office the day I won the state history bee but also set off a firecracker in the teacher's lounge. You never know what they want to talk about.

We stepped onto the porch. Tsotsie brought out mugs of coffee and handed them to us. We kept our eyes on Hartman and blew the heat off our aromatic mugs of java.

He took a sip and lowered his mug and pulled his chin up. "Tough sleeping for me last night. By daylight I come to the conclusion there ain't no way in hell Jacob Stearne done what they said. I don't know you at all, ma'am, but if Jacob's traveling with you, that's good 'nuff. So I got to thinking—if they're saying these things, you must be in a world of trouble. Thought you might need some wheels."

"We don't want to sound ungrateful," Ms. Sabel said, "but that's your car now."

"What good is it to me? Don't carry no hay."

CHAPTER 53

BIANCA DOMINGUEZ STARED AT THE agent and the agent stared at her in the meeting room above the data center at Sabel Technologies while bright sunshine poured in the windows. Both had their arms crossed and frowns squeezed tight. The FBI's geek squad stood to one side, watching and waiting for a definitive outcome as if it were a prize fight.

"You have to comply with the warrant," Special Agent in Charge John Glover said.

"I have. It's not my fault your systems are incompatible with our technology."

Tyler, Sabel Tech's chief nerd, passed by outside the open door for the third time in sixty seconds. She ignored him.

"You must have an interface somewhere. How else could this system work with the rest of the world?"

"We've been over this." She tightened her arms. "We analyze the data and send the client a report."

"That's not acceptable."

"If you don't know how to use our systems, why not ask Mr. Roche to give you the same access he granted us?"

Glover uncrossed his arms and waved them in frustration. "Roche refused. Says he doesn't trust us."

"Wonder why? Maybe because you ignored Jacob's intel and a major candidate died?"

"We need that information." His nerds flinched at his shout.

"Then let us do our jobs and we'll send you the same report we send him." She opened her arms wide. "We know what we're doing."

The Sabel Tech attorney stormed in, waving a court order over his head. "Judge just revoked your warrant. Clear out."

The agent grabbed it, skimmed, then hurled the papers into the air and paced away. When he reached the window, he put his palms on the sill and stared out. After a moment, he turned around and said in a soft voice. "Can my people sit in with you at least? We're on the same team here."

"You guys fucked up and now you want us to cover your ass?" the attorney yelled. "Why not call your dogs off Ms. Sabel? She's fleeing for her life from your jack-booted thugs."

"That's Counterintelligence. Nothing to do with my task force. If I could stop them, I would." He softened his tone. "Look, we want to prevent the next terrorist attack. You want to stop the next terrorist—"

"You want to cover up the American who financed it—" the attorney pointed his finger at the agent "—so the woman who pulls your strings can have her little war."

"I'm a career agent. Presidents come and go." Glover's face exploded in crimson. "Truth—that's what I'm after. Nothing less."

His nerds nodded their heads, looking defiant.

The attorney started to charge across the room.

Bianca put her hand across the attorney's chest. "The Sabels believe in teamwork. Your squad can stay right here. I can't bring them up to speed on how our proprietary system works without slowing the process. But we'll update you every step of the way."

She turned the attorney around and marched out the door with him. As they began to part ways in the hall, she grabbed him. "'Jack-booted thugs'? Are you one of *those* guys?"

"Hell no." He laughed as he walked away. "I am an advocate for my client. If it works—I'll say it."

Tyler stepped in. "We need you in the Guild Hall. We were making progress, then bam—hit a wall."

She followed him. "We're calling the meeting room a Guild Hall? As in World of Warcraft 'guild'?"

He glanced her way, assessing what she knew about online gaming's biggest multiplayer system.

"Method Guild," she said, "Master for two years, but the time commitment was killing me. I'm an officer now. You?"

"Whoa." Tyler grinned as they walked. "I'm impressed. I'm in

Paragon Guild, officer."

She fist-bumped him as they turned into Guild Hall. Three laptops sat in front of every member of the team. Some had UHD screens, others used the wall display. Fiber optic cables ran everywhere.

She pointed at the cables. "We use fiber?"

"10 GigE. Ternary systems use a ton of bandwidth." Tyler glanced her way, started to say something, got one syllable out, then clamped his mouth shut and turned away.

Bianca touched his shoulder and raised an eyebrow when he met her gaze.

"Well," Tyler stammered, "it's just that, we've always been the good guys here. Sabel Tech has always been on the right side of the law one hundred percent. But lately, things look a little … off."

"You mean since I came on board?" She sensed everyone in the room slowing their typing, trying to eavesdrop.

"It's not just you. We know the NSA is used to trashing the Constitution and the rule of law. We're worried about Pia. She ran away when the FBI wanted her for questioning."

"Pia didn't run." She raised her voice to address the team. "She's a chess-player, thinking ten moves ahead. She pulled Jacob out of an FBI witch-hunt seconds before they tossed him in jail. We don't know what political forces are working behind the scenes, but you know Pia, which means you know she went to ground for a reason."

The team rolled her words around in their heads for a moment and, one by one, nodded and went back to work.

"Where are we?" Bianca asked Tyler.

He flagged Teri, whose gaze bounced across three screens.

Teri clicked a few things, then pointed to the big screen, where she displayed a map she had been working on. "We traced the Artist's calls coming from Cambodia. The calls are being generated from an ancient analog system. Our tracer packets stopped there because the only way to trace analog systems is to go there and do it manually. It's like driving a car across land then coming to a body of water—you need a boat. Everything we do is digital. We need a boat to ferry us across the analog bay in Cambodia."

"Clever move." Bianca walked around the large table. "Do any of the Sabel companies have people in Cambodia?"

Teri shook her head. "I tried the Cambodian phone company. I tried the IT guys at our embassy. With the time change and the language barrier, I got nothing. Right now, we're dead in the water on the trace."

"Ideas?"

"What about your boyfriend?" Tyler smirked.

Everyone in the room looked up and held their breath.

Bianca caught their gazes. "He means the FBI guys parked in the other room."

Everyone went back to work while Bianca looked up something on her phone. "Teri, could you walk a layperson through what needs to be done?"

"I'm not sure I know what needs to be done." She shrugged and raised her voice to the group. "Anyone know analog phone systems?"

The team looked up collectively, their noses crinkled as if something smelled foul.

One older woman raised her hand. "PABX and PMBX in my early days."

"I think it's a Fujitsu PMBX. Can you walk someone through the process?"

The woman nodded.

Bianca ran down the hall to the room full of FBI agents and approached the leader. "The FBI has a legate in Cambodia. I need his help."

He looked her up and down. "Where is Pia Sabel?"

"We've traced the Artist to a trunk line in Cambodia. We need your man to visit the phone company. We can walk him through how to trace the call from there."

"You've been in touch with her." He crossed his arms. "The task force wants her for questioning."

"The next attack could be any minute. We need your man now."

"We know you and Pia have exchanged information since she disappeared. Withholding information could lead to charges of aiding and abetting a fugitive."

"Our email wasn't covered by your last quashed warrant." Bianca sighed. "Want me to bring my wingnut-lawyer back in here to explain the Constitution to you?"

The man blew out an exasperated breath.

"What will it take to get the Cambodian on the line?" she asked.

"Either cooperation or an executive order."

Bianca pulled her phone and dialed Veronica Hunter. It went to voicemail. She redialed three times before Hunter picked up.

Hunter hissed, "Whoever you think you are—"

"I stood in the Oval Office and heard you promise Pia anything she needed."

"Oh. You." Hunter hesitated. "Talk."

After a hasty re-introduction, she explained the situation and the need for help in Cambodia.

"I'm not involved in that level," Hunter said. "And don't call this—"

"Ma'am, respectfully, I will hold a press conference laying out everything we know so far. Including that Pia is acting at your request. I'll tell them who helped and who hindered—"

"You're just difficult as your boss." President Hunter sighed.

"I'll take that as a compliment."

"Put the FBI man on."

Bianca handed the phone to the agent.

Even with the phone pressed to his ear, she could hear Hunter's shrill voice ripping into the man. He turned his back on Bianca and snapped his fingers at his geek squad. They began typing away on their laptops. He stuttered a few syllables of apology before looking at the screen. Bianca could see it from where she stood: *Call ended.*

He faced her and tossed the phone. "How do you have the President's cell number?"

"When can we talk to your man?" She caught the phone one-handed.

"As soon as they locate him and wake him up." He crossed his arms again. "You have our full cooperation, Ms. Dominguez."

"Call me when you have him onsite."

CHAPTER 54

THE ARTIST CHECKED THE TWO vagrants with disdain and paid for his coffee and muffins and glared at Schwartz and pushed through the café patrons into the foggy Chinatown lane. He glanced left and right. They crossed the narrow street and huddled in the alcove of a closed electronics store.

Safe from the flow of pedestrians, the Artist examined his little gang. "Why on earth would I go with you to the warehouse district?"

One of the vagrants stepped menacingly close to the Artist and scowled.

"Enough of this farce." The Artist poked the vagrant in the chest. "How much did he pay you?"

The two men glanced at each other, then at Schwartz.

"Show me the bill he gave you and I'll double it just to make you go away, you stinking scum."

One man pulled a fifty out of his filthy pea coat.

The Artist took out his wallet and found a couple hundreds. "Here, be gone."

The men snatched their bills and fast-walked down the sidewalk.

Schwartz sipped his coffee while the Artist held his gaze. The accountant offered nothing.

"Tell me why I shouldn't kill you right now." The Artist stamped from one foot to the other, trying to calm himself.

"You wouldn't have a clue how to do it." Schwartz took another sip. "And you don't have a weapon."

"What happened to the program?"

"I told you. They were working the DNA from the guys at Stearne's place. An FBI agent named Verges is all over it. I can't contact anyone without going straight to 'life without parole'."

"Nice." The Artist set his coffee on the store's narrow window ledge and examined his blueberry muffin. "You'll have to do it yourself. We already know you can."

"He has my kids." The thin man hissed spittle as he spoke. "Your monsters are holding them."

He nodded. "Let's fix that. Give me your phone."

Schwartz scowled and hesitated before handing it over.

The Artist entered a long stream of numbers and waited while the call to Syria went through. The phone rang several times before being picked up. "Give me Ahmad."

"There is no one by that name," the voice on the other end said.

"Tell him the Artist is calling."

"Wait moment."

After a few minutes, the other end picked up.

"What you want!" Ahmad's thick accent crackled over the connection as the call bounced through several countries. "You fucked up everything. We give you ten men, we have only one attack."

"The man I chose for the job did not live up to expectations. I need to make a change in management. How do I tell them not to listen to the Slager anymore?"

Ahmad paused. "The Commander says your people never picked up the last oil shipment—and you never paid."

"There's been a temporary problem there. Roche sold his refinery to Pia Sabel. Now I have to find a new one that doesn't care where the tankers come from."

"Is that my problem? You pay your goddamn bills or I come out there and kill you myself."

"All right. I'll wire the money this morning. It will land in Riyadh by this afternoon." The Artist took a deep breath. "I need to get your men back under control. How can I do that?"

"With two words: *ruyaan nabwyiya.* It means, Apocalypse."

The Artist repeated it to get the pronunciation right. He waved for Schwartz to join him in repeating the word.

Schwartz rolled his eyes and joined in while they tried it several more times.

"What a schmuck." Artist laughed after he clicked off. "Does he really think I'm going to send him more money?"

He took a deep breath and looked skyward to see the fog clearing early. "This is going to be a great day. President Hunter is finally going to start a war with those fucking maniacs and in no time, those oil fields will finally be ours!"

Schwartz's mouth fell open. "Is that what this is all about?"

"Don't be shocked, you imbecile. Why do you think we invaded Iraq? Everyone knew Osama bin Laden was a thousand miles away. After that war, guess who won services contracts for more than two million barrels a day?" The Artist smiled up at the sky and reveled in his memories. "But the fucking government clamped down on ownership and all we get is a dollar a barrel. We took it, but we could've had more. This time, those fields will be mine."

Schwartz was mute.

"Well, Schwartz," the Artist patted him on the shoulder, "now you know how to get your children back. Commandeer them, and you have three Moroccans to kill the Slager. So, go get 'em, Tiger."

The Artist pushed the phone back in Schwartz's shirt pocket and walked away.

★ ★ ★

IN A NONDESCRIPT MINI-WAREHOUSE NEAR the bay, the Slager kicked Schwartz's body and saw no sign of life. The two bullet holes in the thin man's forehead didn't leave any expectation for a miracle recovery, but he'd seen weirder shit go down. He stuck his head out the narrow warehouse door and squinted into the bright morning sun to check the street. No one. Only the thin man's car. That would come in handy.

He closed the door and faced Youssef. Smoke still wafted from his man's pistol.

"What's the matter?" he asked. "You never killed a man before?"

Youssef turned his drained face slowly to the back of the small space. Schwartz's children stood with taped mouths and bound hands, tears streaming down their faces. "Not in front of his children."

"He was a Jew," the Slager lied. The name was a fake ID. The accountant couldn't spell Hebrew if you spotted him a *Yodh* and a *Tsade*.

Youssef trembled.

Not good. A reluctant martyr was of no use to anyone.

The Slager stepped to him and patted his back. "Not exactly the way I expected it to go down either, buddy. When I told you to kill anyone who said *ruyaan nabwyiya,* I was thinking … after we interrogated him. But then I never clarified that, so, yeah, my bad."

He knelt at the body and began going through Schwartz's pockets. "Fuck. We had a deal, Schwartz. Why did you turn on me?"

He glanced over his shoulder. His crew huddled halfway between the front rolling door and the kids in back, whispering Arabic in terse tones. Hanging with martyrs was like carrying nitroglycerine: to stay alive, make no sudden moves. He turned back to Schwartz.

"Sorry, pal," the Slager said to the corpse, "but you never told me things I need to know."

Like, who had his goddamn kids? And, who is the Artist? If there were any clues, he needed them desperately. He pulled two phones, a wallet, and a Beretta Nano. The small pistol was the perfect weapon for concealed-carry: no external bumps, levers, or slides to get stuck in your clothes. Schwartz had given his mission some serious thought. Just like the Slager, he was intent on getting his children out of the mess they were in.

The Slager checked the kids huddled in the corner. They were a couple years older than his own. Shame they had to watch their father die. He couldn't imagine his kids going through that kind of horror. But that's what happens to disloyal assholes like Schwartz.

He pushed the dead man's finger across the first phone's sensor and looked it over. The recent calls list included a long one starting with the international code for Syria. That wasn't good. The NSA would be all over this guy. They had minutes to bug out. Scratching a shred of paper with the remains of a broken pencil, he transcribed several numbers. Then he went to email. Nothing recognizable except a company name, Energy Outfitters. Damn. Schwartz's paycheck came from the same bullshit company as his. He'd tried to find the owners, but every time he tried, all he found were more shell companies.

The second phone revealed something else, but he wasn't sure what to make of it. A Google map with a place marked "Mildred Ridge" ten miles as the crow flies outside of Tahoe. Zooming in closer, he saw a twisting road that was twenty miles long. He pocketed the phone.

The voices of his Moroccans grew louder by the moment. Some kind of fight in Arabic. They started pushing each other and pointing at the Slager. He gave them his look. This time, they scowled back.

"We have to get out of there." He pointed to Schwartz. "This guy was a Fed. They're going to be all over us in minutes. Grab the ammo, the guns, leave the kids."

No one moved.

"Youssef, we have to move right—"

"They say I am woman. I was scared. They came to meet Allah. They want the attack to happen now."

The Slager took a deep breath and waded into their triangle. He stuck a finger in the face of both the others. "Listen up. Youssef is no woman. He made an executive decision. He killed an important American. Now we have to leave. Yesterday, your brothers killed several of the wealthiest Americans. Many people died in their glorious attack! See how the flags are lowered again. The mayor is wearing a black arm band." He showed them Schwartz's phone and pulled up old posts on Maddox's killing. "We have one more mission. But first, we need to go into hiding. Security is tight everywhere. We'll lay low, wait until the infidels feel safe again. Then we strike!"

After Youssef translated, his boys were back on track. But god only knew when they'd come unglued again. The warehouse had been a cache stocked with supplies for them: assault rifles, magazines, suicide vests, and bombs. The crew loaded up Schwartz's car with the goods.

The Slager stood over Schwartz's corpse and stared at the kids. He remembered his lesson: kill the kids first. He raised his gun and aimed. The boy looked up, the face of innocence. Just like Ethan.

When the boy's eyes, clouded with tears, focused on the barrel, he screamed into the tape.

"We are ready." Youssef tapped the Slager's shoulder. "You will kill them?"

"Yeah, start the car." He looked at his young suicide bomber. Another innocent in a rapidly unraveling world. "We'll need to get out of here fast."

Youssef ran outside.

The Slager shoved the last burner he'd used to contact the Artist into Schwartz's pocket. With any luck, the cops would call Schwartz the ringleader and stop looking for him. That would take a lot of luck. He contemplated the other two phones.

From Schwartz's NSA-tainted phone he thumbed out an email to Jacob Stearne. "After-parties are for losers. It's OK though. Some guy showed up with his two kids. One of the three is dead right now. The other two … well, maybe you shouldn't turn down my invitation next time. Swing by soon and you can be the hero who saved their lives. But the air is thin in here. Don't wait too long. Ciao, motherfucker."

He dropped the phone next to Schwartz. The last one, the one that might hold clues to the Artist's identity, he tossed in his hand a couple times. As dangerous as it might be, he put it in his pocket.

He fired four times, ran out, locked the warehouse door, and jumped in the van.

CHAPTER 55

MY ARM SPANNED THE CENTER console and Ms. Sabel's seatback, my feet were spread wide in the roomy footwell, and the wind whirled around my head in a Pontiac GTO with the top down as we flew south on a beautiful summer morning. Mercury had warned me about roadblocks on the I-5. We went the long way to the 101 and drove through redwood country. Ms. Sabel knew how to make the Goat fly. Someone told me she took driving courses with an eye on racing in her youth. She could've won Indy or Monaco from what I saw. We leaned through the gentle curves and hills winding through the Coast Ranges and soaked up the sun when we reached the coastal flats south of Fortuna.

But a 400 cubic inch V8 with a four-barrel carb and four on the floor sucks enough gas to make Saudi princes stand up and cheer when you drive by. We stopped for fuel near Rio Dell and decided to grab some water and coffee for the long drive ahead. Ms. Sabel went inside while I pumped the gas.

Mercury hopped out of the back seat and stretched his arms in the air. *Weehoo, is this a nice day or what? Dude, you know what happens on nice days like this? Everything goes to Avernus. Am I right?*

I said, *To what?*

Mercury said, *Avernus, the volcano. The entrance to the underworld. Do you ever read those books I gave you? No. Of course not. Holy Diana, what am I gonna do with you? Avernus is what you pansy Christians call hell.*

I ignored him. Sometimes I have no idea what he's talking about. But I did read one of the books once. Some of it. Boring.

Mercury stuck his arms out and twirled his toga. *Reminds me of that beautiful day in Abritus. They call it Bulgaria now. I told that smartass*

Emperor Decius not to do it, but he was like you—he had it all under control. He won himself a small skirmish and chased his enemy into the swamp. That's when Cniva, King of the Goths, brought his legions out of hiding. Oh, it was ugly, bro. UG-lee. I lost twenty thousand worshippers that day, including Decius. First emperor to die in battle. Beginning of the end, man.

The pump handle clicked off. I squeezed in a few more drops.

A hulking shadow stopped next to me. "Hey, ain't you the guy they're looking for in the city?"

I squinted into the sun at the silhouette of a guy as big as a redwood. "Huh?"

"Yeah, you're that terrorist-hugger." He shoved me with a meaty hand and yelled at a truck ten yards away. "Jonesy, Trevor, we get a reward for this here guy."

I fell against the pump. I tried to throw a punch but still held the nozzle in one hand and ended up tripping over the hose.

"Where you think you're going?" He grabbed a fistful of my shirt and yanked me upright.

I took a swing at him and hit granite. He laughed.

I kicked his shin and kneed his balls. That combination always works. He let go of me and staggered back, gasping to regain his strength. I landed an uppercut that did nothing but piss him off. His retaliatory charge started from his back foot like a guy who actually knew how to fight.

Not good.

I backpedaled. Sometimes the best defense is to run away really fast.

Ms. Sabel's legs, covered in purple yoga pants, flew between the pumps, her hands on the machine tops, her full body weight in concentrated motion. Her feet hit the side of the monster's head. He fell across the trunk of our GTO. She landed a powerful kick between his legs.

The second time in as many seconds was too much, even for a redwood. The man crumpled into a ball by the back tire.

Ms. Sabel vaulted into the driver's seat and I dove in the passenger side. She put her toe on the brake and her heel on the gas. Her other foot held the clutch, which she dropped when the revs ran up. The back tires broke loose, swinging the back around, pointing us out of the station and down the road. The tires gripped, the drift stopped, and we were thrown forward like a rock from a slingshot.

The Goat growled down the pavement. Nothing sounds like a 60s muscle car.

Although the hot-rodded pickup truck behind us carried a pretty throaty note of its own. The monster's buddies revved their jacked Chevy while the leviathan staggered to the back door. The chase was on.

Ms. Sabel flew down a side street, looking left and right for a way back to the highway. Single-level ranch houses with big yards lined the sides. Kids' toys scattered across the lots. The pavement we were on headed deeper into the woods on a track too narrow for a U-turn.

"Can you pull up a map?" she shouted over noise. "We need a cross street."

I pulled her phone and turned it on. While I waited for the link up with Sabel Satellites, I rummaged around in the back seat and pulled some weapons out of my backpack. I laid two Glocks on the center console up front before assembling my MP5SD. Scanning the road behind us, rifle raised and ready, I caught a glimpse of our pursuers. Naturally, they had a rifle rack in the back window. Empty.

Mercury rode the Pontiac's rear deck like a surfboard. *Are we having fun yet, brutha?*

I said, *How do we get out of this?*

Shoot your way out. There's only three of them. He turned and gave me a mean glare. *If you're expecting my help, just remember how you promised to introduce me to Pia-Caesar-Sabel last time you were about to die. Where's that promise at now, homie?*

Later, OK? I swear. I can't believe how he waits until I'm about to die before he reminds me I owe him. *I can't shoot these guys. Look at all the toys in front of these houses. A stray bullet—*

The first incoming round zinged by my ear and cleared the windshield. We swerved into a bend before they could fire again. I jumped in the back and stretched over the convertible's tonneau cover. I tried to aim when they came around the corner. All I could see was a tricycle in the background.

A volley of shots went to our right as Ms. Sabel swerved left.

Then, suddenly, they were gaining on us.

Ms. Sabel was slowing.

I looked forward. The pavement ended, the road was dirt, but a quarter mile ahead was a long stretch of mud.

She downshifted. "We can make it through that. Hang on."

"No!" I grabbed her shoulder hard. Beyond the muck, a jacked-up Toyota waited for us like King Cniva. "Swing it around. I'll pin them down."

She glanced at me over her shoulder but didn't argue. She did that thing again, toe on the brake, heel on the gas, clutch to the floor, and release. Boom. Our back tires lit up, spewing smoke and the stench of burning rubber, and the back end swung around in the narrow strip. We faced the monster.

I stood up on the back seats for better footing and fired over the windshield on full-auto, aiming into the pavement beneath them. The ricochets pinged off the metal undercarriage, dissipating their deadly energy.

The GTO lurched forward again. I leveled my rifle at them as we approached. The Chevy driver did what civilians always do when facing certain death: he tugged the wheel away from my muzzle, sending his vehicle off-road. The front end folded around a tree trunk. We sped past them as their foreheads banged off exploding airbags.

I dropped to the back bench seat and spread my arms wide. "That was a ponderosa pine. No redwoods were hurt in the making of this getaway."

Mercury dropped in the small space next to me. *Get your scrawny ass over on your side, bro. You think I wanna snuggle with you all the way back to 'Frisco? And quit smiling like you've done something good. You haven't even read the latest email from Larson. Kids' lives are at stake.*

I worked my way up front to the passenger seat and grabbed the phone. I read the last email from Larson and felt my stomach turn. Would he kill children?

After a quick discussion with the boss, I called Special Agent Verges.

"Quesada & Fitch, get the Terrorism Task Force down there. Do *not* bring your buddy Watson."

I filled him in on the details. He complained that Watson was his boss, asshat or not, and that he couldn't run around without permission. I assured him the end would justify the means. I reiterated that he would need a massive SWAT team in case Larson had it rigged to blow or was waiting in ambush. I clicked off.

Ms. Sabel sped through the Humboldt Redwoods State Park so fast we didn't have time to properly admire the massive trees. Even at ninety miles an hour, they were impressive. So were the startled faces of the tourists we wove through like an obstacle course. Our tires chirped as we crossed the double yellow lines to pass RVs. She hunched over the wheel, her knuckles white, her eyes focused on the road ahead with single-minded intensity.

As we flew south, I called Captain Behan, the only connection I had to Admiral Tilden. This time he picked up on the first ring. "Who asked Tilden to pick up Michael Larson?"

"I don't know," Behan said. "Navy's Inspector General has Tilden's equipment locked down. I don't have answers for you."

"Bullshit. You peeked before the IG's crew came in."

"I swear; I don't know anything."

"Won't matter, that video's going live in an hour. Explain it to your friends." I paused for effect. "Or tell me what you saw when you looked through his phone."

He didn't say anything. I didn't say anything. I let the silence hang there, eating at his conscience.

"I don't know what it means," he said finally. "He was getting texts from someone listed as 'the Artist.' It appears they were good friends in high school. The Admiral went to Deerfield. Maybe you can find something out from that angle. But I did see a text where this 'artist' talked about the Admiral picking up an employee of Energy Outfitters."

CHAPTER 56

SUNSHINE STREAMED IN THE WINDOWS of Guild Hall, the temporary hacker's enclave in Sabel Technologies' headquarters. It warmed Bianca's shoulders as she stared at the caller ID on her phone. After a quick glance around, she stepped out into the corridor before answering.

"Have you reconsidered?" she asked.

Stefan hesitated. Something on the line added a barely-perceptible high-pitched whine. "The purpose of my call is to urge you to tell the FBI where they can find Pia."

"Which FBI?" Bianca knew that whine. A cheap Bluetooth tap to a recorder or a second phone. "David Watson of Counterintelligence, who has offered a reward for Jacob Stearne—dead or alive? Or the Terrorism Task Force?"

"He never said 'dead or alive'."

"May as well have. 'Heavily armed and dangerous'. If the cops pull him over, what are they going to do when he reaches for his driver's license?"

Stefan hesitated again. All his calls had been like this; she asked a question, someone gave him guidance on the answer.

"Who's with you?" she asked. "Is it Watson?"

Another hesitation.

"Stefan, we're very close to unmasking the Artist. We know he's routing calls through six countries."

"Where is Pia?"

"If I knew, I would tell the Terrorism Task Force." Bianca had an idea. "You have to ask yourself why Watson wants her. This isn't the first time their paths have crossed. Who do you trust, Pia or Watson?"

Stefan clicked off.

She stared at her phone and wondered about Stefan's position during the call. Was he acting alone? Was he handcuffed to a chair with Watson holding a phone to his ear? Was he with someone else?

She turned in time to see Alan Sabel approaching down the long, marble hall. "Mr. Sabel, could I speak to you privately for a moment?"

He pulled up a yard short with a puzzled look. "I'm expecting your team's progress report in Guild Hall."

"If you don't mind." She pointed to a small, empty meeting room next to Guild Hall. Her heart raced. Talking to Pia was easy, but Alan was not just physically intimidating, he was older and harder with a famously quick wit and an equally famous low threshold for employee mistakes.

He ducked in, she followed, closed the door, and faced him. "Thank you, Mr. Sabel. What I—"

"Please, call me Alan." The big man smiled weakly. He shifted his weight.

She rubbed her palms together and paced into the corner for no reason. She turned around. "Alan, then. Um. I've heard you say things on the news about Pia. I know you're disappointed in her situation. You made that—"

"Despite what the anti-business crowd thinks, there is no room for equivocation in business. She cannot rearrange the truth to suit her wishes. Owning a company like this gives her tremendous power, but with it comes great responsibility. What separates Sabel Industries from—"

"Thanks for the dad-lesson on morality." She hadn't meant to snap at him. "It was my idea."

Alan's head tilted slightly as he digested the implication.

"I talked her into tapping the phones." Bianca threw her arms out wide. "She was against it, thought it was unethical. I thought we might find some answers to a lot of questions."

"But you worked at the NSA. You know better."

"I know. At the NSA we never did that kind of thing because everything is signed off three times over. No warrant—no tracing, no tapping. I felt a little freedom here. It went to my head. The team already gave me an earful." She crossed her arms. "I just can't listen to you blaming her in the press when I know it's my fault."

"I see." He nodded and regarded her. "She looks to you for guidance. Surely you can provide better advice that."

"Tania is her counselor. I'm just an employee."

"Tania is good in a bar fight. But Pia thinks of you as her intellectual peer."

Bianca's gaze snapped up to his. "But she has Jacob—"

"Jacob's not a ... Jacob has certain..." He shuddered. "Let's not talk about Jacob."

Her phone chirped, tugging her gaze to the incoming text. She tried to keep a poker face but felt herself scrunch up with concern.

Alan said, "What is it?"

"Pia. She wants me to trace Energy Outfitters' contractors."

"The company she just bought from Royal Devoor?"

Bianca felt her mouth tighten into a thin line as she nodded.

"When we deliver our report, the team will have a location for Pia and Jacob." She felt him watching her pupils with the same intense stare Pia often used. "It'll be a few minutes old—she'll turn the phone off—but with California's geography, it won't be hard to figure out where they are."

"I see what you're trying to tell me." He paced the room, ending up in the opposite corner from her. "We'll have to report her location to the FBI. Watson will find out. He'll bring a SWAT team in. They'll end up like Bonnie and Clyde. Jesus."

They both paced the small room, one on each side of the center table.

Alan rubbed his chin as he paced, then stopped and caught Bianca's gaze. "Watson's a professional. If I tell him we're bringing her in, he'll stand down, right?"

"Possible." Bianca shrugged. "But I wouldn't put my daughter's life in the hands of a man who's been questionable from the start."

They resumed pacing and picked up speed.

Bianca stopped. "If we tell the Terrorism Task Force, are you sure they'll tell Watson?"

"It depends on how many of Watson's former staff have crossed over.

In a group as big as those two divisions, there would have to be plenty. One of them would find out and tell him." Alan pushed his hair back with both hands. "How close are you to finding the Artist?"

"We can't be sure. At this point, we need him to make another call on the last phone he used, or text Roche again. He's gone two days without texting and he rarely uses the same burner twice. If we could get just one break on physical clues, like who he works for or who else he's been in contact with, we could nail him."

Alan paced again.

"Can Hunter order Watson to stand down?" Bianca asked.

"Tried that." Alan shook his head. "She admitted Watson's division is semi-autonomous now. Partly her lame-duck administration and partly—"

A knock on the door startled them both.

The knob turned and the door opened and Special Agent Glover stepped in. "We understand you located Jacob Stearne."

Two more agents stood behind Glover.

Bianca said, "What makes you think we've located—"

"Because NAVSUP's Captain Behan got a call from Jacob. Which means he has a phone. Which means you know where he was at the time of that call. Don't try to—"

Alan stepped in front of Bianca. "I have instructed my employees not to share any further information with you or anyone at the FBI until we have satisfactory guarantees for the safety of Pia and Jacob."

"You can't do that." Ten seconds of silence passed, then Glover tilted his head back. "You know damn well this is an important investigation into terrorism. You cannot withhold information from me. That's obstruction of justice." He shook with rage, yet took a few seconds and a deep breath. "You have to explain that one."

"I will only explain it to a judge with my attorney." Alan crossed his arms and planted his feet.

"You're forcing me to get a court order?" Glover looked at his men behind him in disbelief.

Alan said nothing.

Glover looked at Bianca. She looked out the window.

"Begging your pardon, sir," Glover stooped a little. "You're forcing my hand. I don't want to do this, but I'll have to take you in."

They stared at each other like territorial bears.

"Hold on." Glover wagged a finger at Alan. "You're stalling. You know you're going to lose, but you know it's going to take a day or two to untangle. That means you know something. With all due respect, you need to tell me what you know."

Alan didn't move.

Glover looked at Bianca. She stayed silent.

"You'll end up going to jail, sir." Glover sighed.

Alan stuck out his wrists.

"Behind your back, sir."

Alan Sabel turned around and offered his hands behind his back.

Bianca faced Alan. "Mr. Sabel, I'm sure there's another—"

"If you can take some blame for her, so can I." He winked. "I bought you the time, now you need to find the Artist. Get on it."

Bianca ran out the door and into Guild Hall. She banged her fist on the table to get the attention of her group. "Two things, people: first, Alan Sabel is going to jail to protect Pia and Jacob; second, there are three terrorists out there. We have hours—maybe minutes—to find the Artist. What have we overlooked?"

CHAPTER 57

THE ARTIST ROLLED HIS EYES at the butler's back while the man made his formal announcement to Chuck Roche, who stood at the end of the hall in his library at 740 Park Avenue in New York City. The Artist's fingers twitched, he bounced on his feet, he rubbed his palms against his leg while he waited in Roche's gallery. A sweeping staircase that led to Roche's bedroom floor curved up and away to his left. Glancing at it made him seasick. He swayed until he stopped looking at it. He had nothing to be afraid of. He would just lay out the reality of the situation. Roche was smart enough to know when to get on board.

The butler opened the double doors with a hand on each knob. "Mr. Roche will see you now."

Chuck Roche stood in front of floor to ceiling bookcases wearing a dress shirt and slacks, as if he were about to have his portrait taken. "I thought you stayed on in the Bay Area."

"Too many terrorists running around." He laughed and stuck out a hand.

Roche looked shocked.

"We have to switch gears." The Artist pulled his unshaken hand back. "We have to back Veronica Lodge Hunter and NEXT USA."

Roche crossed to his bar and went behind it. "What on earth for?"

"The war. We stand to gain all those oil fields."

"That's what I thought when we invaded Iraq. Only a few per-barrel contracts came out of it." He looked his friend up and down. "Besides, even if we win the war, no one can hold onto the region. The Ottomans never had control. The British, French, Russians—all failed. And so did we, if you look at the results."

"This time we'll be committed." The Artist looked at the bar and fought an urge to ask for a scotch. "She'll build bases throughout the region."

"She turned her back on us when she headed up the CIA. She refused to talk to us when she headed up Treasury. She never met with us in her first term. We can't work with her. Is she going to keep Maddox's ridiculous fusion idea?"

"She won't bring it up until after the war."

"But she'll bring it up and then where are we? No. We won't support NEXT USA. End of discussion." Roche grabbed a glass and poured orange juice. "Is that the only reason you came out here?"

"You have to reconsider. We need to get—"

"Do I need to repeat myself?" Roche gave him a withering look. His sharp words hung in the air.

The Artist exploded with internal rage. How dare he rebuke his loyal friend and hand-picked successor? Who did he think he was? He'd turned over the reins of power. He was in no position to give orders. But losing one's temper never works.

Roche took a sip of his OJ. "Sorry. Where are my manners. You want one?"

The Artist nodded. Roche poured another glass.

"Nonetheless," the Artist said, "we need Hunter's help."

Roche stepped out from behind the bar, eyeballing him with silent concern. "You've done a great job carrying on my legacy since you took over the APA. Surely you understand by now: we don't need the president."

Roche stood in front of the American Petroleum Association plaque listing his name as chairman for thirty years until the current one, where the Artist was listed. They both reflected on the inscriptions.

"What is your real problem?" Roche patted his shoulder.

"I've tried Watson and the Counterintelligence group. He's a bureaucrat. They were reluctant and ineffective."

"You don't say." Roche stepped back, his brow furrowed with concern. "Ineffective at what?"

The moment of truth.

There was no getting out of it now. After all, this was the reason he came here. He needed help. He gulped his orange juice to steady his nerves. "Sabel is closing in on us."

"What do you mean? Why worry about Sabel? She's a good kid. Spirited, maybe, and brash, but she owns a refinery now. She'll come around soon enough."

"How the hell could you sell her that refinery?" The Artist tried to rein in his rising voice. "That was your family's first refinery. Your great-grandfather built that."

"An aging pile of brick and rusting pipes. No one wanted to send oil there anymore. She'll lose millions."

"Maybe out of date, but ISIL oil has been running through its pipes for months."

"Are you mad? My people would never allow such a thing."

"She bought your refinery to trace the shipments. I'm telling you, she's closing in on us."

"Closing in on what?"

"Us! I've been shipping ISIL's oil to that refinery. Your people never asked about origins. They were just happy to make a profit for a change. But now you've gone and sold it to her and she's going to figure it all out."

"Have you been drinking?" Roche scowled. "What do you have against her, anyway? Her people saved our asses in—"

"She didn't save us!" His voice reverberated through the room. "She stopped my operation in its tracks."

"What operation?"

When he didn't reply, his friend came to the realization slowly. The Artist expected more cognitive quickness from someone considered the top shelf of business savvy.

Roche staggered back a step and paled. "You're not aiding those ... terrorists?"

"Not 'aiding', Chuck." The Artist poked a finger in the old man's chest. "They're mine. I bought them from ISIL. I brought them into the country. I drew up the plan. I am the one who neutralized NEXT USA." He moved in close to Roche's face. "And you didn't even say thank-you."

Roche stumbled backward and tripped over an ottoman. He landed awkwardly on his elbows, halfway into a silk-covered wingback. His horrified look amused the Artist.

"Now you need to help me." He leaned over the trembling man and snatched away the silver-handled cane. "Since you won't work with Hunter, I need some of your security guards. The ones who aren't afraid to kill."

Roche's face twisted left and right, slowly, while he tried to form the simple syllable "no".

The Artist hoisted the cane to examine the fine handle. The cane felt good in his hand. He raised it high and whooshed it down hard.

Roche raised his trembling hands to ward off his blows. The old man's fingers cracked and snapped.

The Artist struck again and again, reveling in each hiss the cane made through the air. Blood and heat rose to his head. It felt good to get it out. All the pent-up anger. Blow after blow. Why had he ever listened to the sniveling little bitch? Blood spots appeared on Roche's fingers and from under his shirt. Broken ribs, probably. Fine. Exactly what the bastard deserved. This would be as good a time as any to just kill him. He could do it right now.

But he didn't have what he needed.

He stopped, his breathing ragged and hard. His lungs heaved and sweat rolled down his face. "I need your men. The ones who kill. Do I need to repeat myself?"

Roche shook his head. The man's eyes had gone feral with fear.

The butler gasped from the door. "Oh my god. What…"

"You should call Chuck's doctor." He realized he still held the bloody cane in his hand.

"I'm calling the police." The butler turned to run away.

"NO!" Roche managed to shout his directive. "No cops."

The butler stood frozen in the doorway with his mouth hanging open.

The Artist extended his arm and gave the man a dismissive gesture. "Go away now."

"Your men, call them." He turned back to Roche. "Don't tell me you don't have any. I checked the books. The APA paid Roche Security far too much for simple bodyguards. I want those men. There are a few undesirables who need to be excised from the social register."

Roche fumbled for words but managed only a few pained grunts. He gasped for air and finally got his breathing under control. "You're insane."

The blood and heat rose again. He struck blow after blow.

"Insane? You taught me everything I know. But who is the student and who is the master now?" He paused and laughed. Then brought the cane down hard on the old man's shoulders and arms. Striking over and over again. "I am the master. I am the master!"

He thrashed more blows with the cane. "Does your new girlfriend know what you and Hunter did to her parents? You should've killed her then. But how were you to know she'd grow up to become such a powerful young lady."

"Nothing..." Roche gasped. "Nothing to do with it. How could you think such a thing?"

"Watson."

"Watson..." The old man gasped again and stared at his broken arm. "Watson was in high school."

"I don't care." The Artist stepped back. "Call your men. Have them meet me at the executive airport. Tell them to bring guns."

CHAPTER 58

I WORE SUNGLASSES WITH A cowboy hat pulled low and Ms. Sabel wore a scarf over her wind-whipped ponytail as we caught up with late afternoon traffic in Marin County heading south with the top down. Santa Rosa disappeared in the mirrors and Petaluma filled our windscreen. Chrome and glass sparkled up and down the highway. Thousands of people going here and there with no idea that an armed and dangerous man sparkled among them. I smiled and waved.

Mercury stretched his arms across the back seat a foot in each footwell, and soaked up the sun like a frat boy on Spring Break. *Yo dawg, you going to call Special Agent Verges any time soon? He has some clues for you.*

I looked back. *Why don't you just tell me what the goddamn clues are?*

Mercury leaned forward with a scowl. *Hey now, don't be taking Jupiter's name in vain. Show some respect. We could use a little worshiping from you, ya feel me?*

I felt every muscle in my face tighten. *What clues might I expect from Verges, oh great and powerful god?*

Mercury turned his nose up. *Oh. That was so nasty. When you disrespect me, you disrespect the whole Dii Consentes. You think I'm going to help you? Huh-uh, you're going to have to propitiate us now, bro.*

I risked going online again and turned on the phone. First thing I did was look up *propitiate*—and hoped it didn't involve sex. Then I called Verges.

"What did you find?" I asked.

"A dead guy and his two kids. Kids were traumatized, suffered wrist and skin burns from being taped up for a couple days, but no permanent injuries. Local cops are processing the scene."

"Muscular guy, slightly bigger than average with a cowboy belt says 'freedom' on it?"

"No, scrawny." Verges paused to speak to someone in the background. "Grandparents are on the way to pick up the kids. The dead guy was going by an alias of Schwartz, but his real name was Andy Biggs."

"Any chance this guy worked for a company called Energy Outfitters?"

"How did you know?"

"There's an admiral back East who exfiltrated Larson, then shot himself." I explained the whole complex scenario to Verges and gave him Behan's name and number for confirmation. "We need to know the Admiral's roommate at boarding school."

"Thanks for the lead, but it won't do me any good." Verges sighed. "Watson put me on administrative leave."

"Something wrong with that guy."

"No shit." Verges huffed. "He gets pushed around by an industry associations called APA."

"Ms. Sabel will get you transferred." I glanced at her. She shrugged her willingness to try.

"Something else," Verges said. "This guy called a number in Syria before he died."

"HOLD everything right there. Let's get Bianca on the phone and have her contact the NSA. They can—"

"Betcha can't guess who stormed in, grabbed the phone, and promised to deliver it straight to the NSA."

"Watson."

"You're not as dumb as Ms. Sabel says." Verges laughed.

Only the pathetic laugh at their own jokes, my grandmother used to say. Then she would laugh.

I clicked off.

Ms. Sabel and I synched our earbuds and conferenced in Bianca.

"What's Tania's status?" Ms. Sabel asked.

"Guarded. Still on a ventilator, still in ICU, but she cursed Doc Günter this morning."

Ms. Sabel and I breathed a sigh of relief. Tania was back in form. That was a good sign.

Bianca brought us up to speed on Alan buying us twenty-four hours by going to jail. We could keep our phone on until the FBI got a court order. But the real pressure came from knowing the terrorists were overdue for another attack.

"Dad said people won't do business with a criminal. I can't let him do this." Ms. Sabel chewed on a fingernail as she drove.

"He's not a criminal unless he's convicted." I'd intended to make her feel better but from the look on her face, I'd said the wrong thing. So I doubled down. "First thing they have to do is arraign him. That won't happen until tomorrow. Then the attorney will get him out on his own recognizance. Then they'll set a court date. And so on."

Ms. Sabel squinted at me. "How do you know so much?"

I shifted in my seat. "Uh, knew a guy who got in trouble once. Probably."

"I hope you're right. Let's focus on Energy Outfitters then. Do we have access to their systems?"

"They don't have any," Bianca said. "It's a paper company, old school. The accounting is handled by an outside firm that does everything manually. Nothing accessible online. I sent a team to scan their files. They dug up some preliminary items of interest. One is a boatload of phones purchased in Estonia and shipped to Lawrence, Kansas."

"Why Estonia?" I asked.

"Money laundering capital of the world—and the most untraceable phones."

"What's in Lawrence?"

"Last known address for Michael Larson before he jumped parole."

Ms. Sabel and I shared a glance. She was driving fast; her gaze went straight forward a split second later.

"Have you tracked down the phone numbers yet?"

"We're working on it," Bianca said. "Their top priority is to find the invoices for the SIM cards."

She had her team working to trace the list and promised to send me the phone number I needed as soon as they had it.

"Do they have a contractor named Schwartz?" I asked.

"Yes." After Bianca answered, none of us said anything.

The next question was going to be painful no matter what answer Bianca gave us. It wasn't my place to ask the big question, so I left it for Ms. Sabel. She avoided asking it by asking everything else first. There were no other questions left. We needed to know. I cringed and waited.

Ms. Sabel gripped the wheel hard enough to turn her knuckles white. She broke the silence. "Who ran the company?"

"Luuk Devoor."

"Was Stefan involved in any capacity?"

"The accountants said they only communicated with Luuk." Bianca hesitated. "Pia, it would not be wise to assume Stefan is—"

"I know." Her knuckles were still white, her grip still hard enough to break the wheel.

There was another long, awkward pause.

I broke the silence. "We know what we need to do, then. Ms. Sabel will go after Watson, I'll go after Larson. You need to pull enough evidence together to get Mr. Sabel out of jail. Then we go after Devoor."

"Luuk Devoor's jet went to New York early this morning," Bianca said. "He stayed about an hour, and headed back with five extra passengers. He's due to land in a couple hours."

Ms. Sabel looked at me. "I'll take Dhanpal, you take Miguel."

She gave Bianca instructions to contact President Hunter.

We made arrangements with our field agents and drove into the heart of the city. Before long we made it to the warehouse district. We pulled into a parking space half a block from our destination near the shipyards. She gave me a kiss on the cheek for luck, then handed me the keys. She walked up the sidewalk to meet Verges and Dhanpal at the Crepe and Brioche (only in San Francisco can you find a café by that name nestled between the docks).

Miguel appeared out of the ether with a duffel bag full of soldier-candy: C4, MP5SDs, flashbangs, grenades, secure phones, earbuds, and an RPG. We stuffed them in the trunk and drove out to San Francisco International Airport.

Many airports have their executive terminals in nice clean places. SFO makes you drive around an access road behind the fuel storage tanks and the backsides of shipping transfer stations. No wonder the cool people, like Ms. Sabel, fly into Moffett. We pulled up in the visitor's parking at Signature Executive Terminal and waited. My phone app said Devoor's tail number would land in an hour.

Sunshine poured over us like a warm hug. We leaned back. I tilted my cowboy hat over my nose. All we had to do was wait for Devoor to land, beat the crap out of him, and ask him nicely where he stashed Larson and the Moroccans.

Mercury leaned up by my ear. *Remember what I said about beautiful days, bro? See, y'all are taking a nap here when some serious shit is going down. You're thinking you got this—but you don't.*

Without moving a muscle, my eyes slid to my long-lost god. *What do you mean? What's Devoor going to do, ask his butler to hold up on our lemonades?*

Mercury leaned back and crossed his arms. *Oh, so it's back to that is it? You think I'm going to help you out of this one? No fucking way, scrub.*

Whatever.

We snoozed a little because the one thing a foot solder can tell you is: you never know when you'll sleep again.

Half an hour later, Mercury was banging on my head like a bongo. *Go, go, go! Put it in reverse! Flight came in early.*

Without thinking, I fired up the old car and backed up. Miguel opened one eye and looked at me.

Two bullets whizzed by the windshield, slicing through where our heads had been a second earlier. The glass on the car next to us exploded into gravel-sized shards.

I yelled at my forgotten god. *I thought you weren't going to help me.*

Don't think we're all cool now, homie. I just didn't want Miguel's nice clean shirt getting trashed by your brains being splattered all over it.

I tried Ms. Sabel's trick: clutch in, toe on the brake, heel on the gas. Smacking the selector into first, I dropped the clutch. The back tires lit up, the back end came around, we shot forward out of the lot and onto the access road. Behind us, through a cloud of tire smoke, came a black Suburban with a guy standing up through the sunroof holding a rifle with a scope. Another black Suburban followed him.

Miguel crawled over the seatbacks and leveled a rifle over the trunk.

Zig-zagging across the road, I got us around the bend before Miguel or our assassin could get a shot off. The Pontiac didn't handle like one of Ms. Sabel's exotic sports cars. The suspension was crap, the oversteer horrendous, and the engine had more power than the tires could hold down. After two corners, I learned to jab the gas and tap the brakes at the same time to drift around the corners. Modern cars have ABS brakes that prevent drifting. We wove through traffic with Miguel leaning over the trunk trying to find a shot.

Too many innocent bystanders. And jet fuel tanks.

We flew by the Coast Guard base and rounded the bend to find a huge tanker stretched sideways across the road and traffic cops urging everyone to stop.

The Suburban closed in behind us, the shooter still aiming from his sunroof-turret.

CHAPTER 59

PRESIDENT VERONICA LODGE HUNTER SAT on one of two facing couches in the Oval Office listening to Chief of Staff Ron Bose argue with her campaign manager. She sipped her tea.

Her campaign manager turned to her. "The committee asked you to take over the party twice, but if you turn them down a third time, they'll think you mean it."

"What Ron is keeping from you," she said, "is that Pia Sabel and her henchmen are about to catch the remaining terrorists. If they do, there is a potentially explosive ending to that entire episode. We have to wait one more day to see how it plays out. String NEXT USA along for a couple days. Tell them whatever you have to, but make them wait."

The campaign manager stared at her with his mouth hanging open. "That would be a good thing, catching the terrorists. Right? We don't even need to spin that one to boost your candidacy—"

"There could be complications," Bose said.

The campaign manager looked from one to the other, hoping for an explanation. "Do you mean, something could blow back on the president?"

"I have nothing to do with that atrocity." Hunter emphasized her point by clattering her cup on the table. "There are things we don't know. Unknown unknowns." She shared a glance with Bose. "That reminds me: tell the Chairman of the Joint Chiefs to push the timetable back. Nothing happens in the next forty-eight hours."

Her mobile phone rang. She looked at the caller ID and looked at her men. "Sorry, I have to take this."

The men lowered their voices but kept talking.

"Chuck," she twisted away, "why are you calling?"

"Luuk's gone crazy." Roche wasn't breathing as much as panting. "Completely insane. You need distance. Lots of distance from him."

"You turned your back on me twenty years ago and suddenly you care about me?" She laughed. "If your friend's become a problem, call Watson. Isn't that what he's there for?"

"Luuk runs the APA now." Roche groaned in pain. "Watson answers to him."

"Why are you making such sickening noises?"

"Luuk broke my arm and beat me with a cane. The doctor's stitching me up." He breathed hard. "You have to neutralize Luuk."

"Neutralize?" Hunter stood and looked out the window. She felt sick. "Luuk? He's just another trust-fund alcoholic, a *cause célèbre* for raising inheritance taxes."

"He's done something that could bring us all down." Roche groaned again. "It's time to bury the hatchet, Veronica. If we don't start working together, Sabel could ruin us."

"You maybe, but I have her right where I want her." She watched the wind blow leaves across the Rose Garden. "I have important things to attend to, Chuck. Good luck with your Luuk-problem."

"Wait." Roche paused. "It gets worse."

She floated to the window, unsettled by the desperation in his voice. "What has he done?"

"You don't want to know. You need to trust me when I say that."

"Is Watson involved?"

"Luuk called Watson ineffective. I'm guessing that means Watson is unaware of the bigger picture. He's in deeper than he knows. But that raises another question. Answer me straight up, Veronica: did Watson ever work directly for you?"

"He was a college intern at the CIA when I was there. He worked for McCarty." She sucked in a breath. "Oh my god. Did Watson tell Pia something?"

"Not yet." Roche let a sharp yelp escape and cursed the doctor on the other end. "Is Sabel still out in California?"

"You're thinking what I'm thinking?" Hunter traced an invisible heart on her window. "She can take care of both of them for us?"

"That's what I've always loved about you, Veronica." He sighed. "You're a mind reader. I'm assuming you're angling to take over NEXT USA. You know you can count on me... if you're willing to drop—"

"Oil is our only future, Chuck. Fusion will never work. Consider it buried."

She clicked off and retook her seat on the sofa. Holding up a hand, she stopped her aides mid-sentence. "Something big is going to happen today. We can have an unseen hand in the outcome. Who should we back, Chuck Roche or Pia Sabel?"

"Sabel," Ron Bose said without hesitation.

Her campaign manager gave Bose a disdainful glance. "Roche could give more to your party than Sabel could possibly raise."

Hunter squinted at Bose and canted her head for an explanation.

"Roche and Devoor have money," Ron said. "But Sabel plays to win. Cross her and she'll destroy you."

The manager looked Bose up and down before turning back to Hunter. "Cross Chuck and he'll—"

She cut him off with a raised hand. "When Ron says she'll destroy me, he doesn't mean figuratively."

The campaign manager looked stunned.

"Besides," Hunter said, "I can keep Chuck under control."

She called FBI Director Shikowitz. "Your friends, the Sabels, are working on something big for me and some of your people have been getting in their way. I'm going to send you orders, directives, whatever you need to make things happen, but I need them to start happening right now. First, put David Watson on administrative leave, effective immediately. Second, get Alan Sabel out of jail. Third, rescind those wanted bulletins—I don't want Pia or Jacob obstructed in any way. And finally, move Special Agent Verges from Counterintelligence to the Terrorism Task Force as liaison to Pia Sabel. Consider these directives as my executive orders. You'll see why in twenty-four hours."

For a moment she heard only silence and wondered if the old man had fainted. Then Shikowitz said, "I'm glad you finally had a change of heart. Pia's been one step ahead—"

"Quit talking and start moving. Tell the Task Force to back off and let her do her thing. If something goes wrong, she was acting on her own. If she saves the country, she was working for me. Got it?"

★　★　★

STANDING ON A STREET CORNER in San Francisco, Pia held the phone to her ear, half-listening to President Hunter prattling on about what great Americans the Sabels are and how proud she was to have personally freed Alan and how much it meant to her that Pia still took her calls, even if she'd been forced to go through Bianca to get connected.

Hunter's voice became background noise when Stefan Devoor emerged from the Fairmont Hotel across the way and into Pia's visual range.

She turned her hoodie away and nodded at Dhanpal. He tracked Stefan and alerted Verges.

"So naturally," Hunter was saying, "I thought of you when I told them, 'nuclear fusion is my highest priority.' And one of them asked—"

"I gotta go." She heard Hunter trying to squeeze in something about Watson and the CIA, but didn't care. She clicked off and shoved her phone in the pocket of her hoodie.

Stefan scanned the people on all four corners of Mason and California streets. She caught his glance and nosed toward the approaching cable car. He turned and adjusted his speed. She hopped aboard while it rolled to a stop near him. He stepped onto the running board next to her and gripped a handrail.

She examined him closely. No beads of sweat formed on his forehead; his pupils were not dilated. His face was tight and grim.

"Why did you let me buy Energy Outfitters?" she asked.

"You must turn yourself in."

"You knew I'd find out what they were doing."

"The FBI has assured me you will get a fair hearing."

"How long have you known Michael Larson?" she asked.

"I will stay with you to make sure you're treated with respect."

Still no beads of sweat. No dilation of the pupils. No nervous twitches. "Does your father know you sold the company to me?"

"You've not heard a word I've said." He crossed his arms and almost fell off the car. He reached out and grabbed a rail.

"Watson's been put on leave." She leaned close enough to kiss him, her eyes scanning every pore of his skin. "Your father financed the terrorists who killed Marty Maddox."

"Don't do this, Pia. I'm not listening to your fantasy stories. Watson told me you would—"

"Sorry, folks," the conductor's voice boomed from overhead speakers. "The FBI has a roadblock up ahead."

CHAPTER 60

THE SLAGER PULLED THE NISSAN Pathfinder into a gas station outside of Sacramento. The former owner's body—wrapped in a carpet—was starting to stink. When a body dies, there are no more commands from the brain telling the sphincter muscles to keep everything in the bowels. It all comes out, all at once or slowly but surely, depending on the built-up pressure. The old lady must've been constipated for a week. It hadn't been a problem on the road; they cracked a few windows and a breeze flowed through. But he couldn't have inquiring minds asking about it at the stop, so they rolled the windows up tight.

He snuck a glance at the pictures of Ethan and Emma on Schwartz's phone while he pumped gas. It took all his self-control not to call the number back. But he had problems to solve before he knew how to approach the foster parents. Questions like, why did Schwartz have two phones? One to call Syria and one to call the guys from his program? One owned by Energy Outfitters and one owned by who, the Artist or Schwartz? When he tried to commandeer the Moroccans, was he going rogue or working for the Artist?

The Slager had done plenty of drug deals with guys like Schwartz. Mobsters and cartel men are nothing like movie gangsters. There are no blood oaths. No life-time allegiances. No honor codes, and no honor. They work for whomever was least likely to kill them that day. If you could convince a guy that you could protect him, he was yours. The Artist must have promised him refuge—all he had to do was control the Moroccans, grab his kids, and run off to Mildred Ridge. Schwartz miscalculated that gamble.

Oh well.

Google maps had a Street View of the driveway at the Artist's ranch.

Nice brickwork and a solid gate. But the road behind it disappeared into the woods. The satellite maps showed a big spread a few miles in and little else for miles around. A great place to ambush one's enemies.

The pump clicked off. He got back in the car, sniffed once and rolled down four windows. Youssef drove the rest of the way, including the stop off a side road where they dumped the body. The stink outweighed the risk of someone discovering her, and therefore the stolen car.

Mildred Ridge was only five miles from Tahoe as the crow flies, but nearly sixty miles by road. The Sierra Nevadas provided a dense and impassible wall. They drove up and around and behind and over the western side of that wall for hours until they neared the last turn. There he switched places with Youssef and rolled to a stop at the entrance.

"Mildred Ridge" was chiseled in big letters on the wall that ran twenty yards beside the road. The stout iron gate rested on big rollers. A camera and microphone were mounted in an obvious place for visitors. The split rail fence on either side looked fancy, not safe. He could scale it and hike in. But his philosophy: try the easy way first.

He pressed the call button and waited. After a minute, he pressed the button again. On the third ring, a man answered. "Help you?"

"I'm Schwartz. Was told to come up here and wait."

"You guests of Mr. D?"

"Didn't he tell you?"

"Mentioned one guy and some kids."

"Believe me, they're kids." The Slager looked into the camera. "Teenagers."

"Oh."

The gate rolled straight backward, leaving the road open.

He accelerated hard, charging forward before any phone calls checking up on Schwartz could blow his cover. The drive was long and twisty, with dense stands of trees punctuated by meadows and a creek. Several cameras kept watch over his progress so he tried to look casual. When he arrived at the main circle in front of a massive log cabin, a man in a ball cap waved him to a parking space.

The Slager got out, walked around the hood, and stuck a pistol in the caretaker's face. "Where's your wife?"

"I'm not marr…" The caretaker trembled too hard to finish his sentence.

"How many men on the grounds?"

"Just me and Fernando."

"Where is Fernando?"

"In the kitchen." The man swallowed hard.

"Who is Mr. D?"

"Mr. Devoor." Sweat dripped from the caretaker's forehead. "Wait, you don't know him?"

He was sick of working with the Artist's stooges. They can't be trusted. The Slager put a bullet through the caretaker's head and told Youssef and his friends to drag it away. He went inside, found Fernando, and dispatched him as well. After the crew took care of that mess, he gave himself a tour. The control room was perfect for his plans. Cameras monitored the gate and every curve of the driveway. No one would be sneaking up on him.

While the Moroccans ate like pigs in the over-stocked kitchen, he explained the shifts and positions for each man. He left them to eat and talk in their native language.

He sat in a leather executive chair in the study and stared out the window and dialed the number.

The man who answered grated on his nerves. From the sound of his voice, he was white trash, uneducated, and probably living in a trailer park.

He took a deep breath. "Schwartz told me you have Ethan and Emma."

"So?"

"I'm their dad. Tell me where you are and I'll come get them."

"They ain't here right now." The arrogance in the man's voice chafed.

"I meant—" the Slager gripped the chair "—when I can get there. I'm still some distance away."

"Oh. You better get here real quick then. I'm sick of these fucking rug rats."

"I'll repeat my original request: tell me where you are—"

"Hold up now. We gotta work out payment first. You owe me."

"How much?" He glanced at his online balance in the Caymans and estimated at least three days to move a hundred thousand or more to the US.

"Hundred and fifty."

"A hundred and fifty what?"

"Dollars, numb nuts. We ain't taking no pesos." The man took a drag off a cigarette.

The Slager squeezed the arm of the chair harder and decided the foster parents would have to die. They were simply too stupid to live. Besides, they were from the program. No doubt the FBI would be questioning them before long. "Cash OK with you?"

"Heck yeah." He muffled the phone. "That's per day. Hey, where's Schwartz?"

"He's no longer available."

"Oh yeah? What happened?"

"He asked too many questions." The Slager waited for a reply but heard only background noise. Some kind of conversation with a woman.

"Hey, they're back." A note of concern tainted his voice. "Ya wanna talk to 'em?"

The Slager's heart stopped, a pang of guilt and fear stabbed through him like a lance. What if they didn't remember him? What if they hated him?

"Daddy?" Emma's sweet voice melted him.

"I'm here, honey. I'm coming to get you."

"Tonight? I don't like it here."

In the background he heard the foster dad say, "We don't like you either, bitch."

"Not yet. I'm pretty far away." His knees buckled. "Soon. Very soon."

He talked to both of them, sad and slow until the foster dad grabbed them away.

The Slager clicked off and stared out at the valley beneath the study. A creek ran through it, big enough to fish, big enough to swim in the pools. Farther down, a beaver dam flooded a small meadow. A moose stood at the edge.

This would be a perfect kind of place to bring them. He'd find a ranch just like this one in Argentina. Maybe he could blackmail Devoor for a few more million. Schwartz had said there was plenty more.

He turned the chair around and picked up a pen and pad. First thing he had to do was get clear of this whole mess. He wrote out a list of ideas, then scratched out the bad ones and started a new page with better ideas and clarified priorities. Then he scratched those out and started a third page with the best plans on it. When he finished, he reviewed it and liked it. It would work. In the end, he would have his kids and land in Argentina by the weekend.

He thought about his bank balance. He'd siphoned off and extorted more than he'd dreamed. Seven million plus Schwartz's balance of five. That would give him a good start. Maybe he could do better in the Ukraine. Anywhere with beautiful women and fluid paperwork.

Then he saw it. A letter stuck between two books on the desk. He teased it out and looked at the addressee. Luuk Devoor. A Dutch name. When he took this gig, the Artist told him "slager" means butcher in Dutch. His competitors used to call him the Butcher.

He dialed the Artist. "You failed, Luuk. Schwartz is dead. Meet me at Mildred Ridge tomorrow morning."

"You're a dead man, Larson." The Artist sounded like he'd grown some balls since they'd last spoken. "Why wait? I'm downtown."

"I said Mildred Ridge." He clicked off and blocked Luuk Devoor's number.

CHAPTER 61

DRIVING INTO THE RAPIDLY SHRINKING space between a giant fuel truck and an assassin, I heel-toed the brake and gas, downshifted, dropped the clutch, slid sideways toward the traffic cop, and shot right across all four lanes, parallel to the big rig. Bullets raked the silver tanker behind us as we shot over the curb and into the sparsely populated parking lot next to the road. We fishtailed into a U-turn that left some of our chrome on a few parked cars. I looped around in front of oncoming traffic to land back in our lane, tires screaming and burning rubber filling our noses. We roared off just as the fireball erupted.

The modern Chevy Suburban is a remarkable vehicle. It accelerates well. It stops well. But it's not so keen on sliding sideways. Our adversaries skidded to an angled stop, their high center-of-gravity nearly rolling them over before they could make the turn. The driver cranked his wheel over and powered into the parking lot, following my lead. The second vehicle had the advantage of seeing his compatriot's mistake. He swerved into the lot without having to stop. But the lead, with its rifleman on top, kept coming. The image of them—one inch in front of the expanding explosion—filled my rearview mirror.

The road ahead widened into a half-mile stretch of straight pavement. Not what I wanted for our moveable gunfight. Miguel, leaning across the convertible's retracted top, pinged their bumper while trying to hit a tire. They kept coming. I powered up the ramp to the 101, slinging between slower cars, temporarily safe behind the curving concrete barriers.

Mercury sat in the passenger seat, holding his helmet on his head with one hand. *Whooee! I love running for your life in these monster machines. So much better than chariots, y'know what I'm saying, homie? Hey. Wouldn't you like to know who those guys are?*

We merged into with traffic on the crowded highway, northbound.

I shouted over the wind noise, *Who are they?*

He levitated above the car, pulled his feet up, and stuck his arms out as if they were wings. *Sorry brotha—you know I don't tell non-believers anything. Especially useful things like how to lose these guys.*

I took my eyes off the road and looked up at him. *Aw. C'mon. I believe! Kinda.*

What do you believe, exactly?

My eyes came back to the road in time to slam on the brakes and swerve around a slow-moving minivan filled with a third-grade girls' soccer team. The mom flipped me off and—judging by the astonished looks on the little girls' faces—uttered a very loud four-letter word. I told Mercury, *I believe I'm either totally mad or in the presence of a great and powerful divinity. How can I lose these guys?*

All you gotta do is perform the rite of Parilia.

In my left mirror, I saw the second Suburban swing way out to the HOV lane and fly past us, heading north. I counted four heads inside.

I had a vague idea about the Parilia rite. Something about sheep. I could probably figure it out—as long as there's no sex involved. The Romans were, ehm, unpredictable. I said, *OK.*

Just 'OK'? Not, 'I'm dying to do that one'. He waited for me to respond. I shrugged. Mercury said, *You vow to do the ceremony?*

I said, *Yes! As soon as I can find a flock of sheep. Or whatever. I swear.*

Mercury said, *No, not a swear, a vow—as in a defixio vow.*

I vowed the *defixio*, promising to deliver the souls of my adversaries to my murderous god, and he told me what to do.

I slowed up, let the Suburban get within a car length, and pulled between two slower cars in the right lane. He made his move, sliding into the lane next to me. The rifleman popped back up. He looked into Miguel's barrel and dropped back down. They lost a couple car lengths. I veered right to avoid a sudden swerving car, which caused Miguel to lose his balance and drop his weapon.

The killers saw their opportunity and sped up.

Drivers around us were freaking out about the guns. Horns honked. People waved cell phones. Some slammed on their brakes. I pointed at the Suburban and shouted, "He started it."

The civilians were not appeased.

The assassin closed within a few yards. Can't-miss distance. Our nemesis took aim.

With a last-second tug of the steering wheel, I swerved into the off-ramp on two wheels.

The Suburban flew past my exit at seventy.

I slammed on the brakes to make the stop at the bottom of the short ramp. When I caught my breath, I eased into traffic on a large street and wandered through a series of turns to make sure they couldn't find us.

Miguel retook the passenger seat. "Military. Too calm and focused for anything less."

"Great."

During the heat of the chase, I ignored a call from Bianca. Now that things were calmer, I called her back. She had a list of Larson's remaining phones. Whatever the guy's plan was, he was low on phones. Only three remained. I tried the first and got an out-of-service recording. I tried the second and heard him pick up on the fourth ring. He didn't speak. He waited.

"Yo, Larson." I waited but he still didn't respond. "Tell me where you're planning your little ambush and I'll walk into it for you."

"Why would you walk into an ambush?"

"Easier to kill you that way."

"It's beautiful out here." Larson tried to lower his voice to sound scary but the hitch in it gave him away. "A great place to contemplate your final thoughts."

"Yeah, yeah, yeah. Just tell me where I can relieve you and your miserable martyrs of your need to breathe."

He gave me GPS coordinates. Miguel plugged them in and showed me a long road to the middle of nowhere. He forwarded the map to Ms. Sabel and Bianca.

"How much did Luuk Devoor pay you for this operation?"

On the other end of the line, I heard him choke on the fact we'd put it all together.

He hesitated, then inhaled enough courage to brag. "Seven million."

"Do yourself a favor: download a Last Will and Testament. Fill it in."

CHAPTER 62

TOURISTS GROANED AND GRABBED AT handholds as the cable car's brakes screeched and shimmied down California Street's steep grade. The carriage swayed side to side. It slowed across the Stockton Street overpass, pitching forward, delivering the sensation of a terrible accident in the making.

Stefan tightened his grip on the grab handle and turned his steely gaze to Pia. "Surrender. I promise you will be well treated."

"You didn't trust me." Pia pulled a fist from her jacket and shook her head in dismay. "Your father used Energy Outfitters as a slush fund for selling ISIL oil and importing terrorists."

"That's low, Pia. My father is many things, but he's not a terrorist."

"Think about it. Was he pissed when you traded the company to me?"

Stefan leaned back, then composed himself. "Only because you withheld the patents from the company you traded me. You cheated me."

"Sorry, I don't have time to explain."

She shoved a handheld version of the Sabel Dart into Stefan's stomach and grabbed a fistful of his jacket. Lowering him to the step, she propped him against the framework to keep him from falling to the street.

She stepped off, walking backward. His confused gaze strained in her direction, unable to find her due to the paralysis. He slumped into the pathetic posture of a drunk.

When she was satisfied he wouldn't have an adverse reaction to the poison, she quickly glimpsed the street in front of the car. Twenty yards ahead, at the intersection of Grant and California, men with automatic weapons and body armor massed behind two Suburbans parked crossways. She took off running in the opposite direction, uphill.

Dhanpal ran alongside her.

A voice, booming through a bullhorn, ordered passengers to freeze.

She stayed within the rails, using the cable car for cover. It took twenty strides to reach the cross street, Sabin Place. They made a crisp right turn in unison, exposing themselves to FBI fire for a short period. While they weren't considered armed and dangerous, they knew how jumpy SWAT teams were in tense situations.

As they crossed the sidewalk, Special Agent Verges passed them running toward Grant Avenue and the FBI SWAT team. He saluted them on his way to do his part.

Once they were spotted, the bullhorn attacked them with unintelligible orders. Watson's voice.

They wove between the parked cars and scaled a chain-link fence. In the planning stage, Google maps made it look like a shadowy alley, but in reality was a dense garden. They pushed through large leaves until they came out on Brooklyn Place. They leapt the fence and traversed the Baptist Church's playground. From there, they scaled another chain-link fence to land on an upper-deck basketball court. They edged to the street side and stood with their backs to the wall.

"Your plan was off by a block," Pia said.

"Close enough." Dhanpal put his hands on his knees and bent over, breathing hard. "You're fast."

"Air's up top." She tugged his arm to make him stand up straight. "You compress your diaphragm, limiting your air intake, when you bend over."

He gave her a don't-lecture-me-mom glance, but stood up.

She asked, "How did they know we'd be on California Street, not Sacramento or Mason?"

"Forward observer, probably in Stefan's room." He smiled. "Double the bet? Watson ignores Verges."

She nodded. They shook on it and moved closer to the corner. Three trees obscured the second-floor court from the street below, but allowed an unobstructed view of Sacramento Street. After two full minutes, an armored FBI agent walked up the sidewalk, his assault rifle resting on his hip, his eyes alert and scanning. He continued west. They pulled back from the edge.

"Did we have a time limit?" Pia asked.

"Face it, you lost."

A text came in from Verges. "Watson going rogue. Working on the SWAT team leader now."

Dhanpal grinned. "See?"

"DO NOT MOVE! PUT YOUR HANDS OUT WHERE I CAN SEE THEM!" The voice came from the street below.

Pia glanced down and saw the officer between leaves, across the street. Dhanpal had a three-stride head start. She followed. A bullet caromed off the brick behind her, showering fine dust on her back. Dhanpal was halfway up the high surrounding fence when she joined him. They scaled down to the playground, crossed to the nearly three-story fence surrounding the tennis court and clawed their way up.

As they carefully lowered their weight to the second level, three FBI men identified themselves fifty yards behind them on Sacramento. Pia dropped and Dhanpal followed her, landing hard. They gave their feet a few seconds to recover from the stinging impact. But as soon as they were ready, another fence loomed between them and their chosen escape-alley. Pia looked around and found the exit for tennis players. It was a longer route, closer to the agents on the street, but less observable. They ran for it and turned into a dog-leg pedestrian walkway.

At the end of the block, they threaded between gridlocked cars to Spofford Street, a pedestrian avenue. Pia ripped off her hoodie, reversed it from yellow stripes to black, and sat on one of the concrete stools built into the sidewalk. Dhanpal did likewise and pulled out a pocket chessboard. The blend-in plan.

Above them, an electric drone hovered at the end of the street.

Pia looked at Dhanpal. "They don't use helicopters anymore?"

"Keep your head down."

Several moves later, the game was still open, but their chances for escape dwindled fast. One FBI agent stood on one end and two on the other, examining them. The agents leveled rifles at them and approached, slowed by the bulk of their armor.

Pia's phone, set out next to the chessboard, buzzed with a text from

Verges. "SWAT Team Leader checking in with HQ. Should be settled shortly."

Pia smiled at Dhanpal. "Told you he'd come through."

He shrugged. "It's not over—"

"That's her," Watson called out from the Clay Street side. "Watch her, she just killed Stefan Devoor. She's armed and dangerous."

Pia and Dhanpal raised their hands, their fingers spread wide.

"Go ahead, Sabel." Watson approached. "Reach for your weapon. I'd love to see you try."

An agent began barking commands to get on the ground, face down. Moments later, they were handcuffed and shackled at the waist. Anonymous hands yanked them to their feet. One of the agents said, "No weapons, sir."

Watson glared at Pia. "Lucky for you."

The group walked back to Grant and California, where Watson had a traveling command post in his Suburban. The Team Leader kept up a phone call punctuated with, "Are you 100% certain?" and "Can you verify that for me, please?"

Pia and Dhanpal were pushed against the vehicle, photographed, and their rights read to them.

Watson stepped up close to Pia's face. "I've got twenty tourists who witnessed your assassination of Stefan Devoor. This time, you're going down."

Pia stared.

"Excuse me, sir." An agent approached. "We found out Devoor isn't dead. He's breathing normally. Heavily sedated, I think."

Watson glared at the man with an intensity that would melt steel. Before he could say anything, a black Suburban stopped on the hill a block above the cable car. Four men got out. They ran to Stefan and crowded around him.

"Your boss is here." Pia nodded at the men. "Did you know Luuk Devoor brought the terrorists in?"

Watson's red face snapped back to her. "Watch your mouth."

The SWAT team leader rounded the back of the truck with a serious look and posture. "Mr. Watson, sir. I've been instructed to collect your sidearm and credentials. You've been suspended. My superiors tell me you were told this on the phone earlier today and have since switched the phone off."

Watson cursed and dug his ID out of his pocket. He pulled his weapon and looked at it for a moment. His shoulders tensed, his arms shook with anger. He slapped his credentials into the leader's outstretched hand. After a last glare at Pia, he marched up the hill.

"You have to apprehend those men up there," Pia told the SWAT team leader. She nodded up the hill where Luuk Devoor and three men carried Stefan to their truck. "They were the ones who planned—"

He scowled and barked, "You don't give the orders here."

CHAPTER 63

LUUK FELT HIS HEART COLLAPSE like a sheet of paper crumpled into a ball. His son was out cold. His only son. He waved the useless FBI agent, Watson, into the third-row seats at the back of the Suburban, cramped as it was for a man of his size. But Watson's companion for the ride didn't take up much room; the short, wiry warriors of Roche Security could've fit in the cracks between seats. The only normal-sized guy from Roche Security was the driver, a man who looked as if he'd had his ears removed with a butcher knife.

Luuk took the second row with Stefan. The driver sped away, heading over the bridge and out of town on the long drive.

He stroked Stefan's head, willing the young man to wake up strong and ready. He needed Stefan now. The boy had gone from being a burden on his money, patience, and time to a critical problem-solver. And to think, he once had hated children. Still did, but Stefan was the exception.

The whore who sued for child support hadn't bothered to file until Stefan was three. Until then, Luuk had never thought about the consequences of his lifestyle and had himself snipped immediately after the suit was filed. His lawyers advised a financial settlement, but Chuck Roche offered a more cost-effective answer. After the woman's funeral, the boy came to live with him. Stefan was unrelenting with his upbeat attitude, no matter how many insults Luuk threw at the awkward child. Eventually, the young man's relentless charm grew on him. All these years later, Stefan had saved the company from a few disastrous decisions made by management.

Now he couldn't imagine life without Stefan by his side.

And that ungodly bitch, Pia Sabel, had drugged him. If anything happened, he would kill her for it. He would unleash his terrorists on her. Let them do whatever. She would regret breaking the boy's heart before she died. Not that her death would ease his headache. He hadn't had a drink since before lunch and there wasn't one in sight. The driver said there wouldn't be any either. Have to stay frosty, clear-headed. Fuck that. He hired these killers to stay frosty for him.

Stefan's eyes opened with an unfocused stare.

"You're awake!" Luuk shouted. "Oh thank god. What happened? Why didn't she turn herself in?"

He shook Stefan but his handsome son only stared upward.

"Everything's going to work out now, Stefan. We're going to be fine. Only Roche knows about the Moroccans." He stared at his son. "Are you OK? Stefan? Can you hear me?"

Stefan remained unresponsive.

Watson leaned over the back of the seat. He reached past Luuk and closed Stefan's eyelids. "He's not awake, it's a form of parasomnia, like sleepwalking. Sabel Darts use a medication similar to Ambien."

Luuk pushed his son against the B-pillar and tucked a sweatshirt under his head. He did his best to keep the boy comfortable. Drugged up, he looked pitiful. Luuk settled back in his seat. He wanted to cry or kill someone, he wasn't sure which.

Late-afternoon traffic bunched up and slowed their progress across the bridge.

Watson leaned up uncomfortably close to his ear. "What did you mean about Roche and the Moroccans?"

He twisted to face the FBI man. Here was a hard, career agent who'd done plenty for the APA, but could he be trusted with the biggest secret in the country? Luuk glanced at his new bodyguard. The Roche man instinctively understood Luuk's position, raised the barrel of his rifle and gave Watson a nasty look.

Watson looked properly intimidated.

Luuk liked controlling Roche's personal version of the Praetorian Guard. "When you need to know, I'll tell you."

"The whole country is looking for a bunch of Moroccans—"

"When you reported to Roche, who do you think he called to solve problems outside the FBI's scope?" He glanced toward the Roche Security man.

Watson followed his gaze. The former soldier kept up his heartless stare.

"Has the APA's board approved whatever you're doing?" Watson asked.

"You don't ask questions here." The Artist twisted around to face him. "You do as you're told or I'll leave you holding the bag for the whole operation. Understand?"

"Yeah. Yeah, sure." Watson leaned back into his cramped space and looked out the window. "Where're we going? I'm a busy man. I need to get back."

"You might be busy, but you have one more thing to do for me before you go home."

"Oh?" Watson waited, but Luuk chose to say nothing. "What do you need—"

"You told me you knew something about Roche and Pia Sabel's parents. But he pointed out you were too young." Luuk faced his man. "Tell me what you know."

He loved these guards. He didn't even know what they were called, agents? Soldiers? Sentries? Whatever. The man next to Watson kept his iron-stare hard. It was like working with an extra arm.

Watson squirmed. "I was a freshman at Georgetown, got a gig as an intern at the CIA. A guy named McCarty—"

Luuk lifted his new, silver-handled cane across the seat and smacked Watson's cheek hard. "I know about McCarty. I'm asking about Roche."

"I didn't know anything specific." Watson rubbed his cheek with a trembling hand. "Just rumors. Office gossip."

Luuk rolled his hand. "C'mon, I haven't got all day."

"Hunter was the big cheese there." Watson took a breath. "Word was, she and Roche did it in her office all the time. They say she gave him access to McCarty. Then something went off the rails. They had a nasty falling out. I'm guessing that's when McCarty killed Sabel's parents. After that, Hunter and Roche didn't speak much. Then I graduated and went to the FBI."

They rode in silence. McCarty left out that all-important detail about Roche and Hunter. Luuk had always known Roche called the shots with McCarty's guys, but how deep was Hunter? He double-checked Stefan, made sure he was comfortable, pushed another sweatshirt where he leaned against the door.

The Suburban cruised on, leaving Berkeley and heading northeast up I-80.

Half an hour later, Watson collected the courage to speak again. "So what's the job? What are we going to do?"

"We have a little problem at the ranch. My Moroccans have gotten loose and need to be rounded up. There's a man there. You'll get all the glory for killing him and the terrorists."

THE SLAGER STOOD IN THE tower, surveying the compound and the buildings around him. The afternoon sun ducked behind a mountain, but it would keep the area lit for a couple hours or more. The air was warm and dry.

He wondered if he would know when they were near. Stearne was a Ranger, Special Forces no doubt, and they always attacked just before dawn. Night vision helped them own the night, along with practiced control of their sleep habits and prescription stay-awake drugs. They would be alert and ready all night long. He had studied the Rangers and SEALs through books. He took those lessons to heart before he took on the Sinaloa Cartel. He won that fight without night vision. Even though he'd never been through Ranger School, he felt he'd learned enough in the ultimate pass/fail class.

He could do it again.

Luuk Devoor would be an erratic fighter. He would marshal his forces and come at him as soon as he could get there. You tell a billionaire 'tomorrow' and he changes it to 'now' because he's used to getting whatever he wants. Therefore, Devoor would show up first. An easy fight. Undisciplined fighters were lost when the shooting started. Substituting passion for planning was a losing strategy. In those situations, it was always the leaders who figured out how screwed they were and gave up. They wanted to scream "no fair!" but instead ran and hid, watching their people die like flies under a swatter. He always found them cowering in some hidey-hole like Saddam Hussein. Devoor would be that kind of leader, no doubt about it.

The ranch map he brought from the study helped, but looking out at the land from the tower did not. The treetops obscured everything beyond the parking circle. Anyone stationed up high would be more target than spotter. He rolled it up and went back downstairs.

The Moroccans were playing some kind of game in the main room. He thought about making them catch some sleep but decided it wouldn't do any good. They were just young guys on a holiday with no idea they were the most hated and hunted men on the continent. Nor could the boys comprehend the fury that would descend on them before dawn. They were as good as dead already. He only needed them to slow Stearne down enough to get a shot.

He kept going, back to the security office, where all the video displays kept tabs on the sprawling ranch.

He placed the map on the desk in front of the screens and lined up the angles. One camera was trained on the gate. A series of cameras allowed him to change the view, watching anyone coming up the mile-long driveway. No need to waste a guard on that approach. After fiddling with the software, he set it up to stream video to his phone when any vehicle came up. He would be two minutes ahead of his enemies.

Next up was posting a nice little trap for unwelcome visitors. The main house would be an obvious draw. So he stationed a man outside the guest house on the left. He would run inside when the visitors arrived, using his motion to draw their attention. He and Youssef would keep watch from the deck of the guest house across the parking circle. When the visitors' eyes followed the running man, the two of them would step out and blast away. He'd station the mean one, Nabil, in the barn to open up a third front. A three-way crossfire that would kill Devoor and Stearne, and anyone else who wanted a piece of the action.

He marched back to the living room and grabbed the men. He showed them their positions and rehearsed the routine several times. It worked nicely. Turning off certain lights and others on, he created strategic shadows and light pools. He armed each man with a small arsenal and a large pot of Turkish coffee.

He and Youssef took up their position, standing in a deep shadow on the guest house's front porch. He sipped from his own thermos of American coffee. Not the syrup-sweet stuff the Moroccans drank.

"What is next for you?" Youssef asked.

"Tonight, we rid ourselves of those who would foil your quest for martyrdom. Then, I have to get my kids."

"Is that what you live for? Your children?"

The Slager faced the young man. "What do you live for, Youssef?"

"To protect my people from the incursions of the infidels. There is no higher calling than to give your life to protect your people."

"True words if there ever were any." The Slager nodded. "I would give my life to protect my children."

If it weren't for Stearne's unrelenting pursuit, he'd kill these godforsaken terrorists right now and take care of Devoor single-handed. But he was in too deep. Up against insurmountable odds. How did he ever get wrapped up in this? The promise of a clean start proved irresistible. The money, the kids, a new life. He wanted it all. And he was hours from having it. This time, he'd sell insurance—but in Argentina or Estonia or Thailand. Somewhere his kids could grow up nice and safe. He'd keep clean this time. Do it right. Forget these assholes.

But the question Stearne raised ate at his nerves as the sun set and darkness surrounded them. What if Stearne won this round? What if he died? Who would take that money and raise his kids? Who could he trust?

Michael Larson shook his head. Damn it, the bastard was playing mind games with him. No more.

Michael Larson was going to win. Stearne was going to die.

CHAPTER 64

MIGUEL AND I TRADED OFF driving and dozing on the five-hour drive. We kept the top down because it was—as Mercury kept reminding me— a beautiful day. My eyes opened a squint when, after most of an hour driving down a winding mountain road, Miguel slowed to a crawl and stopped. In front of us a herd of sheep filled the road, the shoulders, and the mountain on both sides of us.

"What the hell is this?" Miguel asked. "They wouldn't budge when I tried to push through."

"Damn it." I opened the door and got out. It was a long and dark dusk because the Sierra Nevadas towered over us, casting deep shadows long before sunset.

Miguel turned off the headlights, switched the engine off, and got out to stand beside me at the front of the car. He asked, "Know anything about sheep?"

"We need some laurel branches."

He looked at me funny.

I wanted to die of embarrassment. How do you tell your brother-in-arms you're about to perform a ritual for a god no one has prayed to for fifteen hundred years?

Miguel pointed at a bush beside the car. "Laurels like those?"

Mercury stood behind the bush with his arms stretched wide. *Your god provides, bro.*

I said, *I don't have time for a Parilia right now. There's a bunch of terrorists planning—*

Hey now, a deal is a deal. If you want god on your side, you do the rite thing. Get it? The rite ... aw, you suck, Dawg. You could wither up a Dr. Drake party by just knocking on the door.

A few seconds later, Miguel had his knife out and three branches cut. "How many do we need?"

Mercury pointed at my main man. *See this guy? Now this here is what you call a beee-liever. You could learn a thing or two from him.*

I said, *If he's so great, why don't you infect him?*

I be trying, homie. He's plugged in with the Dineh way. Sa'ah Naaghai Bik'eh Hozhoo, harmony with the universe, and all that bullshit. Hey, before you start thinking of joining up with them, you should know: they make you dance. And I mean that literally.

Nothing wrong with dancing in my book. I'm just not particularly good at it.

I faced Miguel and stammered. "Two each, I think."

"Don't you study this stuff?" he asked.

"Not really. I mean, I think the Romans pretty much made it up as they went along."

"Rituals only work if you believe." He stood up and handed me two laurel branches. "Now what do we do?"

My comrade was too casual with his acceptance. A little religious skepticism is healthy—especially where Mercury is concerned. I explained what little I knew and we set out down the slope, clearing a path for the sheep to follow. And they followed like dogs on a leash. Two hundred yards away, on a little mountainside meadow, we found a small pen with split-rail fencing. We were going backward through the rite, but I wasn't going to wait until dawn, which is when you're supposed to start. We decorated the pen with green branches and shook the laurels all over the place. We built a small fire at the entrance and carried the sheep over it, purifying them, before placing them in the pen. Then we set out an offering of the granola bars we'd saved for our dinner. I dipped my hands in the water trough and shook them toward the east.

Mercury stood with a manly woman, or a feminine guy, I wasn't sure which, watching us. *See how easy that is, my brotha? You could do this kind of thing regular like.*

Alarmed by his companion, I pointed. *Who the hell is he—or she?*

Mercury looked as if I were the stupidest human around. *Pales, god or goddess of shepherds, naturally.*

I said, *Which is it? God or goddess?*

He looked exasperated. *What is with you Americans? No one cared about gender roles for thousands of years, but a couple hundred Puritans land on Plymouth Rock and all of a sudden everyone wants to know what's under the toga. As long as you don't fuck the sheep, no one cares. Hey, wait a minute, you didn't—*

No. And if that's part of the ritual, I'm not going to, either.

A religious experience should include a little dignity. No wonder the *Dii Consentes* has a tougher time scrounging up a Sunday morning congregation than Jehovah's Witnesses.

Miguel and I climbed back up the slope and drove on. We parked two miles short of the driveway and hiked overland. With the lingering twilight, we didn't need our night-vision visors until the end. Our path formed a large letter J, bringing us in at the rear of the property. The least-expected point of attack. On the backside of the ridge overlooking the compound, Miguel sent our silent drone into the sky and donned the virtual reality goggles. I kept watch at ground level.

He surveyed the site and the number of men deployed. We expected more than the four our drone's thermal camera picked up. But another half hour of searching left little doubt there were only four of them.

"Let's get some sleep," Miguel said. "Start shooting at oh-three hundred."

I thought about it. Larson slipped out of my grasp too often. I elbow-crawled to the top of the ridge, Miguel reluctantly alongside me.

It took about a minute to find them using my scope. Larson and a Moroccan sat in deck chairs with their feet up on the railing. They looked relaxed. Too relaxed for my tastes. Call me old-fashioned, but I don't believe killers should have one second of relaxation.

I put a bullet into the dirt twenty yards in front of them. With my silencer, they never heard the shot, only heard the bullet buzzing and saw the dirt pop. Could've been a squirrel for all they knew. But it alarmed them. Took them out of their comfort zone. They jumped out of their chairs and scanned the area around them.

I dialed Larson's number.

He picked up.

I said, "Did you know I'm one of those Special Forces guys they make movies about? I have hours of training and years of experience behind me. Want to know how we operate? I'm going to come for you about an hour before dawn. In that tired time when your muscles have gone slack, when your mind wanders every time your eyelids close, when a blink lasts until your chin hits your chest—even though you know I'm going to attack, you can't keep focused."

"Ha. Nice one, Stearne. Think you can get inside my head?" Larson toed the deck beneath his foot and snapped a look left, then right.

"I don't care what, if anything, is in your head, Larson. I'm going to get inside the head of the guy standing next to you."

I pulled the trigger. My bullet left the barrel with as much noise as a cupboard closing and traveled 285 meters in the first second. Halfway through the next second, it pierced the skin of the Moroccan's head just above and slightly forward of his right ear. After crashing through the bone of his skull, it forced its way into the soft tissue of the brain, where the heavier back end of the projectile overtook the forward end, tumbling into the fleshy matter of his mind. The shockwave that followed my small but supersonic bullet liquefied his brain tissue. In that instant, the synapses that once formed thoughts, like *killing innocent civilians is OK*, stopped functioning. The weak electric pulses fired into an empty void. His heart stopped. His brain ceased all functions. He discovered the true meaning of life—or the lack thereof. The bobbling scrap of lead then blasted a hole in the left side of the Moroccan's head about the size of an orange, splattering bits of brain and blood and bone on Larson's nice clean shirt.

CHAPTER 65

ON A SUNNY CALIFORNIA AFTERNOON, Pia stared deep into the SWAT team leader's eyes through the thick visor on his helmet. He looked like a bug-creature out of science fiction in his body armor; his neck and chin were his only exposed flesh. He said, "You don't understand, ma'am. You cannot commandeer an FBI SWAT team. Caution and patience—"

"There are at least three terrorists on the move." Pia's voice echoed off the buildings and down the street. "Patience will get a lot of innocent civilians killed. We need—"

"So could a running gun battle in downtown San Francisco." The agent pushed his face to hers. "I have eyes on the vehicle carrying Special Agent in Charge David Watson. He might be suspended, but I find it highly unlikely that any FBI man would be working with terrorists."

"Director Shikowitz gave us carte blanche." Special Agent Verges leaned in on their conversation. "You're supposed to help us."

"I am helping you." The team leader glared at him. "But I'm tactically responsible for this op and endangering the citizens of San Francisco is not going to help you."

"Wouldn't it be smart to bring Watson in?" Pia asked. "Because I'm telling you, the guy who grabbed Watson also funded the terrorists."

"I see your passion for this case, but you're not in law enforcement. Let the Anti-Terrorism Task Force handle the fight. Besides, you're making accusations against a man with over twenty years of service. You're not—"

"Damn it, give me the keys to Watson's car." Pia stuck her hand out. "I'll return it to him."

"I'll ride along to make sure he gets it," Verges said. "Keep that drone following them. And provide me turn-by-turn updates—"

The FBI man held up a hand and looked them over. He reached in his armor's vest pocket and pulled out the keys and slapped them in her open palm and waved them off with a good-riddance gesture.

Before they got two steps away, he caught up with them.

"Before you run off half-cocked—" he pulled her arm gently "—I urge you to use caution and patience. We have technology and time on our side."

"There is no time." She pulled away.

Pia drove, Verges rode shotgun, Dhanpal sat in the back with a stack of weapons and opened the sunroof. She weaved the unwieldy beast, oversized for narrow city streets, through startled FBI agents writing up their reports, past reporters snapping pictures, through yellow crime-scene tape, and up the hill.

Verges connected his phone to the FBI SWAT team's surveillance system and kept Pia updated on directions. Despite losing valuable time, they began to gain on Devoor and Watson. As they crossed the bridge into Berkeley, growing rush-hour traffic impeded them and slowed to stop-and-go.

Verges discovered a hidden button for lights and sirens, and they were soon plowing ahead using the shoulder. They broke through the gridlock outside of Berkeley and shut off the lights. Pia powered the truck into the city of Vallejo, gaining on the unsuspecting Devoor. Just outside of Fairfield, they made visual contact and closed in, weaving through heavy traffic. They debated using the lights to pull them over.

Before the debate concluded, a man with an automatic rifle popped up through Devoor's sunroof and fired three shots. Pia swerved. One bullet hit the windshield, creating a dense spider's web in white directly in front of Verges's face. Dhanpal raised his rifle through the sunroof, forcing their attacker to duck down.

"Good thing he has bulletproof glass." Verges ran his fingertips over the inside surface.

"Don't shoot!" Pia yelled.

The wind noise above the vehicle cut off her ability to reach him. Dhanpal fired three shots of his own, all three spider-webbing Devoor's back window.

Pia tugged on Dhanpal's shirt. He ducked down.

"Don't shoot." She glanced above the highway. "Too risky—collateral damage."

"I don't miss." He pointed.

The shooter appeared again and aimed. Pia swerved, nearly wiping out a small car next to her. She swerved back and accelerated. She grabbed the lane next to Devoor. "Can you get his tires without missing?"

"Not safely, but I'll try." Dhanpal rose and fired immediately at his adversary.

The other man fired back, splintering the passenger window and ricocheting off the roof. Pia dropped speed to throw off his aim, but Dhanpal fell back inside.

"I think we have collateral damage now." Dhanpal pointed out the window.

Pia didn't follow his point. Instead, she jammed the emergency brake, forcing the all-wheel drive into a four-wheel drift. She cranked the steering wheel over and released the brake. Her large vehicle shielded three of the four lanes from errant bullets. Traffic around them also skidded to a stop, fearful of the open gunfire. Jerking the wheel back and forth, she dragged the SUV hard to the shoulder.

"What are you doing?" Verges yelled. "We almost had them."

"The SWAT team guy was right." She brought the car to a stop. "Patience and technology. Keep tracking them. I have a feeling they're going to the same place Jacob left for an hour ago."

She jumped down and ran across three lanes to the car with a bullet hole in the windshield. Dhanpal followed while Verges made an urgent appeal to his new boss, John Glover, for support.

Pia and Dhanpal rendered first aid to several civilians caught up in accidents. The car hit by a stray bullet fared well with no injuries, but several collisions piled up behind them. Ambulances came to ferry the injured to the nearest hospital. Pia and Dhanpal left the assistance to the professionals and rejoined Verges.

"We lost them." Verges held up apologetic hands. "We were cobbling together FBI short-range drones with local ground surveillance, traffic cameras. But there are few of those outside the city and they slipped out of the net."

"We have a good idea where they're going."

"Due to the city's team attending training this week, the SWAT team we met in San Francisco was actually from Sacramento. Meaning, the most logical support team is an hour behind us. The Tahoe office is on the wrong side of the mountains from Devoor's Mildred Ridge estate. The terrain is too rugged to land choppers. In other words—"

"We're in the best position to take them down." Pia blew out an exasperated breath. "Roadblocks?"

"Going up in three key areas now. But if Devoor's guys have any tactical sense, they'll be on an alternate route by now."

"The shooter was military," Dhanpal said. "Jacob and Miguel think they're taking on four guys. They're going to be overwhelmed very soon."

Pia squeezed their arms. "Let's get moving."

CHAPTER 66

SOMETIME AFTER DARKNESS DESCENDED AND headlights marked the oncoming cars, Luuk saw groggy stirrings in Stefan. His eyelids batted around, followed by a wandering gaze. The young man sat up, took a deep breath, and looked around. "What happened? Where is Pia?"

"Don't worry about that stupid girl." Luuk offered a bottle of water.

Stefan took it and sipped. "Where are we going?"

"To start a new life." Luuk beamed. "We've relied on Chuck Roche far too long. Our oil fields have poured into his refineries for the last time. We're shedding his yoke."

"Dad, I promised Pia she would be treated fairly." Stefan leaned forward.

"Why should you care about her? She tried to shoot us earlier."

"Why would she do that?" Stefan recoiled with a frown. For the first time, the boy noticed the others in the truck. He turned to Watson in the back. "What are you doing here?"

"Like I said," Luuk continued, "we're starting a new life. All these years, I've been trying to impress Roche. What good did it do me? In his eyes, the rest of the world is just part of the household staff to be ordered about, used and fired at will. Do what he says and everything's fine—but just try to help him once and suddenly, you're an outcast, a radical extremist."

"Roche Refineries are integral to our strategy." Stefan inhaled and rubbed his face.

"I had to beat some sense into that old idiot. He failed to understand—I did it for him. Did he appreciate the sacrifices I made? The money I spent? No. I had to take matters into my own hands. I alone saved this country from Maddox and that ridiculous NEXT USA party.

Fusion energy, ha!"

Stefan and Watson gasped in unison.

"What the fuck?" Watson's shout rattled everyone in car. "Are you telling me Jacob Stearne was right about you this whole time? Are you insane?"

"Dad, what are you talking about?" Stefan's eyes searched his father's. "Pia said it was—"

"What's the matter, boys?" Luuk looked back and forth at both men. "Didn't want to believe the ugly truth, did you? Don't worry about it. The ends always justify the means."

Stefan looked out the window. "Where is Pia?"

"I told you, forget that stupid bitch!"

"Where are we going?"

"To set up an ambush for her." Luuk patted his son's knee. "First loves always turn out badly. But women are a dime a dozen. You'll see."

THE SLAGER CROUCHED ON HIS hands and knees behind a firewood box on the front porch as splattered blood and bits of brain and chunks of Youssef's skull dripped off his face. His eyes darted from side to side. Then up the mountain. Into the trees. Somewhere within half a mile, Stearne was out there with a scope. Death could come at any moment.

Ethan and Emma stared up at him from the deck. He snatched the picture off the pine plank and stuffed it back in his pocket.

Stearne was playing mind games on a whole new level. The Cartels sent messages—heads in gunny sacks, fingers in beer bottles—but they didn't blow the head off the guy standing next to you and let you live. Stearne wanted his prey to be afraid.

Two could play that game.

The Slager's pulse raced like a hummingbird on meth. He needed to calm down and find a way to beat the veteran. He could do it. The Slager never loses. First, he had to get off that porch and regroup. He inched himself backward, deeper in shadows, sensing Stearne's eyes following every movement he made. Paranoia? Probably, but a healthy dose of that could keep him alive.

He sped up his backward shuffle. His path would take him out of the shadows and into a slice of light for a moment, but going forward was out of the question. He made it through the yellow triangle and slid off the end of the deck into blackness.

A hand wrapped around his mouth and an arm circled his chest. His body weight was hoisted into the air.

Damn it. Played right into their hands.

Either Stearne or his Indian friend had caught him. He was a dead man.

His captor ripped the weapon from his hands and the knife from his boot. The man released him and pushed him against the building with a knife to his throat.

When the Slager focused on the man's face, it was neither of the Sabel Security agents. "Who the hell are you?"

"At the moment, Slager, I'm your lord and savior." The man chuckled and looked left, then right with quick, all-encompassing, practiced glances. A professional. "Where are Stearne and Rodriguez?"

"I don't know." The Slager stood on his tiptoes to keep the man's blade from slicing through his larynx.

"The man just shot your lieutenant and you didn't see where the bullet came from?" The man looked into the Slager's eyes with contempt. "Ever hear of situational awareness?"

"Uh—"

"Useless." He pressed a button on his collar. "Benjie, we're on our own."

The Slager could hear a squawk coming from the soldier's earbud. The man grabbed him by the shoulder and pushed him back toward the deck.

"Who are you guys?" He dug in his heels and turned around.

"Stearne got lucky back at the airport. Got away from us. I hate when my victim gets a head start. Puts me in a bad mood. Now we have to deal with you and your worthless excuse for an ambush." The man shoved Larson's shoulder, pushing him back toward the deck and the light. "Get back out there where he can see you."

"He'll kill me."

"Face it, Larson. You're going to die tonight." The man's voice grumbled like an earthquake in a cave. "But if Stearne kills you, Ethan and Emma will live. If I have to kill you, I'll make sure the Larson family tree is pruned right down to the roots. Feel me?"

The Slager froze. Disarmed, exposed, trapped between opposing forces, the reality of his situation became undeniably clear. The Slager had lost. The Artist won. His grand delusion was over.

It was not the ending he envisioned. He'd always believed he would die in a blaze of glory. Fighting the Feds, Sinaloa, the Mob, somebody worthy. But emasculated, helpless, the pawn between opposing special ops soldiers? Humiliating. And somehow, this ignominious end seemed fitting for a man who'd sunk to the depths of shepherding terrorists around the world to kill his countrymen.

In that split second, while the black-clad soldier pushed him, the memory of a jailhouse preacher came back to him. "Hell is not a destination. It's not an afterlife. Hell is the life we enter into willingly right here on Earth. Hell is the result of our self-interested decisions. Like heroin addicts, we make our own Hell each time we put our interests before our higher calling—to comfort the afflicted, to feed the hungry, to stand up for the oppressed."

Michael Larson had comforted no one, fed no one, and stood up only for himself. Michael Larson had damned himself to Hell.

He had been digging his grave deeper and wider since he first listened to Schwartz. Instead of taking his punishment, he'd put his interests above everyone else. Now Ethan and Emma would pay the price for the sins of their father.

Unless.

Unless Stearne killed him. If the man in black could be trusted, he could sacrifice himself to save the kids. Maybe that would lead him out of Hell.

CHAPTER 67

SPARKLING STARS DOTTED THE MOONLESS California sky on the darkest of nights. After the sun's last rays had faded from the stratosphere, the moon was not yet shining, and the light from Tahoe was blocked by a mountain range towering ten thousand feet high—it was the darkest hour. I was ready for the fight. I didn't feel like waiting.

Miguel didn't agree. He gave me a look of disapproval. Then he slipped into the shadows. Moving to his position. Because he knew I'd started things and he had to go along with it.

But that nasty look could've been because I wasted the Moroccan.

Miguel and I have a fundamental disagreement on how to treat terrorists. He likes to deprive them of martyrdom by locking them up for life. I'm more of an instant-gratification guy. Dispatch them now, see what happens. When time allows, I ask them, "If this whole Paradise thing turns out to be true, send me some proof."

So far, no proof.

(In all fairness, my grandfather, who died of a heart attack while we were cleaning the corn harvester, never got back to me either.)

Mercury sat on a nearby rock adjusting his stripper-toga. *You weren't paying attention, homie. You want to live, keep your eyes open.*

I looked through my scope and saw Larson snaking his way back across the deck. *What do you mean? The moron can't live without his phone, like every other first-world inhabitant. And it's under the dead guy. Gonna be fun watching him wipe the blood off ... ew, he's using the dead guy's shirt. Disgusto.*

Mercury scoffed. *Staying alive is not about what you see and feel and touch and smell, brutha. It's about the shadows. You feared the shadows in your childhood bedroom for a reason. Human fears evolved to train*

*and hone your defenses. Wolves, tigers, spiders—and really bad men—
live in the shadows.*

I said, *I am the shadow. They fear me. Right now, Larson's shaking
like a guy in an electric chair.*

Mercury shrugged and rolled his eyes.

You know that feeling you get when some random god speaks to you
and you think he's wrong but you don't want to hear him say, *I told you
so* later? I hate that. Especially since Mercury is the kind of god who
would rub it in my face for eternity. I used my scope to watch Larson.
The man stood stock still, staring at his phone as if he were weighing a
big decision.

Then Mercury's words turned over in my brain. A warning light went
off in my basal ganglia which caused my limbic system to search through
all known past experiences and send the analysis to my neocortex for
final evaluation. The result: Mercury used the past tense. *You weren't
paying attention.* My short-term memory dredged up Larson's departure
from the scene and his re-emergence. Something odd happened. Why
would he come back and stand next to a dead body? What was he
thinking about that left him staring at a phone? Why stand where he
knew I could shoot him? What was wrong with his shadows?

My real question was, what the hell was wrong with Mercury? Why
can't gods just tell you what you need to do and skip the whole free-will
crap? I mean, would it have been that hard for God to tell Moses, *Oh by
the way, illnesses are not caused by witchcraft, so don't go burning
women at the stake every time something goes wrong. It's these little
germ-thingys that got away from us in the lab. My bad. Anyway, have fun
wandering the desert.*

Miguel reported in over the comm link. "In position for phase one."

I moved my scope to the Moroccan who lurked by the big house. Just
as I found him, he turned, surprised and disappeared around the corner.
"Hold up. My target disappeared. Taking a leak, maybe."

"Move in closer. Better shot when he comes back."

I worked my way down the rocky slope. My path took me under the
trees. For two hundred yards, I would be working blind. Larson could
disappear on me. My anxiety level went up a notch. Every battle plan has

holes in it. You improvise, but stay as close to the original idea as possible. Our plan was to take out three terrorists and capture Larson alive. Miguel even had a pistol with Sabel Darts just for the occasion. It was a simple plan. But trudging down the mountain, I had a sick feeling about how it was going down.

Shadows.

I came up near a horse paddock at the back of the main house. The ranch house was huge, maybe ten bedrooms or more. But unused. The paddock didn't smell of horses. The corral didn't have that chopped-up look that hooves leave. I edged around the house between the main building and Larson. My nemesis still stood like a statue contemplating the meaning of life.

Something was wrong. No one invites you to a firefight, loses a man, then stands around waiting to be killed.

Unless that's what he wants.

I stood in the shadow, replaying Larson's bizarre behavior in my mind. After I killed his man, he crept out of range. Smart. I visualized his return. His shadow was longer on the way back than the way out.

Mercury stood in the turning circle of the driveway. *Y'know, I feel like the Marlboro Man. Oh, you don't remember him, do ya? He was a macho guy for the cigarette companies back—*

I said, *Why was Larson's shadow longer when he came back?*

Mercury stuck his hand out as if he were shoving someone.

I ran back along the side of the main house, passed the paddock, into the trees. I put five trees between the compound and me before I contacted Miguel. "Back off twenty yards, buddy. We have additional hostiles."

Miguel's breath surged through the comm link as he hoofed it into the trees. When you work with a guy long enough, you do what he tells you and ask questions later. That's what I liked about Miguel. We were a telepathic team.

A rifle shot cracked through the night air.

"I'm hit." Miguel bit down his pain. "Pinned. A hundred meters east of the flagpole."

"I'm on him." I jogged through the trees until I could see the flagpole.

Leaning against a tree, I scoped the darkness.

A shadow widened the base of a tree along the main drive. Full body armor, thermal reduction system, all black. A helmet to boot. My shot would have to be straight into the base of his neck. I'm no sniper, but Miguel needed help. I held my breath, pressed into the tree trunk next to me, pointed the crosshairs.

He moved. Ducked down and crawled behind a car.

I could tell a soldier when I saw one. He felt my presence. He knew I was there.

Dropping to the ground, I elbowed my way forward until I could see his feet under the car. They don't make bulletproof boots.

He went down screaming.

I put a second bullet in his quadriceps. The third went through his hand. Not dead but no longer part of the fight.

Uprange, Larson had no interest in the injured man. He'd heard the scream and watched from his deck, fifty yards away. With my scope trained on him, I could see him better. He held the phone in his limp left hand, dangling by his side. In his right was a piece of paper. Maybe a note or a picture.

To the side of his dark figure lurked another shadow. I switched my visor to thermal only to see the side of him disappear around the building.

A bullet puffed the dirt a second before the bang arrived in my ear. With a quick push up, I was back in the trees, circling for a shot at one of the Moroccans. When Miguel and I made our plans, we had one terrorist at the main building and the other across the driveway. I caught my breath.

Mercury pointed at Larson. *You could put the guy out of his misery, y'know.*

I said, *High-value targets first. I'm going for whoever's hiding behind him.*

Scrambling around in the dark, I found a good vantage point deep in the forest. My adversary circled somewhere nearby for his vantage point. He wasn't showing up on thermal.

Another gunshot rang out. This one farther away, in the direction of

DEATH AND THE DAMNED

Miguel. The terrorists were closing in on him to finish him off. It was a squeeze play. I could kill my rival or save Miguel. Not both.

But it spoke volumes about how to find my man.

I bolted for Larson on the deck. Running at full speed, I made more noise than I needed. Larson looked in my direction with a resigned expression. I jumped on the deck and tackled him. He landed against the dead man without resistance. His phone clattered on the deck. It was buzzing.

I shoved my knee into his chest and leveled my rifle at the corner of the building. A split-second later, a face took a peek. I fired three shots; one went wide, one nicked his helmet, but the third drilled through his visor and into his eye. He fell backward with a death grunt.

Headlights swept up the drive.

The human eye is drawn to motion. I froze.

"You have to take …" The voice came from beneath me.

I refocused my peripheral vision downward. Blood poured from the side of Larson's head. The action was quick but my adversary had gotten a shot off. Larson had taken a bullet meant for me.

We were in a dark corner. The car pulled around the bend in the drive, its headlights sweeping the buildings. A bright flash crossed me, too quickly for recognition. I hoped.

"Take … children." Larson pushed a piece of paper under my body armor. "My money … access on the phone. Unlocked."

The car stopped. Four doors opened.

I raised my scope. Five men. Three of them heavily armed with the same uniform as my last victim. Then they pressed their eyes to thermal binoculars and scanned the grounds. I rose to leave.

Larson shoved his phone in my pocket. "Please."

He exhaled and died.

For a moment, I worried the phone was a bomb. Then his plaintive tone rang in my ears. What he said hadn't registered, but I didn't have time to analyze it, and I didn't sense any threat. I scrambled off the deck.

As I moved to a better position, it hit me. My whole reason for being here was to get Larson. I wanted to drag him back to justice. I wanted the FBI and the White House to know that Maddox's murder was committed by terrorists-for-hire. Larson and Devoor represented a whole new world where the gulf between rich and poor has grown to feudalistic proportions. Democracy means nothing when generational wealth—like ancient royalty—can buy anything, including people. Devoor bought Larson and managed to get him to do unthinkable things. But now it would never be proven because, in the absurdity of a random world, a bullet meant for me crashed through his skull. Everything we fight for hangs in the balance of this fragile thing called life.

Mercury ran alongside me. *Dude, get your head in the game. After you die, I'll guide you to the afterlife and introduce you to Kierkegaard and Nietzsche; y'all can whine about existentialism for days. But right now—*

Yeah, I get it. Sometimes the lonely god is right. I focused on assessing the car.

Miguel hailed me on the comm link. "Two guys coming for me. You saw the new arrivals?"

"You OK?"

"Bleeding, upper thigh. Think my hip's broken. Not steady enough to aim."

"I'll take 'em down."

I rounded a machine shed and a small barn and found a solid redoubt behind a boulder. The new guys were checking the compound as if they owned it. Their survey took them in the opposite direction from me.

I located Miguel up the hill. Approaching him were two figures. The last of the Moroccans.

Shouting coming from the ranch distracted me for a second. The new guys had found their wounded comrade at the flagpole. They exchanged field instructions and medical supplies.

When I returned my sights to the hillside, one of the Moroccans was missing.

The one who wasn't missing went down in a heap.

I waited and listened. Downslope, they were still administering aid. Upslope, the last guy was moving in on Miguel. Since he was covered by a rock outcropping, the only thing I could do was jump him. Close-quarters combat.

My favorite.

I crouch-ran through the trees.

A pile of loose granite slid under my feet.

I stopped in my tracks and trained my thermals toward the compound. The entire group, mostly obscured by trees, was motionless. If they had thermal vision, I would be a series of distinct red and yellow blobs between the branches. The Sabel liquid armor hid most of my body heat. Since it extended the thin, flexible armor to the arms and groin, only the face, hands, and some of the legs would be picked up as heat sources. But body heat also poured out of the suit around the neck and arms. Even when I hid behind a rock, some of that heat signature escaped. Only a pro would know what the small blobs meant.

The bullets started flying my way.

I scrambled over the granite scree, spraying a trail of rock beneath my churning feet. Crossing the heap of gravel, I made it behind a denser part of the woods. The shooting stopped and the hunt began in earnest. I could tell because they went quiet. Like the first two, these were soldiers whose tactics rivaled my own.

From down in the compound, a voice shouted. "Stop. FBI. I am Special Agent in Charge David Watson. Come out with—"

The sound of an unprotected gut being pounded with a rifle butt followed.

They would not be following the rule of law that evening.

Fine with me.

I crossed another outcropping and found a scared teenager perched on a slice of rock across a small cliff from me.

Not a hardened veteran. Not a religious fanatic with excessive devotion. Just another kid like Hakim. Scared and disillusioned and far from home. Larson had not kept up the ardent religious propaganda required to keep the martyrs thinking their calling was a divine idea. Without constant reinforcement of dogma, humans revert to their hardwired survival instinct.

Dressed in week-old clothes and smelling like he hadn't showered in days, every part of him trembled. The gun in his hand clattered to the ground ten feet below him. His jihad was over. I'd seen it many times.

Mostly with Sadam's Republican Guard, but sometimes with the Taliban and al Qaeda. Once a soldier realized he was abandoned and alone, he wanted out. Many of the men I'd taken prisoner went back to productive, peaceful civilian lives. I felt sorry for this kid.

"Take it easy," I said in Arabic. "Do what I tell you and everything will be fine."

His eyes grew three times in size. He never expected to hear Arabic. He said, "You're going to kill me."

His knees shook so hard he slipped off his rock, remaining above the short but ugly drop by hanging on with his fingers.

"Give me your hand." I held mine out. "I'll help you."

He shook his head. He didn't trust me.

He jumped to his rifle and picked it up. When he tried to aim up at me, I was standing next to him.

I grabbed the rifle out of his hands. "Take it easy. You'll be fine."

He ran. Down the slope, stumbling, running, falling, staggering between the trees.

It was too late. There was nothing I could do to save him.

The men in the compound lit up the area with their automatic weapons. Three bullets sparked off rocks, but I heard eighteen shots fired. Three men with AR15s set to triple-burst mode, each firing two bursts. Eighteen rounds. Based on those numbers, I faced one hell of a well-trained squad. When they'd raised their rifles, one fired a pattern of left-to-right, another right-to-left, the third down-to-up. The method ensured they would annihilate their target. Each man's first round hit wide of their target but the next two found him. No one could've survived.

My chances for continued existence went from slim to none.

Mercury swung from a tree-branch over my head. *See? That's what I'm talking about, homie. Stinking thinking. Always with the negativity. Why not look at the positive side? You're going to die in a blaze of glory. You could take out one of them and maybe wound a guy before they blow your eyeballs out the backside of your skull.*

I said, *Is there someone else I can talk to? Is Mars busy right now?*

Mercury grinned and spread his arms wide. *You're in great shape with me, dude. Check out who's checking out Nabil.*

Between the trees downslope, an armor-clad soldier inspected his kill, oblivious to my presence. They miscounted and thought they'd bagged their last man. On pure instinct, I raised my weapon and squeezed off a three-round burst. My eyes met the scope a split second after the bullets left. All three rounds were direct headshots. One of them must have knocked his helmet off, because he was running but his helmet lay on the ground behind him. His comm link buzzed. I couldn't make out the words.

"Miguel, you good for now?" I asked over our comm link.

"Yeah." He grunted in pain. "Got myself wedged in a good spot. I can cover the north end of the driveway. Herd them to it."

Running again, I circled our enemies, staying east and south of their perimeter. They would be assessing the situation and using thermal imaging to find me. This would not be an easy night. It was down to cat and mouse. Three veteran soldiers plus Watson and two unidentified men.

New headlights swept up the road. This remote and uninhabited ranch was fast becoming Grand Central Station.

I fell into a bush by the driveway, a hundred yards south of the circle. As the new truck passed my position, I saw Pia Sabel in the driver's seat. Next to her, Special Agent Verges. No sign of Dhanpal. Which meant he was probably fifty yards south of me.

I flashed my ID beacon to the south. An infrared frequency visible only to our Sabel Night Vision Visors. As expected, Dhanpal flashed back. We linked up.

"Why is she driving into the enemy camp?" I asked.

"Verges wants to talk them into surrendering." Dhanpal's tone of voice indicated his objection to Verges' plan had been overruled. "The SWAT team is half an hour behind us."

Mercury lay in the grass next to me. *Dawg. You are not going to let Pia-Caesar-Sabel become a hostage, are you?*

I said, *I'm thinking. There has to be a way to solve this without dying.*

It's been nice knowing you, but her only chance is a human sacrifice. Charge like the Light Brigade, brutha!

Sadly, he was right. From the look on Dhanpal's face, he knew it too. That was our boss, charging ahead—against the advice of her battle-hardened warriors.

Dhanpal and I jogged behind the SUV, our heat signatures masked by the vehicle's mass.

She stopped twenty yards south of five men.

We ran up and pressed against the back bumper. "I shot one guy's helmet off. You take him out. I'll take one of the others. If either of us survives, we go for the third."

"You're figuring Watson remains neutral?" Dhanpal asked.

"He's a bureaucrat; he'll side with the winner."

The passenger door opened. I used my telekinetic skills to keep him in the car. Unfortunately, I suck at telekinesis. Verges stepped out and held his FBI credentials aloft and shouted for everyone to lay down his or her weapon.

A single shot echoed between the buildings.

Dhanpal and I spun around the vehicle, blasting away.

I jumped Verges' lifeless body. In an instant, the frailty of human existence is exposed for the fleeting, beautiful, and delicate thing that it is. He was probably still technically alive. A single bullet had severed his spinal cord. He might survive another ten minutes. But no longer.

My shots pinged off body armor. My aim was center mass and up, letting the MP5 rise on full auto. Five bullets smashed into the man's armor. The first just above the groin. The second, abdomen. Third, center chest. Fourth, shoulder. Fifth, helmet. I was becoming an expert at dislodging helmets.

But what I saw when his helmet flew off made me stagger. A man with no ears. Kasey Earl. In a bar in Kabul, he admitted to me that he'd raped an Afghan woman. His captain had destroyed the rape kit before the MPs could get there. He bragged that he'd gotten away with it. So I cut his ear off before six other soldiers pulled me off him. Tania shot off his other ear a few years later. Somehow the son of a bitch kept getting away from me. Not this time.

I stopped to take aim.

Kasey's eyes blew wide open. He began to twist away.

His wingman put three slugs in my chest. Center mass.

Liquid armor is new. It's better than Kevlar. Lighter, more flexible, and more responsive to impact, it disperses a projectile's penetrating energy over a greater area, thus softening the blow more than Kevlar, even Kevlar with ceramic inserts. Liquid armor radiates the energy like ripples on a pond. The waves expand outward. Old-fashioned armor uses forty or more layers of Kevlar sandwiched between as many layers of cotton or nylon. It blunted the impact in a cone-shape, like a net catching a tightrope walker. Kevlar armor saved your life from a bullet to the chest but still allowed significant damage in the impact area.

But my assailant chose armor-piercing rounds. And we were at close range.

He may as well hit me with a baseball bat. Hard. Several times.

My lungs collapsed as I put a round through the shooter's face.

Dhanpal had a similar exchange with his target. He killed the man but had the wind knocked out of him as well.

I landed face-first in the dirt and tried to push up. In my peripheral vision, I saw Kasey Earl and Watson running for their vehicle. They jumped in and burned rubber out of the area.

With the high-value targets neutralized, I rolled on my back and tried to breathe.

Ms. Sabel ran to my side and knelt beside me. She leaned down to give me a hand up. In her haste, she put her weight on my weapon.

She was about to ask about my condition when Luuk Devoor pressed a pistol to her temple.

My rifle was stuck. She and I froze.

"You stupid bitch!" Devoor thumbed the safety off the Smith and Wesson SD9. "You've ruined everything. I'm so sick of you always—"

"Dad!" Stefan's voice came from behind him. "Put the gun down. It's over."

Luuk looked over his shoulder with pure hate in his eyes. "We kill her, get out of here. We can still make this work."

"There is no 'we', Dad." Stefan's voice trembled. "Don't make me … just put the gun down."

"You're taking her side?" Luuk turned back to Pia. His index finger tightened. The metal began moving. The travel of an SD9's trigger is short. The springs and levers moved in the direction they were built to move.

The bang reverberated through the compound like a cannon shot.

CHAPTER 68

THE PICTURE WINDOWS IN THE guest wing overlooked Sabel Gardens' flowerbeds and drenched the living area in bright morning sunshine. Jacob was little more than a silhouette gesticulating wildly when Pia strode through the room. She thought it best not to interrupt. She waved good morning to him. He frowned and turned away. Hoping he was arguing with a real human on an unseen phone, she kept going into the Lavender Room.

Seeing the pile of white gauze around Tania's head made Pia flinch. A reaction she quickly masked. Tania read a book on a stand, her bed tilted halfway up. "How is my favorite agent this morning? Oh, hey, I like the eye shadow."

After a delayed reaction, Tania returned a weak smile. She gripped the sheets in her fists. "The black eye ... mmh ... came from f-f-f-falling ..."

"Something like that." Pia smiled and kissed her cheek. It wasn't the first traumatic brain injury recovery Pia had seen. Talking was aggravating for TBI victims. "Your memory will come back. It just takes time."

"Phht."

Pia couldn't tell if Tania had tried to make a word or a noise.

She noticed a benign lump in the corner. Jaz Jenkins, a young man who once had an awkward and unrequited crush on Pia, sat like a pile of laundry, unformed and unmoving. "Jaz, so good to see you."

"Get OUT!" Tania slapped her book with both hands.

"Thanks for the reminder." Pia squeezed Tania's hand and returned her scowl with a smile. "I'm late for my appointment. I have to run, but

I'll be back later."

She turned for the door. Jaz moved to cut her off but she motioned for him to follow her out.

"She's not herself," he said.

She pulled the door closed behind them. "It's the recovery process. Erratic and emotional behavior is normal."

He flushed. "I wanted you to know ... I mean, you and I explored some, uh, interest a while ago. I didn't want you to—"

"Let's not worry about ourselves." She caught his gaze and squeezed his arm. "This is about Tania. You're the best man to help her recover. She needs you."

"Thank you." He smiled. "I'm not family, so Doc Günter won't tell me anything."

"The bullet grazed the top of her skull. It cracked open a chunk about the size of your index finger. She's lucky it wasn't a quarter inch lower, but the shockwave it sent through her head was significant. The mood swings are normal. She's expected to make a recovery—in time. Whether it's a full recovery or not depends on her care. That's why you're the best man to help her right now. You have patience—and you can maintain a cheerful attitude when she's agitated."

He lifted his chin in silent agreement. His smile broadened from formal to genuine. They nodded a tacit understanding of their newly defined relationship. He returned to Tania.

A text from Stefan pinged her phone. "Mind if I pop over? I have a couple friends I'd like you to meet."

His tone struck her as odd.

The police investigation had been brutal. The press advocated lynching him for his father's treachery. Even though he'd killed his father, no one in the community would speak to him. Their relationship had been on hold since Mildred Ridge while he sorted things out with attorneys. Was he trying to brag that he had any friends left at all? Was he ready to rebuild their relationship? Was she? The very thought of seeing him again twisted her stomach so tight she squeaked.

She texted her reply. "Sounds delightful. I'm open all morning."

Across the room, Jacob stood braced against a pillar, staring out the window. She tucked her phone away and crossed to him. "Everything OK, Jacob?"

"Sometimes closure just ... closes in." He sighed without looking at her.

"Yumi won't negotiate?"

"There's nothing to negotiate." He glanced her way with a sheepish look, as if he wanted to apologize for snapping at her. He realized he didn't have to and turned back to gaze at the garden stretched out before him.

"I imagine you're a fine chef." She patted his shoulder. "But I *know* you're the best agent in the world."

He shrugged. "Oh. Hey. Um. Would you ever kinda have maybe an interest in meeting a used god? Nah. Forget I asked. Stupid—"

"What an honor." She smiled. "I'm excited just to be invited. Let's talk next week and schedule some time."

Jacob looked sick and turned away.

Some days, no one is happy.

She went to her library to receive Stefan. She checked her hair and makeup, considered changing, but didn't want to be in the wrong end of the house when he arrived. It shouldn't be about her looks anyway.

Theoretically.

Her father knocked on the east door and entered without waiting for an invitation. "Just saw Doc. He said Miguel's in recovery, the surgery went well. He'll be the bionic man when he heals."

"Dad..." She wasn't ready for the conversation she needed to have. She wanted to write down how she felt, what she'd learned, why she thought certain things. But sometimes it's better to just get it out there raw and unscripted. She crossed the room to him and put out her hand, palm up.

He looked at it and slipped his big hand around hers.

She took a deep breath. "I forgive you. Not because of the love and kindness you've shown me, but because I need to. I can't bear the weight of distrust anymore. You saved me. I love you."

Planted in a casual position half-turned to exit after delivering his news, he cleared his throat and faced her. "I appreciate that. Now that we have the air cleared, if there's anything else you want to know, I'm ready. If you want the full details—"

"I'm not ready for details. But soon." She gave him a hug.

He wrapped his arms around her and kissed her. They held each other and didn't speak for a long time. Then his phone buzzed with a text. They broke and gave each other awkward looks, regretting they couldn't hug longer. He tossed his phone in his hand, smiled, and left.

Pia looked around the library, picking which seating area might work best. It should be a formal setting that could become casual in case they spontaneously decided to pick up the passionate side of their relationship. She wanted the passion between them rekindled. The wingbacks by the fireplace were too stiff. The chaise near the globe looked too suggestive. The facing loveseats in the reading nook— perfect. No coffee table to get in the way.

She considered making the first move since relationships scared the hell out of her. That would force her to think about the moment and the future at the same time.

No way. He could make the first move. If a move was going to be made. Urgh. Why is love always so hard to—

"Pia?"

She turned to find Stefan, tall and handsome, framed by two objects that didn't fit her expectations. She blinked, but the objects remained. Each of his hands descended from his shoulder to the hand of a small child. Toddlers. Two of them. Wow.

Stefan left out a few details about his past. Or maybe it was on her: she should've asked. Or not?

"I'd like you to meet Emma and Ethan." Stefan's smile twitched in anticipation of her response.

She willed herself to respond but instead heard herself in the middle of one long, continuous inhale.

"Emma is the one with the long hair." Stefan lifted his brows.

Finally, her brain kicked back into gear. "Oh. Hi. Uh. Nice to meet you. Come in. Please. Come in. Would you like some chocolate milk? Or toys? We have toys here. Somewhere. I'm sure. I'll have someone bring them. Or buy some. Or candy? Do you like candy?" She looked to Stefan. "Sorry, are they allowed to have candy? Maybe a healthy snack. Ha ha. You'd think an athlete would understand the importance of healthy snacks. You can never start celery too early. Right?"

The boy backed up behind Stefan's leg and hid his face. The girl stared with her mouth open and looked to be on the verge of screaming for help.

Stefan laughed.

Pia looked up. People never laughed at her. Ever.

"I needed that." Stefan reined in his amusement. He squatted next to the kids and pointed to the globe. "Check it out guys! I'll bet that thing spins. Want to find out?"

He hoisted Emma to his hip and pulled Ethan around Pia to the five-foot globe. "Want to try it?"

Ethan buried his face in Stefan's leg again.

She came up behind them and patted her legs. "Um."

Emma looked over Stefan's shoulder at her, then hid her face.

Stefan squatted to the boy's level, and pressed Ethan's finger to the globe, and gave it an effortless push. The giant ball turned silently on smooth bearings. Ethan's eyes grew. He let go of Stefan and gave the globe another push, three fingers this time. It turned faster. Emma squirmed down off Stefan's shoulder and stood next to her brother. Together they watched the globe turn.

"Sorry. I'm usually good with kids." She fidgeted. "I got a little nervous. I didn't know you had any children."

"I don't." He motioned for her to squat down next to the three of them. "Not yet. I've filed adoption papers, but it takes time. There is a process."

The realization of whose kids these were came to her. She dropped to her knees and watched them spin the globe. "Michael Larson's kids? Jacob told me about his dying request, but neither of us—"

He nodded and smiled. "Perhaps, had I been more vigilant, or inquisitive, I might have discovered what my father was doing and stopped him. But guilt like that can kill a man if he lets it. Before you say it, I know—I am not responsible for my father's sins." He gestured at the children. "Nonetheless, I am responsible for my neighbors."

The children giggled and gave the globe a bigger spin. They looked over their shoulders at the adults to see if they were in trouble, but found only approval.

"I came to say good-bye for a year." Stefan took her hand. "I've instructed the lawyers to pay the survivors triple for their losses. Money won't settle the true losses, but it shouldn't stand in the way of recovery. I'm selling the company and donating the proceeds to the Gates Foundation. Maybe they can do something useful with it. The Devoor family certainly didn't. When the paperwork is done, I'm taking my new kids on a world tour."

Pia couldn't hide her shock.

"I thought it through." He gave her hand a reassuring squeeze. "The United States exists today because General Washington refused to become a monarch. Yet we allow generations to preserve more wealth than King George ever had. Why? What was my contribution to society? What have I done to deserve a massive fortune? Not as much as Bill Gates' doorman. So, I'm getting rid of it. I don't want another Luuk in my family."

"You're selling everything? How are you going to tour the world?"

"Almost everything." He laughed. "One of the trust funds my great-grandfather set up I can't get rid of, so I'm stuck with a fortune bigger than the lottery. Do you feel sorry for me?"

"No." She pushed him. "Why the kids?"

"You." He examined her gray-green eyes for a moment. "Your father built a fortune from nothing. You won championships. One could argue the two of you deserve your wealth. But what have I done? Nothing. So that led me to the question, what can I do? What contribution can I make to the world?"

"I'm sure you have many talents. You could—"

"You said it yourself—there are millions of children who need to be wanted. When I heard about these two, I tracked them down. In the ashes of every horror, there is an opportunity to make the world a better place. Maybe it will be a down payment on paying for my sins."

They took the children to the kitchen for chocolate milk, and took them to the Sabel Gardens playground and wore them out. When they were too tired to walk, Stefan carried Ethan and Pia carried Emma back to Stefan's car. They buckled the kids in car seats and stood staring at each other by the open driver's door.

"Write if you find work?" she teased.

His arms circled her waist. "I thought about inviting you on our trip and decided against it. The kids and I must find peace in our lives first. The next time I see you, I hope to be a better man. I also hope I won't have lost you to someone else by then."

She hugged him and kissed him and watched him drive away.

A full minute after his car exited the long drive and disappeared from view, she still stood in the same place, wondering why she hadn't stopped him.

Her butler approached and stood some distance away. "Your appointment, David Watson, has been waiting for half an hour, ma'am. Shall I send him away?"

Pia took a deep breath. "No. Make him wait a few more minutes. I'll be there in ten."

After she changed into a formal business skirt suit and pumps that accented her height advantage over the former FBI agent, she went to her home office and had Watson brought in.

She parked her butt on the forward edge of the sprawling desk and motioned him to a chair in front of her.

Too far to extend a handshake, he gave her an awkward glance and sat. She stared at him. Dark suit, gray crew-cut, inquisitive eyes, large frame, slightly overweight but fit. He squirmed in his chair.

He said, "I wasn't aware you interviewed your prospective employees, Ms. Sabel."

She folded her arms across her chest.

"Should I take this as a good sign?" He tried to chuckle. "The Major went into my background pretty—"

"The Major handles all employment matters. This is not an interview."

She allowed a long silence to stretch out between them. Her gaze remained focused on his pupils. She watched his eyes sweep the room, come back to her, then dart away again several times.

She pushed off the desk and took a step toward him. "Did you watch Director Shikowitz's press conference this morning?"

"I heard he scapegoated me." He shrugged. "All I needed to know."

"You don't believe your termination was justified?"

"If you don't mind my asking, why am I here?" He frowned. "If you're not involved in the hiring process, that is."

"Is that a 'no'?" She circled him. "It would've been nice if someone with a law enforcement background attempted to make Luuk Devoor stand down. You chose to cut and run."

"If you called me here to ask me questions about that night, or any part of it, my attorneys have—"

"Shikowitz terminated you for failure to act. If they intend to prosecute you, that's up to them. What interests me is that you applied for a job at Sabel Security the same day you were terminated. Why?"

Watson's mouth opened, but no sounds came out. He took a deep breath and chewed his cheek. Outside, a leaf blower started up a good distance away. Then he met her gaze. "Sabel is the best. Where else would I go?"

"Any number of agencies or security companies." She leaned back against the desk and crossed her arms again. "Who to trust is the scariest decision we can make in life. Stefan Devoor proved reliable. How could Sabel Security trust you?"

"I know things." He leaned forward with a desperate look. "I was an intern for McCarty. I can help your investigation."

"What investigation?"

"I know what Hunter told you was only the half of it."

"How do you know what Hunter did or didn't tell me?"

"By who is still alive." He leaned back, fighting to keep a smug look off his face. "Do you want help investigating the people who murdered your parents?"

CHAPTER 69

I WAS SICK OF SITTING around waiting for Chuck Roche to say something I could hear through the bug we placed in his home library, but not enough to trade shifts with Dhanpal. "Why, you got a girl or something?"

Dhanpal looked away with an expression devoid of mirth and slid into the kitchen.

We were sharing a giant apartment at 737 Park Avenue in New York City that would make one hell of a party crib if it had furniture. All I could think about was Yumi—but she wasn't interested. I was in the process of forcing myself to move on.

I'd begun the search for someone worth cooking a gourmet meal for. So far, none of Manhattan's prime Mrs. Stearne candidates showed any interest in my offers to try my lemon rice chiffon cake. But I'm not the kind of guy to let a couple hundred rejections get me down.

Ms. Sabel bought the place so we could keep an eye on Roche for a few days. She had a premonition about the guy after speaking to Watson three days ago. Nothing she wanted to share. Sometimes, she's as mysterious as Mercury.

I took the other route to the kitchen and cut Dhanpal off before he could mope off to his futon in the back room.

"Dude, what's up? Why the swap?"

"It's a thing I…" He turned away. "Forget it."

"C'mon, brother, tell me what you're up to. I'll decide if it's worth swapping."

He straightened up, his eyes hardened for battle. "Brent put a bullet through his brain."

I could feel Dhanpal's deep pain. But, while the name was familiar, it wasn't clicking for me.

"Hey, that sucks." I put my hand on his shoulder.

Mercury stood behind him feigning concern and wiped a fake tear from his eye. *You don't know Brent from Frosty the Snowman, do you?*

Through clenched teeth, I said, *Would it kill you to just toss me a line once in a while?*

Mercury leaned back as if I slapped him. *No need to get all up in my face, yo. Think Virginia Beach. The SEAL who clued you in to following the Moroccan trail. Without Brent, you never would've been on the front page of the Post.*

And then, once in a while, gods actually help you. I thanked the ancient deity with a nod.

"I never should've pushed him," I said. "I'm sorry, Dhanpal. It was my fault."

He looked up with red eyes and gave me a long, hard bro-hug. He'd lost a battle-buddy—that's high on the failure scale.

"Just take off, right now." I didn't want to see him cry, and he didn't either. "His family needs you. Bianca can figure out a way to help me monitor Roche. We got this."

Dhanpal started to object.

"Go now, before you feel guilty or get hung up on something trivial. You need to be there."

He nodded and sniffled and grabbed his backpack. He stopped by the door. "It's not about you. He had demons before you came along."

"If you have demons," I said, "bring 'em here." I pointed to my heart.

He fisted his chest, flashed a peace sign, and left.

Bianca hooked me up by monitoring the site herself. She would alert me if anything needed direct observation. From previous conversations, we expected Roche home in an hour for an important meeting.

I'd been cooped up long enough, so I grabbed an earbud, the leash, and Anoshni. My one-year-old pup loved Central Park. Besides, it was a beautiful Saturday, prime time to hunt for women-in-search-of-a-personal-chef. Anoshni introduced me to a couple Columbia University juniors who stopped wrecking their kite long enough to pet him. They were adorable young ladies enjoying the attention summer shorts and tank tops brought them. But they were philosophy majors. I get enough of that crap from Mercury. I moved on.

Next, we met a nice lady walking a Pekingese. Unfortunately, the fur-pile on legs said something abusive to Anoshni. He took exception. It didn't go well after that. Our conversation ended with the lady's chin turned up, a nasty reference to mutts, and she was gone.

I was still scoping and hoping when Bianca buzzed me. "Watson just arrived at Roche's. Roche Security just closed his street to bring someone in. You need to get back to the binoculars. Pia wants visual confirmation on the third party."

Having reached the North Woods section of the park, I considered hailing a cab, but the audio feed started streaming into my ear.

Roche's distinctive nasal voice came first. "Nothing to be sorry about, young man. You managed a meeting with Pia Sabel, that's a success right there. What did she tell you?"

"She didn't tell me anything. She asked questions." Watson's voice. "Oh. Pardon me, ma'am. I didn't know you were going to be here."

I kept my head down to block out the sights and sounds around me. I walked quickly, trying to visualize the setting in Roche's library. A couple chairs with ottomans, a bar on one side, big windows, a balcony, floor to ceiling books. Who was the mystery woman? She said something my sensors didn't pick up.

"No ma'am," Watson sounded submissive. "But I should get an Oscar for my performance."

Watson and Roche laughed. If the woman joined with them, they drowned her out.

Roche's voice again. "The question is: did she believe you?"

"I'm sure she did." Watson.

"For your sake, you better hope so." President Hunter's voice. The mystery woman. "As long as her home is destabilized, we're safe."

Roche. "Now that you've accepted the nomination, you can pull her into your circle. Only then will we be safe."

Hunter. "Can I count on you this time? You're not going to throw another tantrum and withhold campaign funds when I need them?"

Roche. "Stop being jealous and petty. You brought Sabel into this, she's your problem."

"What did you expect me to do when you refused to fund us? We needed someone with money. Now she's *our* problem."

"We can make friends with her." Roche again. "Bring her into our group."

"If she finds out—"

"Don't get hung up on her. She's quick, but young and naïve."

"You guys are underestimating her." Watson this time. "She'll never stop coming after us. She's a time bomb. Our only option is to infiltrate Sabel Security and kill her."

Mercury snapped his fingers in front of my nose. *Yo dude, you see what I see?*

Walking toward me were two mothers with baby strollers, side by side. Their mouths were wide open in horror, their eyes focused on something behind me.

I spun around.

Kasey Earl charged me, brandishing an eight-inch knife.

Mercury grinned. *You got this, right?*

THANK YOU!

Thank you for choosing my book. I hope you enjoyed reading it as much as I enjoyed writing it. As an independent writer, I am dependent on word-of-mouth referrals and book reviews. If you liked this book, please tell everyone, and leave reviews all over the place. I will be eternally grateful.

When you do write a review, send me a link to it and I'll put you in the next drawing for an autographed book. I run at least three or four drawings a year.

If you can't get enough of Pia, Tania, Miguel and Jacob*, checkout the series at SeeleyJames.com/books. While you're there, join my newsletter to get discounts, drawings, fun, news, outtakes, and more about the Sabel Agents club on Facebook! Every week (or so, sometimes I'm lazy), I'll let you know about the book in progress, personal triumphs & tragedies, what I'm reading and other fun stuff. I even had one person write to me to say, "I don't like your books, but I love your newsletters." To which I replied, "Thanks, Mom." Yeah ... whatcha gonna do?

I'd love to hear from you. Please write, message me on Facebook, let me know what you think.

*I like you already.

NOW THAT YOU'VE READ THIS BOOK, WHICH ONE SHOULD YOU READ NEXT?
HTTPS://SEELEYJAMES.COM/BOOKS

ACKNOWLEDGMENTS

My heartfelt thanks to the beta readers and supporters who made this book the best book possible. Alphabetically: Melissa "Iceterrors" Capo-Murray, Alun Humphreys, Ken Newland, Jeannine Chatterton-Papineau, LoriAnn Shisk, Gloria Smith, Gail Weiss, and Sue Whitney.

- Amazing Editor: Mary Maddox, horror and dark fantasy novelist, and author of the Daemon World Series http://marymaddox.com
- Extraordinary Editor and Idea man: Lance Charnes, author of the highly acclaimed *Doha 12, SOUTH,* and *THE COLLLECTION.* http://wombatgroup.com
- Medical Advisor: Louis Kirby, famed neurologist and author of *Shadow of Eden.* http://louiskirby.com
- Romantic Ideas Editor: Pam Safinuk

A special thanks to my wife whose support, despite being reluctant to say the least, has been above and beyond the call of duty. Last but not least, my children, Nicole, Amelia, and Christopher, ranging from age sixteen to forty-three, who have kept my imagination fresh and full of ideas.

About the Author

His near-death experiences range from talking a jealous husband into putting the gun down to spinning out on an icy freeway in heavy traffic without touching anything. His resume ranges from washing dishes to global technology management. His personal life stretches from homeless at 17, adopting a 3-year-old at 19, getting married at 37, fathering his last child at 43, hiking the Grand Canyon Rim-to-Rim several times a year, and taking the occasional nap.

His writing career ranges from humble beginnings with short stories in The Battered Suitcase, to being awarded a Medallion from the Book Readers Appreciation Group. Seeley is best known for his Sabel Security series of thrillers featuring athlete and heiress Pia Sabel and her bodyguard, unhinged veteran Jacob Stearne. One of them kicks ass and the other talks to the wrong god.

His love of creativity began at an early age, growing up at Frank Lloyd Wright's School of Architecture in Arizona and Wisconsin. He carried his imagination first into a successful career in sales and marketing, and then to his real love: fiction.

For more books featuring Pia Sabel and Jacob Stearne, visit: SeeleyJames.com.

facebook.com/seeleyjamesauthor

instagram.com/seeleyjamesauth

bookbub.com/authors/seeley-james

www.ingramcontent.com/pod-product-compliance
Lightning Source LLC
Chambersburg PA
CBHW030644120726
47905CB00001B/56